Snow Angel

Mark A. Roeder

iUniverse, Inc.
New York Bloomington

Snow Angel

iUniverse books may be ordered through booksellers or by contacting:

iUniverse
1663 Liberty Drive
Bloomington, IN 47403
www.iuniverse.com
1-800-Authors (1-800-288-4677)

ISBN: 978-1-4401-0885-3 (pbk)
ISBN: 978-1-4401-0886-0 (ebk)

Printed in the United States of America

iUniverse rev. date: 11/18/2008

Acknowledgements

I'd like to thank Ken Clark, Kathy Staley, and Robbie Ellis-Cantwell for proofing this manuscript. Their task is a tremendous one as grammar, punctuation, and I never get along.

Dedication

This book is dedicated to all my friends in Bloomington, Indiana and especially to Marc…

Six Months After *Outfield Menace*…

November 1952

Kurt

I sat in Ryan's garden staring down at Angel's letter. A chill breeze blew across my neck, making me shiver. The letter trembled slightly in my hands. I'd been trying ever so hard not to miss Angel, but I yearned for him with all my heart. I had read his letter so often in the past weeks it was beginning to separate at the folds. It had been six months since Angel left, and I felt as if a hundred years had passed. I looked down at the letter and read it once again in the bright autumn sunlight.

Dear Kurt,

I hope you get this letter before you go to school. I had a talk with Noah Taber last night, and I gave him a letter to pass around at school. I know you're not going to like it, but the only way I could think of to make everything okay for you is to make everyone think I'm the queer. I couldn't bear seeing you abused any more. I've been a coward. I know I should've stood by you when all this started, but I just didn't have the courage. I couldn't take everyone hating me. It wasn't all cowardice, though. You see, Adam and the others killed Matt Taber because they found out he was like us. I was afraid they'd come after you, and the only way I could think to save you was to pretend I hated you, too. I even managed to convince Adam that I especially had it in for you and made him promise I'd get to be in on the "fun." Adam bought it and said it was a chance for me to redeem myself and prove my loyalty.

I was there the night they killed Matt, but as I told

you, I didn't do it. I tried to stop it and nearly got myself killed. I didn't know what they were going to do to him until they started beating him. That's when I tried to put an end to it, but they held me back. I fought, but with them holding each of my arms I couldn't break free. There wasn't anything I could do. I had to just stand there and watch them kill him. I really think they would've killed me, too, if Adam wasn't so obsessed with baseball. Jesse wanted to kill me. He argued hard for it, but Adam told him 'no,' and what Adam says goes. If I wasn't a kick-ass first baseman, I think they would've offed me. It's kind of weird, isn't it, that baseball saved my life?

I had to watch it after that. I wanted out of Adam's little gang, but if they even suspected I might tell about what I'd seen, they would've killed me for sure. That's why I wouldn't talk to you about the night Matt died. I didn't want to put you in danger. I would've taken the secret to my grave, probably, if it hadn't been for them coming after you.

I know I should've gone straight to the cops after they'd killed Matt, but I was too scared. I just didn't know what to do, and Adam said he'd make sure he took me down with them if I ever opened my mouth about it.

I sent a letter to the cops before coming here tonight, telling them exactly what happened the night Matt died. I gave them all the names. Hopefully, it will be enough to put Adam and all those assholes behind bars for a long time, but who knows? If not, they'll kill me for sure, so I have to leave.

I'd take that risk to stay with you, because I love you more than anything, but there's more to the situation than that. Me being here wouldn't stop the name-calling and abuse. Even if I admitted to being a homo, too, it still wouldn't stop it. Maybe it would be easier to take because we were in it together, but it wouldn't end it. The only way I could think of to end it is to take the blame myself. In the letter I gave to Noah, it says that I'm the queer, not you. It says... well, you'll read it, so you'll know.

I told Noah who killed his brother. I told him how I had wanted to stop it, but couldn't. He actually thanked me for trying to save his little brother. I wish I could've. Anyway, it feels good to get it all off my chest.

I love you, Kurt, more than anything else. I'll always love you. I'd give my life to stay with you, but Blackford isn't ready for two boys in love. Even if there was a way to save you without everyone thinking I'm a queer, they'd catch onto us eventually. I mean, they're not that stupid. Maybe the world will change some day. I hope so. Anyway, what I want most of all is for you to be happy. I love you, Kurt. Be happy.

Angel

P.S. Look for me on graduation day. I know it's a long time off, but I'll be there. No matter where I end up in the world, I'll come back, and maybe when I leave again, you'll come with me.

A shadow fell across the letter just as I finished reading it. I looked up into Ryan's wise eyes. I did my best to smile, but my heart was breaking. I put the letter aside, jumped up, and grabbed Ryan around the waist.

"It will be okay, Kurt. He'll come back," Ryan said.

I cried softly into Ryan's shoulder. He wrapped his arms around me and held me close. As always I felt safe in Ryan's embrace.

"It's a little chilly to be sitting out here. Let's go inside. We'll talk and have something hot to drink," Ryan said after I'd gotten myself under control.

I nodded, still too choked up to speak. Ryan led me from the stone patio into his Frank Lloyd Wright style house. I sat in one of the comfortable club chairs while Ryan walked on to the kitchen.

"Hot cocoa or hot tea?" Ryan asked.

"Cocoa, please."

"Good choice."

I loved Ryan's home. It was one-story, with a high, peaked roof, and it looked as though it had just kind of grown there instead of being built. The lower halves of the walls were rough stone in a reddish-orange hue, and the upper parts were some sort of dark wood I didn't recognize. There were lots of windows, adding to the beauty of the house. The patio extended out from the back porch, flowing into the garden, so that it was difficult to determine where one ended and the other began. Even in November, the garden was beautiful.

I looked out the windows into the garden. It was dormant now, but the statuary of beautiful youths, small spruce trees, and boxwood made it far more cheerful than most other gardens at this time of year. In the summer, Ryan's garden was no less than a paradise. Its beauty had helped ease my heart since my boyfriend left. I'd worked among the hostas, geraniums, and black-eyed susans, losing myself in their beauty so as not to dwell on the sense of loneliness that had threatened to overwhelm me.

There were so many plants inside near the south-facing windows that it looked as if the garden had crept inside to spend the winter near the fire. Ivy crawled up the walls and above the windows. A large banana tree, a dwarf lemon tree, and something Ryan said was a kumquat tree added a touch of summer to the indoors.

Ryan's living room felt like something out of a ski lodge, with its great stone fireplace, exposed wooden rafters, and huge art-deco rug. The room was filled with comfortable, leather club chairs and love seats. I snuggled back in my chair and extended my hands toward the crackling fire. The scent of wood smoke tickled my nostrils.

I heard Ryan's familiar step behind me and turned to see him carrying a tray holding two extra-large mugs of steaming cocoa and a bowl of marshmallows. He set the tray down on a low, wooden table between our chairs and handed me a mug.

"Thanks," I said as I plopped a marshmallow into my mug.

That was the last word spoken for quite some time. We just sat there sipping cocoa and gazing at the fire and the indoor garden. My eyes wandered to Ryan from time to time. He was looking very handsome in his black-wool, cable-knit sweater. There was a time when I'd had some sexual thoughts about Ryan, even though he was old enough to be my father. My heart belonged to Angel now, however, and Ryan had become my mentor. He was like a second father, too, and I could talk to him about things I'd never dare speak of with my dad.

"I really miss him," I said, stating the obvious. I felt as if I might begin crying again.

"I know you do, Kurt, but Angel will come back."

"At graduation? I'm a sophomore! I feel as if he's been gone forever. How can I survive waiting three whole years?"

"By taking it one day at a time, Kurt. Don't look so far down the road. Hold your love for Angel in your heart. Think of his return as a wonderful, distant event, to be anticipated with joy. Until you can be together once more, focus on your own life—school, work, and fun. Time will pass much more quickly if you don't dwell on Angel's absence. Enjoy what you can of your life now, Kurt, and the days will speed by. You only get to be fifteen once, after all."

"Yes, but three years!"

"Look at it this way, Kurt. There is nothing you can do to change the situation. Angel made a great sacrifice to turn back the clock, so to speak. I'm sure I don't have to remind you what your life was like when everyone believed you were a homosexual. Now, only a few of us know the truth. You're safe now, Kurt, because of Angel.

"You owe it to Angel to be as happy as you can be. You know he wants you to be happy. You won't be able to help missing Angel from time to time. I'm sure he'll miss you, as well. Things are as they are, however, so you must make the best of the situation. Life is too short to waste even a moment, Kurt. I know. I feel as if I was your age only yesterday. The years fly by, Kurt. I'm not saying you should forget about Angel. You can't and you shouldn't, but do your best not to be so sad. Remember the good times with Angel, and look forward with eager anticipation to when you can be together again. I know you don't feel like it now, Kurt, but you're a very lucky boy. You've found love when you're young. Some people go through their entire lives without finding love. It's especially hard for guys like us. Even though he can't be with you right now, Kurt, you still have Angel. Remember that."

I nodded.

"You're right, of course, but it's still hard."

"I know it is. The important thing is to look at the situation as positively as you can. The difference between happiness and sadness is most often perception. You are only as happy or as unhappy as you believe yourself to be. You have a wonderful, handsome boyfriend who loves you so much he sacrificed himself to save you. Beyond all hope, the nightmare you were living has ended. Angel saved your life—literally and figuratively. You can walk through the hallways of your school now without being hated. You're free to enjoy your life as you have not been since the trouble began. Look around you, Kurt, smell the flowers, and gaze upon the trees. Enjoy your friends and your family. Spend time with your coin collection. Do all the things you enjoy. Angel sacrificed himself so that you could enjoy your life, so do so until you can share your life with him."

"Thanks, Ryan," I said.

"You're very welcome. Dispensing wisdom is what we old guys are for."

I laughed. "You're not *that* old."

Ryan was right. I missed Angel terribly, but there was nothing I could do to change the situation. Angel and I simply could not be together right now. Even if I knew where he was, I couldn't just run away and join him. To do so would be to undo the sacrifice he'd made for me.

"I hope he's okay," I said.

"Angel is a very bright and resourceful boy. He's also the most courageous boy I've ever had the honor of knowing. Angel can handle anything life throws at him. I'm sure he's treating his life right now as a big adventure. You can rest assured that he'll keep his promise. He will return to you, Kurt."

"I know he'll come back," I said. "I can feel it in my heart."

"Trust your heart, Kurt. It will never lead you wrong. Even when your thoughts attempt to lead you astray, your heart will remain true."

I nodded. Ryan had a way of putting things in perspective. He never tried to sugarcoat anything for me, but he helped me look at things in the proper way. I didn't know what I'd do without him.

Every young homo needed an older mentor like Ryan—someone more experienced and wiser who wouldn't take advantage.

I shuddered to think that Ryan had very nearly been lynched by a mob for the murder of Matt Taber. Ryan was entirely innocent, of course, but Danny Mackwoods had turned him in because his car matched the one supposedly seen trailing Matt shortly before Matt was brutally murdered. It was my own fault Danny found out about that. He overheard me talking to Angel about the car in Ryan's garage. Even before I found out who really killed Matt, I didn't truly believe Ryan was guilty. Still, I'd nearly cost Ryan his life. Thank God he had forgiven me.

Angel had saved Ryan, too. He was still on the inside of Adam's gang then, pretending to be one of them. It was Angel who called the cops and tipped them off that a lynch mob was coming for Ryan. Angel had saved my life and Ryan's. He was a hero.

Ryan and I sat and sipped hot cocoa for a good long time in silence while thoughts of Angel flowed through my mind.

Eventually, we stood. I gave Ryan a hug and thanked him for helping me through another dark hour. I felt a good deal better as I walked toward home. It would be many long months before I laid eyes on Angel again, but he was with me in my heart, so he wasn't truly gone. I wondered what Angel was doing at just that moment and if he was thinking of me.

Angel

A mile isn't far when speeding down the road in a car, but it seems a good deal farther when one is walking. Oh, how my feet ached in those first days of my flight from Blackford, Indiana. I walked all night, every night, for an entire week before I felt safe enough from prying eyes to venture out in the daylight. I couldn't even begin to guess how far I'd walked during those nights. Distance didn't mean much in the dark.

My heart ached in those early days, for each step took me farther away from Kurt. My departure meant he could go back to living his life unmolested, and that made our separation worth it. I loved Kurt with all my heart and would have done anything to take away his pain. Exiling myself from Blackford for a few years was a small price to pay for his happiness. If only we could have remained together…

There was no use dwelling on "if only," so I gave that up quickly. Although my heart ached with longing for Kurt, I was happy. I'd saved him: first, from Adam, Chuck, Danny, Jesse, Travis, and Joshua, who would have happily murdered him for being homosexual; and second, from all the other jerks who were making his life a living hell for the same reason.

With any luck, Adam's gang was behind bars now and wouldn't have the chance to murder again. I was sure the family of Matt Taber would do all they could to see that the gang was punished. I was concerned for Kurt's safety, but if Adam's gang wasn't already in jail, they would avoid Kurt like the plague. Adam wasn't stupid. He'd know the cops were watching Kurt just in case the gang came after him. Kurt was too obvious a target. If the gang wasn't behind bars, I was sure the cops had Kurt's house staked out. It was quite a different story where I was concerned. If I'd stayed in Blackford, Adam would have come after me no matter what. I'm sure he would gladly have risked prison to make me pay for turning him in. I halted for a moment. What if he saw Kurt as an opportunity to punish me? It was a chilling thought. No. I knew Adam. He wouldn't risk his own neck or that of any member of the gang for anything less than me. Kurt was safe. I was not.

No matter where the situation with Adam stood, I couldn't go back home. My name was mud back in Blackford High School. I'd publicly announced I was a homosexual with the letter I'd left behind and had told all my classmates they could go fuck themselves for being prejudiced bastards. I smiled when I thought of their rage and frustration at not being able to lay their hands on me.

I wondered what my parents thought of me. I'd left them a letter, too, but one quite different from the letter I'd left for my classmates. I told my parents I loved them and that I was sorry to have to leave. I told them the truth about me: that I was attracted to guys instead of girls. I hoped they wouldn't hate me for that, but if they did hate me, then they weren't the parents I thought they were. I was sure my mom, at least, was worried about me. I was sorry for putting her through that worry, but I had no choice. The only way to save Kurt was to leave Blackford behind.

My stomach growled. I'd tried to save as much of the money I brought with me as possible, and I'd picked up odd jobs here and there, but it was hard for a vagrant like me to find work. As a result, I skimped on meals even when I had a fair supply of cash. My future was uncertain, and I didn't want to find myself with nothing. Better to skimp now than starve later. Besides, as long as I had a little money in my pocket, I wasn't broke. Having absolutely nothing would've left me feeling too desolate. I'd read somewhere that Mark Twain was down on his luck for quite a spell and refused to spend his last dime. He kept that dime no matter what, so he wouldn't be penniless. Who would've thought that Mark Twain and I would have something in common?

I had enjoyed walking in the night during those early days, with the stars above and the owls hooting in the near and far distance. It was still more pleasant to travel in the daylight. After a week of nighttime travel, I'd figured I was far enough away from Blackford to risk hiking along in the daytime. I wasn't a fugitive after all. The police might want me to testify against Adam's gang, but I doubted they would expend any great effort to find me. They would just have to make do with the letter I sent naming Matt Taber's killers.

I was sure one of Adam's gang would crack under the pressure and tell all. That would seal the fate of Adam & Company. My parents might be searching for me, but I'd figured they would give up after a week. After reading my letter and discovering I was a homosexual, they might be glad to be rid of me. I wondered how Mom and Dad were holding up under the stares of the townsfolk of Blackford. Most people there couldn't bring themselves to say the word "homosexual," much less think one had actually walked the streets of their hometown. I hoped I hadn't caused my parents too much trouble, but I couldn't help being what I was. God had made me attracted to boys instead of girls, and I could no more change that than I could change into an eagle. If only I *could* change into an eagle! Then I could fly instead of walk! My mind took many flights of fantasy as I walked along lonely stretches of dusty road.

Six months had passed. All those long weeks of travel, of never staying in the same place for more than a few days, had made my legs strong and my feet accustomed to long hikes. Still, my legs, feet, and the rest of me were tired by the time the sun dipped below the horizon. The nights were becoming cold, and I wondered how I'd get on when fall truly gave way to winter. I guessed I'd deal with that when it happened.

I left the gravel road and lay down under the stars, hidden by a few small cedar trees that filled the air with their woodsy scent. Nearby, wisps of fog twisted and rose from a small pond. The fog crept up the slope toward me like small, insubstantial spirits.

I thought of Kurt as I lay there. I wondered if he was snug and warm in his bed at home. I was tempted to write him a letter, but I wasn't sure it was wise. My parents could force me to come home if they found me. I would not be so foolish as to include a return address (even if I had one), but the letter would be postmarked.

No one had a clue as to where I was now. I wanted to keep it that way. I had traveled first south, then east, and finally north again just to jumble any attempt to find me. Of course, there might be no one searching for me at all, especially after all this time, but I just couldn't risk it. If I was forced back to Blackford, I'd be forced to attend school. A living hell awaited me if I ever returned to B.H.S. No, I couldn't risk a letter or even a phone call. Phone calls could be traced—at least they could be traced on radio cop shows and probably in real life, too. I wished I could let Kurt know I was okay, but it was just too risky.

I thought about the day when I would return. There would be Kurt, eighteen-years-old instead of fifteen. He'd be taller. He might look quite different. How he looked didn't matter, but it would feel odd meeting him again after all that time. Would he even be the same person? We would both legally be adults, and no one could stop us from going wherever we wished then. Would Kurt wait for me all those years? Three years was a very long time. I felt as if an eternity had already passed, and yet only a sixth of our waiting time was over.

"He'll wait on me," I said out loud to the darkness. "I can feel it in my heart."

***

I awakened the next morning to the singing of cardinals. Birds and animals were often my companions on the road. I had awakened before to find raccoons, rabbits, and deer nosing about. I often spotted them as I walked along. They paid me little mind, as if they knew I was no threat. Once, I'd awakened to find myself face to face with a skunk. He was quite a beautiful creature really, but I dared not move a muscle. I watched him as he slowly waddled away. I was glad he hadn't taken a dislike to me. I had no idea how long it took the stench of skunk spray to wear off.

Great fluffy flakes fell from the sky. The fragrant cedars had kept most of the snow off me, but the ground was covered in white. I stood, stretched, and zipped up my leather jacket as far as I could. I dug in my pocket and pulled out a hard roll I'd purchased two days before. I nibbled at the stale, buttery roll as I made my way back to the road. I hoped I'd come across some sign of civilization soon or I'd have a hungry day and night. Going without wasn't so bad really, but I didn't like missing too many meals in a row. That had happened a handful of times when the little towns and farms had been too far apart or when everything was closed because it was a Sunday or a holiday. I tried to carry a supply of food in my pockets, but sometimes one outpost of civilization was too far from the last.

I was chilled from sleeping on the ground, but I began to warm up as I walked along. I was heading north. I was many, many miles north of Indianapolis already. I'd stayed there a few days, but it was too big a city for me. I preferred small towns like the one I'd left behind far to the south.

The wind got up, turning the chill into a deep freeze. Fall turned into winter before my eyes. I shivered and was thankful for my warm leather jacket, my flannel shirt, and my long hair. I had considered cutting my hair to disguise myself, but I just couldn't bring myself to do it. I wouldn't feel quite like myself if I didn't feel my long blond mane on my neck and shoulders. Hair as long as mine was quite a rarity so it would probably have been wiser to cut it, but I'd made it six months without doing so, and I wasn't about to chop it off now. I got quite a few odd looks as I traveled and I was sure it was the reason I was seldom offered a ride, but I'd never been bothered by what others thought of me. Now, I was doubly glad I hadn't cut my hair. It helped keep me warm in the growing cold.

I trudged along through the snow, mile after mile. I was hiking through some beautiful, if rather flat, country. I wasn't entirely sure where I was, but I was somewhere north of Logansport. I guess my location didn't matter all that much as long as there was some kind of town not too far ahead. The problem was, I didn't know if the next town was two miles away or twenty. Even a map wouldn't have helped a great deal. It would be hard to figure out how far I was from the next town when I wasn't sure where I was.

I kept on walking. The movement helped me keep warm. Fond thoughts of hot cocoa, hot tea, hot *anything* danced in my head. What I wouldn't have given for a steaming bowl of chili, or vegetable or potato soup.

I heard a car coming up behind me. It was only the third one of the morning, and I'd been walking for some hours. Not many souls were brave (or stupid) enough to venture out into the falling snow. As it drew nearer I looked back and saw it wasn't a car at all, but a shiny-green Ford pickup. The driver slowed as he neared and pulled the truck to a halt as it came even with me. He motioned for me to open the passenger-side door.

"Would you like a ride?"

"Definitely! Thanks!"

"It's turning nastier out there by the minute. You shouldn't be outside. The radio says we may get a regular blizzard in a few hours."

"I'll ride it out in the next town."

"So, where are you headed?"

"Anyplace that's warm where I can get something to eat," I said.

Perhaps I should've lied, but I hated lying. The truth was probably as good as any story I could make up, and it was a good deal easier to remember.

"Oh, I didn't introduce myself. I'm Jack. Jack Selby."

"I'm Angel."

"Angel," Jack repeated. A look of profound sadness crossed his handsome features, but it was gone almost before it appeared. "Now, that's an interesting name."

"Yeah, there aren't many Angels around."

Jack put the truck in gear. I could hear the snow compacting under the tires as the truck moved slowly down the road. I looked at Jack as he steered. He wasn't quite thirty. He was younger than my dad, in any case. He had dark hair and was rather good-looking. His face was a bit stern, yet kind. I liked him. I could just tell he was a good person. I felt completely at ease riding in his truck.

The snow fell steadily down, sometimes whipped around by the wind. The wipers were kept busy keeping the fluffy white stuff off the windshield. I reveled in the warmth of the cab as I watched the passing scenery.

"Nice truck," I said.

"Thanks. I'm very proud of her. She's only a few months old. This is my first new vehicle. She's quite a step up from the old Model A truck I had before."

"Model A? From the 30s?"

"Yeah, she was almost an antique, but a vast improvement over my first car."

"What was that?"

"A Model T."

"Really?"

"Yeah. The top speed was twenty-five miles per hour, downhill. On a flat road I was lucky to get her up to twenty. It was all I could afford at the time. I bought her at an auction for $35."

"That's all? Wow, $35 for a car!"

"Well, she'd seen better days. She ran perfectly, though. I fixed her up until she looked like new. I actually still have her stored in the barn. I'm not quite sure why I keep her."

"Does she still run?"

"Probably not. She had a few problems near the end, and she's been sitting for a long time. That's not good for a car."

"What happened to your old truck?"

"It's sitting out behind a shed on the farm. She was my dad's. He was a farmer, like me. He drove that truck everywhere. When Dad passed away I inherited his truck, along with everything else. I used her until this spring. She threw a rod, and that was that."

"Where do you live?" I asked.

"Outside of Verona."

"Is Verona far?"

"No. It's just a few miles up the road, although it will take a while to get there in this snow. It's the next sizeable town."

"Is there a restaurant?"

"Oh, yes. More than one. There's a drive-in. It's the hangout spot for teenagers, but it's closed for the season. There's also Rector's Soda Shop, which serves burgers, hot dogs, and sandwiches in addition to ice cream. The best place to eat is Edna's Diner on Main Street. No matter what you like, you'll find it at Edna's. If she doesn't have it, she'll get it."

"That's where I'm headed then. Edna's sounds like Heaven."

"How old are you, Angel?"

"Fifteen."

"What are you doing out all by yourself on a day like today?"

"That's kind of a long story. I, uh, had to leave home."

Jack didn't ask me why. He just nodded. I liked the way he didn't pry into my business. He didn't treat me like an ignorant kid. He treated me as if I was his age.

"So, what are your plans, Angel? Beyond Edna's that is."

"Well, I, uh, usually look for someplace to sleep. I'll see if I can pick up some jobs shoveling snow or doing whatever. I do a lot of odd jobs to pay my way."

"Have you been doing that long?"

"For a few months now."

"That sounds like a rough way to live."

"It's not so bad. The cold is the only real problem. I guess if I was smart I would've headed south for the winter, instead of north."

"It's warmer down south, I'm sure. I hear Florida is nice this time of year. I've never been there myself, but I've read about it." Jack paused. "You know, I could probably find you some odd jobs to do around the farm tomorrow. Maybe I can save you the trouble of looking for work."

"Really?"

"Why not? There's a spare room. You can sleep there tonight if you'd like."

"That sounds wonderful."

We drove on through the snow. It was warm enough inside the cab that I unzipped my jacket. Even my toes were toasty warm. I was relieved I wouldn't have to sleep outside or in a barn tonight. Cold is bad enough, but the wind would've made my night miserable. Thank God Jack came along and was kind enough to give me a ride.

We passed through a small town that wasn't terribly different from Blackford. It did seem a bit larger, with more stores, but it could've easily been named Blackford-North.

Soon, Jack turned off on a winding gravel drive. I could just make out a large farmhouse and a big barn beyond. The driveway wasn't terribly long, but the swirling snow reduced visibility a great deal. I was relieved when we'd reached our destination. The snowstorm was growing more intense by the minute. Soon, Jack wouldn't have been able to see past the hood of his Ford.

I followed Jack around to the back of the house. He led me inside.

"Emma! I brought something home!"

"Not another stray," said a woman's voice coming down the stairway. Soon, the voice was followed by Emma herself, who must've been Jack's wife. She was rather pretty, with beautiful blonde hair and blue eyes. She was obviously surprised to see me, but she smiled.

"Hmm, not the kind of stray I was expecting."

"Emma, this is…Angel."

"Angel?"

Emma and Jack exchanged a look, but I couldn't figure out just what kind of look it was. Emma looked back to me.

"It's very nice to meet you, Angel."

"Angel is going to help me out with some odd jobs tomorrow. I thought he could use the guest room tonight."

"I was just about to start supper. Do you like fried chicken, Angel?"

"I love it."

"Good. It will be an hour or so before it's ready. You look tired. Perhaps you'd like a bath and a little rest. I'll come for you when it's time for supper, or send Jack."

"Thank you," I said.

"Come on. I'll show you where everything is," Jack said.

Jack led me upstairs to a large bedroom. There was a big double bed, an old dresser, and a rocking chair.

"Here it is," Jack announced. "I hope you like it."

"It's great!"

"The bathroom is just down the hall. I'll set out everything you need."

"Thank you so much, Jack. I really appreciate this."

"Think nothing of it."

With that, Jack departed, closing the door behind him. I sat on the bed for a moment, trying it out. I sank back into it, nearly toppling over. It was a feather bed. I struggled to my feet and walked to the window. There was nothing to see but swirling snow. Jack was right; a blizzard was coming, if it hadn't arrived already.

I shivered as the wind shook the window panes. The very sight of all the blowing snow made me cold. I was truly grateful to be inside out of the wintry storm. I'd really lucked out when Jack picked me up—fried chicken, a hot bath, and a warm place to sleep! Life didn't get any better than that!

I left my cozy room and walked down the hallway to the bathroom. There I found not only a towel and washcloth laid out, but a set of clothes as well. I stripped and filled the tub with water as hot as I could stand it. A couple of minutes later I eased myself into the tub. Ahhhh!

I'd warmed up on the ride to the farm, but the hot water really did the trick. I could feel the heat penetrating me, easing my muscles. I sank down in the old-fashioned tub until the water was up to my chin.

I had a good wash, shampooing my hair twice, and then I lay back and relaxed in the tub. Pure luxury. I think I could have stayed forever. I grew sleepy after a few minutes and nearly nodded off, so I thought it wise to climb out. I didn't think drowning in the Selby's tub would be a good way to repay their hospitality. *Oh look, a dead boy in the tub. How nice.*

I stood and let the water run off my body as the tub drained. I grabbed the towel and dried off. The clothes were rather too large for me, but they were clean, warm, and comfortable. I took my belt out of my jeans and used it to hold up the jeans Jack had left for me. Without the belt, the jeans might've fallen down. That would be truly embarrassing.

I gathered my dirty clothes and carried them back to "my" room. I set them on top of the dresser. Jack had included a flannel shirt in the pile of clothes he'd left for me, and I snuggled into it gratefully. I had so much to be grateful for that I felt like it was Thanksgiving.

I lay back on the bed, telling myself I'd just rest for a bit. I must've fallen asleep, for I was awakened by a rap on the door what seemed only moments later. I rose up on my elbows, more or less. It was rather difficult raising myself off the feather bed.

"Yes?"

"Supper is ready," Jack said.

"I'll be right out!" I said.

I was famished. I squirmed my way to the edge of the bed and quickly pulled on my shoes. I rushed to the door where Jack was waiting.

"Thanks for loaning me the clothes," I said as I followed him down the hallway.

"I thought yours could probably use a wash. We couldn't have you running around naked, now could we? For one thing, it's much too cold."

"Too embarrassing as well," I added.

Jack laughed.

I caught the scent of fried chicken and freshly baked bread halfway down the stairs. I was suddenly twice as hungry as before. Real food!

The scent was even more heavenly in the kitchen itself.

"Have a seat, Angel," Emma said. "Iced tea?"

"Yes, please."

"Help yourself, Angel," Jack said.

Never one to be shy, especially not when I was starving, I reached out and took a drumstick. Next, I put a small mound of mashed potatoes on my plate, followed by green beans, and cooked apples. Emma cut me a thick slice of hot-from-the-oven bread. I smeared butter and strawberry jam over it.

I took a bite of chicken.

"This is so good," I said, forgetting not to speak with my mouth full.

"Thank you, Angel."

"Emma is an excellent cook," Jack said. "Her blackberry pie takes first prize at the county fair every year."

"I've only entered for the last two years, Jack. To hear you talk, you'd think I'd won annually since I was six."

"If you had entered, you would have won. I'm merely giving credit where it's due."

I liked the easygoing way of Emma and Jack. They seemed just right for each other. They seemed appreciative of each other, too. There was a touch of sadness to the pair. It was subtle, yet detectable. Perhaps it was something in their eyes as they looked at each other. Perhaps it was their tone of voice. I don't really know, but a sense of shared tragedy was noticeable even when they were smiling. I didn't give it a great deal of thought. It's a wonder I even noticed. My attention was almost wholly focused on my plate.

It was only with effort that I was able to keep from devouring everything on my plate like some wild boy. It had been some time since I'd had a real meal. I couldn't remember the last time I'd eaten so well.

I found myself talking more after I refilled my plate with everything. I didn't even realize I was doing it at first, but I was telling Jack and Emma the whole tale of my troubles with Adam and his gang. I'd shot my mouth off about Kurt before I could stop myself. When I realized I'd given myself away my eyes widened in surprise.

I've done it now. They'll kick me out for sure. One just doesn't announce he's a homosexual to people he's just met.

"It's okay, Angel," Emma said.

I realized I must have had a look of shock and terror on my face.

"I didn't mean to tell you that," I said. "I'm sorry. Do you want me to go?"

"Of course not," Emma said.

Jack said nothing. I wasn't quite sure what he thought about my announcement. He didn't look pleased, yet he didn't look ready to toss me out on my butt, either. Emma gave him a look, and he finally spoke.

"You're welcome here, Angel. Don't worry about that. Now, why don't we try some of Emma's blue-ribbon blackberry pie?"

"Thanks," I said.

I breathed a sigh of relief. How could I be so reckless? I didn't usually let my mouth run off like that. I wasn't one bit ashamed of what I was, but I wasn't stupid, either. I knew what most people thought of homos. In all the months since I'd left Blackford, I'd never once told anyone about me until right there in the Selby kitchen. I guess I was just so comfortable and relaxed I forgot myself.

Our talk shifted to the Selby farm while we ate dessert. I could easily understand why Emma's blackberry pie won a blue ribbon at the county fair every year. I was quite stuffed, but I just couldn't quit eating that pie. It might just have been the best pie ever. It was even better than Mom's, although I'd never tell Mom that. I felt a touch of sadness as I thought of my mother, but I let it pass.

Jack excused himself to take care of the animals when we'd finished. I offered to help, but he told me to stay put. Emma made us some hot tea, and we sat in the table and drank it out of Golden Wheat cups. I remembered that Kurt's mom had a set of that china pattern. It had real gold around the edges.

"Do you think Jack's okay with…what I told you…about my… boyfriend?" I asked.

"I think you took him by surprise, that's all."

"You're a lot nicer than most people."

"My father once told me there were two rules to judging others. Rule number one is to judge others by what they do, not by who or what they are. Rule number two is not to judge others."

I smiled. "I like that."

"I get a feeling about people when I meet them. You seem like a nice boy, Angel. You're not the first homosexual I've met, either. I must admit my first encounter was disturbing in the beginning. I'd heard so many nasty stories. I have to see something for myself before I believe it, and well, what I saw was a kind, considerate soul, not unlike you. I learned to relax, and when I got to know him a bit, I discovered he was much like everyone else."

"A lot of people hate me for what I am, but I don't understand it. I know in here," I said, pointing to my chest, "that I am as I was meant to be. I've always been completely comfortable with who and what I am."

"You're a smart boy."

"You really think Jack's okay with it? He's been so nice to me. You both have."

"Don't worry about it, Angel. Jack isn't the judgmental type. That's one reason I married him. Knowing Jack, he's already forgotten what you said. He doesn't consider things like that important. Now, if you'd said something about growing corn or raising chickens, *that* he would remember."

Emma gave a small laugh. She was very easy to talk to, so I ventured to speak with her about something I'd been wondering about.

"Both of you reacted to my name," I said. "I know it's an unusual name, but I feel like there's more to your reaction than that."

"You're not from around here, so you don't know, but...there was an Angel in our lives for a short time: our son."

I swallowed. I was suddenly fearful I'd brought up a painful topic.

"I guess he's…not here anymore." I chose my words carefully.

"No. We lost him to pneumonia when he was five. He had blond hair and blue eyes, just like you. His hair wasn't as long, of course, but…"

Emma was on the verge of tears. I took her hand.

"I'm sorry. I shouldn't have asked."

"No. No. It's okay. Angel is in our thoughts always. You're not bringing up painful memories. Those memories are always there. I try to remember the happy times with him and be thankful that we had those five years with him."

Emma looked into my eyes.

"Your features are quite similar to his. I wonder if our Angel would've looked like you if he'd survived. If so, he would have been a handsome young man."

I squeezed Emma's hand.

"That's why you and Jack seem sad," I said. "Even when you're laughing, there's a little bit of sadness there."

"You're more perceptive than I thought. Yes. Even happy times have an edge of sadness, because our Angel isn't here to share them with us. We keep him alive in our hearts, however, and always will."

I wondered if losing their son made Emma and Jack more accepting of me. I don't mean because our names were the same, but rather that they would probably have given anything to have their son back. They wouldn't care if he was heterosexual or homosexual, as long as he was there. Maybe people really did have to lose something before they understood its worth. Of course, Emma and Jack might have been just as accepting if their son was alive and well and sitting at the table with Emma and me. I wasn't the first homosexual to cross their path, either. I wondered about that, but I'd already asked too many questions. In any case, the Selbys were one in a million, or at least one in a thousand. The world needed more people like them.

Kurt

I followed the scent of bacon downstairs and found not only bacon, but scrambled eggs and toast waiting on the kitchen table. My dad was already out and about. My sister, Ida, was sitting at the table. None of this was a surprise. My older brother, Sam, was still in bed, which was even less of a surprise. Most weekday mornings were the same in the James household.

Mom filled a plate for me with too much, as usual. She was convinced I was too thin. I thought I was just about right at 5'8" and 125 pounds. I would like to be more muscular, but eating too much breakfast certainly wasn't going to help with that. I put some of the scrambled eggs, toast, and bacon back when she wasn't looking. Ida grinned at me and stifled a giggle.

I loved my family, although my mom could be overprotective at times. Dad was forever telling her to back off and not smother us. Dad himself wasn't around as much as I would have liked, but he was there when I really needed him. Sam thought himself to be hot stuff. He had caused some problems when Angel was around, but he was only looking out for me. Once my big brother understood that Angel wasn't taking advantage of me, he'd been supportive. Sam was one of the three people who knew that the rumors about me being a homosexual were actually true. Ryan knew, of course. Tommy, my best friend, knew about me, too. Everyone else believed the letter Angel had left behind.

That letter saved my life, or at least the quality of it. As soon as Angel's letter was passed around at school, the insults and abuse stopped cold. Some of the guys who had been such jerks actually apologized. I was glad Sam and Tommy knew the truth. It felt good to know that my older brother and my best friend knew I was a homo and still cared about me. If the truth got out some day, I would at least have those two in my corner.

I had nearly revealed the Golden Wheat pattern on my plate when Sam finally lumbered in. He mussed my hair, said, "Hey, Squirt," and took a drink directly from the milk bottle while Mom wasn't looking. I grinned. Sam and I were actually closer now than we had been before he found out about me. I think those days when I was in such danger made him realize how much he loved me. The way he tried to look out for me made me realize how much I cared for him, too. The big jerk.

Sam had been down on homos before he found out I was one. He'd suspected Tommy was a homo, which was not true. He also thought the Nudo twins were homos, which was *very* true. His distaste for homosexuals disappeared when he found out the truth about me, and that made me feel good inside.

I finished the last of my scrambled eggs, toast, and bacon as Sam began his. I pulled on my coat and toboggan, kissed Mom goodbye, and began walking toward town. Oh, yeah, in case you aren't from Indiana, a toboggan is a knit cap. I don't know why we use the same word for a cap and a sled, but we do. I just thought you should know.

Our farm wasn't far south of town, but it was a cold walk to get there on a windy morning. Sam would have driven me if I'd asked, but I didn't like to pester him for a ride more often than necessary. Besides, Tommy expected me to show up at his house so we could walk to school together.

I breathed in the fresh, cold air. I liked living in the country. A lot of my friends couldn't wait to get away from "hick country," as they called it, but I was happy here. If only Angel could've been with me.

I stopped, pulled out my wallet, and flipped it open. I took out the small black-and-white photo that was carefully hidden between school photos of Sam and Ida. If anyone saw that photo, I was dead meat. I probably shouldn't have carried it with me at all, but I couldn't bear to be parted with it. I took it out to look at it so often it was a bit worn. The photo was of Angel and me kissing. Ryan had taken it and given it to me. When I looked at it, I felt closer to Angel. I gazed at it for several moments and then tucked it away again.

My cheeks were getting numb by the time I reached Tommy's house. I reveled in the warmth when his mother let me inside. Tommy grinned at me when I entered the kitchen. We'd been friends for a long time, but we were even closer now. Tommy hadn't deserted me during the hard times of a few months before. He was a true friend.

Tommy had flaming red hair and freckles, which he was convinced would keep him from ever finding a girl. He was cute, though, and I had little doubt he could find himself a girlfriend. Tommy was a year younger than I, and I was just fifteen, so he had plenty of time.

Tommy wasn't quite finished with his breakfast, but I didn't mind the wait. I sat in the kitchen and talked with Tommy and his mom. Mrs. Brody was almost like a second mother to me. She even hugged me whenever I stopped in for a visit.

I felt at home in Tommy's kitchen. The old, yellow wallpaper with tiny shamrocks was as familiar to me as the wallpaper in my own kitchen. The old Hoosier cabinet was just as familiar. It had sat in the corner forever, a relic of the olden days, and was still used by Mrs. Brody. They had some dishes that were made during the depression. I liked the vibrant green and the small, three-leaf clovers that decorated the plates, cups, and bowls. I wondered if the dishes had been selected because they matched the wallpaper.

Soon enough, Tommy and I were on our way to Blackford High School.

"Are you going out for varsity baseball next spring?" Tommy asked as we stepped out the door.

"It's November, Tommy. Why are you thinking about baseball?"

"Well, I was just thinking. Adam, Travis, Chuck, Jesse, Danny, and Joshua are all in jail. That's six members of the varsity team gone. With Angel, there's seven gone. It's the perfect opportunity to make the team. It will be totally different now that Adam's crowd is out of the picture."

"I guess you're right. I hadn't thought about it. I might try out next year, but that's a long way off."

"I like to plan for the future."

"Have you picked out Mrs. Tommy Brody yet?" I teased.

"I'd settle for my first date. There are plenty of girls I'm interested in, but the problem is none of them is interested in me. Who can blame them? I'm pathetic."

"Oh, you are not pathetic."

"Yeah, well. Stand me up beside the likes of Adam Voegerl and decide who's the hottest."

"Need I remind you Adam is a murderer? That's not an attractive feature."

"You know what I mean! He's tall, handsome, and strong. I'm none of the above."

"Tommy, you're only an inch shorter than I am."

"Yeah. You're short and I'm shorter."

"Thanks."

"Hey, you have someone," Tommy said in a low voice even though no one was near.

"Yes, but I'll be eighteen before I see him again."

"You still have someone."

"That's true. I wish I didn't have to keep it such a big secret. Maybe then I could keep Alicia Tulleyfield off me."

"Aww, poor Kurt. Has a scary girl been flirting with you again?"

"Yes, she wants me to ask her out. I just know it."

Tommy laughed. "Talk about barking up the wrong tree."

"Hey, why don't you ask her out?" I said.

"Me? Why would a girl like Alicia be interested in me? She's beautiful."

"I thought you just said she was scary."

"That was sarcasm, if you didn't notice."

"So, ask her out."

"Yeah, and get shot down."

"So what if you do get shot down? You won't be any worse off than you are now."

"I guess that's true, but I'd never have the nerve."

"Just ask her out. If she says yes, you'll be doing yourself and me a favor. She won't be hounding me if she's dating you."

"Oh, so I'm supposed to take your rejects?"

"She's not my reject. You know good and well why I'm not interested in Alicia Tulleyfield."

Tommy grinned. He was messing with me.

"I don't know about asking Alicia out."

"Come on. She's interested in dating, or she wouldn't be after me."

"Yeah, but I'm not cute like you."

"You think I'm cute, huh? You homo."

Tommy laughed.

We were nearly at the school. Tommy didn't say whether or not he'd ask Alicia out, and I didn't press him. Most likely, he'd take some convincing and probably a good shove. There was time enough to get my best friend a girl, however.

Tommy and I parted as we entered the school and made for our lockers. I would've thought that after six months I would have adjusted to everything that had happened in the spring, but it still gave me an odd sensation to be on friendly terms with classmates who had treated me like dirt when they thought I was queer. It was especially weird being around Doug Finney and John Hearst. I'd never forget the little scene in the boys' restroom. When they thought I was queer, they actually tried to force me to blow them. If Coach Douglas hadn't come along, they would have made me, I'm sure. I was still frightened of Doug and John even though they'd never tried anything like that again. Neither of them looked me in the eyes now. I think that after the rumors about my homosexuality were quashed, Doug and John were uncomfortable about what they'd tried to force me to do. Sometimes, I hated having to hide the real me, but it was far too dangerous for my classmates to know the truth.

There had been way too much excitement in Blackford in recent months. There was the disappearance of Matt Taber in March, the discovery of his body in April, and the unmasking of his murderers in May. I'd very nearly become the next victim myself. I still had nightmares about that night. The nightmare always ended when Angel came to save me—just as he had in real life. In late September and early November had come the trial for those accused of killing Matt. I didn't attend at first, because I did not want to see Adam and that crowd again. I followed the trial in the weekly paper, however. There was a battle over Angel's letter being used as evidence, but the prosecutor used it to frighten the defendants. I was called in to testify, since Adam and his gang had kidnapped me and made it clear they were going to kill me in a very nasty way. They even made me dig my own grave. I had no doubt that if it wasn't for Angel I'd be rotting away in that grave right now.

Danny Mackwoods cracked under the combined pressure of Angel's letter and my testimony. He admitted everything. His testimony took down the whole lot of them. Adam and his thugs were put behind bars, despite their youth. I was able to do one good turn for my boyfriend. My testimony, combined with that of Danny, established with absolute certainty that Angel had nothing to do with the death of Matt Taber. He had even tried to save him. I also made it clear that he saved my life. There was still some ugly talk about Angel because he was a homo, but some people had changed their minds about him. They no doubt decided that being a hero made up for being a homo. Most people simply didn't believe he was queer—despite the letter he wrote saying otherwise.

I wished I had a way to let Angel know the outcome of the trial, and especially how at least some of the residents of Blackford didn't hate him so much anymore. I had no way to contact him, however. Unfortunately, it still wasn't safe for him to come back. I dreamed of the day we could live together in peace. I knew in my heart we would be together again someday. I wasn't so certain about the living-in-peace part.

I put such thoughts out of my mind. I just wanted to be a normal boy. I guess most people wouldn't consider me normal if they knew I had a boyfriend. I'd certainly be labeled as queer. I felt normal, however. More than that, I was quite certain I was normal. True, most boys were heterosexual, but I was confident that I was exactly as I was meant to be. Angel had made me understand that. He'd done so much for me! I felt as if graduation would never come. That's when Angel had promised to return. I wanted it to be May of 1955 right now!

The calendar stubbornly remained on November of 1952, however. At least it was late November–nearly Thanksgiving, in fact. Then, Christmas would come and the New Year. I wanted very much to take Ryan's advice and enjoy my life so that time would pass faster, but I so wanted to be with Angel again!

I spotted several of my J.V. teammates as I sorted through books in my locker—Bart, Derek, Edgar, Fred, Sidney, Horace, and the Nudo twins. I wondered how many of us would make varsity next year. I grinned. Tommy had affected me. He had me thinking about baseball.

I headed toward my first-period, American Literature class with Mrs. Kendall. I was determined to immerse myself in the class and make at least fifty minutes pass quickly. I wasn't thrilled with Mrs. Kendall when I had her for English my freshman year, but I found it was the subject, and not the teacher, that I disliked. Lit was so much more fun than English! We had just finished reading several poems by Robert Frost, which I enjoyed immensely. We were on the second chapter of *The Country of the Pointed Firs* by Sarah Orne Jewett. I had never heard of her before, but enjoyed her writing enough that I'd been reading ahead. Several of my classmates, most of them guys, didn't care for Jewett's book at all. Of course, most of the guys didn't like reading anything if it wasn't a comic book. Most of the girls were into the novel, and I wished I could discuss it as eagerly as they did. I had to pretend disinterest, but at least I could intelligently answer questions in class. I wondered if Ryan had read the novel.

My next class of the day was World History. I rather liked it, probably because Mr. Brooks wasn't big on names and dates. He told us back in August that he didn't think exact dates were important. "One can always look that up," he said. Instead, Mr. Brooks focused on the events themselves, how they came about, and how those events changed history. We spent a good deal of time on people, too, not just the famous, but the ordinary people of Ancient Greece, Rome, and other civilizations. Mr. Brooks made history into a story, which is what it should be. Far too many of my teachers reduced exciting times and places to dry, dull facts.

Mr. Brooks was no pushover, and his tests were mostly essay. Each test also had a section where one had to put key events in chronological order. While Mr. Brooks taught us that remembering exact dates wasn't important, it was important to understand that Julius Caesar ruled Rome before Augustus and so on. Mr. Brooks was a popular teacher, despite the difficulty of his tests.

I shared second-period World History with Tanner and Tyler, the Nudo brothers. They were identical twins and I could only tell them apart by the desks they occupied. Both had unruly black hair, tanned faces, dreamy brown eyes, and nice builds. Even their gestures and mannerisms were exactly alike. More than once I'd asked them a question and they both answered at the exact same time, in the exact same words, with the exact same facial expressions. It was freaky.

It was widely rumored that the Nudo twins were not only homos, but had sex with each other. It was one of those rumors that had been around so long that no one really thought anything about it. I think most didn't believe it, even though the brothers were extremely close. I knew for a fact that the rumors about them were true. Tanner and Tyler were homos. What's more, they had kissed right in front of me! I'd been simultaneously aroused and turned off by that. The very thought of incest was about more than I could stand—eww! Yet there was something intensely erotic about exact duplicates making out. I had bolted from their bedroom right after they kissed, mainly because I was overwhelmed and madly turned on. It was just too much to handle.

Poor Tanner and Tyler thought they had made a major mistake kissing in front of me. They had strongly suspected I was homosexual like them, but my reaction made it appear they were wrong. I promised never to reveal what I knew about them to anyone, but left them with the impression I wasn't like them. I could have told them the truth, but something held me back. Then came Angel's letter and everyone again believed I was heterosexual. I guess it would be safe enough to tell the

Nudo twins I was like them, but it was just easier to keep everyone in the dark. The fewer people who knew the truth, the fewer would be the chances for someone to slip up and reveal that I was, indeed, a homo.

I would have been tempted to reveal the truth to the Nudo twins if I didn't have Ryan. Without Ryan I would have been totally alone as far as having someone to talk to about homosexual feelings. Sam and Tommy knew my secret, but neither of them were like me. They couldn't begin to understand what was going on in my life. My conscience was eased by the fact that the twins had each other.

Even though he believed I was heterosexual, Tyler couldn't help but check me out now and then. There was something in his gaze that indicated more than casual interest. Of course, I knew both of the twins were interested in me. The proof of that had come months back when they'd invited me out for ice cream, and they'd ended up kissing in front of me in their bedroom. I am quite sure that, had I been up for it, we would all have been naked on the bed. Perhaps one of the reasons I didn't reveal the truth to the twins was to keep myself safe from their advances. I loved Angel dearly, but the Nudo twins were extremely attractive, and I hadn't had sex for months—at least, involving more than myself. There was no reason to tempt fate.

My mind had been wandering. We were several minutes into class and I couldn't remember a thing before that moment. I forced myself to pay attention. Mr. Brooks was talking about the Black Death and how many people in the Fourteenth Century believed it was caused by bad air. They actually thought that burning incense and wearing perfumes would help them. That seemed quite ridiculous now, but I wondered how many of our own beliefs would seem just as ridiculous far in the future.

I liked the way history put things in perspective. So much of what was accepted as truth in the past turned out not to be true at all. In my own time, homosexuals were considered to be on the same level as murderers. Just think about it. Many people, perhaps even most, thought it was just as bad to love someone of the same sex as it was to kill someone! Where was the logic in that? I had the feeling that some day that particular notion would be considered ridiculous. I just hoped I lived long enough to see it.

I was glad I'd met Angel and Ryan. Angel was completely at ease with his homosexuality. He accepted it and didn't let the opinions of others sway him. Ryan had lived long enough that he was at ease with himself, too. He'd told me about how he wrestled with doubts and self-hatred early in his life. I felt like I didn't have to struggle like that, because Angel and Ryan were there to teach me. Ryan was doubly valuable to me now that Angel was gone.

I somehow managed to focus on the present. Ryan was right—time did seem to pass faster. Soon, it was lunch. I sat by Tommy, as usual, along with several others from the junior-varsity baseball team. Baseball was long over, but we still sat together. The Nudo twins had taken to sitting directly across from Tommy and me. They had always sat in the general vicinity, but they had moved in closer. I think it had something to do with their physical attraction to me.

I wondered why they were interested in me at all. I definitely wasn't as attractive as they were. Perhaps they were seeking a change, however. If things had been different and Angel wasn't in my life, I would have been interested in one twin or the other. I don't think I could have stomached them together, but then again, I wasn't sure. The whole idea of their incestuous relationship both repelled and attracted me at the same time. I definitely couldn't picture myself having sex with my older brother, Sam. Yuck! He was quite attractive, but he was my brother. It just seemed…wrong. I'd seen Sam shirtless plenty of times. He thought he was hot stuff and loved to go around with a bare chest when he could get away with it. I'd seen him naked, too. Seeing him in various states of undress didn't inspire lust, however. The attraction just wasn't there. Don't get me wrong. I'm glad I'm not attracted to my brother, but I sometimes wonder why I'm not. The Nudo twins were definitely into each other, but then maybe it was a twin thing. Everyone knew twins tended to be extremely close. It was almost as if they were the same person. I don't know. Maybe that made it okay.

Our lunch was particularly good. It's hard to go wrong with burgers and fries, even when the burgers don't quite taste normal. B.H.S. had some pretty good food, but it did usually taste a little off, as though it wasn't made quite right or from quite the right ingredients. There were rumors that the stray dogs around town ended up in the hamburger, but I didn't believe that. I guess I couldn't expect cafeteria food to taste like Mom's. After all, Mom cooked for five, not a few hundred.

I gazed over at Martin Wolfe as I chewed on my burger. As always, he was sitting alone. I'd once tried to get him to sit with us, but he'd refused my offer. Well, refused sounds too strong. He just mumbled a "no thanks." He acted kind of suspicious of me. Some guys did give him a hard time, although I'm not entirely sure why. I guess Martin thought my offer wasn't genuine and that I was up to something.

I thought about Martin as I sat there. He was kind of invisible. I was sure he was sitting at the same out-of-the-way table every single day, yet I didn't notice him more than once every week or two. No one paid much attention to him other than to torment him. No one even did that very much. Mostly, they just ignored him.

I had Lit with Martin. I'd almost forgotten. Isn't that weird? You'd think I'd know who was in my class. Martin never talked, though. Even the teachers had given up trying to draw him out.

I wondered why Martin was like that. Was he a homo like me and hiding it? Was he extremely shy? He would've been likable enough if he talked more. There didn't appear to be anything wrong with him. He didn't stutter. He wasn't short, or too tall. He was rather plain looking, even a bit homely, but he wasn't what I'd call ugly. He was just sort of there. I felt sorry for him. How could he go through life not talking to anyone, sitting alone day after day, being so inconspicuous that he just kind of faded into the background? When people swept their eyes over Martin's table, I really think most of them didn't see him. I wondered if it was possible for someone to just fade away until they couldn't be seen or heard at all. If it was, Martin Wolfe was a prime candidate.

My afternoon classes weren't quite as enjoyable as my morning classes. I didn't mind. The events of a few months ago had given me an appreciation for the true value of not being a target. The absence of pain is pleasure. I thoroughly enjoyed sitting in class and walking about B.H.S. without being molested.

I walked Tommy home after school, even though I planned to take a look inside Whitney's Antiques. Tommy lived so near B.H.S. walking him home didn't create much of a detour.

After Tommy walked through the open gate of the white picket fence that surrounded his home, I crossed the street and headed for downtown Blackford.

Blackford is by no means a big town, but everything one could possibly need is there. There is a bank, a post office, a barber shop, and a drug store, of course. I guess every town has those. There is the *Blackford Chronicle* office, the home of our local newspaper; the Black Heifer Diner, a general store, Merton's Ice Cream Parlor, the Marathon where Sam pumps gas, The Delphi Theatre, and my personal favorite, Whitney's Antiques. That is just the downtown area. There are other businesses around town. One of my favorites, on the edge of town, is the A&W that I pass on the way to and from school every day.

I was just passing the Black Heifer when a Nudo twin cut across the street and made a beeline for me.

"Hey, Kurt."

"Hey…"

"Tyler."

"You guys should really wear name tags or something."

"Where would the fun be in that? What's up?"

"I'm heading for the antique store."

I expected Tyler to immediately become disinterested. Few teenaged boys, other than I, were into old things.

"Yeah? Can I come?"

"Um, yeah. Sure, if you want."

Tyler seemed genuinely enthusiastic. Perhaps the fact that he was a homo explained his interest in the antique store. I loved to look around in there. Ryan had some antiques in his house. Maybe all homos liked old stuff. I wondered momentarily if I was giving myself away by going into Whitney's.

The sleigh bells on the door rang as we entered.

"Hello, Kurt. I haven't seen you for almost a week," Mrs. Whitney said.

I flushed slightly with embarrassment, but if Tyler thought it odd I visited the antique store frequently, he said nothing.

"Yeah, you know how it is. Oh, this is Tyler. He's a friend of mine from school."

"Hello, Tyler."

"Hi, ma'am."

"We just came in to have a look around, but I guess you know that."

Mrs. Whitney laughed. I was in the shop so often I would have memorized the location of everything if Mrs. Whitney didn't have a fondness for rearranging.

Mrs. Whitney had lots of old books. Tyler and I spent a few minutes browsing through those. I always kept my eye out for any on the outlaw, Jesse James. He was one of my ancestors, believe it or not. I also looked for books on the west. Great, Great, however-many-times Grandfather James had given me an interest in the old west.

There was a lot of beautifully decorated china in the shop. I liked to look at it, but I didn't have the least interest in buying. I had no use for dishes, and some of the better pieces of Victorian porcelain could cost as much as $5! Mrs. Whitney also had furniture from Colonial days. I was more into it, but couldn't afford it. I would've liked the old flintlock she had on display that once belonged to a Revolutionary War captain, but it was priced at nearly $100!

Coins were my thing. Before long I gravitated to the display case near the old cash register. I spotted the 1828 large cent I'd been eyeing for a few weeks. I nearly had the $2 saved to buy it. I knew I shouldn't spend all my money on old coins, but I just couldn't help myself. My most expensive purchase to date had been a silver Tetradrachm of Alexander the Great. I'd paid $15 for it, but that was a cheap price, especially for a coin over 2,000 years old! Mrs. Whitney had found it at an auction and sold it to me at cost. Thanks to working for Ryan, I'd been able to buy it right away.

I gazed at the large cent again, fearful someone would walk in and buy it before I had $2 saved up.

"Could you hold this for me?" I asked Mrs. Whitney, looking at the coin. "I can bring you a dollar tomorrow, and I should have the rest soon."

"Just take it with you, Kurt. I trust you to pay me."

I smiled.

"Thanks! I'll bring you the dollar tomorrow after school."

"That will be fine, but there's no hurry. You are my best coin customer after all."

I was quite fond of Mrs. Whitney.

Mrs. Whitney gave me the coin, and Tyler and I departed.

"She just lets you take stuff and pay her later?"

"Yeah, sometimes when I don't have enough money. I have more money now that I've been working for Mr. Hartinger."

"That's really great. Mr. Hartinger is the guy they arrested for killing Matt Taber, right? Before they found out who really did it?"

"Yeah. He's much too nice to harm anyone, let alone kill them."

I didn't tell Tyler that Ryan was a homosexual. It was a secret I was not at liberty to divulge. Besides, since Tyler didn't know I was a homo, he'd probably wonder how I knew about Ryan. I guess I could know about Ryan without being a homo myself, but like I said, I wasn't at liberty to give out information about Ryan. He was like a second father to me. I would never harm him.

"You wanna…I don't know…get something to eat or something?" Tyler asked as we walked down Main Street.

"Um, I'd better get home. Mom will be expecting me for supper."

"Oh, okay."

The disappointment in Tyler's voice made me feel guilty.

"We could eat out some time later this week, or maybe this weekend," I said. "Maybe Tanner would like to come, too."

"That sounds great, but I would rather it be just us. I spend more than enough time with my brother."

I nodded. I wasn't quite sure what to say. I knew too much about Tyler and his brother. Perhaps that's why Tyler looked somewhat embarrassed.

"Well, I'd better head for home. I have homework, and Mom will be wondering what I'm up to."

"Okay, well, I'll see you at school, and we'll get together later this week," Tyler said wistfully.

"Bye."

"Bye."

I wondered if spending time with Tyler Nudo was a wise idea. He seemed a little too eager. Maybe I was reading too much into things, however. Maybe he was just looking for a friend. What if I was wrong, however? What then?

Angel

I awakened to morning light reflecting off the snow. For several moments I was disoriented and couldn't quite make sense of the soft mattress and warm comforters. The events of the previous day flooded my mind, and I realized I was on the Selby farm.

I'd visited with Jack and Emma the evening before. When Jack returned from his evening chores, he said not a word about the bomb I'd dropped. Maybe Emma was right. He seemed to have completely forgotten about it. Perhaps it just didn't matter that much to him. Either way, I was relieved.

Emma had told me about their son, Angel, but no mention of him was made when Jack returned. I had a feeling Jack and Emma remembered him silently, without ever speaking his name. Why would they need to speak of him? With a look they could communicate everything.

I knew from living on a farm that there was less work in the winter months. That's not to say there was no work—not by a long shot. I was sure Jack could find me plenty to do.

I had to get out of bed before I could do anything. I looked at the clock. It was nearly nine! That was extremely late in farm terms. I wondered why Jack hadn't wakened me.

I forced myself to climb out of bed. I dressed quickly because the bedroom was rather cool. It was toasty warm compared to outside, however. I walked to the window as I was pulling on my shirt. It was still snowing, but the blizzard had moved on. I could actually see something more than blowing snow outside the window. A wide view of empty fields spread out before me. In the distance was a forest. Everything was covered in a blanket of white, but now the snow seemed more beautiful than dangerous. The wind had died down considerably. I had little doubt it was still bitterly cold outside, but no longer unbearable.

I finished dressing, made the bed, and then walked downstairs. Jack was nowhere to be found, but Emma was bustling about the kitchen.

"Good morning, Angel. What would you like for breakfast?"

"Oh…uh. Would pancakes be too much trouble?" I was dying for some pancakes.

"Of course not. I'll fry you up some bacon and eggs to go with them."

"You don't have to do that. I don't want to be any more trouble than I must."

"It's no trouble. I'm glad to have your company this morning. How do you like your eggs?"

"Scrambled, please, and thank you for fixing me breakfast. Where's Jack? I should go help him with whatever he's doing."

"Jack is out and about, but don't you worry about that. Breakfast first. Jack said you could help me around the house today. Is that okay with you?"

"Of course."

"Wonderful. I'd like to tackle the living room and give it a really good cleaning, but Jack is usually too busy to help me. I can't move most of the furniture around by myself."

"I'll be glad to help."

We were both silent for a bit as Emma mixed pancake batter in an old crock.

"Angel, I know it's none of my business, but what about school? Haven't you missed a good deal of it already?"

"Yes. Unfortunately. That's unavoidable, though. I hope to make it up someday."

I sat at the table and told Emma about my plans to travel around until I could return to Kurt. The scent of bacon began to fill the kitchen as Emma prepared breakfast.

"That's a very long time to be on your own without a home or family, especially at your age. Have you given any thought to going back home sooner?"

"Sure, but I don't see how I can. I read in the paper that Adam and the gang are locked up, but they aren't my only problem. My name is mud in Blackford. If I tried to go back now, things would get ugly. It might put Kurt in danger, too, although maybe not if we played it right. He could pretend to hate me."

"That is quite a dilemma. I wish I could think of a solution to your problem."

"Fixing me breakfast is help enough."

"You're easy to please."

"I've been dreaming about pancakes for days—weeks!"

"Then, this morning your dream will come true. I'll feed you pancakes until you can't stand another."

I laughed.

Emma soon placed a Golden Wheat plate stacked high with pancakes in front of me. Another held lots of bacon and a mound of scrambled eggs. I spread rich, creamy butter on my pancakes and doused them with maple syrup. I tasted them and moaned.

"These are SO good!"

Emma grinned.

I felt a bit guilty sitting there devouring a huge breakfast while Emma had only hot tea, but she assured me she'd already eaten. She seemed very pleased to be sitting there with me.

"You must be alone a lot," I said. "My parents have a farm. Even with farm hands to help, Dad is busy most of the time."

"Yes, I'm usually alone between breakfast and lunch and between lunch and supper. There's always something to keep Jack busy. He quite often puts in a few hours after supper, too."

"That must get lonely."

"Yes, but it's not so bad. I know Jack is somewhere about. Sometimes I catch a glimpse of him out the windows. In the summer I raise a large garden. I love to work with my vegetables and flowers. I spend hours out there. I'll often see Jack in the distance on his tractor. He'll give me a wave, and I'll wave back. Even when I'm alone, I'm not really alone. It is rather nice to have someone right here with me in the kitchen, however."

I smiled. I also ate and ate. I would've felt guilty for eating so much, but Emma was so obviously pleased I loved her cooking that I knew my appetite was a compliment. Emma was one of those people who derived pleasure from doing things for others. It's too bad everyone wasn't like her. As soon as I finished breakfast, I intended to do all I could for Emma.

I made myself stop eating before I became miserable. It took willpower to turn down more pancakes, but I was already feeling too full. I pushed my plate away.

"What would you like me to do first?" I asked.

"You're certainly eager to get started," Emma said. "First, I'd like you to carry all the smaller pieces of furniture out of the living room and place them out of the way in the next room. Leave the heavier pieces. We'll move those around later so I can clean under them. While you work on that, I'm going to clean up the kitchen."

"I'll get right on it."

The living room was sparsely furnished, but there was still a lot to move. The couch and two large arm chairs would have to stay put, but I thought I could handle just about everything else. I began carrying small tables, lamps, and various small items into the next room where I stacked them to the side. The task took longer than I imagined it would. Emma appeared in the doorway before I was quite finished.

"Next, take all the pictures off the walls. I want to wipe them down before I vacuum."

Emma disappeared again. She was serious about cleaning. I couldn't remember Mom ever taking everything off the walls to wipe them down.

I finished moving the small pieces of furniture. I started in on clearing the walls next. It gave me a chance to admire the old photographs and prints. In one of the photographs was a group of people sitting outside—some standing, some seated on old wooden chairs. I had no idea how old the photo was, but it was *old.* People didn't dress that way anymore, that was for sure. The photo showed enough of the farmhouse that I could tell it was taken right in the front yard. There was an old log barn in the photo that must have been right outside the window, but didn't exist now.

Next, I moved an old print of wolves howling in the moonlight; I loved the rich blues of the background. Another print of an old-fashioned house that had the same blues for the sky was also a nighttime scene. What I liked most about it was the golden glow of the windows casting rectangles of light out into the snow-covered yard. There was something comfortable and homey about that print. There were lots of similar prints and quite a few old photos as well.

Emma entered with a pail of warm water and a couple of clean rags before I'd finished clearing the walls.

"There's a stepladder in the shed out back. Could you get it for me, Angel? If you don't mind, I'm going to have you wipe down the upper portion of the walls. I'm a little afraid of heights."

"No problem," I said.

I went to the shed and located the stepladder with ease. The shed was filled with lots of old stuff—stone jars, a giant iron kettle, and pieces of no-longer-used furniture. I thought I even spotted one of the chairs I'd seen in the old family portrait. I didn't have time to look around, however. I didn't want to keep Emma waiting.

I returned with the ladder and set it up. Emma was already wiping down the walls from the floor to as high as she could reach. I finished taking down the old prints and then joined her.

"Wring out the rag so it's merely damp," Emma said. "I don't want to ruin the wallpaper."

I did as she instructed, climbed up the ladder, and began to wipe down the walls.

"I like this wallpaper," I said. It was a cream color with tiny little roses.

"I think Jack's mother put it up," Emma said.

"Have the Selbys lived here a long time?" I asked.

"Oh, Heaven's yes! Jack's family was some of the first settlers. They arrived back in the 1830s. When Jack's Great, Great Grandfather Thomas Jefferson Selby first settled here, Indians were still living on part of the farm."

"Really?"

"Oh, yes. You'll have to get Jack to tell you about that. It's quite interesting."

"I noticed the old family photos."

"Did you see the one with the family seated outside?"

"Yes."

"Take a good look at it later. The oldest man in the photo is Thomas Jefferson Selby. Standing right next to him is another man. If you look closely you'll see he's an Indian."

"That's really cool. My family has been on the same farm for a long time, too, but I don't know if we have any old photos like that."

"I think you're lucky to have grown up on a farm, Angel. My family is all city people. I grew up in Richmond, Virginia."

"I liked it okay, but I don't know if I'd want to be a farmer. It's a lot of work."

"It is that. Jack works himself to death, but he loves it. Are you okay up there, Angel?"

"Yes. I'm fine. Heights don't bother me much."

Emma and I kept cleaning and talking. Wiping down the walls of the living room was quite a task. Emma was cleaning about six feet or so up from the floor and I had just as much wall to wipe down above her. It was a good thing the ladder was a tall one or I could've never reached the top.

By lunchtime, we'd finished wiping down the walls. Emma had left me to dust off the framed photos and prints while she worked on getting lunch ready. The scent of fried pork chops and mashed potatoes wafted in from the kitchen as I worked.

I took a minute to carefully look over the old family portrait. There was Thomas Jefferson Selby. I looked carefully at the man standing next to him. I'd taken him for a member of the family, but upon closer examination I noted he didn't look like the others. His skin was darker and his hair black. He was a real Indian for sure. I wondered what life was like back in those days when the Indians were still around. I wondered if there were still bears and wolves in the woods. It was a different world.

I started in vacuuming while Emma continued lunch preparations. I looked up after a while to see Emma beckoning me. I turned off the noisy vacuum.

"Go get cleaned up, Angel. Jack is just coming in the back door."

I walked upstairs and washed up before returning to the kitchen. Jack was seated.

"How has your morning been going?" he asked.

"Emma has kept me busy."

"I'm sure. I think there's more work to do in the house than outside. I don't know how she keeps up."

The pork chops that had tempted me with their scent were sitting on a platter on the table. They were a light golden brown and still sizzling. Steaming mashed potatoes and corn rested in bowls nearby. There were applesauce and cornbread, too.

"This is delicious," I said after taking the first bite.

"I agree," Jack said.

"Thank you," Emma said.

Jack and Emma talked for a bit. I sat and waited for my chance to ask Jack what had been on my mind all morning. Before long I had an opportunity.

"Emma said there were Indians on the farm when your great, great, grandfather lived here."

"Yes, there were. All the Indians were supposed to have moved on. A great many were forced out. Great, Great Grandfather Selby didn't care much for that. He figured the Indians were cheated out of their land, which was more or less true. There was even some trouble with the government trying to force the Indians on the farm out, but Great, Great Grandfather stepped in and told whoever was sent that it was his land and he would decide who lived on it. The way he saw it, the land was probably more theirs than his anyway."

"So they were allowed to stay?"

"Yes. From the tales that have been passed down, I'd say Great, Great Grandfather was not someone to mess with. He'd been on friendly terms with "his neighbors," as he called the Indians. After he stood up for them, they were even more friendly."

"That's incredible."

"He even knew Chief Aubbeenaubbee and Chief Neeswaugee personally, although they weren't around for long in his lifetime. Old Aubbeenaubbee was killed by his own son. Chief Neeswaugee left with his band after giving up his land to the government."

"Chief Aubbeenaubbee was killed by his son?"

"Apparently, Aubbeenaubbee killed one of his wives in a drunken rage. He had a less than stellar reputation. A council ruled that a son of the murdered wife should be the avenger and slay his father. Paukooshuck, the son of Aubbeenaubbee and the eldest son of the murdered wife, was given a certain number of moons to execute the death sentence. After some eleven months of hiding, Aubbeenaubbee attended the marriage of his daughter. As was his habit, Aubbeenaubbee indulged in too much liquor. He finally realized that he was in danger and had to get away, but he was too late. Paukooshuck followed him for several miles and caught up with him. The drunken Aubbeenaubbee sat down and fell asleep in a log cabin. When Paukooshuck arrived, he crept in, took his tomahawk from his belt, and well, I'd better not go into details at the table, but he killed him."

"Wow."

"I guess life was a good deal more interesting a hundred and more years ago. Most of the stories that have come down from the early days are a good deal more peaceful. The Indians were just people when you got right down to it, just trying to live their lives like everyone else."

"They've always seemed kind of mythical to me," I said. "There are Indian mounds on our farm. Sometimes when I'm walking along I'll find arrowheads in the fields. I even found a big stone tomahawk in a stream once. It was just lying there. Who knows how old it is? I don't think there have been Indians around Blackford for well over a hundred years."

"We find quite a few things here, too," Jack said. "There's a rather large mound in the woods, but we don't disturb it. That would be like digging in a cemetery."

"Oh, I've never tried to dig anything up. That always seemed wrong somehow. I've just found things lying around. Did your great, great, grandfather write all this stuff down, or has it just been passed down?"

"It's been passed down. I guess I should write it all down, or it will be forgotten someday."

"It's sure interesting. Kurt loves stuff like that. He's big into the old west, so I'm sure he'd like to hear about Indians, too."

I grew sad for a moment when I thought of Kurt, but the sadness passed. I let it turn to a feeling of love. He was far, far away, but I knew he loved me. That meant everything.

After lunch, Emma and I continued our work in the living room. It turned out to be an all-day task. I would never have thought it would take so long, but by the time we vacuumed, dusted, and put everything back as it had been, evening was coming on.

I helped Emma in the kitchen while she prepared supper. I don't think I'd ever realized how much work went into food preparation. The potatoes alone had to be scrubbed and washed, peeled, cut into small pieces, boiled with butter and salt, drained, and mashed while adding milk and more butter. Mashed potatoes were one of the simplest items Emma prepared. Emma must have spent a good deal of each day just fixing breakfast, lunch, and supper for herself and Jack.

After supper, I cleaned up while Emma went and sat with Jack. Emma didn't want to leave it all to me, but Jack and I insisted. I was glad to be able to do something for such a nice lady. Of course, I was getting paid. The meals alone were more than worth the work I put in.

I carried in some firewood after cleaning up the kitchen, but that was it for my tasks for the day. I spent some time with Emma and Jack, but I was tired, so I went to my room.

It was nice to be alone with my thoughts. I'd had more than enough time to think in all those months of travel, but maybe I'd grown so accustomed to being a loner that I now needed time to myself. I just sat in the room and looked out the window. I tried to figure out where I was going next and what I'd do when I got there. I couldn't stay with the Selbys forever, after all. It would've been nice to stay right where I was until it was time to return to Kurt, but if I stuck around too long I'd be in trouble. Sooner or later someone would notice me, and then there would be uncomfortable questions. The nearby town of Verona was small. I had no doubt it was one of those places were everyone knew everyone else. I'd stick out for sure if I stayed any length of time. No, I was doomed to remain on the move. A few days in any one spot was about all I could manage.

If the Selbys had lived in a big city, things would've been different. I could blend in where there were lots of people. Of course, then the Selbys wouldn't be living on a farm and probably wouldn't have needed any help. I felt out of place in big cities, too. So, if I could stay, I probably wouldn't want to stay. Life was like that sometimes.

All I could do is enjoy things as they were. That wasn't so bad. I had a great place to stay for a few days, and I'd definitely be well fed before I went on my way.

In the next few days I helped Emma in the house and Jack on the farm. I wasn't worked very hard at all. I had the feeling the Selbys were just giving me a place to stay and having me do just enough that I wouldn't feel guilty about it. Why wasn't the world filled with people like that?

The weather turned more fall-like again, but it was still rather chilly. I truly appreciated snuggling into a warm feather bed each night. I daydreamed about Kurt and me living together. Perhaps we would have our own farmhouse. Maybe we'd even have kids. Well, not have kids. That was biologically impossible. We could adopt, though; at least, I guessed so. Could two guys adopt a child? I didn't see why not. Of course, if it was known we were homosexuals, it would probably be impossible. Who knew what the future might hold?

My days on the Selby farm were filled with good food, hot baths, and a warm bed. It seemed like paradise. Even so, it was all too soon time to go. I could have stayed another day or so, perhaps, but I felt as if I'd already put the Selbys at enough risk. Having me on the farm wasn't like harboring a fugitive, but the busybody local authorities might not see it so.

Jack and Emma tried to convince me to stay "just a few more days," but I had to leave soon, and the present was as good as any time.

"Stay until tomorrow morning at least," Emma said. "I'll send you off with a big breakfast."

"Do you know where you're heading?" Jack asked.

"Not really," I said.

"Well, I've been thinking. I know someone who owns a big hotel in Fort Wayne. I'm sure he could put you to work—for a while, at least."

"Really?"

"Sure. If you're interested, I can call him tonight."

"I would appreciate that."

It was after supper when I announced my departure, so before long I retired to my room for my last night on the Selby farm. I was going to be very sorry to leave in the morning, but I wouldn't repay the kindness of Jack and Emma by causing them trouble. I settled into the old feather bed and fell fast asleep.

I awakened fairly early the next morning. I took a bath and then dressed in my newly cleaned clothes. I packed up my few belongings and made the bed. I hesitated for a few moments before leaving my room for the last time. It was odd. I'd only lived there for a few days, but I felt as if I'd grown up in that room. I had a last look around and then walked downstairs.

Emma began fixing pancakes the moment I walked into the kitchen. Jack was there, and the three of us had a huge breakfast. I ate my fill. Who knew when I'd have such a meal again?

"I made that call last night," Jack said. "There's a job waiting for you whenever you get there."

"Thank you!"

"When you get to Fort Wayne, go to the Hotel Indiana. Just mention your name, and Bert will set you up."

"I don't know what to say."

"You already said thank you. I think that covers it," Jack said.

"Hardly."

Emma was kind of tearful when the time came for me to depart. She loaded me down with food for the road. One thing was for sure: I'd have plenty to eat for a few days, at least. I didn't know how long it would take me to get to Fort Wayne, but I was in better shape than I had been for a long time.

"Here's your pay, Angel," Jack said handing a small stack of bills toward me.

"Staying here with you was more than enough pay," I said.

"Nonsense. You were a great help, and a Selby always pays his debts. I'll be insulted if you refuse."

Jack scowled, and I took the money. I thought I'd better. When I counted the money later I found he'd given me $40! I felt rich.

"Thank you for everything," I said.

"You keep in touch with us, Angel," Emma said. "I put our address in your pack. I expect to hear from you when you reach Fort Wayne."

"You will," I said. It was too risky to contact Kurt, but not to write the Selbys.

"Would you like me to drive you somewhere?" Jack asked.

"No. You've done more than enough for me. I'll be fine."

Emma hugged me and I hugged her back. Even Jack hugged me, which was kind of a surprise.

"Here. I knitted this for you, Angel."

Emma presented me with a bright-red scarf.

"It's beautiful," I said. "Thank you."

"It will help keep you warm on your journey," Emma said as she wrapped it around my neck.

Emma hugged me again and kissed my cheek. I smiled at her.

"I'd better get going," I said. "Thanks again, for everything. I don't know how long it will take me to get to Fort Wayne, but I'll write when I get there."

"Be careful, Angel," Emma said.

"I will."

We said our goodbyes. I walked outside and then away from the Selby Farm. I felt a tug at my heart as I departed.

Kurt

Tyler grinned when he spotted me in the hallway. At least I thought it was Tyler. Who could tell with identical twins? The Nudo brothers quite often even dressed alike. I don't know if they did so on purpose, or if, being twins, they just picked out the same clothes to wear. It hardly mattered. What mattered a great deal was that I thought Tyler was very, very cute, and I felt very, very guilty for thinking so.

Tyler and I had spent some time together after school the day before. It was his idea, not mine, but I had fun. When we went our separate ways, I was concerned he might be interested in me as more than a friend. Now, I was more worried that I might be interested in him. I belonged to Angel, and I didn't want to even think about cheating on him.

Maybe I was worried about nothing, though. It was okay to have friends. It was okay to think other guys were cute. Lots of guys were cute. I noticed that every single day. Thinking a guy was cute didn't mean I wanted to have sex with him. Sure, if I'd never met Angel, I probably would be interested in Tyler, but Angel was my boyfriend. I was probably reading too much into Tyler's interest in me. I had let the Nudo twins believe I was heterosexual all along. Surely Tyler wouldn't think of me *in that way*. What if Tyler saw through me, though? What if he could tell I was just like him?

A vision of making out with Tyler Nudo popped into my mind. I banished it instantly, but it disturbed me. I should not be having such thoughts about another boy. I loved Angel. He was the one for me.

Six months was a long time. Six months without being held. Six months without being kissed. Six months without making love. Maybe it wasn't unfaithfulness raising its ugly head, but merely frustration, desperation, and sexual need. Maybe I just needed to go home after school and masturbate.

I almost couldn't believe I could think about masturbating without the least trace of guilt. There had been a time when I couldn't even bring myself to think about it, except when I was actually doing it. I was much more comfortable with myself now—thanks to Angel and Ryan.

Tyler was especially friendly at lunch. I knew it was Tyler this time, because his brother spoke his name out loud. I enjoyed spending time with the Nudo twins. Tyler and his brother were witty, funny, and just all-around nice guys. Maybe that's why no one gave them any real trouble—despite the rumors about them.

"Not eating today, Tommy?" Tanner asked as we sat in the noisy cafeteria.

"Just cautious," Tommy said, poking at his fish sandwich with a fork. Tommy took a bite. "Rubbery, bland, and reminiscent of a pencil eraser."

The guys laughed at that, so Tommy proceeded to give us a full review of his lunch.

"The peas are more suitable to a pellet gun than a school lunch," Tommy said pensively after sampling them. "The mashed potatoes can best be described as pasty, the milk as chunky, and…what the heck is this yellowish-green blob anyway? Jell-O salad or congealed fat? You decide. Overall, I'd describe our meal as rancid repast."

Where did he learn words like that?

"You should be a food critic, Tommy," Tyler said.

"Not if I have to eat here."

Actually, lunch wasn't that bad. The fish was rather good, in fact, even though it was a fish sandwich. I couldn't identify the mysterious yellowish-green blob any more than Tommy could, so I just steered clear of it. I have a firm rule. If I can't figure out what it is, I don't eat it.

I enjoyed my time with my friends. I wished Angel was there, of course. Not a day, not an hour went by when I didn't wish for Angel. Oh, how I wished things could go back to the way they were before all the trouble started. Well, I guess they had gone back, with one notable exception: Angel was gone. All I could do was wait for his return.

***

I began to rethink my acceptance of Tyler's invitation as the days passed. Perhaps spending time alone with him was not a good idea. It was fine when others were around, like at lunch, but what if something happened that shouldn't happen when we were alone?

Nothing will happen that you don't allow to happen, I reminded myself. That was certainly true. Even if the worst came to pass and Tyler put the moves on me, all I had to do is say "no." There was no reason to avoid someone who might well become a good friend just because I was afraid he might come onto me. I was probably completely wrong about Tyler's intentions anyway.

I was beginning to think Tyler had forgotten about going out with me, but on Friday he asked if we could catch a movie at the Delphi and have a late supper at the Black Heifer. *Singing in the Rain* was playing at the Delphi, and I really wanted to see it, so I accepted.

We were to meet a little before 7 p.m. in front of the theatre. I couldn't shake the feeling I was going on a date. I very nearly called up Tommy and asked him to come along, but I realized that wouldn't be a nice thing to do. Tyler had asked to spend time with me, not Tommy and me. Perhaps we could get a group together for an outing soon. Maybe Tommy and I could do something with both the Nudo twins. Maybe even some of the guys from the team would tag along. Derek Spradley was always a lot of fun. Of course, he would talk about girls the entire evening, but he was good comic relief.

I took a shower and then sorted through my clothes to pick out what to wear for my…evening with Tyler. Nothing looked quite right on me. After twenty minutes I began to feel guilty. Why was I so concerned with my appearance? This was *not* a date. I quickly grabbed a pair of jeans and a navy, button-down shirt. It was good enough for school, so it was good enough for an evening with a friend.

I began to put on cologne, but then decided against it. It might give Tyler the wrong impression. I half wished he had never asked me, but then again it would be nice to go out. I spent a lot of time with Tommy, of course, but he was often busy, and we didn't want to spend all our time together. I had other friends, too, but we were more likely to play baseball or go swimming together than to catch a movie. Baseball and swimming would have to wait for spring now. Thanksgiving was upon us, and it was too cold outside for sports and especially for jumping in the water. Brrrr!

I forced myself to stop analyzing my time with Tyler. I thought about things way too much sometimes. Nothing bad was going to happen, and Angel himself would want me to have a good time. If only I could have been meeting Angel in front of the Delphi! I sighed. *Some day*, I promised myself.

I pulled on my coat and walked into town a little before 7 p.m. I passed the A&W, now sitting empty. The A&W was usually closed between the beginning of November and the end of March. Its opening every year meant spring was upon us. Winter was coming up fast now, and Christmas was just over a month away.

I grew increasingly nervous as I entered town and approached Main Street. What if… No. I was being stupid. I forced myself to keep moving forward. I couldn't back out now.

Tyler was waiting under the flashing marquee, looking very handsome in a long coat. I wondered why the girls at school weren't after him, but maybe they believed the rumors about him. Maybe they knew those rumors were true.

"Hey, Kurt!"

"Hey, Tyler."

"You're right on time."

We bought our tickets and walked inside. I just stood in the lobby admiring its beauty.

"I love this place," Tyler said.

"Yeah, me, too. It's a bit worn, but I like the sense of history. Just think how many people have come here to watch movies through the years."

"My parents had their first date here," Tyler said.

"Mine, too."

We walked to the concession stand and purchased popcorn and Cokes from Martin Wolfe. Martin barely said a word, just like at school. He did seem somewhat more comfortable behind the glass case filled with candy than he did in the hallways, classrooms, or cafeteria at B.H.S. Maybe he didn't fear being picked on here quite as much. I tried to be friendly with Martin as we made our purchases, but it was hard to get a reaction out of him.

I saw a look pass between Martin and Tyler as Tyler paid for his stuff. I wondered what was up with that.

"Do you know Martin?" I asked as we walked into the auditorium.

"Who?"

"Martin Wolfe, the boy working on the concession stand."

"Yeah, well, kinda. Why?"

"No reason, I guess." I realized I was being nosy. I had the feeling Tyler knew Martin a lot better than he was letting on, but it was none of my business. "I was just thinking it's odd that I rarely notice him at school. I see him every time I come here, but it's like he's invisible at school."

"I have a class with him," Tyler said, but volunteered nothing more.

"Yeah. Me, too."

Tyler and I found seats in almost the exact center of the auditorium. We sat there and looked around at the ornate gilded cherubs and the painted sky overhead.

"This place is really something," Tyler said.

I agreed whole-heartedly, but my mind was still on Tyler and Martin Wolfe. There was most definitely something between them. Was Martin one of us, too? Had he received the same invitation from the Nudo twins as I did? Had he accepted? Martin was kind of homely, but not really ugly. He was just there. Would guys like Tyler and Tanner go for him?

Of course, whatever was between Tyler and Martin might be nothing like that at all. Why did my mind always go right to sex? Perhaps because I hadn't had sex in so long. I should've been used to going without. I'd waited fifteen years for my first time.

Tyler looked at me and smiled as he reached for some popcorn. I was smiling, too. I *really* liked him, and I was excited to see *Singing in the Rain.* I was always excited to see a movie—any movie—but I particularly wanted to see this one. Debbie Reynolds was so cool.

Tyler and I laughed as we watched the cartoons before the show. They were so much better than those on TV—and almost no one had a TV. Being in color helped, but everything was so huge in a theatre. They didn't call it the big screen for nothing.

Finally, the show began, and I was mesmerized. I could sense Tyler beside me, and I could smell his cologne, but I was inside the world of the movie. I watched the images and was enveloped by the dialogue and music as I sat there stuffing popcorn into my mouth. Time flew, and it seemed we had just sat down when "The End" appeared on the screen.

Tyler and I followed the crowd out into the lobby. I spotted my brother, Sam, with his girl, Betty. Sam caught sight of me too and nodded. His eyes drifted to Tyler. I wondered what my big brother thought of me going out with one of the Nudo twins. He didn't know what I knew, but he'd long suspected the Nudo brothers were homos. Sam knew I was one. Did he think I was cheating on Angel?

I put it out of my mind as Tyler and I continued through the lobby and into the rather chilly night. We walked down the street and entered the Black Heifer. We weren't the only movie-goers having supper after the show, so we had to wait just a bit to be shown to our booth.

Emma Schroeder set glasses of ice water and menus on our table as we sat down. My sister did a lot of babysitting for her, and I mowed the Schroeders' lawn, so Mrs. Schroeder knew me. I wondered what she would think about seeing Tyler and me together.

Don't be stupid, Kurt, I told myself. I was far too self-conscious about being with Tyler. I guess that was understandable to a point. My life had been a living hell back when everyone thought I was a homo. I didn't want to go there again.

Tyler and I browsed the menus.

"I'm going to have the Heifer platter," Tyler announced after a few moments.

"Hmm. I don't know if I'm that hungry." The Heifer platter came with a huge burger and three toppings, plus a mound of fries or onion rings. "Then again, that does sound good."

We both ordered the Heifer platter when Emma returned. Tyler grinned at me again. He was *so* cute.

"How did you like the movie?" I asked.

"It was great, but the company was even better."

Uh-oh. That's not the kind of thing I wanted to hear.

"I think it would be wonderful to be an actor like Gene Kelly. Can you imagine being in movies like that? I mean, just think if that was your job."

"That would be more exciting than working in a bank or a garage or whatever. Maybe you should become an actor, Kurt."

"I think I would if it wasn't for two things. I have no talent, and I don't have the type of personality it takes to be a performer."

Tyler laughed. "I can't comment on your acting ability since I've never seen you act, but I don't know if I agree with your second reason. You've played baseball in front of crowds."

"That's totally different. There are two whole teams on the field at once. Even when I'm batting, the crowd is only watching me for a few seconds."

"Yeah, but it's kind of like performing."

"If you say so, Tyler. I'm just glad I don't stink as bad as I used to."

"You were never that bad."

"Oh, yes, I was."

"Well, you aren't now. You're one of the best! You can make varsity easily next year."

"Only because the varsity team has been decimated. It will be mostly new guys."

"So go for it."

"Maybe, but we're getting off our topic. Maybe you should become an actor."

I almost added, "You have the looks for it," but stopped myself in time.

"I doubt I have the talent for it, either."

"You and Tanner could both be actors. You could do the same plays. He could be on one night, and you could be on the next. No one would ever know."

"That's sure the truth. We've switched classes so often it isn't even funny. At home, when one of us wants to slip out when we're not allowed, the other pretends to be both of us."

I laughed.

"That must come in handy. Maybe I could use a twin."

"There is a downside. Most people see us as a set, not as individuals. I'm more often one of the Nudo twins than I am Tyler. Most people call me Nudo because they can't tell if I'm me or my brother."

"I guess that would be rough."

"There are more advantages than disadvantages, but sometimes I'd like to be somewhere I can just be Tyler, instead of a twin. You know?"

"Yeah. I can see that."

Tyler talked about what it was like to be a twin some more. Our food arrived. My burger was delicious! As we ate we talked about movies, baseball, the Delphi Theatre and all sorts of things. I hadn't had so much fun since the last time Angel and I went out…

I paled. Guilt consumed me.

"Kurt? What's wrong?" Tyler asked.

"Um, oh, just a disturbing memory from the past," I lied. "It's nothing. What were you saying about the TV your parents are buying?"

I only half-listened. It was only a movie and dinner, but was I somehow being unfaithful to Angel? Was it right that I be sitting here laughing and enjoying myself with another boy when Angel was who knows where? For all I knew, Angel didn't have enough to eat. He might be cold, lonely, or even sick. Suddenly, my burger didn't taste so good.

"Hey, I should be getting back home," I said. "Let's finish up so we can get out of here."

"Oh, okay," Tyler said with a hint of disappointment in his voice.

"I've had a great time," I said. "It's just that it's getting late. You know how parents are."

"Yeah," Tyler said, brightening up again.

We finished our meals. Our conversation was a bit more subdued, but we still enjoyed ourselves. My enjoyment was tinged with guilt, but I did my best to hide it.

"I'll walk you home," Tyler said after we'd paid our checks and stepped out into the cold.

"Um, how about you walk me to the edge of town? It's pretty far to my house, and it's definitely not on your way."

"Okay," Tyler said, "that's probably a wise idea. I've been having so much fun with you that the hours have slipped past unnoticed. I might get in trouble if I'm too late. I don't know if Tanner is around to cover for me."

"Well, I know no one is covering for me," I said with a grin. "Even if Sam was willing, no one would ever believe he was me."

"Yeah. He's not nearly as cute as you," Tyler said.

I didn't know what to say to that, so I said nothing.

Tyler walked me to the A&W just south of town and there we parted. He hesitated just before we separated. Did he want to kiss me? Or, was he just reluctant for our night to end? I tried not to think about it as I walked home alone. I felt guilty enough as it was.

Angel

A part of me truly didn't want to leave the Selby farm behind. I'd only stayed there a few days, but I was homesick for it as I walked through the little town of Verona. I guess Jack's and Emma's place was so much like my own home that it felt as if it was home. Despite the pain I was now feeling, I was glad I'd met Jack and Emma, and not just because of the warm bed and excellent food. I enjoyed meeting people, especially wonderful people like the Selbys. That was one truly cool thing about my travels: I got to meet lots of different people.

Most people weren't as kind as Jack and Emma. That type of kindness was truly rare. Theirs was the type of kindness that most churchgoers claimed to have, but don't. Of course, one could be a good deal less kind than Jack or Emma and still be a good person. They were one, I guess, or rather two in a million.

"Patrick Bailey get in this car right now!"

I was pulled out of my thoughts by a loud, masculine voice. A man was standing by an old Chrysler yelling at a boy who must've been his son. The boy was rather good looking, with dark hair and eyes. He looked to be about thirteen. He was obviously in trouble.

The man grabbed the boy by the shoulder and shook him.

"When I introduce you to one of my business associates, you look him in the eyes and give him a firm handshake! You were pathetic! I thought I'd raised a son, not a daughter!"

Ouch. I looked at the man and narrowed my eyes, but he didn't notice me. He shoved his humiliated, red-faced son in the car, and soon they were gone. I felt sorry for the poor kid. It's too bad his father wasn't more like Jack.

In only a few minutes I walked past the town limits. The next sizable town, according to Jack, was Argos. It was about ten miles distant. I wasn't quite sure what town lay beyond that, but sooner or later I'd reach my destination: Fort Wayne.

Having an actual goal gave me a sense of purpose I'd lacked. Until now I'd ambled along not much caring when I reached the next outpost of civilization as long as I didn't run out of food before I got there. The winter weather made shelter a necessity, but there were always farms even when there weren't towns. It felt good to be heading to somewhere instead of away from somewhere. It made me feel as though I was accomplishing something.

I still felt as if I was heading away from Kurt. Then again, I could look at every step I took as being one step nearer to seeing him again. I liked that idea much better.

Argos was much smaller than Verona, but it seemed a pleasant-enough place. It had a grocery, a hardware store, and a gas station. There was probably a bit more there, but I didn't explore. I just let the road lead me through town and out into the countryside once more.

The snow started in just east of Argos. Oddly enough, the falling snow gave me a comfortable, cozy feeling. That might not seem to make much sense considering that I was out in the elements, but the snow didn't make me any colder. I was snug and warm in my leather jacket, toboggan, and the new red scarf Emma had given me. The fluffy white flakes fell all around me and upon me. As far as I could see in any direction, snow fell from the sky, covering the ground in a blanket of white. Now and then the sun peeked through the clouds, and the snow lit up like a million sparkling diamonds. That was a rare event and all the more beautiful because of its rarity.

I found myself wondering what the countryside I was walking through looked like in spring, summer, and fall. When I was a little boy I'd first noted how the changing of the seasons vastly altered the appearance of the farm. I could close my eyes and picture what the farm looked like at any time of the year, but I had only a clue as to how the fields and forests that surrounded me now would look at other times of the year. I guess it didn't matter. I loved the falling snow. While I liked to think of other times and places, nothing was more important than the here and now.

It was just as well I was fond of snow. It rarely stopped falling in the coming days. Sometimes, it slowed until it was barely falling from the sky, but it kept on coming down. It might have stopped when I was sleeping, but even under the trees I awakened with a light dusting covering me.

During the afternoon of the third day of snow, the temperature took a dip. My winter wonderland became a good deal less pleasant. The snow fell ever harder and was becoming deep enough to pose a problem. After a couple of hours of heavy snowfall, I was more wading through it than walking. There wasn't a single car traveling along the old road. That didn't surprise me, because the snow was becoming so deep that no car could make it through. Who knew how long it would take a snowplow to make it out on such a lonely stretch of road? I wasn't even sure I was on the right road anymore. I began to fear I was lost. The falling snow no longer seemed comfortable and cozy as it had a few days before, but rather menacing.

The going was hard, but I did okay until the wind got up. At first, I just had some difficulty seeing, but all too soon the snow was swirling around so hard and fast I could barely see ten feet in front of me. I kept going as long as I could, hoping to spot a barn, a farmhouse—anywhere I might find some shelter—but there was nothing. Truth to be told, I could have walked right through a town without knowing it.

I trudged on, no longer sure if I was keeping to the road at all. I got turned around and couldn't even tell in what direction I was traveling. I kept going because I feared to stop. I grew colder and more fatigued with each passing moment. Finally, I could go no further. I knew it might well be the death of me, but I lay down in the snow and closed my eyes. I had to rest, if only for a few moments.

***

"Look Grandma. It's an angel in the snow."

The small voice penetrated my sluggish thoughts as I stirred from a dream of hot vegetable soup and warm bread with butter and strawberry jam. I struggled to return to my dream, but it had already flown away. I tried to remember where I was and how I'd arrived there, but all that came to mind was blowing snow and unbearable cold. Was I awake now, or dreaming again, or had I slipped into oblivion?

I felt a hand on my face, a small hand that must certainly have belonged to the small voice. My right eyelid was pried open and I beheld a girl, no more than six. I blinked away the snow as my eyelids fluttered open. I was half covered in fluffy white coldness. I couldn't feel my fingers, nor my hands, nor my feet.

"He's not an angel, Child, he's a boy. Help me get him up or he'll freeze to death."

The small hands tugged at my shirt collar, but had not the strength to move my much larger body even an inch. They were joined by larger hands, old and wrinkled. I stirred and tried to push myself up. After a few tries I managed to sit up.

"Come on, boy. Get to your feet. I'm too old to be out in this cold."

With the help of the old lady and the girl, I made it to my feet. I was unsteady at first and stumbled along, but it felt good to once again be upright. I got my first good look at the old woman. She was wrinkled and stooped, but kindly looking. She wore a long brown coat covered with a red-and-green plaid shawl. Her head was covered with a blue scarf and her hands with worn, knitted mittens of faded green. She smiled at me, and I returned her grin.

"Come on, the cabin is this way," said the girl, taking my hand in hers as she tugged me along.

I followed, not knowing what else to do. I still wasn't completely sure how I'd found my way into the woods, for woods it was: a thick forest that extended beyond sight in every direction. The limbs were bare except on the scattered pines and fir. The trunks looked black against the white of the snow, and indeed there seemed little color in this place except for the dark green of the pines and firs and the red and green of the old lady's shawl.

My arms and legs were numb, and I still could not feel my hands and feet at all. Even my torso felt cold as if the fire in my chest had gone out. I couldn't remember feeling this weak before, and my stomach rumbled. I wondered when I'd last eaten.

The little girl led me along a path I could not follow with my eyes, but she seemed to know exactly where she was going. Squinting at the snow I could at last make out two sets of footprints going in the opposite direction, but the thickly falling snow had all but obliterated them. I realized that if I'd lain in the snow much longer I would've been hidden from view until the spring thaw revealed my frozen body. I shivered with the thought and felt as if I was freezing solid even as I walked.

Our hike would've been beautiful if it were not for my tired body, the penetrating cold, and the hunger than gnawed at me more with every step. I felt as if my body was trying to consume itself.

Before long, a cabin mercifully appeared on a hilltop, with smoke curling out its stone chimney. It was a log cabin and looked quite old. I'd seen such a cabin before on my parents' farm. Well, the cabin on our farm was actually an old log barn, but it was built the same way, with hand-hewn logs fitting together like a giant Lincoln Log set. The cabin was much smaller than the barn I knew so well, but it looked snug and warm, a truly welcome sight in my current state.

We trudged up the hill and were soon walking across the uneven boards of the porch. The girl opened the door and led me in, still pulling me along by the hand. The warmth enveloped me like a comforter, and I didn't think I'd ever felt anything quite so pleasant before. The girl and her grandmother pushed me into a comfortable, cushioned rocking chair situated right by the fireplace—just in time, too, for my strength had nearly given out. The fire was burning low, but I turned my hands to its warmth, luxuriating in the heat. The grandmother poked at the fire and added another log. Soon there was a merry blaze in the hearth that flooded the room with warmth.

"Take off those gloves and shoes so the heat can get to you," the grandmother said.

I obeyed without hesitation. I pulled off my gloves and then went to work on my shoes. My numb fingers had trouble with the laces, and the little girl came to my rescue, quickly loosening the laces and pulling my old shoes off. I removed my socks as well, and the heat began to warm my bare feet.

My shoes and socks were set close by the fire to dry. As I began to warm, the little girl helped me out of my toboggan, scarf, leather jacket, and finally my sweater. One would think I would've been warm under all that clothing, but I knew if the little girl and her grandmother hadn't found me, I would've been doomed.

Feeling began to return to my fingers and toes, painfully, and it made me wince. Little by little the sharp pain eased, and I began to feel as if I inhabited my own body again. My chest began to feel warm as if the fire within had restarted, and I began to get a little sleepy.

A cup of hot tea was placed in my hands and I sipped it gratefully, feeling its warmth flow down my throat to heat me up from the inside. I cupped it in my hands, reveling in the treasured warmth.

"Thank you," I said when the empty cup was taken away.

I yawned. I had not realized how very tired I was. I was desperately hungry, but I needed sleep more than food. My head began to nod, and I did not resist when I was led from my chair to a bed. I felt thick blankets being pulled over me and a hand on my brow smoothing back my hair. I smiled and mumbled my appreciation even as I drifted off to sleep.

I awakened some hours or perhaps days later, for all I knew. I sat up and peered out the multi-paned window beside the bed. The snow continued to fall outside, covering everything in white. I turned and looked toward the fireplace. The fire was burning lower now, but the room was filled with warmth.

I did not see the little girl, but perhaps she was in the other room or outside. The grandmother was working at an old wood-burning range that was black, trimmed in chrome, and much larger than my mother's gas range back home. The scents of her labors wafted throughout the room, telling a tale of freshly baked yeast bread. My stomach rumbled, but I was not yet ready to rise.

It was my first chance to look about inside the little cabin. The front door was directly opposite the bed so that if the door and the window behind the bed were both opened in the summer time, a cool breeze would flow through the room. To my left, or to the right as one entered, was the large fireplace, built out of fieldstones. In front of it was the rocking chair I'd sat in upon my arrival as well as an old armchair and a wooden bench upon which rested a handmade cushion. Directly across the room, opposite the fireplace was the kitchen range. Just to its right was a doorway into another room. Between the two sources of heat there was a large open space. In the middle was a large, hand-braided rug. At the end closest to the range stood a long wooden table painted a dull red. Surrounding it were four matching chairs. A short distance away, along the wall stood a large, step-back cupboard filled with heavy, white, ironstone plates, platters, and cups. The room's furnishings were completed by a dark-cherry dresser with heavy glass knobs, located near the bed, a dry-sink in the kitchen area, and what I think was called a plantation desk situated along the wall not far from the fireplace. There was also a blanket chest, painted dark green, resting under one of the windows. All in all, the cabin looked more like it belonged in the 1850s than the 1950s.

I climbed out from under the blankets, quilts, and comforters, stood and stretched. My movements attracted the attention of the grandmother.

"I'm glad you're up. It's nearly time for supper."

"How long have I been asleep?"

"For several hours, since late yesterday evening. It's now nearly six p.m.," she said, glancing at an antique kitchen clock.

I had slept nearly a day.

I took a seat by the fireplace and pulled on my socks, now dried and warmed by the fire. The last traces of the cold had left me, and I felt whole again.

"Where's...the little girl? Sorry, but I don't know your names."

The little girl in question entered through the front door just then, toting a bucket of water which was quite small, but still too much for her. I crossed the short space quickly and relieved her of her burden.

"Set it right there if you don't mind," the grandmother said, indicating one end of the range.

I did as I was asked, and upon coming close to the range I discovered a large pot of vegetable soup simmering away.

"That smells delicious."

"You'll find out soon," she said.

The little girl approached me somewhat timidly, looking up at me from far below. At 5'10" I towered over her.

"Are you an angel?" she asked.

"Child," her grandmother said, "I told you before. He's a boy, not an angel."

"But Momma said angels are beautiful and have long golden hair. I always thought of just girl angels, but he looks like a boy angel to me."

I grinned.

"Well, your grandmother is right. I'm not an angel, but my name is Angel."

"Are you sure you're not an angel?"

"If I was an angel, what would I be doing freezing out in the snow?"

"Momma said that angels sometimes disguise themselves. They come as beggars or poor people to see who will help them and who won't."

"Perhaps that's true, but I'm just a boy, not an angel. I'm sorry to disappoint you."

The little girl looked as if she did not quite believe me.

"What's your name?" I asked.

"Laura."

"That's a beautiful name—for a beautiful girl," I said. I meant it. Laura was as cute as she could be, with long brown hair, soulful brown eyes, and a smile that was forever upon her lips. As adorable as she was, I sensed that her heart was where her true beauty lie.

"My name is Adie," the old woman said, "but you can call me Grandmother if you wish; most everyone does."

I smiled. "Grandmother. I like that. Well, Laura and Grandmother, thank you for saving me. I would have perished out in the cold if you hadn't found me."

"Laura is the one who spotted you," Grandmother said.

"I saw you from the window!" Laura said, taking my hand and pulling me to one of the two windows that looked out the front of the cabin. "See, way over there is where you were lying. I saw your red scarf!"

The hill she pointed to looked much like all the other hills to me, but I did not doubt her word. The cabin had not been visible for most of our journey, but had I looked, I could have seen it from where we started out.

"I'm very glad you spotted me, Laura. You saved my life."

Laura shyly grinned and turned a bit pink with embarrassment.

"How did you come to be on that hill?" she asked.

"Well, the last thing I remember is trudging through a blizzard. I was so tired, so hungry, and so cold I just couldn't go any further, so I lay down in the snow. I was terribly cold for a long time, but then I began to feel warm. I fell asleep, and then you awakened me."

"You nearly froze to death, then," Grandmother said. "Those who are freezing began to feel warm just before they die."

"I really saved your life, then?" Laura asked, quite pleased.

"You really did, both of you, and I'll be forever grateful."

Grandmother smiled, but said nothing. She turned her attention back to her soup. Laura looked up at me and grinned.

"Now, if you'll set the table, Laura, we'll have supper."

"I'll help," I said.

Laura led me to the step-back cupboard. There we gathered thick bowls, bread plates, glasses, cups and saucers, spoons and knives. Laura pulled linen napkins out of a drawer and then set salt and pepper on the table. We were done in a flash, and it was not too soon for me. I was ravenously hungry.

Grandmother filled our bowls with soup. While they cooled, she pulled a loaf of freshly baked bread from the warming oven above the range. She set out butter and strawberry jam, making my mouth water. Lastly, she put a pot of hot tea and a stoneware pitcher of cold water on the table, and we all sat down to eat.

I tasted the soup, careful not to burn my lips because it was still quite hot.

"This is delicious!" I said.

Grandmother smiled and cut me a large piece of warm bread, which I smeared with butter and jam. I took a bite, and it was heavenly.

"I just remembered," I said. "Just before you found me I was dreaming—dreaming of hot soup and freshly baked bread. This is my dream come true."

"I helped make the bread," Laura announced. "I helped make the jam last spring, too."

"Well both are delicious, Laura. I can't say as I've ever tasted better, and that's the truth."

Laura smiled so sweetly I wanted to take her in my arms and hug her.

We ate in silence mostly, engaging only in polite conversation, giving most of our attention to the soup and bread. Perhaps it was because I was starving, or perhaps not, but it was the best vegetable soup I ever tasted. I could just picture Grandmother preparing it–cutting up potatoes, carrots, cabbage, and corn, seasoning it and simmering it long on the old wood-burning range. The whole cabin filled with its scent, mixed with that of the bread. I breathed it in as I devoured spoonful after spoonful.

When my bowl began to get empty, Grandmother refilled it. When my first slice of bread was devoured, it too was replaced. It was all so delicious. Even the water tasted wonderful, and the hot tea was just right with the bread. I thoroughly enjoyed my meal.

I emptied three bowls of soup before I was full and consumed four thick slices of bread covered with butter and jam. I offered to clean up, but Grandmother wouldn't hear of it and banished me to a seat by the fire with a cup of hot tea. Laura sat across from me, rocking in the chair I'd occupied when first brought to their cabin. She had a special teacup and saucer, smaller than the others and just her size. She sipped from the cup quite properly as she rocked back and forth by the fire, a true little lady.

Soon, Grandmother joined us. Laura surrendered the rocker to her and sat on the padded bench by my side. I noticed that Grandmother was never quite idle. Even as she sat by the fireside and talked, her fingers were busy repairing stockings so they'd last a little longer.

"Where do you come from?" Laura asked. "We almost never get visitors here."

"I came from a little town called Blackford, in the southwestern part of the state. It's near Kentucky and Illinois."

"That is far!" Laura said.

"Yes, I've been traveling for many months, since May."

"That is a long time! Why aren't you still in school?"

"I had to leave home," I said.

"Why?"

"That's none of our business," Grandmother said.

I was thankful for Grandmother's interruption, for I was not eager to give details of my past.

"It's a long story," I said, "but I had to leave to protect someone very special to me. I'm going back some day. For months I've traveled from place to place, making my own way, meeting new people, and having adventures."

"It sounds terribly exciting! You must be very brave," Laura said. I noted she didn't press me for details. Apparently, a single reproach from Grandmother was enough.

"It can be exciting at times, but it can also be lonely, and as I learned quite recently, dangerous. I came to be in your woods by accident. I took a wrong turn in the blizzard and became lost. It was nearly the end of me."

"I'm glad you're safe. It seems so sad you're alone, though, especially with Christmas coming. How can you bear to be away from your family?"

"I'm not looking forward to it, but I'll get by."

"Not looking forward to Christmas!" Laura said, putting her hands to her cheeks in shock. "I've never heard of anyone not looking forward to Christmas!" She turned to her grandmother. "Can he stay with us for Christmas? Please? It's only a few days away."

"Don't be silly. Of course, he's staying for Christmas," Grandmother said, as if there had never been any doubt.

"I don't want to be any trouble," I said.

"Nonsense. It's rare we get a visitor. We're delighted you're here."

"Well, I would like to stay until Christmas very much. When I said I wasn't looking forward to it, I didn't mean Christmas itself. I meant being alone on Christmas."

"Ohhhh," Laura said.

"I insist on helping out while I'm here. I'm sure there's lots I can do for you."

"We get by just fine on our own," Grandmother said, "but if you insist."

"I do."

It was settled that simply, and I was quite pleased. We passed an enjoyable evening by the fire. I related some of my adventures, and Grandmother and Laura told me something of life in the woods. I learned that Grandmother had lost her husband long ago and that Laura was orphaned when she was only four. She'd been taken in by her grandmother and had lived with her ever since.

At bedtime, Laura offered me the use of her bed again, but I refused, opting for the pallet in the loft instead. There was no electricity in the cabin, but Grandmother provided me with a little lamp, and I carried it in one hand while I used the other to pull myself up the ladder into the half-loft. Once safely in the loft, I stuck my head back down into the cabin and bid Laura a second goodnight. She giggled and snuggled into her blankets.

The loft extended over half the main room of the cabin, allowing me to look down and see the old kitchen range. There was a pallet all made up with sheets and comforters, just as if I'd been expected. Perhaps it had been made up during my long sleep in anticipation of my spending the night. There was an old wooden trunk on one side of the loft, and on the very edge was a line of old stoneware jars, ready for use. A large antique spinning wheel sat at the edge as well, a remnant of days gone by. It wouldn't have surprised me too much to discover that Grandmother still used it. After all, my surroundings seemed lost in time.

Despite my long sleep, I was still tired. I undressed in the privacy of the loft and snuggled down into the pallet. I soon discovered I had no need of the comforters, for the heat from the fireplace and cook stove wafted up from below, making the loft the warmest room in the cabin. I lay there shirtless, quite comfortable even though it was late December. Soon, I was fast asleep.

I awakened in the morning to the scent of frying bacon. I climbed to the edge of the loft and looked down to see Grandmother stirring milk gravy. Enticed by the sights and scents, I grew instantly hungry. I stood and dressed, made up my pallet, and then climbed down the ladder.

"Good morning," I said.

"Good morning," Grandmother said and Laura echoed.

"I need some more water, Laura," Grandmother said.

"I'll get it, if you'll show me where," I said.

Laura and I pulled on our coats, and she led me outside. There on a bench were two old galvanized buckets. I picked them up in my gloved hands and followed Laura a short distance down the hill. I could see a small roof that seemed to be growing right out of the hillside. The snow-covered path led right to it.

"This is the springhouse," Laura said, opening an old wooden door.

It was well-named; there was an actual spring inside that filled a small well and then overflowed into a small stone trough that led to the outside. Shelves on the walls stored eggs, milk, butter, and anything else that needed to be kept cool. At present, it was warmer inside the little shed than out. I guessed the earth insulated the little structure, since it was mostly underground. I bet it felt nice and cool in the summer.

I dipped first one bucket and then the other into the well, filling them with crystal- clear spring water.

"You're strong," Laura said as I lifted the buckets, and we left the springhouse to make our way back to the cabin.

"Do you usually carry all the water for your grandmother?"

"Oh, no, she carries most of it, but I try to help."

"I'm sure you're a great help."

I noted on our return trip that there was a smokehouse and a woodshed out back. The woodshed didn't look as if it contained enough wood to make it through the week, let alone the winter.

"Where do you get your wood for the fire?" I asked.

"From fallen trees all through the forest. We have a little wagon to carry it in and a sled for the winter."

I knew then what I'd be doing after breakfast.

The scent of bacon seemed even stronger as we returned to the cabin. Soon, we sat down to a breakfast of scrambled eggs, biscuits and gravy, and bacon. There was ice-cold spring water and hot tea, as well. The scrambled eggs were especially good, because Grandmother had mixed in herbs, giving the eggs a taste I'd never experienced before. I ate and ate until I was quite full.

"Are there tools in the woodshed?" I asked. "I thought I'd get in some firewood."

"You don't have to do that, Angel," Grandmother said.

"I want to. Besides, it's the least I can do after this fine breakfast and that wonderful supper last night."

"Yes, all the tools you'll need are hanging on the walls."

"Good, I need some exercise."

"Can I go, Grandmother?"

"No, Child, you have lessons."

Grandmother must have noticed my confused look, for she explained.

"We're rather isolated here, so I teach Laura at home as much as possible."

"We have loads and loads of books!" Laura said, pulling me across the room to show me a shelf full of school texts on every subject imaginable, most of them far too advanced for a six-year-old.

"Well, I'm going to get started. It's a beautiful day. I'm itching to get outside."

Grandmother and Laura bid me goodbye, and I made my way out into the cold December air. I was wrapped up in my coat, scarf, and toboggan, but was still a bit chilly. I imagined the work would heat me up soon enough.

I found an ax and a saw hanging on the woodshed wall. A large sled leaned in the corner. I gathered up the tools and set out to the north of the cabin in search of fallen logs. I pulled the sled along behind me as I made my way through the trees. It didn't take me long to find a big log that would likely keep me busy the whole day long.

I'd lived on a farm. I hadn't done all that much farm work back home, but I knew how to handle an ax and saw. I got right to work with the saw, cutting the log into sections just the right size for the fireplace. The limbs I cut into smaller pieces suitable for Grandmother's kitchen range. The large logs for the fireplace would need to be split, but I'd spotted steel wedges and a sledge hammer, so I knew I could perform the task later.

I felt like a pioneer as I sawed through the tree. I soon became warm enough that I hung first my scarf and then my toboggan on the sled. The air was cold and crisp, but the sun shone down brightly. It might seem odd, but I enjoyed the work. I thought of the nearly empty woodshed and what a hardship it must be for Grandmother and Laura to chop wood for the fire. I could do so with ease, and my mind was filled with visions of a woodshed filled to the roof.

My muscles began to ache after a while. I didn't foolishly push myself in the cold, but took frequent breaks to catch my breath and give my biceps and back a rest. During those times, I looked out over the countryside. There was little to see beyond trees, trees, and more trees flowing over the hills, but when I looked carefully I noted that Grandmother's cabin was not the only home in the woods. Far to the west I spotted a clapboard farmhouse and to the south another. In a couple of locations to the east, I could see a spiral of smoke rising that no doubt indicated a dwelling of some sort hidden in the hills. In no way was the area densely populated, but Grandmother and Laura weren't completely alone. They did have neighbors, however distant.

I was not alone during my labors. One of Grandmother's cows, whom I later learned was named Bessie, walked right up to me as I was sawing on a log. She looked at me with her soulful brown eyes, and I stopped my work to pet her. I stroked her muzzle and her flank as I told her what a beautiful cow she was. I swear she could understand. I don't know if cows can smile, but Bessie seemed to be smiling. Bessie made me a little homesick for my own farm; she even had the same name as my favorite cow back home. In the past months, however, I'd learned to appreciate what I did have rather than moan about what I didn't.

I stopped petting Bessie for a few moments as I became lost in thought. I laughed as she nudged me, clearly telling me I wasn't finished. Bessie reminded me of a very large dog. From that very first day, Bessie stayed nearby most of the time I was working, as if she was glad of the company. She lived in the old barn with other cows, a few chickens, a horse, and a couple of goats, but perhaps she liked being around someone new.

Sawing wood is hard work, but I truly didn't mind. The breakfast I'd eaten had fueled me up for the day, and my labors kept me warm. I thought fondly of what might be awaiting me when I returned to the cabin later—perhaps some more of that wonderful vegetable soup.

I filled the sled and pulled it to the woodshed. I set the largest logs to the side and stacked the others neatly. When the sled was empty, I turned to the task of splitting wood. The sledgehammer was heavy and drove the wedge deep into the log with each swing. Some of the logs I split right down the middle with a single swing. Others were far more stubborn, especially those with knots.

With my task completed, which took quite some time, I assure you, I pulled the sled back to my workplace in the woods and continued. I worked steadily until lunchtime and then returned to the cabin. There was indeed hot vegetable soup waiting on me as well as more of the delicious bread. I'd worked up quite an appetite and ate ravenously.

After lunch, I returned to my work and continued right until dark. Night comes on early in the winter, especially in the forest, and I was not sorry to lose the light. I was quite pleased with what I'd accomplished, but I was also quite tired. My muscles weren't accustomed to being used so. I turned my hand to the same task whenever I could in the following days. I was determined to leave Grandmother and Laura with enough firewood to last the winter.

I carried an armload of wood back to the cabin with me, as I had earlier at lunch and added it to the stack on the porch. I stepped into the cabin to find it filled with golden lamplight and the scent of ham. For supper Grandmother had prepared thick ham steaks, with biscuits, jam, and even pumpkin pie! If it wasn't for my labors in the forest, I was quite sure I would've grown fat from eating so well.

After supper, we sat around the kitchen table where Grandmother and Laura instructed me in the art of making a wreath of balsam pine. While I was cutting firewood, little Laura had gathered pine boughs and then patiently waited for my return so I could join in the fun. By the light of lamp and candle, they showed me how to bend an old coat hanger into a circle and then attach boughs one after another until they formed a wreath. My fingers grew a bit sticky from the sap, but the scent of fragrant pine filled the air, reminding me Christmas was near. I felt truly lucky I'd get to spend it in that little log cabin in the woods, with Laura and Grandmother.

I was the last to finish my wreath, which was a surprise to no one. There was no hurry, however, as we had all the evening and night before us. Laura had gathered a basket full of pine cones, bittersweet, and winter berries, and with these we decorated our wreaths. Laura asked if I knew any Christmas stories, and I think I did a rather good job of reciting *The Night Before Christmas*. I might have gotten a line or two wrong, but if anyone noticed or cared, they did not say.

Grandmother brought out long strips of red cloth from a drawer, and these we used to fashion bows for our wreaths. When they were finished, they were quite beautiful, although mine had a slightly awkward look to it. Laura noticed my slight frown and pronounced my work "rather good for a boy." I smiled and then laughed.

Laura and I helped Grandmother hang two of the wreaths in the front windows. The other, fashioned by Laura, had a place of honor on the outside of the front door. There it would greet us as we entered and add an extra touch of Christmas cheer.

"Can we get a tree tomorrow, Grandmother?" Laura asked as we were scrubbing off the pinesap with hot water and lye soap.

"Yes, I think it's time. Christmas is only a few days away."

Laura smiled and then turned to me. "Will you come with me tomorrow? We'll find just the right tree, and then you can chop it down!"

"I'll be happy to. How about just before supper?"

"Yes, then we can decorate the tree once it's all set up."

"It sounds like a plan," I said.

I was tired from my day's exertions, but content. We spent the rest of the evening and night talking by the fire. I'd forgotten how enjoyable just talking could be. Here, there was no radio, and certainly no TV. There was no phone, nor any other distractions of the modern world. I did not think I could permanently live like that, but it was rather pleasant for a while.

The next day I spent sawing, chopping, and splitting firewood. I stacked a good deal of it right on the porch of the cabin, for winter was only beginning, and all the logs would be cleared away long before spring. Most went into the woodshed, however, a sort of bank account against the cold. I was pleased I'd found a way to contribute.

I stopped working early enough so that Laura and I would have plenty of time to find a Christmas tree. It began snowing again just as we set out, pulling the sled behind us. There were scattered pines throughout the woods and denser stands here and there. We headed for the nearest of the pine groves, and Laura and I circled trees, trying to decide which was just right.

I knew from experience that trees looked much smaller outdoors than indoors. I reminded Laura that a tree that was much taller than I was would be too big. The open end of the main room of the cabin could hold a tree more than fifteen feet tall, but how would we have decorated it? If it were to be placed under the loft, a height of eight feet was about it.

Laura fell in love with a tree that was just a bit taller than I was. While she stood back, I took a swing at the trunk, showering myself with snow. It took several swings to bring down the pine, but it was no harder work than I'd been doing all day. Soon, the tree was lying on the sled, and I was pulling it home, while Laura walked by my side and sang carols in the falling snow.

We had not taken long to harvest our tree, but even so, the shadows were deepening fast. The windows of the cabin shone with a warm, golden glow as we approached, promising both warmth and hospitality. I abandoned the sled just in front of the porch, grasped the trunk of the tree, and pulled it inside.

Grandmother already had a large stoneware jar, partly filled with pebbles, sitting before one of the front windows of the cabin where she desired the tree to be placed. I lifted the tree, set it in place, and held it there while Laura added more pebbles to keep the tree from tipping over. When she was finished, I stood back and the tree stood all on its own, more secure that it would have been in any tree stand.

The balsam pine began to fill the air with its scent, even before we began to decorate. This Christmas tree would have no lights, but Grandmother produced a box of old ornaments that we began to hang on the tree with care. Some of the ornaments were plain round glass bulbs in blue, gold, pink, red, silver, and green. Others were shaped like little Christmas trees, snowmen, Santa, angels, birds, and fruit. There were paper decorations with deep rich colors such as I'd never seen before. Grandmother said they were very old and had originally come from Germany.

Little by little, the tree took shape. The light of the candles, lamps, and the fire at the other end of the cabin reflected off the shiny ornaments, making them sparkle. Once we had added a couple of boxes of icicles, the tree was a beautiful sight to behold. I couldn't remember ever having enjoyed decorating a Christmas tree quite so much.

That night, after retiring to the loft, I lay looking at the rafters, thinking of my own family and even more of Kurt. I wondered how he'd been getting along all these months and if he thought of me daily as I did him. I hoped his life had gone back to normal. No doubt nearly everyone in my hometown hated me, but it was worth it to give Kurt back the life he'd lost. I knew he wouldn't have allowed my sacrifice if he'd know about it in advance. That's why I hadn't told him. I had just taken the blame and slipped away before anyone could stop me.

I wish we could have spent Christmas together. It was at times like this that I missed him the most. I reminded myself we wouldn't be parted forever. We would be together again some day. I did not know what would happen upon my return, but at least there would be Kurt. That was more than enough. Perhaps someday we would travel back to Grandmother's cabin, and I would show Kurt where I'd spent a happy Christmas when I'd expected to be alone. I went to sleep with that pleasant thought dancing in my head.

I spent my days sawing, chopping, and splitting fire wood. I realize that might sound like drudgery, but it was anything but. I was outside, in the fresh air, surrounded by beauty, and no more than a few hours away from a delicious home-cooked meal. Laura frequently pulled me away to help her gather pine boughs, berries, and other necessities for her Christmas decorations. At other times she, or Grandmother, brought me a mug of hot tea. Bessie kept me company, too, searching through the snow for grass and watching me work.

The meals served by Grandmother were delicious, beyond even my own mother's home cooking. Grandmother was an artist. Each soup, ham, pie, biscuit, or cake was an edible work of art. Every bite told me she put a great deal of care into everything she cooked and made me feel lucky to have nearly frozen to death in her woods.

Christmas came quickly. When I was younger, it seemed as though Christmas would never arrive; the days crawled by, and I had thought Christmas would never come. Perhaps it was because I was older now–I was fifteen after all–but the days sped by, and then it was Christmas morning.

"Happy Christmas!" Laura announced as I climbed down from the loft.

"Happy Christmas, Laura," I said. "Merry Christmas, Grandmother."

"Merry Christmas, Angel."

I grinned. It was snowing outside again, perfect weather for Christmas day. All was snug and warm inside the cabin, and the air was filled with the scent of pine, hot pancakes, and maple syrup. The fire popped in the fireplace, and my eyes turned to its merrily dancing flames. At the moment, I didn't wish to be anywhere else. The only thing that could have made the day better was to have Kurt at my side. I wasn't going to worry about Kurt, however, for he was home, safe and sound with his family. I knew we would someday be together each and every Christmas.

Grandmother beckoned us to the table. We followed the scent of bacon, pancakes and hot maple syrup and sat down. There was a crock of fresh, creamy butter, provided, no doubt, by my friend Bessie. The chickens had made their contribution, too, in the form of eggs, which Grandmother had fried sunny side up. It all smelled so delicious that I became instantly hungry.

Grandmother and Laura didn't have a lot of money, but I had the feeling that rich men with piles of gold would've traded places with them in an instant—if they had any sense at all, that is. Grandmother and Laura were focused on the business of living. They spent their days milking Bessie, gathering eggs, tending their animals, churning butter, making jam, and creating what they needed with their own hands. In the summer they grew fresh vegetables to be put away for the winter. They weren't concerned with making money or building an empire. Their only concern was life itself. I felt truly lucky to be a part of that. I knew I'd learned something I could take with me when I went on my way.

After breakfast, we cleared up and then gathered around the tree. I was eager to watch Laura open presents. I even had one to give her myself. The first gift she opened was a teddy bear. I had no doubt Grandmother had made it herself. He was small and brown and cuddly, just the kind of thing Grandmother would make. Laura also received some pretty ribbons for her hair. She was so excited over those she squealed. Laura presented Grandmother with a new apron. How she'd managed to buy it, I did not know. I was very surprised when Laura handed me a package. I unwrapped it to find a pair of red mittens.

"Grandmother helped me with them—a lot," Laura said, smiling.

"They're beautiful," I said. "Thank you so much."

I hugged Laura and smiled at Grandmother.

Grandmother presented me with a second unanticipated package, and I opened it to reveal a dark green, hand-knitted sweater.

"I'll put this to good use I'm sure," I said. "It's beautiful."

I gave Grandmother a hug this time.

I pulled out the single package I'd placed under the tree and handed it to Grandmother.

"It's not much," I said, "but I thought you might like it."

She tore away the green paper decorated with pine cones to reveal a wooden spoon. I'd whittled it myself with my pocket knife while I was taking breaks from chopping wood.

"It's wonderful," Grandmother said, "one can never have too many spoons. This one is the perfect size for stirring soup."

Laura had a few more presents to unwrap and sent the paper flying as she tore into them. She received some Christmas candy, books, and a pretty needlepoint pillow with an angel on it. Soon, it was bare beneath the tree.

"I think there's one more present for you somewhere," I said to Laura.

Laura looked under the tree, confused.

"Ah, here it is," I said, pulling a small package wrapped in bright red paper from my pocket.

Laura opened the package, stared at her present, and then back at me. She was speechless.

"Here, let me help you put it on," I said.

"But, it's your gold chain!"

"Was mine, now it's yours."

"But…"

"No, buts. I want you to have it."

Laura held her hair up while I put the chain around her neck and closed the clasp. She grinned at me and ran to the mirror.

"I look like a princess!"

"That's much too expensive a gift, Angel," Grandmother said quietly.

"It cost me nothing. I already had it, and I truly don't need it. I thought it would make Laura happy."

Grandmother made hot cocoa and we all sat around the fire, while admiring the Christmas decorations. It felt good to have the whole day to do with as I pleased. I could just sit there in front of the fire and drink hot cocoa and talk with Grandmother and Laura. It was a wonderful Christmas Day.

Laura and I helped Grandmother make Christmas cookies later in the morning. We cut out angels, trees, bells, reindeer, and snowmen with cookie cutters and then decorated the cookies with colored sugar. Grandmother baked them in the old range, and the scent of sugar cookies intermingled with all the other delicious scents of the day. We devoured them with cold milk as soon as they'd cooled enough to touch. Even Grandmother feasted on cookies, so that when the time came for lunch, none of us was hungry.

Grandmother made us a feast for supper, however. The large ham had been tantalizing me with its scent all day, even when I was stuffed with cookies. Grandmother glazed it with brown sugar and herbs, and when I tasted it, I nearly moaned with pleasure. In addition to the ham, there were mashed potatoes, corn, sweet potatoes with caramel sauce, green beans, and freshly baked yeast rolls with the ever-present butter and jam. For dessert, Grandmother had baked a Christmas cake, chocolate on the inside, but frosted with white icing and decorated with green and red sprinkles. It was nearly too beautiful to eat, but we didn't let that stop us. By the time we were finished I was so stuffed I was nearly miserable. I almost felt as if I was too full to walk, but I made my way to the fire anyway, where we all sat and watched the falling snow through the windows. It might just have been the best Christmas ever.

I stayed on with Grandmother and Laura until New Year's, but at last it was time to go. I'd filled the woodshed to the roof. Grandmother and Laura wouldn't want for wood this winter for sure, and perhaps they were set for the next as well. Part of me didn't want to leave, but I couldn't stay there forever, and I knew in my heart it was time to go on. Jack and Emma were no doubt already wondering why it was taking me so long to reach Fort Wayne. The sooner I set out, the sooner I could set their minds at ease.

Laura had tears in her eyes as we stood just inside the cabin door saying our goodbyes, but I assured her I'd return someday.

She smiled at that and gave me a hug. Grandmother hugged me as well. I thanked them for taking me in, feeding me so well, and making my Christmas a wonderful experience.

"No," Grandmother said, "thank you."

I couldn't resist hugging them once again.

"I was wrong about something on the day we found you in the snow," Grandmother said.

"Oh?" I asked.

"Yes. I told Laura you weren't an angel, but I couldn't have been more wrong."

Kurt

Tyler had *that* look in his eyes whenever we were alone—a yearning, almost pleading desire for love. That look wasn't just about sex. If it had been, I could far more easily have ignored it. No. Tyler needed someone to love and someone to love him back. He needed what I had with Angel.

I felt guilty for letting Tyler believe I was heterosexual, yet what might he do if he knew the truth? I already felt as if he was pursuing me. I also felt guilty because I was interested. Not that I'd cheat on Angel. No. I would never do that. I did like the attention and the companionship, though. Tyler helped to fill an emptiness that Angel left when he departed. Of course, the better part of the emptiness could never be filled—or rather could only be filled by Angel's return. Still, the emptiness was there, and I needed someone to help me fill it.

The Nudo twins had each other. That was something. I couldn't begin to understand the complexities of their relationship. I didn't think they could be to each other what Angel and I were, however. Brothers couldn't be boyfriends; at least, I didn't think so. Tanner couldn't give Tyler what he needed, but I couldn't, either. As attractive, sweet, and kind as Tyler was, my heart belonged to Angel. Perhaps what Tyler needed even more than a boyfriend was a friend who could understand—someone who wouldn't think of him as a freak because he was attracted to guys instead of girls. I felt as if I was cheating Tyler by not opening up to him.

Would it really be so dangerous to tell Tyler I was a homosexual, too? I knew for a fact he was one of us. He had kissed his own brother in front of me, after all. That still made my head spin. True, Tyler might pursue me more vigorously if he knew I was like him, but all I had to do was say "no."

Could I say "no"? Was I strong enough? Tyler was undeniably attractive. If Angel wasn't in my life, I'd jump on Tyler in a second. Angel was in my life, however, and I would never cheat on him. That was the bottom line. That was what would give me the strength to say "no" to Tyler Nudo. I decided it was time to tell the Nudo brothers the truth.

Just after lunch, Tyler asked if I'd like to go out for a bite to eat after school. I knew this was my chance. Now that I'd made my decision, I wanted to say what I had to say and be done with it. Otherwise, I'd agonize over my decision and rethink it until I drove myself insane. I accepted Tyler's invitation but asked him to bring Tanner along, too. Tyler wasn't thrilled with that idea, but he agreed the three of us would go to the Black Heifer for an early supper.

The time and place were set. That was the easy part. Now I had to tell the Nudo twins the truth. That would be a good deal harder. I just hoped we would be able to talk in the Black Heifer. I couldn't take the slightest risk of being overheard. Of course, I could have gone home with the twins, but that wasn't completely safe. I was reasonably sure my willpower would stand up to temptation, but why tempt fate? I wanted to spell things out clearly before I risked being alone with either of the twins again.

Tyler met me at my locker after school, but there was no sign of his brother. This wasn't good. It wasn't good at all.

"You did ask Tanner to come, right?" I asked.

Tyler laughed.

"I am Tanner."

"Oh! There is just no way to tell which of you is which!"

"Sure there is," Tanner said. "I'm the cute one."

I rolled my eyes.

Tanner's twin hurried toward us.

"Sorry, I got held up by Mrs. Kendall. I had to hand in some makeup work."

"No problem. You guys ready?"

The twins nodded. Wow. They were adorable! Somehow, they looked even cuter together than apart.

The three of us walked the short distance from the school to the diner. Normally, I would have walked home with Tommy after school, but he'd stayed home sick today. I needed to remember to call him after I got home to check on him. Tommy knew my secret, of course, but he didn't know about the Nudo twins. This conversation had to remain between Tyler, Tanner, and me.

"Christmas is coming up fast," Tanner said as we crossed the street. "I can't wait."

"Thanksgiving vacation sure went by fast enough," his brother noted.

"Tell me about it."

"Just think, though. Soon we'll have more than a week off, and it will be Christmas, too!" Tanner said.

"Well, it's beginning to look a lot like Christmas," I said, half singing the words. I nodded at the falling snow, the decorated tree outside the bank, and all the decorations in the store windows.

Tyler and Tanner both moaned at my bad pun.

"Why do you hang out with this guy so much?" Tanner asked, rolling his eyes.

"Because I'm funny! Sometimes," I said. "Right, Tyler?"

"Um, yeah. Whatever you say, Kurt."

"Hey, no fair ganging up on me."

We reached the Black Heifer and walked inside, shaking the snow off our coats. The place was practically empty. Perfect. I chose a booth isolated from the few other customers, and we sat down.

The Black Heifer was decorated for the season with pictures of cows and other farm animals surrounded by tinsel and garlands. A freshly cut tree was on display in the window, its multicolored lights blinking on and off. Christmas music played softly in the background. I was so caught up in the Christmassy feeling I almost forgot why I was there.

I allowed myself to be distracted by the menu for a couple of minutes. To be honest, I was stalling. I wasn't at all sure how to tell the twins the rumor about me had been true. At least I knew they wouldn't kick my butt for it. Then again, they might be plenty angry that I'd let them believe I was heterosexual when I was really a homo.

Tanner and Tyler both ordered a cheeseburger, fries, and a Coke. Did twins eat the same things all the time, or what? I followed suit. I wasn't especially hungry, so anything was fine.

"Um, there's something I wanted to tell you guys," I said as soon as our waitress departed. I knew if I allowed myself to stall any longer that I might never work up the courage to speak. "That's why I wanted both of you to be here. Before I tell you anything, though, you've got to promise that this will remain between us."

"You've kept our secret," Tanner said, "so we'll definitely keep yours. You can trust us."

"Yeah, and I bet your secret isn't nearly as big as ours," Tyler said.

"That's where you're wrong."

I paused. Tyler and Tanner gazed at me expectantly. I had trouble making my voice work.

"I lied to you guys before. Well, I didn't lie. I just let you believe something that wasn't true. I had a reason for doing it then, which I hope you'll understand. That reason has been gone for months, though, so I guess I should have told you the truth sooner, but…well, it's complicated."

"You should come with subtitles. Like on those foreign films I heard about," Tanner said.

"I guess I'm not making much sense, huh?"

"You're making some sense," Tyler said.

"I guess I should just say what I have to say. You weren't wrong about me. I am like you guys. That day when you invited me to…your room…well, I didn't get all nervous and hurry away because I was freaked out. I acted like that because I was already seeing someone and I was tempted. I knew I had to get out of there."

Tyler smiled.

"I knew it," he said quietly.

"I couldn't tell you the truth then because the secret wasn't mine alone. Things were kind of messed up then, too."

"So the rumor about you was true," Tanner said. "Why did Angel leave the letter saying it wasn't? Unless…"

Both twins gazed at me.

"Angel was, and is, my boyfriend," I said.

"You're kidding!" Tanner said. "Angel Egler and you! Wow!"

"Keep it down will you?" I said.

"Sorry."

"Yeah. Angel and me. Unbelievable, but it's true. The thing is, Angela Yates started the rumor about me. It was based on nothing but the fact that she wanted Angel for herself. She had no idea anything was up between Angel and me except friendship. She wanted me out of the way, so she started that rumor about us so Angel wouldn't hang out with me anymore."

"That cow," Tyler said.

"I'm sure you guys remember the letter Angel left behind. He wrote that letter to save me. I didn't know he was going to do it. I didn't know he was leaving, either. But, he sacrificed himself for me. I didn't think my nightmare of a life would ever end, but Angel changed things back to the way they were before the rumor started. The thing is, the rumor is true. I am a homosexual. Only Angel, Tommy, my brother Sam, and now you know the truth." I didn't mention Ryan, as it might bring up uncomfortable questions.

"That's so Romeo & Juliet," Tanner said. "Well, you know what I mean. He loved you so much he gave up everything for you."

I nodded, close to tears.

The waitress brought our food just then, so we grew silent for a bit.

"You know, I never believed that letter Angel left behind," Tyler said. "I just didn't see how a guy like him could be one of us."

"Maybe you need to have a higher opinion of yourself," I said.

"Maybe, but it's not easy. You know the things they say about us at school."

"I don't think anyone really believes that stuff," I said.

"Yeah, but, it is true you know—some of it."

"I know," I said.

"Do you think we're…okay," Tyler said.

I took a sip of Coke to stall.

"I don't really understand your relationship," I said. "I understand that you're homos, and I think that's perfectly okay. As for… as for the incest," I said just above a whisper, "well, I could never think of my brother like that, but… I just don't know. What I do know is that you're great guys. You're twins, too, so I guess that makes things different. I guess I'd have to say I think you are okay."

Tyler and Tanner looked at each other. I could read love there, but also a trace of guilt. Tyler's question cued me in that he had reservations about his physical relationship with his brother. I had the feeling Tanner shared those reservations. I'd been as truthful with the twins as possible. I wasn't entirely sure how I felt about their incestuous relationship. Like I've said before, it both attracted and repelled me at the same time.

"I hope you guys will forgive me for not being honest with you before," I said. "I really couldn't tell you the truth at first, and later… well, maybe I just remained silent out of habit. I've never feared you guys would spread rumors about me, but things were so bad when that rumor was going around I just didn't want to go back to that."

"We understand," Tyler said, looking at his brother for a moment.

"Yeah, I know those were rough times for you, Kurt. No one would want to go through that. We're just sorry we couldn't help you out more then."

"I know why you couldn't," I said. "I understand."

"Wow. Angel Egler," Tyler said. "I've had fantasies about him! He's such a bad boy. That really gets me going."

"Down, Tyler," Tanner said. "You're talking about Kurt's boyfriend."

"Oh, sorry."

"It's okay," I said, grinning.

"I hope you'll forgive me for saying this," Tyler said, "but it's really hard picturing you and Angel together. He was such a badass, and you're, well, you're kind of quiet, sort of the sensitive type."

"You never knew Angel as I did. You didn't get to see the real Angel. He's tough. There's no denying that. He's also the sweetest, kindest, most loving boy that ever was."

"He's got it bad," Tanner said to Tyler. "This boy is head over heels in love."

I nodded and began to tear up.

"Hey, it's okay, Kurt," Tyler said, reaching across the table for a moment to take my hand.

"I just really miss him," I said, blinking back tears. "He left a letter for me. He said he'll return when I graduate, but that's so far away!"

"At least you know he is coming back," Tanner said.

"Yeah, anyway, I wanted to tell you guys the truth, and there it is. I hope we can still be friends. I thought maybe we could talk to each other about things we can't talk to others about. I can talk to Sam and Tommy, but they don't really understand. They're not one of us."

"Hey, we homos have to stick together," Tanner said.

"No one else will stick with us. That's for sure," I said.

"We are the outcasts, the despised, the ridiculed," Tanner said. He laughed weakly. There was too much truth to what he said for it to be funny, but I guess it's better to laugh than to cry.

Tyler looked at me thoughtfully, but I couldn't tell what he was thinking. Would he back off now that he knew about Angel and me, or would he pursue me harder? I guessed I would just have to wait and see.

"I'm glad this is over with," I said.

"You hate spending time with us that much?" Tanner teased.

"I don't mean that! I mean telling you the truth."

"Lies are easier," Tanner said. "I prefer fantasies myself, usually about the entire boys' baseball team making me—"

"But anyway!" Tyler said.

Tanner laughed.

"Let's talk about something easier," I said.

"And something Derek Spradley can hear," Tyler said. "He's coming our way."

"Uh-oh, girl talk," I said.

The twins laughed.

"Hey, what's up, guys?" Derek said.

"We were just sitting here waiting for you, Derek," Tanner said with a grin.

"Sure, you were."

"Join us. We're about done, but maybe we'll force ourselves to get dessert and keep you company," Tyler said.

"Yeah, we're selfless when it comes to our friends," Tanner said.

"Uh-huh," Derek said skeptically.

"Hey, did you guys see Alicia Tulleyfield in that sweater today? That thing was so tight. Mmm," Derek said.

The rest of us laughed.

"What?"

"We just knew you'd talk about girls," I said.

"I can't help it! I love girls!"

"If only one would love you back, right?" Tyler asked.

"Yeah," Derek sighed. He looked at me. "Alicia wants you bad. You know that, right?"

"Yeah, I know, but—"

"But what? She's so hot!"

"She's not…quite my type," I said. The twins exchanged a look and smiled at each other. "She's all yours, Derek."

"I wish!"

"You fantasize!" Tanner said.

"Nightly," Derek said, wiggling his eyebrows.

"Let's not delve any more deeply into *that* topic," Tyler said.

"Actually, Tommy has it bad for Alicia," I said. "I'd really like to see those two get together. I think Tommy's really lonely, if you know what I mean."

"Aren't we all!" Derek said. "Tommy can only have her if I don't work up the courage to ask her out first!"

"Well, I guess Tommy can have her, then," Tanner said.

Derek stuck out his tongue at Tanner.

"Um, what do you guys want for Christmas?" I asked to change the subject.

Tyler gazed at me for a moment, as if to say I was what he wanted for Christmas. Maybe I was just seeing something that wasn't there, however. Soon, we were all talking about what we hoped to find under the tree on Christmas morning. I smiled. Spending time with my friends made me feel good inside.

I called Tommy after I got home. He was doing better and would be back in school the next day. That was good news. Things weren't the same without my best friend around. I told Tommy about hanging out with the Nudo twins after school. He laughed when I told him some of the things Derek had said. He wasn't so pleased that Derek wanted Alicia, but then he wasn't surprised, either.

"What girl doesn't he want?" Tommy asked when I told him. I laughed.

I climbed into bed that night feeling a good deal better about many things. If only it was graduation day and I could look up and see Angel smiling at me. I went to sleep dreaming about just that.

***

I feared Tyler would pounce on me when he found out I was a homo, but as it turned out, I had nothing to worry about. His yearning glances in my direction made it clear he was interested in me, but he didn't try anything. I knew I was safe from unwanted advances when Tyler said, "If you weren't taken by Angel, I'd be after you in a heartbeat." You can just imagine how good that made me feel about myself. First Angel, now Tyler—guys actually thought I was hot!

I became closer to the Nudo Twins than ever. The three of us belonged to a secret club of sorts. We got together sometimes to talk about boys—who we think is hot, who we think might be one of us, and things like that. I didn't feel so alone now. I could talk to the twins about things I couldn't discuss with anyone else. I just wished I had told them the truth months ago.

The twins, Tommy, and I started hanging out together a lot after school. Tyler and Tanner even told Tommy they were homos. Tommy wasn't too surprised, but he was cool with it. I knew I was lucky to have such an accepting and understanding best friend.

Christmas vacation arrived at last. Dad and Sam bought a tree and brought it home tied to the top of the car. Dad was in charge of the lights. We never started decorating before he got the lights working. If one bulb was out that was it for the whole string. Sometimes it took half an hour to figure out which bulb had burned out. Occasionally, Dad had to walk away from the task for a few minutes to avoid saying words that wouldn't fit with the holiday season at all.

Decorating the tree was a family tradition. While Dad was sorting out the lights, Mom and Ida were busying making hot cocoa and sugar cookies. Sam and I went to the attic to bring down all the boxes of ornaments. Once Dad had the lights sorted out, Mom and Ida brought in the hot cocoa and cookies. We tuned the radio to a station playing Christmas music, and all of us joined in decorating the tree.

The old ornaments had become familiar over the years. There were some Mom and Dad bought before Sam was born. There were even ornaments that my grandparents had purchased. Dad pointed out the glass bulbs that had no silvering. He said those were made during World War II when the metal was needed for the war.

The snow fell down outside, making me feel as if our farmhouse was inside a big snow globe. Perhaps our whole world was nothing but a snow globe sitting on someone's mantel in an unthinkably huge house. Okay, I know I'm weird, but sometimes I think things like that.

We took our time decorating the tree, frequently stopping for some hot cocoa or a cookie. One by one the ornaments went on until the boxes were empty. Next came the icicles. We used four boxes! Icicles have to be put on just a few strands at a time or they don't look right at all. With five of us working away at the task it didn't take long. Soon, all that remained was putting on the star.

As the baby of the family, the honor of putting the star on the top was mine. Sam helped me get up on Dad's shoulders and he held my legs while I put the star on the very top of the tree. I was fifteen now and hardly a little boy anymore, but I still liked getting up on Dad's shoulders to put the star on the top. I felt as if Sam and Ida had kind of been cheated, for neither of them was the youngest in the family for very long. I would be the youngest forever, unless Mom and Dad decided I needed a little brother or sister. I seriously doubted that would ever happen!

Once the star was in place Dad plugged in the lights and the whole tree was brilliantly illuminated in an instant. The tree was beautiful with no lights, but with them—wow!

I loved the whole holiday season. It seemed like the entire town of Blackford was decorated inside and out. There was not a house that didn't have at least one string of lights across the porch, and many were lit up all over. Our entire porch was outlined with lights, and Dad put lights on the little spruce in the front yard, too. The front windows were outlined with lights, and it was a beautiful sight.

Walking downtown was like strolling through a winter wonderland. Every storefront was decorated for the season with lights and often with moving figures, too. There was a set of elves in the General Store window, busily making toys. The bank had a life-sized Santa that waved to those who passed by. Merton's Ice Cream Parlor had a Victorian skating scene in the window. Merton's also offered peppermint ice cream during the holiday season and everyone stopped in for a taste.

There were big, lighted wreaths hanging on the street lamps and a huge decorated Christmas tree near the town hall. Everywhere one turned there was something to see. In the evenings, a lot of people drove slowly around town, admiring all the lights. The most impressive decorations were to be found downtown, however.

As Christmas drew ever closer and gifts began to appear under the tree, I wondered where Angel might be and how he would spend his Christmas. I hoped he wasn't all alone somewhere. I wished he could be with me, or at least with his own family. I took out the photo of Angel and me that I carried in my wallet and gazed at it often.

During the last few months I'd learned to not dwell on what might be happening to Angel. Instead, I assured myself that Angel could take care of himself, no matter what he came up against. He had survived his involvement with Adam's gang. He'd saved my life. I couldn't completely stop myself from worrying about him, but I did the best I could. When I thought of Angel, I thought about how much I loved him. I knew he was out there somewhere, loving me right back.

Christmas morning was wonderful! We weren't allowed to get up before 8 a.m., but you can be sure Sam, Ida, and I were downstairs in front of the tree about a minute after. There were presents for everyone. I received the inevitable sweater and a few other clothes, but mostly I received stuff I truly wanted. Clothes on Christmas is a dreaded gift, yet wrapped up in Christmas paper even underwear can seem exciting.

I received a new coin guide and a bunch of coin-collecting supplies. There were folders to hold pennies, nickels, and dimes. There were individual coin holders for special coins. Even better were the coins themselves! I actually received a Carson City silver dollar made in 1881! I was so excited I about wet myself.

Sam and I received a huge train set. It had a locomotive that puffed out steam as it went around the track. There was even a train station, little trees, and a tunnel to go with it. I couldn't wait to get it set up.

We unwrapped gift after gift until not a single one was left. Then, it was time for breakfast. Mom made us French toast with special cranberry syrup. I know cranberry syrup might not sound all that tasty, but believe me it is! There was also bacon, scrambled eggs, and raisin toast.

After breakfast, Sam and I set up our new train set under the tree. Sam was too busy to spend time with me most of the time, but Christmas was different. He seemed like a boy again. We spent a whole hour laying out the track and arranging the little buildings. Then, we switched on the train and it chugged around the track. There were even lights in the passenger cars, making it seem as if there were little people inside. I couldn't wait to show Tommy!

Christmas Day was given over to general laziness. I spent quite a while up in my room placing coins in the folders I'd received. There was a little space for each year and each mint. I also looked through my new coin guide, dreaming of $20 gold pieces and early Colonial coins.

People came in and out all day long—friends of the family and relatives, too. I spent most of my time downstairs visiting and eating my weight in Christmas cookies and candy. I did a fair amount of napping, too. It seemed to go right along with overeating.

Tyler called in the late afternoon and asked if I wanted to go to the park. I, in turn, called Tommy and invited him along. Tommy and I met up with Tyler and Tanner about an hour later. Some guys from school were building a big snowman, so we pitched in to help. Someone threw a snowball, of course, and soon snowman building was replaced by a snowball fight. Tommy, the twins, and I teamed up. We ducked down behind a bank and popped up all at once to deliver a deadly volley. I got a snowball right in the face, but luckily the snow was just wet enough to compact into a ball and the snowball exploded on contact. It was freezing cold, but didn't hurt much.

We had a blast pelting our enemies with snowballs. Eventually the fight degraded into every man for himself, and that's when it became truly crazy. By the time we finished we'd all been nailed multiple times.

The cold, as well as a good deal of snow, had made its way under my clothes, so I felt a good deal like a snowman myself. I think everyone else was just as chilled. When the fight was over, we all went our separate ways. Tommy and I walked together, and he told me all about the racetrack he'd received. I couldn't wait to try it out, but I needed to get home before I turned into a popsicle. There would be plenty of time to spend with Tommy later. Christmas vacation lasted through New Year's Day.

I felt a little guilty for having so much fun over Christmas break. I was so busy spending time with my family, Tommy, and the twins that I didn't even think about Angel that much. Oh, I thought about him, but I kept getting distracted by life. I knew Angel himself would tell me not to feel guilty, though. I could only hope he was having so much fun he didn't have much time to think of me. That was probably unlikely, though. I just hoped he wasn't alone.

The problem with good times is that they go by way too fast. Before I knew it, it was 1953 and I was sitting back in a classroom. New Year's Eve had more meaning than ever before. When the clock struck 12 it meant I was one year closer to be reunited with Angel. If only 1955 would get here!

I realized as I was sitting in second-period World History that today, January 2nd, was Angel's sixteenth birthday. Mine didn't come up until the 18th of February, but my boyfriend turned sixteen today! I wished I could be with him. I'd give him a cake with sixteen candles. I'd sing *Happy Birthday* and give him presents. Most of all, I'd hug him close and tell him how much I loved him. I closed my eyes and wished Angel a happy birthday, hoping that somehow he would know I was thinking about him.

I grew a little depressed because Angel and I couldn't be together. He would only turn sixteen once, and I was missing it. I would miss his seventeenth birthday, too, and his eighteenth. Life was so unfair!

I couldn't be completely angry with life, however, for life had given me Angel in the first place. I just wished that he had never left. As bad as those days had been back when everyone hated me, I'd gladly go back if I could be with Angel. I wished I could go back in time and run away with Angel. That wasn't going to happen, so I guessed it was best to just continue on.

Angel

I awakened under a pine tree on my sixteenth birthday. I didn't even realize it was my birthday until later in the morning. If I had thought about it in advance, I would have stayed with Grandmother and Laura just a bit longer. I was sure Grandmother would've baked me a cake. It was too late for that now, however, so I plodded along. Oddly enough, it wasn't so bad spending my birthday alone. Somehow, I just knew Kurt was thinking of me and wishing me a Happy Birthday. That's all I needed to be happy.

Nothing of great note happened on the rest of my journey to Fort Wayne—just lots of walking and lots of cold, cold nights and not much warmer days. Had it been summer, the trip would've been enjoyable. Even in early January, it wasn't too unpleasant. I enjoyed being out in the sun, watching the countryside slowly go by. I hitched a few rides, as well, which sped me along to my destination.

Had I been back home, the temperatures would've made me shiver, but I'd grown acclimated to the cold. I had my coat, my toboggan, the scarf Emma knitted for me (and which had saved my life), the mittens and sweater Laura and Grandmother made for me, and my long hair to keep me warm. I was far more comfortable than seemed possible in the frigid air.

I reckoned I was only about twenty miles from Fort Wayne when I awakened to an especially cold January morning. I stood, stretched, and walked back to the narrow highway I'd been following for the last several days. I pulled a paper bag out of my pocket that contained two donuts. I had my breakfast as I walked. I loved donuts, even stale ones. They were sooo good.

Only a few vehicles passed as I walked along at the side of the road. After I'd hiked along for an hour or so I heard the loud whir of a motor. I looked back to see an old Dodge business coupe plodding along. It looked like a '39. At least it looked a good deal like the old Chevy that Kurt's older brother, Sam, owned. His car was a '39, as well. I think.

The old car slowed as it approached, but I kept on walking. The car pulled up level to me, veered a bit off the road, and stopped. The driver motioned for me to open the door.

"Could you use a ride?"

I was expecting someone older, but a guy of about seventeen or eighteen was driving. He wasn't especially handsome, but he looked kind.

"Yeah, if you don't mind," I said. "I would appreciate it."

"Climb in."

I did so and closed the door. The old Dodge took off again, and soon we were sailing down the road at thirty miles per hour, a vast improvement over my walking speed.

"I'm Clarence."

"I'm Angel."

"I've never met anyone named Angel before."

"I'm the only one I know."

"I can believe it."

Clarence began to steal looks at me right away. At first, I thought he was just checking out my hair. Many people couldn't stop looking at my hair when they first met me. I lived in a world of crewcuts after all. It soon became apparent that Clarence was checking out more than my hair, however. When he realized I'd caught on, his face turned red and he looked away.

"Sure is cold out," Clarence said. "We're supposed to get freezing rain this afternoon and snow tonight."

I shivered despite the warmth being pumped out by the heater.

"Brrr! Just hearing you say that makes me cold. Hey, how far are we from Fort Wayne?"

"Um, maybe eighteen miles. It's not too far. I live there."

"Great. That's where I'm heading. I have a job lined up."

"Aren't you a little young to be working?"

"Yeah. Aren't you a little young to be driving around instead of being in school?"

"It's Saturday."

"Oh! I lose track of what day it is sometimes."

"So, if you don't mind my asking, what are you doing out all by yourself?"

"I'm just traveling around and seeing the sights, and, like I said, I have a job lined up in Fort Wayne."

"Are you a runaway?" Clarence asked.

"Yeah, sort of, but that's a long story. Let's just say I needed to get away for a while. Don't worry, I'm not a desperate criminal."

Clarence grinned. His eyes roved over me again.

"You sure don't look like a desperate criminal." Clarence paused. "You have a girlfriend where you come from?"

I could see where this was going. It was as obvious as could be.

"No. You?"

"Me? No. No girlfriend."

We rode along in silence for a few moments.

"Listen, Angel, I'd never dare to say this if I knew you, but…you're really good-looking."

Clarence turned completely red. I was shocked he was bold enough to say such a thing. Guys just didn't talk like that. Sure, Clarence was from a big city, but still—

"Um…thanks."

"I'm sorry. I can't believe I said that."

"It's okay."

"Is it?"

"Yeah."

"Well, you're *really* good looking."

Clarence actually became so bold as to put his hand on my knee. I was shocked he had the nerve. He seemed timid as a mouse.

"Clarence, you're a really nice guy, but—"

Clarence quickly withdrew his hand.

"I'm sorry. I'm *really* sorry."

Clarence trembled. I think he feared I'd belt him in the mouth. Most guys would have, I'm sure.

"It's okay, Clarence. I understand."

Clarence jerked his head toward me and nearly ran off the road. I had to grab the wheel and steer to keep us on the pavement.

"You understand?"

I'm sure Clarence was shocked right down to his toes. The subject we were broaching was just not talked about. Well, I guess it was. It almost had to be. Still, I'd venture to say that most homosexuals probably went to their graves without revealing what they were to another living soul.

"Yeah, but listen, nothing can happen between us. Okay?"

Clarence looked more embarrassed than ever.

"I'm sorry. I…I shouldn't have…I'm sure you not…I mean."

"Clarence, relax. I understand."

"You mean you're…you know—"

"Yes."

"Wow. I never thought I'd meet another…you know, but…"

Clarence suddenly looked very unhappy.

"What's wrong?"

"It's because I'm ugly, isn't it? I knew if I ever found someone like me that he wouldn't want me because I'm ugly."

"You're not ugly, Clarence, and your looks have nothing to do with it."

"I don't understand."

"I have someone. I have a boyfriend."

"A boyfriend? Wow. Why isn't he with you? Doesn't he want to be with you while you're traveling?"

"I'm sure he wants to be with me, but he can't. It's a long story, but I love him, and some day I'm going back to him."

"This is exciting," Clarence said, laughing a little. "You really have a boyfriend? That's incredible! Have you and your boyfriend ever…you know?"

"Yeah," I said.

"Wow. I've never. Well, I don't know anyone else like me. That's why I put my hand on your leg. I shouldn't have, but you're a stranger, and you're so attractive. I just couldn't control myself. I thought, well, that this might be my one chance."

"You'll find someone."

"I doubt that."

"Hey, I come from a much smaller place than Fort Wayne, and I found someone."

"Yes, but you're the most beautiful boy I've ever seen." Clarence turned red again.

"Thank you. You're good looking in your own way, Clarence. You'll find someone."

"Do you really think I will?"

"Of course. They say there is someone for everyone."

"But, does that include guys like us?"

"It includes everyone."

"You know I didn't even know what guys like me are called until I looked it up? I thought something was wrong with me. I mean, all the other guys are always talking about girls—in the locker room. You know? I never got it. The thing is, when I looked at guys, well…you know. I thought I was sick, but I didn't want to tell my doctor about it. It was just too embarrassing. So, I started trying to find out for myself.

I looked through all these medical books, then psychology books. I didn't want to be what those books said, but I knew there was no use in denying it. I tried to deny it, believe me, but I couldn't."

"Of course not. You're meant to be the way you are."

"I don't know about that."

"Well, I do."

"The books say it's a mental illness. I'm thinking that someday, when I can afford it, I'll try to get myself cured."

"Clarence, it's not a mental illness. You can't be cured, because you don't have a disease. Nothing is going to change you. Nothing can."

Clarence looked upset. My stomach growled loud enough for Clarence to hear it.

"It sounds like you're ready for something to eat."

"Yeah. Getting something to eat is the first thing on my list once we get to Fort Wayne."

"Could we…eat somewhere together?"

"Sure."

"Great! I know this place where the food is good and they give you mounds of it. You'll be stuffed by the time you leave, and we'll have lots of time to talk. We'll get an out-of-the-way booth."

"That sounds wonderful."

"I'm curious. Has your hair always been so long, Angel? It's beautiful."

"I started growing it out when I was little, about three or four. I wouldn't let anyone cut it. My parents tried everything, but I was a stubborn little kid. They eventually gave up. Dad said at least it saved money on haircuts."

Clarence laughed.

"I've never seen a guy with long hair like yours. I would love to grow mine long, but my parents would kill me."

"How old are you?"

"I'm seventeen."

"Well, someday you'll be out on your own, and you can grow your hair as long as you want."

"How old are you, Angel?"

"Sixteen."

"Really? I thought you were my age."

"Nope."

"What's it like to kiss? I've always dreamed of a man taking me in his arms and kissing me."

Clarence turned red again, but he was as hungry for information as I was for food. I tried my best to explain what kissing was like, but it wasn't easy. Clarence asked me quite a bit about sex, although his face reddened with every single question. Clarence was very naïve, but that wasn't a surprise. It wasn't exactly easy to learn about the things I was telling him.

We pulled into Fort Wayne, and Clarence parked his old Dodge in front of an old restaurant called Sarah's. It was an ordinary-looking place on the outside, but wonderful scents began to tease my nostrils even before we were through the door. The ambiance could best be described as "well worn." Sarah's had obviously been in operation for a good many years. The booths, tables, and chairs were all scuffed, but clean. The interior was plain, but homey. Clarence picked out a booth way in the back, well away from the few other customers.

I gazed down through the menu. I practically licked my lips as I read each entrée. It didn't take me long to settle on the chicken dinner. It had been ages since I'd tasted fried chicken. Well, I hadn't had any since I was on the Selby farm, and that seemed like ages ago, even though it was only a few days.

Our waitress brought us ice water and took our orders. I went all out and even ordered myself a Coke.

We sat there in the booth and quietly discussed what it was like to be homosexual in Indiana. Clarence was full of questions, and I answered each one as well as I could. Just before our meals arrived, I began to tell him the story of Kurt and me.

I was amazed when my chicken dinner arrived. There was at least half a chicken on my plate! There were extra-large portions of mashed potatoes, corn, and cooked apples, too. There was also a large basket of rolls with plenty of butter and jelly to go with them. I talked and ate—mostly ate. I told Clarence about meeting Kurt and all that had happened. Our waitress refilled our basket of rolls twice before I even neared the end of my story. I was so full by the time I'd cleaned my plate I thought I might explode. Clarence absolutely insisted that we order dessert, however, and soon a big piece of coconut cream pie was set down before me. I thought I'd died and gone to Heaven.

"I wish I could take you home with me," Clarence said when we'd nearly finished dessert. "I don't like thinking of you out in the cold."

"I'll be all right. There's a job set up for me. As soon as I make some cash, I'll look for a cheap place to live."

"Hey, how about I buy you breakfast tomorrow morning?"

"I can't let you buy me breakfast. You've already given me a ride. You saved me a ton of walking in the cold."

"Please, let me buy you breakfast. I so enjoy talking to you. I swear it's more than worth it to me. Please?"

I couldn't take those puppy dog eyes gazing at me.

"Well—"

"Please?"

"Okay," I said. "And, thank you."

"I have to be home soon," Clarence said. "Can I give you a ride somewhere?"

"Do you know where the Hotel Indiana is?"

"Of course, everyone knows that. It's right downtown."

"If you could give me a lift there, I'd appreciate it."

"That's where your job is?"

"Yeah."

"Wow. What will you be doing?"

"I don't know, but you can bet I won't be running the front desk."

We paid our checks and climbed back into Clarence's old car. He drove me several blocks south. I could see what appeared to be a huge courthouse and some rather tall buildings. I hadn't seen buildings that big since I passed through Indianapolis. We drove right down among the multistoried structures.

"There it is," Clarence said.

"Wow."

"Yeah. Cool isn't it?"

I looked through the windshield at a beautiful seven-story building. Above one end was a massive sign that read "Hotel Indiana." At the other end was a marquee with "Embassy Theatre" in big letters.

"There's a theatre, too?"

"Yeah. It was the Emboyd until just this year. Somebody new leased it and changed the name to the Embassy. It's incredible inside. You've just got to see it. I go to see movies there sometimes."

"It's hard to tell where the theatre ends and the hotel begins."

"Yeah. It's all in one building. The theatre kind of wraps part way around the hotel like an L, but you'll see that for yourself soon enough."

Clarence pulled up in front of the hotel lobby.

"Meet me at Sarah's tomorrow morning at eight, okay?" Clarence asked.

"I'll be there."

Clarence waved as he drove away.

I took a few moments to look up and down Jefferson Boulevard. The snow plummeted so hard and fast it was nearly a blizzard. I couldn't make out a great deal other than vague outlines of tall buildings. Fort Wayne was a lot bigger than Blackford.

I turned and walked into the lobby of the Hotel Indiana. I just stood there for several moments taking it in. It was as fancy inside as the Delphi Theatre back home. There were chandeliers hanging overhead and rich, intricately detailed, gaily colored carpet underfoot. There were sconces on the walls and beautifully detailed work on the moldings. The furniture was plush and fancy—the kind that looked extremely comfortable but far too nice to actually sit on.

I walked toward the front desk, somewhat unsure of myself.

"How may I help you, sir?" the desk clerk, a young man in his twenties wearing a crisp white shirt and a black tie, asked.

"I'm Angel Egler—"

"Ah. One moment, please."

The clerk picked up a phone, pushed a single button, and spoke.

"Mr. Howard, Angel Egler is here."

I knew Jack had arranged a job for me, but I didn't know the desk clerk would be watching for me. After all, no one knew when I would arrive.

"Mr. Howard will be right out."

"Thank you."

The clerk eyed my long hair as I stood there admiring the lobby. He was quite good-looking, with curly black hair and green eyes. He seemed a bit stand-offish in a way. When he'd spoken to me he was stiff and proper. Perhaps that was just his work persona, however.

"Angel?"

I turned at the sound of an unfamiliar voice.

"Yes."

"I'm Bert Howard. Jack Selby told us to be on the lookout for you. I'll talk with you later about your job, but you'd probably like to rest first. Pearce will show you to your room."

My room? I had a room? I felt more like a guest than an employee.

"That will be…great," I said.

Mr. Howard snapped his fingers, and the desk clerk, who was obviously named Pearce, came around the counter. He led me to a small elevator. Once the doors closed he pressed the button marked "7".

"You'll be staying on the top floor. We like to keep the guests as close to the ground floor as possible, for their convenience."

I nodded. I wasn't quite sure what to say. I followed Pearce down the hallway after the elevator opened. He didn't walk far before he stopped and unlocked a door. He stepped aside and gestured toward the room with his hand.

"Here you are: home sweet home."

"Thanks," I said.

Pearce handed me the key and left without another word. I stepped inside and closed the door behind me. The room was small and had only one window, facing Jefferson Boulevard, but it was neat and clean. There was a bed with a small lamp stand and lamp beside it. There was a low, wide dresser with a mirror, a small desk with a chair, and another comfortable looking armchair. The room had its own bathroom. I supposed it was exactly like all the other guest rooms. It was much nicer than most hotel rooms I'd seen. Best of all, it was warm! For someone who was used to sleeping outside or in a barn, the room was paradise.

The first thing I did was take a shower. The hot water felt indescribably luxurious. I lingered as I shampooed my hair and soaped up my body. It was the first real wash I'd had since leaving the Selby Farm. I almost couldn't believe I'd be able to have a wash every single day now, that I had a warm place to sleep and my own room in a big, fancy hotel! It really was too good to be true, and I feared I'd wake up soon, shivering in the snow under a pine tree.

I didn't wake up, however. I continued right on reveling in the hot water, the shampoo, and the soap. I stayed in the bathroom for a good long while, then dried off, and lay naked on my bed. I could actually lie there naked and be warm!

I pulled a blanket over me to feel comfortable and extra warm and settled in for a nice little nap. I felt safe, as I hadn't since I'd left Grandmother's cabin. I had a roof over my head, a job, and I didn't have to worry about where my next meal was coming from. I fell asleep with those pleasant thoughts drifting through my head.

I'm not sure how long I slept, but when I awakened it was dark outside. I looked out the window to see the lights of Fort Wayne spread out before me. I gazed down at the street below. The headlights of cars moved slowly up the street, past the hotel. I liked the feeling of all those other people out there. I'd spent more than enough time alone.

I dressed and headed down to the lobby in search of Mr. Howard. Now that I'd rested, I was eager to see just what I'd be doing in the hotel. Pearce wasn't at the front desk, but I asked the clerk there where I could find Mr. Howard. She directed me toward his office.

"Come in, Angel. Sit down."

"Thank you, Mr. Howard."

"Do you like your room?"

"It's wonderful."

"I've called Jack to let him know you arrived safely. I'm sure you'll want to call him yourself before long, too."

"Oh, yes. Jack and Emma were so kind to me."

"Jack had only nice things to say about you. We wouldn't normally hire someone so young here, but I owe Jack quite a few favors. If it wasn't for Jack Selby, I wouldn't be where I am today."

"I promise I'll do the best job I can at whatever you want me to do."

"Let's talk about that. I'm sure you're curious about your job. I'm going to use you as a jack-of-all-trades, so to speak. You'll be a bellhop, carrying guests' luggage for them. That can be a tough job, but it will give you a chance to pick up tips in addition to your regular pay. You'll be working with the cleaning staff when needed, making up rooms for guests, vacuuming the hallways, etc. You'll work some in the Café Coffee Shop, busing tables, waiting on tables, cleaning, and so forth. I'll probably have you running some errands. Eventually, I may put you on the front desk. You can expect to move around a lot, and you probably won't know what you'll be doing until the need for you comes up. You'll be filling in wherever an extra hand is needed."

"That sounds great."

"You'll put in eight hours a day. We're open around the clock, of course. The hours you work will vary. Some days you'll be on during the day; others you'll be working evenings and nights. You won't be working late-night hours, because things generally aren't as busy then."

"When do I start?"

"I'm going to start you out tomorrow morning at ten. Why don't you meet me back here then?"

"I'll be here," I said.

"Do you have any questions?" Mr. Howard asked.

"I can't think of any right now, but I'm sure I'll have questions later."

"Never hesitate to ask. We have a good group of people working here. We're committed to giving our guests the best service possible. If I'm not around, just ask whoever is near when you have a question. I'm sure they'll be glad to help."

"Oh. I do have one question. Say I'm vacuuming or whatever and a guest asks me to do something for them, like—I don't know—get them extra towels or something. Should I drop what I'm doing to take care of them?"

"Definitely. The guests come first. Making them happy is our number-one priority. Their needs always take precedence. You'll never get in trouble for dropping what you're doing to help a guest."

"I thought so, but I wanted to make sure. I don't want to mess up on my first day."

"Oh, you will. Everyone does. Just do the best job you can do. That's all I ask. That's all anyone can ask."

"I'll definitely do my best."

"I'm sure you will. You come highly recommended. Now, if there's nothing else..."

"Thank you, sir. I'll see you tomorrow morning at ten."

Mr. Howard smiled. I liked him. He was business-like, yet kind. He never quite smiled, but I could tell a smile was just under the surface. I had the feeling I'd enjoy working for him.

Despite my nap, I was tired. I wanted to be fresh for my first day of work, and I'd promised to meet Clarence at eight a.m. for breakfast so I headed back to my room. I intended to make an early night of it. I was lucky Mr. Howard didn't want me until ten a.m. because I hadn't thought to get a phone number for Clarence. I would have hated to have stood him up. I guess I could have asked for the morning off, but that didn't seem a good way to start a new job.

Once in my room, I gazed out the window again. It was snowing hard. I felt so warm and cozy standing there in my room with the elements on the other side of the glass. My room. I liked the sound of that. I felt as though I was starting a completely new life. If only Kurt was there with me, everything would have been perfect.

I undressed, set the alarm for 6:30 a.m., turned off the light, and climbed into bed. I went to sleep with visions of Kurt dancing in my head.

***

The alarm clock rang, pulling me out of a dream of pancakes and maple syrup. I experienced a moment of disorientation, but then I realized I was in the Hotel Indiana. I smiled. I was meeting Clarence for breakfast at eight. I could make my dream of pancakes and maple syrup come true. I climbed out of bed and walked to the window. The blizzard of white continued outside, piling snow on the city streets.

I took a quick shower and made myself as presentable as possible. I needed to buy some clothes suitable for work—and soon. I could manage that now that I had a job. I could even take my meals right in the hotel for free. Most employees didn't have that fringe benefit. I had little doubt that Jack Selby arranged it for me with Mr. Howard. The angels were sure looking out for me when Jack stopped to give me a ride. I was becoming more and more certain our meeting was not an accident.

I bundled up and headed out into the winter wonderland. The snow fell so thickly and fast it was difficult to see. It wasn't overly cold, however, just a little below freezing. I tried to catch snowflakes on my tongue as I walked. I laughed. If my old classmates could see me now, I doubted they would recognize me. I'd played the badass back at B.H.S. No one at school, except for Kurt, knew the real me.

It was a short drive from Sarah's to the Hotel Indiana, but it was quite a hike. I moved along at a brisk pace and made it to Sarah's just before eight. Clarence was waiting on me. He grinned when he spotted me.

"I was afraid you wouldn't show."

"I always keep my word."

"I'm beginning to learn that. Come on, let's go in."

The scent of bacon greeted us as we entered Sarah's. Thanks to the extra large portions of the evening before I hadn't awakened terribly famished, but I began to grow more and more hungry as the wonderful scents of the restaurant assailed me.

"Let me suggest Sarah's Breakfast," Clarence said as we took a seat in a remote booth. "It comes with pancakes, bacon, sausage, ham, biscuits, gravy, and eggs. You eat it, and I guarantee you won't be hungry all day."

"Sounds good. Oh, this might be better," I said, gazing at the menu. "The Pancake Feast—all the pancakes you can eat with bacon or sausage. I was dreaming about pancakes this morning. *This* is what I want."

"Dreaming of pancakes, huh?" Clarence said. "I was dreaming about something else, or rather someone." Clarence grinned shyly at me.

I ordered the Pancake Feast. Clarence ordered a western omelet and French toast.

We continued our discussion of the evening before, but talked more of our lives than purely homosexual matters. Of course, much of our talk was about dealing with our desires and feelings. Poor Clarence had been so alone. I felt sorry for him. He was such a sweet guy, too. In another place and time I could have fallen for him, but my heart belonged to Kurt.

I almost couldn't understand why Clarence was so isolated. Fort Wayne was several times larger than Blackford. There had to be way more of our kind here than back home. Such a large city offered a certain anonymity that wasn't available in Blackford. By all rights, Clarence should have been far more worldly than I. He was rather shy, however. That probably explained it. I still had no idea how he worked up the courage to rub my leg in his car. Perhaps he was so desperate for contact with another guy he'd pushed his fears aside. Intense need could sometimes substitute for courage.

I felt at ease around Clarence. I'd known him only a short time, yet he felt like a friend. I was neither timid nor fearful by nature, but it was still comforting to know at least one person in such a big place.

I told Clarence about my room at the hotel and about my job. He told me about his school and some of the characters there. His high school reminded me a lot of B.H.S. We talked and laughed until our food arrived. We were a good deal quieter while we ate, but we still kept up a conversation. I was already beginning to feel at home in this new place.

"Can you meet me for lunch?" Clarence asked when we'd nearly finished our breakfast.

"I start work at ten. I don't know when I'll get off for lunch, and I'll only have an hour."

"Supper, then, please?"

"Well, I don't know when I get off for the day. If you'll give me your phone number, I can call when I get off work, and we can have supper together. This time I'm buying."

"Oh, I wouldn't want you to do that."

"Hey, I've got a job now. I owe you for the ride you gave me yesterday."

"Getting to talk to you was more than payment enough."

"I disagree. I'll buy, just this once. No arguments."

"Okay. I surrender!"

Clarence wrote out his phone number and gave it to me.

"You will call me, won't you?"

"Of course, I will. I'll call sometime this evening. I'm just not sure when. If I don't call by eight p.m., call the Hotel Indiana and ask for me. I'm in room 712."

We continued talking and eating. Clarence seemed so happy to talk with me that I began to wonder if he had any friends. There was no doubt he had a crush on me, so that likely explained his enthusiasm. I was thankful I'd already told him I was taken.

After breakfast, Clarence and I climbed into his car. The snow had slackened its pace until it merely fell gently from the sky. Still, it was far more pleasant to ride than to walk. I'd had more than enough walking for a while.

It was a good thing Clarence drove me back to the Hotel Indiana. We'd lingered so long over breakfast I would have had to run all the way back otherwise.

"I'll call you when I get off work," I said as I stepped out onto the sidewalk in front of the hotel.

"I'll be waiting."

Clarence drove up Jefferson Boulevard, leaving me alone on the sidewalk. I liked my new home. It was a big city, but Fort Wayne seemed a friendlier place than Blackford. I hadn't expected that.

I had just a few minutes before ten. I hurried up to my room, took off my coat and toboggan, and checked myself in the mirror to make sure I was presentable. I paused for a moment to look around my small room. I smiled. Already I felt at home. I looked at the alarm clock. It was getting close to ten. I made for the door, ready to start my new adventure.

I rode the elevator down to the lobby. It was weird how life worked out. A year ago, I would've never thought I'd someday be living in Fort Wayne, working in its finest hotel.

I knocked on Mr. Howard's door.

"Enter."

I stepped inside Mr. Howard's small office, crowded with ledgers, guest books, and lots of envelopes and papers all neatly organized in cubbyholes near his desk.

"Ah, Angel, and five minutes early. Good. Good."

"I'm always on time," I said. "If I'm ever late, it means I'm in serious trouble somewhere."

"I'll remember that. Today, I'm going to have Mrs. Edwards show you the ropes in housekeeping. There are times when we get more guests than the maids can handle. In such a situation we need every pair of hands we can get.

"Whenever a guest arrives today, you'll be called down to the front desk. Fife is our bellhop/kitchen boy. He'll be showing you how to handle guests and their luggage."

"Fife?"

"Interesting name, isn't it? Scottish, without a doubt. Fife Kirkcaldy. He's an excellent bellhop. He'll teach you everything you need to know. Just watch and learn when you're with Fife."

"Yes, sir."

"Mrs. Edwards is expecting you. You'll find her on the second floor. Just look for her cart."

"Thank you, sir."

I left Mr. Howard's office and went in search of Mrs. Edwards. It took no time at all to find her. Her cart, filled with linens and soaps was sitting in the hallway outside one of the rooms.

"Mrs. Edwards?" I said, walking into the room. "I'm Angel."

"Nice to meet you, Angel. Help me strip this bed, will you? Then I'll show you how we make the beds here in the Hotel Indiana. And call me Greta."

I instantly took a liking to Greta. There was a no-nonsense aura to her, but just under the surface was kindness and a sense of humor, too. Greta was a couple of inches shorter than I was and much heavier. She had white hair that had likely been blonde in her youth. Her eyes were blue. I soon learned that although she didn't smile a great deal, her smiles were well worth seeing. Greta seemed to me like a kindly aunt.

We quickly stripped the bed. Greta pulled clean linens from her cart and showed me how to make hospital corners. It was rather easy after she'd showed me, but I would've have had a nasty time trying to figure it out for myself. It was all a matter of tucking the sheet under the end of the bed properly. Once that was done, the rest was simple.

"There are often a lot of rooms to clean," Greta explained. "You shouldn't spend any more time than necessary in each room, but it must be prepared properly. Soon, it will become second nature to you, but in the beginning you might want to keep a simple checklist in your head—bed, dust, sink, tub, toilet, floor. The bed will always need to be made up with fresh linens. The room won't always need dusting, but always check and dust if necessary. The sink and tub will nearly always need a little work. The toilet won't always need cleaning, but must be checked. Also don't forget to make sure there's plenty of toilet paper. Last, clean the floors with the hand sweeper. I'll have you assist me in a couple of rooms, then we'll see how you do on your own."

Mom handled most of the cleaning at home, but I'd helped some. I watched Greta carefully as I assisted her. The job didn't seem too hard, but required attention to detail.

Soon, Greta assigned me a room to clean on my own. It was harder making a bed alone than it had been with the two of us, but I thought I did rather well. I nearly forgot to check the toilet paper, but remembered at the last moment. I went through the checklist in my head—bed, dust, sink, tub, toilet, floor. I memorized the list by thinking up a short phrase that used the first letters of all the words—"Ben did sink to the floor." Not highly original, but it kept me from forgetting the list.

In a very short time, I was ready for inspection. I called to Greta, and she entered the room.

"Excellent," she said. "You're a bit slow, but that's to be expected on your first day. I think you'll do just fine. I'll be happy to have your assistance whenever things get hectic around here."

I followed Greta back out into the hallway, ready to start on the next room on the list. A boy came hurrying up the hallway, but as he drew close, I realized he wasn't a boy at all, just a rather small young man.

"Angel, a guest is checking in. You're needed at the front desk."

Fife's Scottish brogue was so strong I had a bit of trouble understanding him. Even if I hadn't already known his name, Fife's heritage couldn't have been more obvious. He might as well have been wearing a kilt. I followed him toward the elevator.

What I noticed most about Fife was his small stature. He was shorter than Kurt by some four inches. He was 5'4" at most. I wondered if he even weighed a hundred pounds. I was a full half foot taller than Fife.

I'd only glimpsed his face for a moment, but Fife was cute. He had curly brown hair and brown eyes. His height and face made him look like a boy, but his body made it obvious he was no child. Fife was rather well built. His shoulders were broad for his body. His chest and arms were thick. I was willing to bet he could bench press me.

"I'm Fife," he said, holding out his hand once we were in the elevator.

"I'm Angel," I said, shaking his hand.

"It's nice to make yer acquaintance."

That's as far as we got before the door opened and we stepped into the lobby.

"May I show you to yer room, sir?" Fife said.

He was speaking to a man in his forties who was standing by three suitcases. Fife quickly grabbed up two of them, and I took the other. If the suitcases Fife carried weighed as much as mine, he was indeed strong.

I followed behind the guest as Fife led him to the elevator, trying to remain unobtrusive.

"Two bellhops?" the man asked.

"Angel's going through a wee bit of training today," Fife said.

"Ah, I see."

I didn't know what to say, so I said nothing. I smiled instead.

Fife led the way to the room and ushered our guest inside. I followed, placing the suitcase by the others on the bed. The guest gave Fife a tip, and I was surprised when he gave me one, too.

"Thank you, sir," I said.

"If there's anything you need, just call the front desk," Fife said.

With that we were gone.

"Bein' a bellhop is rather easy. Ya just have to come running when called. It's all about being polite and getting the guest to his room quickly. I can see yer've got the polite part down already."

"I try."

"So yer'll be working here, I'm told," Fife said.

"Yes. I'm to be the jack-of-all-trades. In fact, I'd better be getting back to Greta."

"I'll see ya later then, Angel. Welcome to the Hotel Indiana."

"Thanks!"

There was something really sexy about the way Fife spoke. I loved his accent. I wondered how long he'd been in the States. Hopefully, I'd have the chance to get to know him, but at the moment it was back to work. I didn't mind. I was enjoying my first day on the job in the Hotel Indiana.

Kurt

I kept gazing at Martin Wolfe during lunch. He was sitting alone, as usual.

"What are you looking at?" Tommy asked.

"Martin. He just sits there all alone, day after day. You know, I almost never hear him talk."

"Who?" Tanner asked.

"Martin Wolfe, that boy sitting over there."

"Oh, that guy who works at the Delphi. He does go to school here, doesn't he?"

"Yeah, but it's like he's invisible. Even I usually don't notice him. It's so sad the way he sits there alone."

"Maybe he wants to," Tommy said. "Didn't you ask him to join us once?"

"Yeah. He barely acknowledged my existence."

"Well, there you go," Tommy said.

"He's kind of scary in a way," Bart, one of my J.V. teammates from last year, said. "He doesn't talk to *anyone*. I've had classes with him, and he'll barely answer teachers. I actually thought he was mute for the longest time. It kind of freaked me out when I finally heard him speak."

We were all gazing at Martin. Unfortunately, he looked up just then. He quickly looked back down.

"I think we scared him," I said.

"Yeah, we're a real scary bunch," Tommy said, rolling his eyes.

"Maybe to him we are. I'm going to ask him to sit with us again."

"It's your time to waste," Tommy said.

I left my half-eaten corn dog and orange Jell-O sitting on my tray and walked over to Martin's table. I stood there for several moments, but he didn't look up.

"Hey," I said. "I'm Kurt. I've seen you at the Delphi, and I'm in one of your classes. My friends and I were wondering if you'd like to sit with us."

Martin looked up slowly, but he never quite looked into my eyes.

"No, thanks," he mumbled. It was a replay of the first time I'd asked him.

I started to leave, but instead I turned back.

"Why not? It can't be very fun sitting here by yourself. We'd really like you to join us."

Martin stared at me. He looked simultaneously frightened and furious.

"I said NO!"

I think every head in the cafeteria turned in our direction. The boy who almost never spoke had just yelled at me. I was embarrassed and frightened. Bart was right; Martin Wolfe was kind of scary.

"Um, if you change your mind..."

My voice trailed off, and I quickly returned to my seat. Some kids were still looking at me, but more were looking at Martin. I don't think he knew it. He was just staring down at his plate.

"You'd better leave him alone, Kurt," Tommy said. "I think he's crazy. There's no telling what a guy like that might do."

I frowned. How could I help someone who didn't want to be helped? Why didn't Martin want to sit with us? Why did he push everyone away?

I tried to put Martin Wolfe out of my mind, but fate had other plans. Just after lunch I spotted my old enemies, Doug Finney and John Hearst, harassing Martin in the hallway. They had him backed up against the wall. They weren't hitting him, but they were talking at him. I was too far away to hear what they were saying, but I was sure it wasn't very nice. Martin just stared straight down at the floor, refusing to react at all. John grabbed his chin and forced him to look up. There was murder in Martin's eyes. John gave Martin a shove, called him a queer—I was close enough to hear by then—and walked on. Martin was visibly upset.

"Are you okay?" I asked.

Martin just looked at me. He said nothing, but I could see tears in his eyes.

"I heard what those guys called you. Just ignore them. They're jerks."

Martin shot me a look that seemed to say "mind your own business" and then walked away as if I hadn't spoken to him at all. I could not figure that boy out.

After the Doug and John incident, I experienced an increased number of Martin sightings. Perhaps it was merely because Martin was on my mind, but I began to notice him far more often. The invisible boy had lost his invisibility, at least to me.

Martin began to frequent the more populated parts of the school. I don't know where he usually hung out, but it was no place I'd ever been. I pictured him skulking around back hallways, avoiding his classmates the way a vampire does sunlight. Martin had altered his routine. I wondered if Doug and John had anything to do with that. I spotted them giving Martin a hard time twice more in the next couple of days. I recalled seeing them push Martin around in the past, but those were isolated incidents. They were on his case about something now. Uncomfortable thoughts about my former days as the school homo flooded my mind. Had Doug and John pegged Martin as queer? If so, he was in danger.

There wasn't much I could do to help Martin, so I turned my thoughts to Tommy. He was mooning over Alicia Tulleyfield again. I guess he wasn't mooning over her again. He was *still* mooning over her. He talked about her all the time and sighed whenever she was near. It was enough to make a young homo sick. Finally, I'd had enough. Something had to be done to end Tommy's torment—and mine.

Tommy and I were walking down the hallway just after school when I spotted Alicia. I clamped my hand down on Tommy's wrist and pulled him toward the girl of his dreams. I knew he might never forgive me for what I was about to do, but if I had to hear him sigh one more time, I was going to drown myself in the toilet.

"Kurt! What are you doing? Lemme go!" he hissed, trying not to speak loudly enough for Alicia to hear.

Tommy struggled against me, pulling me off balance, but he couldn't break my hold.

"Either you ask her out, or I'm asking her out for you."

"Kurt! No!"

"I mean it, Tommy!"

We were getting close to Alicia by then, so Tommy had to quit fighting.

"Please," he pleaded through his teeth.

"Do it," I ordered.

I gave Tommy a final shove in Alicia's direction.

"Hi, Tommy."

That was a good sign. Not only had she greeted him, she smiled.

"I, uh, um—will I go out with you?" Tommy stammered.

Ouch. Not so good. Tommy's face turned nearly as red as his hair.

"I mean…will you go out with you?

"Arrgh!" Tommy said, covering his face with his hands.

"What Tommy is so eloquently trying to say is '*Will you go out with me*?'" I said. "He *really* likes you."

Tommy shot me an angry look, but it disappeared in an instant when Alicia spoke.

"I'd love to. How about tomorrow night? *Abbott and Costello Meet Captain Kidd* is playing at the Delphi."

"I, uh, um…great!"

"You're so cute when you're flustered," Alicia said, pinching Tommy's cheek. "Why don't we meet a little before seven in front of the theatre?"

"I, um—"

"He'll be there," I said.

"Great! Bye, Tommy. Bye, Kurt."

"Later, Alicia," I said.

"I am going to kill you," Tommy said slowly and quietly when Alicia had gone on her way.

"Me? What did I do?"

"Oh! You!" Tommy began to sputter.

"Look at it this way, Tommy. You have a date with Alicia, thanks to me."

"I think I'm gonna be sick," Tommy said and rushed for the bathroom.

Love was sure a funny thing.

Tommy wasn't the most confident or outgoing boy around, but he turned into a quivering mass of uncertainty when Alicia was near. I thought he was going to faint when she walked near our table the next day at lunch. Who knows what he would've done if she'd actually spoken to him?

Mere hours before his date, Tommy rushed up to me as I was getting books out of my locker.

"You've got to go with us, Kurt."

"Huh?"

"You've got to go with Alicia and me."

"Tommy, you do not want me tagging along on your date. Haven't you ever heard the phrase 'three's a crowd'?"

"Please! I'm gonna puke on her or something. I just know it."

"Tommy, why are you so worked up? You wanted to go out with her, and you're going. It's just a movie. It's easy; you sit there beside her and watch the screen. People do it all the time."

"It's not easy! How do I know if she wants me to hold her hand? How do I know if it's okay to put my arm around her?"

"You're asking the wrong guy about that."

"Well, what am I going to say to her? What if I say something stupid? What if I do something stupid?"

"Tommy, relax. Just be yourself. The fate of the world does not rest on this date. So what if you say something stupid? You didn't do the best job of asking her out, and she still said yes."

"Only because you were there to handle the situation!"

"Tommy, I was merely the translator. Alicia said you were cute when you were flustered."

"But what if she finds out what a loser I am?"

"I hate to tell you this, Tommy, but I'm sure she already knows."

"Oh, thanks a lot!"

"All I mean is that Alicia sees you every day at school. She has since the first grade. She knows what you're like. She obviously likes you as you are, or she wouldn't have said yes."

"I bet she would go out with you in a flash if you asked her."

"Probably, but I didn't ask her. You did. She said yes. So quit worrying."

"I can't! Please, Kurt, you've got to go out with us. Please!"

I glanced around the hallway.

"Hey! Laverne! You want to go see Abbott and Costello tonight?"

Laverne was the first girl I spotted that I sort of knew. She slowed and walked up to Tommy and me.

"Would you like to go with Tommy, Alicia, and me? Just as friends?"

"Sure. Why not? If it's just as friends. There's no way I'm dating you, Kurt James."

I laughed.

"Meet us in front of the Delphi a little before seven?"

"I'll be there."

"Great."

Tommy stared at me in wonder. He drew close and whispered.

"How do you do that? You don't even like girls, and you can ask one out without even thinking about it."

"I think you answered your own question. What do I care? If Laverne had said 'no,' I'd just ask another girl. Now, are you happy, Tommy? I'm going with you. I have to sit with a girl. You'd better appreciate this."

"Oh, I do, Kurt! I do."

I smiled as Tommy walked away. He was such a mess. Hopefully he'd gain some confidence on his first date. I definitely didn't want to go along every time he had a date with a girl. That would be some kind of homo hell.

Tommy was a nervous wreck after school. He begged me to come home with him and help him pick out clothes to wear on his date.

"This isn't the prom, Tommy. It's just a date."

"Just a date? Just a date? I'm going with Alicia Tullyfield!"

I guessed that was supposed to explain Tommy's weird, frantic behavior.

"Relax. I'll help you pick out something."

I resisted the impulse to tell Tommy's mom he was going on his first date. The mischievous side of me wanted to do it, but as Tommy's best friend I couldn't betray him. Besides, he was worked up enough.

"Here," I said, pulling a yellow and black plaid shirt out of Tommy's closet. "Wear this tonight."

"Are you sure?"

"No. I picked out the ugliest shirt you have so Alicia will hate you. Of course, I'm sure!"

"Okay, what else?"

"Neutral-colored slacks—tan is good. You have loafers, right?"

"Yeah. Is brown okay?"

"Brown is perfect."

"What else?"

"Socks would be a nice touch."

"And?"

"Underwear, but you can pick those out yourself. I don't think Alicia will be seeing them anyway."

Tommy turned completely red.

"That's a good look. Your face matches your hair."

"Shut up."

I laughed.

"Okay, you're set. I'll meet you back here in time to walk to the Delphi. I'll be here by 6:45 at the latest."

"Should I wear cologne?"

"Yes, but just a little. Don't bathe in it."

"Thanks, Kurt."

"You're welcome. I'll see you in a few hours, Tommy."

I left Tommy in his bedroom and quickly exited his house before he could come up with another question. Were all heterosexual boys like that? If so, how had our species survived so long?

I pictured Tommy obsessing over every detail while he prepared for his date. He was probably second-guessing my clothing choices even now. With any luck he wouldn't change his mind and pick out something stupid. Tommy looked really good in that particular shirt and it was hard to go wrong with tan slacks and loafers. I just hoped he took my advice and didn't use too much cologne.

It was Friday. I walked home and got my homework out of the way so I could have the entire weekend free. While Tommy was no doubt bouncing off his bedroom walls, I wrote an essay for Lit, read a chapter for World History, and delved into my math and science homework. I ate supper with Mom, Dad, and Ida. Sam was already out on his own date with his girl, Betty. After supper, I returned to my homework, finished it, and at 6:15 changed for Tommy's date. I was back at Tommy's house by 6:40.

"Do I look okay?" were the first words out of Tommy's mouth.

"You look fine," I said.

"Oh! I forgot to brush my teeth!"

Tommy took off for the bathroom as if he had explosive diarrhea. I had to fight to keep from laughing. I had the feeling Tommy would be more entertaining than the movie.

Tommy was shaking on the way to the Delphi, and it had nothing to do with the cold. Alicia and Laverne hadn't arrived yet when we reached the theatre. Tommy went ahead and bought two tickets. I waited, just in case Tommy's ultimate nightmare occurred and Alicia didn't show.

Alicia arrived in less than five minutes, and Laverne showed up about a minute later. Laverne and I purchased our tickets, and we all went inside. We headed for the concession counter first. Tommy bought Alicia and himself popcorn, Cokes, and M&Ms. My evening was a good deal cheaper, because Laverne and I were going dutch. We weren't on a date, after all. I bought some popcorn and a Coke, and Laverne bought a big Milky Way.

Martin Wolfe waited on us, but he did so without a word. He wouldn't even look at me. He almost acted as if I'd offended him, but what had I done?

Laverne and I got the giggles at the concession stand. I have no idea why. We couldn't stop ourselves. Alicia and Tommy laughed at us for being such freaks. It helped to break the tension. The tension needed breaking. Before our fit of laughter Tommy looked a bit green. I feared he might indeed hurl on Alicia. That would not make for a good first date.

Tommy seemed more at ease as we walked into the auditorium and searched for seats. His expression turned to one of fear, however, when we ended up with the girls sitting between us. I think he had envisioned sitting next to me so I could offer advice. Things were probably better as they were, however. Tommy needed to fly solo. I gave him a smile and a nod and mouthed, "You'll be okay."

I intentionally ignored Tommy after that. Despite his desire for my presence, I figured he would be uncomfortable if I was watching him. I put Tommy and his first date out of my mind and just had fun. Laverne was a great companion, especially because there was no chance she would become romantically interested in me. She'd made that quite clear when I asked her out.

I sneaked a look in Tommy's direction about half way through the movie. He had his arm around Alicia. I was surprised he had the courage, but he'd managed it. His first date was going well. He had his arm around his girl, and he hadn't hurled on her. I just hoped the remainder of his date would go smoothly. I truly hoped things worked out for Tommy. I wanted him to experience with Alicia what I'd experienced with Angel. I also wanted Alicia out of my hair. If she was dating Tommy, she wouldn't be after me.

I experienced momentary sadness when I thought of Angel. Oh, how I wished I could be with him! I remember Ryan's advice, though: the best way to endure the long wait until Angel's return was to live my life and have fun whenever possible. I lost myself in the movie while the minutes ticked away—each one bringing my reunion with Angel a little bit closer.

At the end of the film I had to pee really bad, so I excused myself and ran for the restroom. When I met Laverne, Tommy, and Alicia in the lobby a few minutes later, they were all talking and having a good time.

"Hey, Kurt, Alicia and I are going to get a bite to eat. Want to come with us?"

I looked at Laverne.

"I really need to be getting home," she said.

"I probably should, too. Tommy, why don't you and Alicia go on without us?"

"I'll see you soon, Kurt," Tommy said.

As the pair walked away, I had no doubt Tommy was glad I didn't accept his invitation.

"Why don't I walk you home?" I asked.

"Just don't get any ideas, Kurt James," Laverne said. I could tell by the tone of her voice she was kidding.

"I promise to behave," I said.

"I really had fun tonight," Laverne said as we exited the theatre and walked under the flashing marquee. "Tommy and Alicia are good together."

"Yeah, they are. Tommy has a major crush on Alicia. I'm glad to see things working out."

"I have no plans to tie myself down with a boy, but if they're happy, I'm happy for them."

"Not interested in dating, huh?"

"There will be plenty of time for that," Laverne said. "Right now, I just want to have friends. Of course, if Mr. Right comes along, I might change my mind."

"Will you know him if you see him?"

"Almost certainly."

I walked Laverne home with no romantic incidents and then turned my steps toward my own home. I smiled. I bet Tommy was no longer angry that I'd forced him to ask Alicia out. That boy owed me. I wondered how they were getting along, but I was quite sure I'd hear all about Tommy's date by tomorrow at the latest.

Angel

My first day of work ended at seven p.m. I'd put in eight hours with an hour off for lunch. I felt like collapsing in my bed, but I'd promised to eat supper with Clarence. I gave him a call, and a few minutes later his car pulled up in front of the hotel. I walked out and climbed in.

"So, how was your first day?"

"Great, but I'm so tired."

Clarence didn't ask where I wanted to eat. He just headed back to Sarah's. I didn't mind, but I wondered if that was the only restaurant he knew in Fort Wayne. There had to be dozens of different places to eat. Perhaps Clarence liked Sarah's so well he didn't even think of eating elsewhere. I had to admit the food was delicious there.

I treated myself to a cheeseburger, fries, and a Coke. The cheeseburger was huge, and there were enough fries for a whole family. I ate them all, of course.

"Did the owner used to cook for giants or something?" I asked Clarence as I eyed his massive plate of spaghetti and garlic toast.

"No. Sarah is like one of those mothers who thinks her kids never eat enough. Her customers are her kids. It's impossible to leave this place hungry. Sarah won't allow it."

"It's a wonder all the regulars aren't seriously overweight."

Clarence laughed. He laughed at anything I said that was the least bit funny. I couldn't help but like him.

Clarence stiffened as a couple of young guys entered. I wondered if the boys were classmates of Clarence, but then I remembered I wasn't in a little hick town anymore. Fort Wayne likely had three or four high schools. It turned out my first impression was correct, however. The boys joined us in our booth.

"So this is why you've been ditching us. You have a new friend, huh?" one of the pair, a rather good-looking boy with dark-blond hair and blue eyes, asked.

"I'm Hal," he said, turning to me.

"I'm Angel."

"This is Eugene," Clarence said, pointing to the other boy.

Eugene had straight black hair and brown eyes. He was about the same age as Clarence and Hal, a couple of years older than my sixteen. Eugene wasn't particularly good-looking, but he wasn't unattractive, either.

"So you're our replacement," Eugene said, not overly friendly.

"Hardly," I said. "I'm just visiting."

The visiting remark wasn't entirely true, but then it wasn't a lie, either. My time in Fort Wayne would be temporary. I might stay until it was time to return to Blackford, but who knew?

"Visiting, huh? Who?"

"His aunt," Clarence said quickly. "She lives outside of town."

"So how do you know him?" Eugene asked.

Clarence didn't answer right away.

"We met right here," I said. "Clarence was nice enough to end my solitude."

"Solitude?" Eugene asked. "You talk kind of funny."

"It comes from reading books. You should try it," I said.

I was quickly taking a dislike to Eugene. There was something in his eyes that spoke of cruel mischief. I think there was more to fear from Hal, however. He let Eugene do most of the talking while he sat back and observed. Hal carefully watched Clarence and me, as if looking for weakness or hidden meanings in our hesitations and our words. Hal gave me an appraising look and then raised his eyebrow at Clarence. I wondered what was up. I looked back and forth between Hal and Clarence. Hal was rather good-looking—cute even. I began to suspect that something might have happened between the pair at some point in the past. Had Clarence put the moves on Hal? I gazed at Clarence, and he turned a bit red, as if he could read my thoughts. I made a mental note to ask him about it later.

Thankfully, Hal and Eugene did not permanently invade our space. They soon departed for their own booth. It was impossible to talk without being overheard, so Clarence and I shifted to non-controversial topics. When I mentioned I'd played varsity baseball, he began asking me all sorts of questions about it. Talking about baseball made me homesick for the game, yet I enjoyed our conversation immensely. I was soon lost in a world of freshly mown grass, crisp uniforms, and racing around the bases at top speed. Adam & Company had sucked much of the pleasure out of the game, but I had enjoyed it even with them. I wondered if I'd ever get to play again.

My mound of fries slowly disappeared as I told Clarence about my life as a first baseman. He seemed as caught up in the tale as I was. I could sense Hal and Eugene listening in, but there was nothing dangerous or revealing in my words.

"That must feel incredible," Clarence said after I'd described tagging a runner just before he reached first when the bases were loaded. "I can't even imagine the adrenaline rush and all those people cheering."

"It's amazing how the crowd gets into it sometimes. You would never know it's just a game."

"It's not just a game to you, though, is it?"

"No. It's not. Whether we win or lose isn't that big of a deal to me. I want to win, of course, but there's just something about playing. I can't describe it."

"I bet the girls were all over you," Clarence said. I would have thought it an odd comment had I not known Hal and Eugene were eavesdropping. Clarence was performing for them.

"Yeah, but they are a little afraid of me, too."

"Why?"

"I have a reputation as a badass back at my school."

"You don't seem like a badass to me. I wouldn't want to fight you, but—"

"I'm not, at least not in the sense of being a bully or looking for trouble. I've been in some fights, but the whole varsity team has a reputation."

I began to tell Clarence about Adam & the gang. I left out Matt Taber's murder, of course, but I told Clarence how everyone got out of our path and how Adam wanted to rule the school.

"A lot of rumors get going around, too. There was one about me getting a girl pregnant."

"I hope your parents didn't find out."

"No. They never heard it, but everyone at school was talking about it for a while. It started up over nothing. One of the girls, Rebecca, moved away. Someone started the rumor that she left to have my baby, or get rid of it. It was just crazy. I barely knew her."

"Rumors are like that," Clarence said. He glanced over at Hal and Eugene, making me wonder if he had a particular rumor in mind.

I enjoyed my time with Clarence, even with the eavesdroppers. In my travels, I'd spent most of my time alone. I never stayed in one spot long enough to get to know anyone, with the exception of my days with the Selbys and with Grandmother and Laura. It had left me feeling a bit isolated.

Until I'd departed, I had spent my entire life in Blackford. It was weird finding myself in someone else's hometown. There was a whole world in Fort Wayne I knew practically nothing about. Fort Wayne itself was just one among a multitude of towns, each one its own little world.

"You ready?" Clarence asked when we had both eaten as much as possible.

"Yeah. I'll pop if I try to force down another bite. That cheeseburger was huge!"

"Later, guys," Clarence said. I merely nodded to Hal and Eugene as we walked to the front counter to pay our checks. I grabbed Clarence's check at the last moment so his buddies wouldn't notice. They might think it odd I was paying. I didn't want to cause Clarence any trouble.

I zipped up my leather jacket as we reentered the wintry wonderland outside.

"Hey, you want to come to my house for a while?" Clarence asked when we were once again in his old car.

"I don't know, Clarence. I'm really tired and I have to get up at 6:30 tomorrow morning."

"Please? Just for a while. I just want to show you where I live."

"Okay," I said. "Just for a while."

Before long, Clarence pulled up in front of his home. It was a newer house, with a large, heavy front porch typical of many of the homes currently being built. I spotted a late-model Packard in the garage, so I guessed Clarence's parents did okay.

Clarence led me inside and into the kitchen, where I met his mother. Her eyes lit on my long hair so I made sure I was extra polite. It only took a few moments for me to put her at ease.

Next, I followed Clarence to his room. A set of shelves completely filled with models covered one wall.

"You have some real talent," I said as I examined a model of a 1950 Dodge Coronet.

"Thanks."

"I mean it. I've assembled a couple of models, but they never look quite right. I tend to have pieces left over, too. Yours look perfect."

Clarence turned a bit red, but I could tell he was pleased. I pulled off my leather jacket.

"Angel, I hope this question doesn't make you mad, but are those the only clothes you have?"

No doubt Clarence had noticed that I always wore the same shirt and pants.

"Yeah. I'm going to buy some more soon. I need something dressier now that I have a job in the hotel. I haven't had the time to go shopping yet."

"Hey, let me loan you some clothes. I've got some dressy stuff you can borrow."

"No. That's okay, Clarence."

"Come on. I'm just loaning them to you."

Clarence walked to his closet and began pushing hangers aside. A few moments later, he handed me a white, long-sleeved, button-down shirt and a pair of black slacks.

"These will be perfect for your job in the hotel. Dressy, but comfortable. Take off what you've got, and I'll put your clothes in the wash for you."

I started to protest, but the clothes I was wearing were getting a bit smelly. I began to strip and immediately felt Clarence's eyes on me. Forgetting himself, he just stared at my bare chest.

"Whew, this shirt does need a wash," I said as I placed it on the bed.

I kicked off my shoes, then peeled off my socks and added them to the pile. My jeans came off next, and finally my boxers. Clarence stealthily checked out my stuff. I pretended not to notice.

"I'll put these in the wash," Clarence said, but he made no move towards the door.

Clarence ran his eyes down my naked body and back up again, lingering slightly on the most interesting parts. He reddened slightly as his eyes met mine again. There was a moment of sexual tension there, and I was once again glad Clarence knew I was taken. Otherwise, I think he would have tried something with me.

I ended the moment by turning and pulling on the boxers Clarence had set out for me. I was quite sure Clarence was checking out my butt, but where was the harm in that?

"You're beautiful," he said as I turned around again. Clarence gazed at my naked torso.

"Um, thanks," I said and grinned.

I pulled on the slacks, the socks, and last of all, the shirt. Everything was a bit big for me, but fit well enough.

Clarence departed to put my clothes in the washer, but he soon returned. He took a seat in his desk chair, and I sat on the edge of his bed.

"So, Hal and Eugene are two of your friends?" I asked.

"Not exactly friends. Hal and I used to be closer. I just know Eugene through Hal."

"Why aren't you close with Hal now?" I asked. I strongly suspected something was up between those two. Clarence's reddening face told me I was right.

"Well, a couple of years ago I kind of—well, you remember what I did in the car. I did that with Hal, too, only here, sitting on my bed."

"What did he do?"

"He shoved my hand away. I passed it off as a joke, but I don't think he believed me. He never says anything about it, but he sometimes hints that he knows something about me—something dark and sinister. Things changed after I ran my hand up his leg."

"I thought as much," I said. "I think Hal is suspicious of us. I don't know if you noticed, but he was watching us when he was sitting in our booth. You don't think he'll make trouble for you, do you?"

"I don't know. Maybe, but…he doesn't really know anything."

"I think we should be very careful about what we talk about when he's around. I don't want to cause you any trouble."

"It'll be okay." I could tell Clarence wasn't entirely convinced about that. There was an edge of fear in his voice.

Once again, I felt sorry for Clarence. Being different wasn't easy. I did okay, but then Clarence wasn't me. I could hear the isolation in his voice, the loneliness, and the desperation.

Clarence turned on his radio, and Doris Day began to sing *A Guy is a Guy*. The title of the song seemed particularly appropriate. Clarence and I lay back on his bed and just listened as Rosemary Clooney sang *Blues in the Night*, and then Nat King Cole sang *Unforgettable*. I couldn't remember the last time I'd listened to music.

"I wish I was different," Clarence said just after Patti Page finished singing *I Went to Your Wedding*.

"How do you mean?"

"You know…I wish I liked girls and not guys."

"I don't."

"You don't? You mean you wouldn't change if you could?"

"No. This is the way I'm supposed to be."

"How can you be so sure?"

"I can feel it in my heart."

"But everybody says—"

"Who cares what everybody says? People say all kinds of things. Most people don't even think about what they're saying. No one can understand what it's like unless they're homosexual, too."

"I never thought of it like that. So you really wouldn't change so you could get married someday and have kids?"

"Hell, no. I have Kurt. Someday, we're going to be together. Maybe we'll even adopt kids."

"You talk about him like he's going to be your wife."

"No. He's going to be my husband."

Clarence was quiet a while. We just lay there and listened to the radio. I knew I should get up and ask Clarence to take me back to the hotel, but I was so comfy and warm I allowed myself to lie there for just a few more minutes.

I awakened some time during the night. I'd fallen asleep. Clarence's arm was wrapped around me. I raised myself up on my elbows, wondering what time it was. My movements awakened Clarence.

"Angel?"

"Yeah?"

"You awake?"

"I wouldn't have answered you if I was asleep."

"Oh, yeah."

"I guess I fell asleep."

"Me, too."

"Angel?"

"Yeah?"

"I really like you."

"I really like you, too, Clarence."

"Do you think we could…I mean…you know…"

"What?" I asked, although I feared I knew the answer.

Clarence raised himself up on one elbow. I felt his fingers on my chest. He began to edge his hand downward, but I pushed his hand away.

"We can't," I said. "I have a boyfriend."

"Could I just…give you a blowjob? You don't have to do anything in return."

"No, Clarence. I won't cheat on Kurt."

"But, if I just—"

"No. Listen, I should leave."

"You think I'm nasty now, don't you?" Clarence said with a sob in his voice.

"No. I don't think that, Clarence. I think you're curious. I think you're a normal teenaged guy. What you've got to understand is that Kurt and I are committed to each other. He may be far, far away, but he's still my boyfriend. I can't be with another guy like that. If I was single it would be different."

"Would you do it with me if you were single?"

"Yes, but I'm not."

"I'm sorry. I shouldn't have come onto you. I knew better after what happened in the car. It's just—"

"It's okay, Clarence, but I think I should leave."

"No, please don't. It's late. I'll drive you back in the morning. I'll set the alarm for six. Just sleep with me this one night, okay? I just want to feel you beside me. I promise I'll keep my hands to myself, and I won't ask you for sex again."

"Then I'll stay," I said.

"Angel? Would you…would it be okay if you held me? If not, I understand, but I just want someone to hold me."

In answer, I moved closer to Clarence and wrapped my arms around him. He lay with his back against my chest. I could hear him softly crying.

"It will be okay, Clarence. You'll find someone to love you. I know you will."

We drifted off to sleep.

The alarm rang. I awakened with Clarence's arms wrapped around me. I jerked away from him, remembering where I was and what had happened, or rather what had not happened, the night before. I relaxed.

"Hey," Clarence said, smiling and rubbing his eyes.

"Hey."

"I guess we'd better get up."

"Definitely. I need to get back to the hotel so I can get ready for work."

"Do you want to have breakfast first?"

"I probably shouldn't."

"Come on. Mom won't mind."

"What will she say about me spending the night?"

"We'll just tell her the truth—that we fell asleep."

"I guess I can stay for breakfast."

"Great!"

We got up. Both of us were fully dressed. The shirt Clarence had loaned me was a bit wrinkled, but I could hang it in the bathroom while I took a shower, and that would get most of the wrinkles out.

"I just thought of something, Angel. What are you going to do about school? Do you think you'll ever finish?"

"Some day, I guess."

"Dad says you can't get anywhere without graduating from high school."

Graduation had preyed upon my mind as I traveled. I'd promised to meet Kurt at his graduation, but what about my own? By the time I returned to Blackford, I'd be three years behind. Could I finish high school wherever Kurt and I ended up? I'd be twenty-one when I graduated! I'd be an old man!

"I'll run and get your stuff out of the dryer," Clarence said.

Clarence returned soon with my old, familiar clothing. I climbed out of bed and changed back into my own clothes. Clarence stole looks at my body, but I pretended not to notice. We'd slept beside each other all night and nothing had happened, so no harm could come of Clarence merely checking me out.

"Angel?"

"Yeah?"

"Thanks for last night. I…I get so lonely sometimes. I know you have a boyfriend and all, but…when you held me, I just felt so safe. I felt like somebody cared about me."

"A lot of people care about you, Clarence. I'm sure your mom cares about you and your dad."

"I know, but…I'm talking about a different kind of caring. My parents are supposed to love me. I'm talking about someone caring about me because they like me for me."

"I care about you, Clarence."

Clarence got a little teary-eyed. I pulled him to me and hugged him.

"Thank you for last night, too, Clarence. I miss Kurt an awful lot. It's been months since he's held me. I think I needed to be held last night, too."

"You love him a lot, don't you?"

"More than I can express."

Clarence sighed. "I kind of hate to hear that. I really wouldn't mind if you just stayed in Fort Wayne forever. I know we could be good friends and…more than friends. Don't take that the wrong way, though. I know you love Kurt. It's just that if you didn't…then there could be something between us."

"I'm sorry."

"Don't be. It's okay. You've given me hope, Angel. If there's one guy like you wandering around, then maybe there's more."

"You'll find someone, Clarence. I know you will. Even though I can't be your boyfriend, I do consider you my friend. We'll always have that."

"I guess that's pretty special," Clarence said.

"Yeah. It is."

"Come on. Let's go. Mom was working on breakfast when I went down for your clothes. I explained why you spent the night. Everything is fine. Breakfast will be ready soon."

We made for the door.

"Hey, I just got an idea," Clarence said. "Why don't I ask Mom if you can join us for Sunday dinner? It will just be Mom, Dad, my grandmothers, my Uncle Frank, and me."

"Um, I don't know."

"Please," Clarence said.

"It's no fair using those puppy-dog eyes of yours against me."

"I'll take that as a yes."

"Okay, but ask your Mom when I'm not here. I don't want her to feel pressured into saying yes."

"Oh, I'm sure she'll be okay with it, but I'll ask her later."

"Cool."

I followed Clarence into the kitchen. The scent of hot biscuits and something sweet wafted toward us before we even made it through the living room. Sausage links sizzled and popped in a frying pan as we walked into the kitchen. The table was already set with Blue Willow china, like Mom used at home. I fought down the wave of homesickness that threatened to engulf me and concentrated instead on the wonderful sights and sounds of the Mason family kitchen. My newly aroused hunger made that task a good deal easier.

Clarence's dad had already left for work, so it was just Clarence, his mom, and me for breakfast. We sat down to scrambled eggs, sausage links, just-baked biscuits, and homemade cinnamon rolls. The cinnamon rolls were the 'something sweet' I'd smelled from the living room. There was orange juice and hot tea, and everything was delicious.

I grinned as I watched Clarence and his mom talk. I joined in the conversation, too, but I was remembering my own mom as we sat there. Mrs. Mason was admonishing Clarence about his grades and his drawn out "Mommmm" made me remember all the times my mom had embarrassed me in front of someone. The thing was, I missed it.

Clarence looked at me and rolled his eyes. I grinned. Clarence didn't know how good he had it. I was sure he was lonely and needed someone special to love him, but he had his family, his friends, and his home. I'd come to value those things more and more since I'd left Blackford behind.

After a most delicious breakfast, Clarence and I bundled up and headed out to his car.

"Angel," Clarence said as we climbed in his car, "Will you tell me why you ran away? What happened? Did your parents find out about you? I know it's none of my business, and if you would rather not tell me, I understand, but I'm curious."

"Well, a whole lot of stuff happened. You know how I told you about Adam and the other guys on my team? Well, I didn't tell you the worst, not even close."

I began to tell Clarence about the murder of Matt Taber, not knowing if he would believe me or not. If he didn't trust my words, he gave no sign. I told him about meeting Kurt. I told him about the rumors that started up about Kurt and how I'd rescued Kurt from Adam and the gang. I told Clarence about the letters I'd left behind and about skipping town. I only gave him the condensed version, but I hit the highlights.

"Wow," he said when I'd finished. I guess I should say he said "wow" yet again, for he'd said it several times during the course of my tale. "That's incredible. You must truly love him to do that for him."

"I do love him. I miss him so much it hurts."

"I'm sorry you can't be with him, Angel."

"Me, too."

Talking about Kurt felt good, yet it dredged up so many painful memories. It multiplied my longing for Kurt and my homesickness tenfold. How was I ever going to make it through all the long years of waiting until I could return to Kurt?

I didn't realize we'd arrived at the Hotel Indiana until Clarence stopped the car. I looked out the window, and there it was: my new home.

"Thanks for letting me borrow the clothes."

"No problem."

"See you later, Clarence."

"Bye."

Clarence drove away. I walked into the hotel, moving quickly toward my room. It was time to get ready for my day.

In my room, I looked into the mirror and checked myself out in the clothing Clarence had loaned me. I looked much better than I had the day before. I planned to go shopping for some clothes as soon as possible. I was sure Clarence would help me find a resale shop somewhere. Even though I had a job now, I didn't see any reason to waste money on new clothes.

I spent most of my morning running errands for Mr. Howard. It was simple stuff mostly: running to the post office, delivering memos to staff, and so on. Mr. Howard even trusted me to go to the bank for change. I was carrying a hundred dollars with me!

An influx of guests in the late afternoon had me working with Fife. I tagged along a couple of times, but there wasn't a whole lot to learn. Soon, I was flying solo. My first experience as a bellhop came when two guests arrived simultaneously. Since I was around, no one had to wait. I carried bags for a nice old lady. She must've had bricks in those suitcases! I don't know how she managed to lift even one of them herself. She gave me fifty cents for a tip. I was pleased.

Fife and I didn't just stand around waiting when there we no guests checking in. We dusted the lobby with feather dusters, swept the floor with push sweepers, and just generally made ourselves useful. I was sent out on more errands as well.

The errands helped me learn my way around downtown Fort Wayne. The area right around the hotel was becoming especially familiar. I was even getting used to the tall buildings. At first I felt a little hemmed in, but that sensation quickly passed. Who knew? Maybe Kurt and I would even live in a big city someday. There was sure a lot more to see and do in Fort Wayne than there was in Blackford.

I had my lunch at one p.m. in the hotel's Café Coffee Shop. I'd been eating out with Clarence, but I intended to take as much advantage of the free hotel meals as possible. For lunch, I had a cheeseburger, fries, a Coke, and a slice of pecan pie. For a boy who had recently been on his own surviving on stale rolls, such a meal was a feast. It wasn't as good as the meals I'd eaten on the Selby farm or in Grandmother's cabin, but nothing could compare to that.

I had called Jack and Emma, as well as written them, to let them know I'd arrived safely. I also thanked Jack so profusely for getting me a job at the hotel that he'd told me to thank him by not thanking him anymore. I liked Jack's sense of humor.

I had Grandmother's address and I planned to write her and Laura soon. I was sure they'd like to know I'd arrived safely. Grandmother didn't have a phone in her cabin, but it wouldn't take a letter long to reach her. I missed Grandmother and Laura and Jack and Emma, too. Most of all I missed Kurt.

After lunch, I got right back to work. I was sent into the kitchen to wash dishes. I also learned how to prepare salads. I did some busboy work as well. It wasn't as fun as eating in the café, but it wasn't a bad afternoon. One thing was sure true about my job: it was never boring.

After work, I retired to my room and took a bath. I had already told Clarence I wanted to spend the evening and night in my room. I'm sure he would have called otherwise. I seriously needed some rest. I wasn't accustomed to putting in an eight-hour day. The hot bath eased my tired muscles. It felt especially good to get off my feet. I just lay there in the hot water, relaxing.

After my bath, I sat down at the small desk and wrote Grandmother and Laura a letter. I enclosed a postcard that showed the outside of the hotel. I smiled when I pictured how excited Laura would be when she heard from me. She was the sweetest little girl I'd ever met.

***

By noon on Sunday, I was ready for a break. I enjoyed my job at the hotel, but I looked forward to dinner at Clarence's house. I'd been hanging out with Clarence now and then, although our schedules made our time together a bit rare. I worked most often on evenings and weekends, although I was needed some mornings when there had been an especially large number of guests the night before. Clarence was busy with school on weekdays. My leisure hours often occurred while he was in classes.

I worked Sunday morning, but I had the whole afternoon and evening off. Dinner at the Mason home was scheduled for two p.m., so I had a chance to clean up and rest beforehand. Clarence offered to pick me up, but I opted to walk instead. It was quite a little hike, but I wanted to get out and enjoy the fresh, if rather cold, air.

Eugene and Hal spotted me as I walked up Calhoun Street. It seemed such a coincidence to cross their path in such a large city that I wondered if it was a coincidence at all. The pair eyed me suspiciously, but neither spoke to me or stopped as we passed each other. I didn't like the way Hal looked at me. He had a sinister edge to him that reminded me of Jesse Offield. Jesse was definitely not my favorite person.

Eugene and Hal were reminders that I had to be careful not to arouse suspicions. I might place Clarence in jeopardy if I wasn't careful. I wondered if I'd made a mistake in accepting Clarence's dinner invitation. I'd been to his home a couple of times now. Did his parents wonder about my sudden appearance?

I might place myself in danger, too. There would be trouble if anyone found out I was a runaway. I was sixteen now, but that didn't legally make me an adult. The trouble could affect those who had helped me. Mr. Howard would definitely be at risk. He'd be in hot water for hiring me if the truth came out. I was smart enough to lie about my age on the all the papers I filled out at the hotel. I claimed to have turned eighteen on January 2nd. That might be enough to cover Mr. Howard. He could always claim he thought I was eighteen. I'd back him up, too. I falsified my age to protect him and the hotel. I was hired as a favor to Jack, but I considered it a favor to myself, also.

I thought about Hal as I walked along. He might be trouble. I feared he was snooping around for evidence that Clarence was a homo. Clarence definitely needed to get new friends.

I arrived at Clarence's home right at two p.m. Clarence himself opened the door and grinned when he spotted me. I had enjoyed my walk, but it was rather pleasant to step in out of the cold. The scent of turkey and dressing wafted through the house. I was suddenly twice as hungry as I had been before.

Clarence introduced me to his grandmothers. They were pleasant old ladies and were quite, well, grandmotherly. Clarence's dad was friendly, and, of course, his mom was, too. I didn't see much of his mother, however, because she was quite busy in the kitchen. Clarence's Uncle Frank arrived about twenty minutes after I did. He was a bit loud, but funny. He teased me about my hair, but he did so in a good-natured way. I liked him.

Sunday dinner was in the dining room, and I sat right next to Clarence. He squeezed my hand under the table as his father said grace, and I thought how, in another time and place, Clarence could have been my boyfriend. I truly hoped he found someone. If he didn't, someone was missing out on a wonderful guy.

The turkey, sage stuffing, and cranberry sauce were delicious! So were the mashed potatoes, the sweet potatoes, corn, green beans, freshly baked rolls, and the pumpkin pie. It was just like Thanksgiving. I gorged myself, but didn't feel guilty, because everyone else did, too.

Clarence had a truly wonderful family. They talked, laughed, and made me feel right at home. They were so kind and thoughtful to each other and me that I found myself missing my own family. A momentary surge of sadness engulfed me, and I took a big sip of iced tea while I attempted to hide the miserable expression on my face. I brought myself under control quickly, but not before Clarence's mom caught a glimpse. She said nothing, but she had seen.

After dinner we were all sleepy. Clarence and I went to his room and took a nap on his bed. The rest of the day was given up to visiting with his family, playing cards, eating, and having fun.

I was truly lucky. I could well have been cold, hungry, and alone. Instead, I was warm, stuffed, and surrounded by laughter and not-so-quiet conversation. I had a job and a warm place to sleep. All things considered, my life was good.

Kurt

The phone rang.

"Hi, Tommy."

"How did you know it was me?"

"Please!" I said. "You would explode if you couldn't talk to me about Alicia. So, start talking."

"Oh, my gosh, Kurt! Did you see how she let me put my arm around her? I didn't think I'd have the nerve to try, but I did and she let me!"

I was going to tell Tommy I had indeed noticed, but there was no opportunity. He barely paused to take a breath. The boy was excited.

"We ate at the Black Heifer. Well, you know that, but we sat in our own little booth and talked for the longest time. She really likes me, Kurt! She said so!"

"I guess there's no accounting for taste."

"Shut up!" Tommy laughed. "She said she thought I was a really nice guy, but not as in I'm-a-really-nice-guy-but-she-only-wants-to-be-friends. She dropped a hint about the next school dance. I asked her to go with me, and she said yes! Yes! Yes! Yes!"

I could hear Tommy's mother in the background telling him to calm down. I hoped he would. I didn't know if my ear could stand up to the verbal assault.

"Do you know she even likes baseball? I think that's why she had a crush on you. You wouldn't believe how much she knows about it.

She even has a baseball-card collection! Isn't that incredible? A girl who collects baseball cards? I told her I was thinking of going out for varsity this spring, and she said I should go for it. As soon as it warms up, I've got to start practicing. Alicia said she'll come to all my games!"

"Hmm, it doesn't sound like you're mad at me for pushing you into going out with Alicia."

"I was, but not now. Thank you, Kurt. Thank you! Thank you! Thank you! I'm your slave!"

Tommy's enthusiasm made me laugh, but I was happy for him. We talked for another forty-five minutes. Well, Tommy talked. I mostly listened. I didn't mind, though. I was very pleased that my best friend was so happy. I knew what it was like to find someone. I would no longer have to worry about Alicia pursuing me. That was a HUGE bonus.

During lunch on Monday, our table was forced to hear about Tommy's happiness. We were a captive audience—at least until we finished our meat loaf, corn, and mashed potatoes. Tommy went on and on about Alicia.

"Have you had to listen to this all weekend?" Tanner asked me when there was a rare pause in Tommy's verbal barrage.

"Oh, yeah!" I said. "He's so disgustingly happy I think I'm going to be sick."

Tommy just looked at me and laughed.

"Oh, Alicia, I love you so much!" Tyler said, trying to imitate Tommy's voice. Tyler held his hands to his heart. He sounded completely sappy. "I'll do anything for you. Let me kiss the ground you walk upon."

"You guys are just jealous," Tommy said, grinning.

"How long do you think he'll be like this?" Derek, who was sitting near, asked.

"Who knows? This could go on for weeks," I said.

"We'll never survive it," Tanner said.

"Maybe Tommy will get mono and have to stay home for days and days. It is the kissing disease you know," Tyler said.

Nothing we said fazed Tommy. His abundant happiness made him invulnerable to all attacks.

"I think we're just going to have to ride it out, guys," I said.

"Well, this is your fault," Tyler said. I'd told everyone how I had forced Tommy to ask Alicia out. I'd left out the way he tripped over his own words.

"Hey, how was I supposed to know she would actually *like* him?" I asked as if the concept were foreign to me.

"True," Tanner said. "I can't picture any girl actually liking Tommy. I guess you aren't to blame. Maybe Alicia is actually an alien or something. I bet she's not human."

"That would explain a lot," Tyler said.

"Oh, did I tell you guys we held hands all the way home after supper?" Tommy asked. My best friend was either oblivious to our comments or just didn't care. The boy had it bad.

***

"Kurt, would you mind if we didn't walk home together?" Tommy asked just after school.

"Who am I to stand in the way of true love? Of course I don't mind."

I didn't have to be told that Tommy wanted to walk Alicia home. I didn't dare mention her name for fear Tommy would start talking about her.

"Thanks, Kurt!"

"No problem."

Tommy disappeared. Since I was on my own, I thought I might stop in Whitney's Antiques. It had been a few days since I'd looked things over. I didn't want Mrs. Whitney to think I'd abandoned her.

I walked to my locker and dumped as many books as possible. Textbooks were heavy! I lightened my load and set off for the exit.

The hallways were all but empty by then. Once the bell rang, everyone rushed from the school as if it was on fire. I spotted a lone figure up ahead and slowed. It was Martin Wolfe. He was crying.

I slowed and then stopped before him.

"Martin?"

He completely ignored me. He just stared down at his feet. I thought I caught a glimpse of a black eye before he looked down. It was a stupid move, but I reached out grasped Martin's chin, and made him look at me.

"Don't touch me!"

Martin slapped my hand away. I thought he was going to strike me. He had a black eye. Both his eyes were red from crying.

"Martin, who did this to you? Was it Doug and John? It was, wasn't it?"

"It's none of your business! Leave me alone! How many times do I have to tell you to leave me alone!"

Martin shouted in my face, but this time there was no one else to hear.

"I just want to help."

"Don't you dare act like you care! Don't you dare! No one cares about me! No one!"

Martin pushed past me before I could say anything. I was still reeling from his anger. I'd never met anyone like Martin. What was wrong with him?

I changed my plans and headed for Ryan's house instead of Whitney's Antiques. Browsing would have to wait for another day.

I thought about Martin as I walked, but I could make no sense of him. If I were all alone I'd sure be happy if someone reached out to me. Every time I tried, however, Martin bit my head off.

I knocked on Ryan's door. As always, he smiled when he saw me.

"Are you busy?" I asked.

"I'm just looking through gardening catalogs. I get a little antsy for spring at this time of year."

"Good. I want to talk to you about something, or rather, someone."

"Well, come on in. Hot chocolate?"

"Yes, please."

It occurred to me that I never entered Ryan's house in the winter months without being offered hot chocolate or hot tea. It was yet another reason why I so enjoyed my time with Ryan.

As Ryan prepared hot chocolate, I told him about Martin Wolfe. I'd described all my encounters with him and the incidents involving Doug and John by the time Ryan and I sat down near the fire with our mugs.

"I just don't get him," I said. "He's all alone. He doesn't talk to anyone. I thought he would be glad when I asked him to hang out with us at lunch, but he barely acknowledged me. Then, when I tried harder, he just got mad."

Ryan sat there in silence for several moments before speaking.

"Martin has chosen to be a loner for a reason," Ryan said at last. "I think most people in his situation would be glad to have someone reach out to them. They would appreciate an offer such as yours. Something is different about Martin, though. I've never met him, but his behavior tells me he probably has some trust issues. It may be that someone has hurt him in the past. Perhaps it was even someone who offered to be his friend, only to turn on him. It could be a general distrust of others. You say John and Doug have been picking on him?"

"Yeah, the way they picked on me when they thought I was queer."

"And everyone else more or less ignores him?"

"It's not so much that they ignore him, it's that he's hard to notice. He kind of blends into the background. He never draws attention to himself. He almost never talks. One of my friends actually thought he was mute for a long time. He really thought Martin couldn't talk. It's no joke. He's *that* quiet. If Martin was a color, he'd be beige."

"Hmm. It sounds like he's almost completely drawn into himself. I've read about individuals who are completely inner-directed. Those individuals are institutionalized because they can't take care of themselves. They live completely within their own mind. Martin obviously isn't that far gone, but what you describe does seem similar.

"I'm not a professional, but I would guess that Martin has been so tormented for such a long time that he's drawn into himself. The outside world is unpleasant, so he lives in his own little world as much as possible and resists any effort to draw him out. Do you remember what Martin was like when he was younger?"

"Not really. All I remember is the other kids making fun of him. He always wore old clothes—hand-me-downs. I can't remember him joining in when the rest of us were doing things together."

"That's interesting that that's all you remember of him. My guess is that Martin decided to avoid the pain of being left out by excluding himself."

"I feel even worse now. I was never mean to Martin, but I should have tried to be his friend years ago."

"Don't feel so bad, Kurt. You didn't realize what was happening. When you took note of his isolation, you tried to help him."

"But he won't let me help him. The more I try, the angrier he gets. He kind of scares me now."

"You've made the effort and have been rebuffed. Reaching out to him obviously isn't working. I think your best course of action now is to leave Martin alone."

"Isn't there anything I can do?"

"Be nice to him, and make sure your friends are kind to him as well. Smile at him. Say "hi" to him when you pass him in the halls. Respect his wish to be left alone, but leave the doorway to friendship open. Martin has to choose to walk through that doorway. You can't force him."

"I wish I could do more than that."

"I know, Kurt. I wish you could, too, but I think what Martin needs is beyond you. Just be kind to him. I think simple kindness has been too long missing from his life."

"That's so sad."

"The world can be a hard, cruel place, Kurt. The best you can do is to help others as much as you can and get as much enjoyment out of life as possible."

Our conversation turned to other matters. I told Ryan how disgustingly happy Tommy was about dating Alicia. We talked about Ryan's plans for his garden, which involved me, of course. Ryan called me his chief and head gardener, which was a rather grand title considering I was the only one who worked for him. I liked it, though.

Ryan had a way of making just about everything seem special. He paid attention to little details no one else noticed. He could sit and look at a plant for the longest time, just enjoying its beauty. Ryan wove his own happiness. I tried to do the same, but I was just learning.

I walked back home in the cold thinking about Martin. Ryan was right. I'd tried and failed to help Martin Wolfe. I'd done all I could do, except for giving him the respect and kindness that everyone deserved. I was going to talk to the guys and get them to be nice to Martin. None of my friends was cruel to him, but like most everyone else, they took no notice of him. He was invisible. Perhaps, if we were nice to him long enough, Martin would join us at our table. Maybe someday we would even become friends.

***

I tried to smile at Martin when our paths crossed, but he never once looked at me. I said "hi," but received no reaction from him at all. It was as if he didn't even hear. Tommy, Tyler, Tanner, and Derek reported the same. I often thought of Martin as the invisible boy, but perhaps we were invisible to him—mere ghosts on the edge of his world.

I never got the chance to become Martin Wolfe's friend. A few days after I talked to Ryan about him, Martin was dead.

I walked into school early on Wednesday morning. I came in earlier than usual because I'd decided I was going to try out for the varsity baseball team. I wanted to track down Coach Marley, my J.V. coach, and sound him out about my prospects. I didn't make it to

Coach's office, though. I turned the corner in the hallway leading to the gym to make a grisly discovery: Martin Wolfe hanging from the neck by a rope. There he was, hanging there right in the middle of a deserted hallway.

I just stood there for a few moments in complete and utter shock. I stared at Martin's lifeless form. His face was bluish. His neck twisted at an unnatural angle where he hung from the noose. A desk and a chair sat under him. The chair was overturned and lying some distance away. I couldn't believe it. Martin Wolfe had hanged himself.

Voices and the sound of shoes scuffing the wooden floor brought me back to my senses. I turned the way I'd come and sprinted around the corner. I spotted Edgar from my baseball team the year before.

"Edgar! Go get a teacher. Tell them to come here right now!"

"What?"

"Just do it! Please! Then get Principal Kinsley. Hurry!"

Edgar could hear the fear and desperation in my voice and did as told.

"Tyler! Tanner!" I cried out when I spotted one of the Nudo twins.

"It's Tanner," said the twin as he walked toward me. He smiled until he saw my face.

"Kurt, what's wrong?"

"Something horrible has happened." Tears welled up in my eyes. "You've got to help me keep everyone out of the back hallway."

"Why?"

"Martin Wolfe hanged himself."

"*What?*" Tanner asked.

Of course, he rushed for a look and came back moments later looking green and nauseated.

"We've got to keep everyone away," I said.

Tanner nodded. As our classmates began to filter into the school, more and more came our way. We told them the back hallway was off limits. Some thought it was a joke. Others could see the grim expression on our faces. Thankfully, Mr. Brooks, my World History teacher, soon arrived on the scene.

"Kurt, what is all the commotion?"

I couldn't speak. I was choked up. I led Mr. Brooks around the corner. He stood stock still for a moment. He turned and hurried back around the corner.

"Everyone stay back! No one goes past the last set of lockers!" he ordered.

The small group that had gathered backed off.

"You two, make sure they stay back," he said to Tanner and me.

I was happy to put a little more distance between Martin's corpse and myself. I couldn't see him where I stood, but I knew his dead body was hanging just around the corner. I was shaking with fear. Tanner looked frightened and ill.

"What's going on?" Iggy, another of my old teammates, asked.

"Martin Wolfe hanged himself," Tanner said before I could stop him. I guessed there was no need anyway. There was no way something like this would remain a secret.

A flurry of discussion and comments broke out.

"Hanged himself?"

"Someone killed himself?"

"Who is Martin Wolfe?"

Principal Kinsley arrived on the scene. I just pointed him in the direction of Mr. Brooks, who was standing guard at the corner. Mrs. Ryan showed up a few moments later. Right after that, the principal went marching back the way he had come, ordering everyone even further back. He disappeared into the growing crowd.

The next hour was an anxious one. The police arrived first; then ambulance drivers came after. Martin was long past saving, but I guess they had to come anyway. The police roped off the back hallway. Everyone was sent to class, except for me, because I'd discovered the body.

I stood off to one side, just around the corner from Martin's corpse. I knew he was dead. There was no doubt about it. No living boy was that color. I tried not to think about what I'd seen, but when I closed my eyes I could see Martin as clear as day—bluish with bulging eyes, his neck broken. I tried not to close my eyes. I tried to think of other things. I fought to get the image of Martin Wolfe out of my mind, but I knew it would haunt me to the end of my days. I wished Angel was there to hold me.

Mrs. Ryan tried to comfort me. She knew I was upset. Soon, the police were asking me questions. I told them how I'd discovered the body. They wanted to know what time I'd found him and if anyone else was around. I answered their questions as best I could.

I saw them wheel Martin's body away, covered with a sheet. I was glad I didn't have to look at him again. I didn't know if I could stand it.

When second period rolled around, Mrs. Ryan walked me to class. I could tell she was shaken up, too. Everyone stared at me when we walked in. Word had spread. Everyone knew I had discovered Martin's body. They all knew I'd seen him hanging there—dead. I didn't look forward to their questions.

I barely listened to Mrs. Ryan during class, which was quite unusual for me. She didn't call on me and said nothing about my lack of attention. She understood.

Martin was dead. I'd seen him only the day before. I'd smiled at him and greeted him in my effort to draw him out. He'd ignored me. I felt as if I'd failed him. All my efforts hadn't made one bit of difference in the end.

I wondered what pushed Martin over the edge. What caused him to decide to take his own life? Was it the slow buildup of years of pain? Had harassment from guys like Doug and John caused Martin to decide death was a better option? What if I was somehow responsible? What if he killed himself so I'd quit bothering him? I told myself that was just stupid. Why would anyone hang himself because someone smiled at him and greeted him in the hallways?

The much-dreaded questions of my classmates came at the end of second period and continued throughout the day. I couldn't go anywhere without being asked to recount my discovery of the body. I was the center of attention. I hated it.

I spotted Doug Finney and John Hearst laughing in the hallway between classes. I felt like they were laughing at Martin. My brow furrowed in anger, but I didn't really know what they were laughing about. It could've been most anything. Still, I hated them for the way they'd treated Martin. He might have killed himself because of them. They didn't even have the decency to feel bad about it.

I was never so glad for a school day to end. Tommy and Tanner took me to the Black Heifer for an early supper right after school. Tyler was noticeably absent, just as he had been at lunch. I knew he was in school. I'd seen him mid-morning, looking upset and haunted. I'd suspected there was something between Tyler and Martin. Now, that suspicion grew stronger.

No one said a word about Martin Wolfe as we made our way to the Black Heifer. My friends knew how I'd been hassled all day to describe how I found his body. I thought the questions would never end.

The guys made an effort to raise my spirits by joking around. No one was really in a comic mood, though, and soon we settled into just talking. It felt good to be surrounded by my friends just then. Tommy had even forsaken Alicia for the moment to be with me.

We devoured cheeseburgers, fries, and chocolate milkshakes as we sat in the booth. It was such a relief not to hear Martin Wolfe's name for a few minutes. I knew I wouldn't be able to get away from all the questions for several days, but at least I had a much needed break.

Tanner took off for home when we left the Black Heifer. Tommy walked with me as far as his house. He spoke about baseball and somehow managed to keep himself from talking about Alicia. He offered to walk me home, but I told him I'd be fine and that I needed to think, anyway.

Think I did as I walked in the biting January air. I felt as if I'd lost a friend, and yet I didn't know Martin Wolfe. We probably hadn't exchanged a hundred words in our entire lives. I'd barely noticed him until recent weeks. Still, I couldn't shake my feelings. Perhaps I was mourning what could have been.

I racked my brain thinking about what I could have said, or done differently, to have prevented this tragedy. I could think of nothing. I had reached out to Martin, but he'd turned away. Maybe if I'd made the effort sooner. Maybe if I'd tried to befriend him back in grade school, things would've been different. I guess it didn't matter. Martin was dead. My opportunity to help him had ended. I felt like a failure.

Sam was sitting in the room we shared when I got home. He wasn't around much, but it was his day off from the Marathon station.

"Are you okay, little brother?"

"I guess I am. I don't know."

"I'm here if you need me. If you want to talk or whatever…"

"Thanks," I said.

Sam could be a cool brother. He was stuck on himself and thought he was hot stuff, but I could tolerate that. Sam had been there when I needed him. He knew how much I missed Angel, and he knew I was messed up now. I felt more secure because he was there.

Angel

My life settled into a nice comfortable routine. Perhaps I shouldn't say routine, because that makes it sound boring. My life was anything but. I rather enjoyed my work at the Hotel Indiana. Mr. Howard was a considerate boss. Pearce and I got on well. Greta was kind and funny in her way. Fife turned out to have a great sense of humor. I spent a lot of time with him. I kind of think he had a crush on me, but he never once voiced it out loud or really flirted with me. I had my own little room, complete with a private bathroom. I had regular meals and was actually making money!

Most of my leisure time was spent with Clarence. He visited me at the hotel. We ran around town in his old car. We spent a good deal of time at his house, too. We watched movies at the Embassy Theatre. It was like the Delphi back home, only more incredible! Just walking in was an event. I think the Embassy was the most beautiful theatre I'd ever seen. The chandeliers, painted ceilings, moldings, ironwork, and tile floors were overwhelming. I loved listening to the giant organ that played before each show. I watched every single movie that played in the Embassy. Mostly I went with Clarence, but if he couldn't make it, I went alone.

Time seemed to pass a little more quickly now that I had a job and friends to keep me occupied. Still, I yearned for the days to speed by so I could once again be with Kurt. He was the one missing piece in my life.

I knew Clarence would have gladly been my boyfriend if I wasn't taken. If I was single, I would have returned his interest. He was witty, funny, and kind. He reminded me of Kurt in some ways. I was not single, however, and had no desire to be. I already had the greatest boyfriend in the entire world.

I was concerned that Hal would make trouble for Clarence. Hal was ever-watchful, and I took extra care when we were around him. Clarence understood the danger and watched his step around Hal, too. If we were dating, Hal might have figured things out, but as Clarence and I were just friends, he wasn't able to confirm his suspicions about Clarence. Still, I was worried.

If it hadn't been for missing Kurt so badly my heart ached, I could've settled right down in Fort Wayne and remained there forever. I knew I was very lucky indeed to find myself in such a situation. I could just as easily have still been on the road, sleeping in barns and under the stars, unsure of where my next meal might be found. My life on the road had taught me to value security. Not once did I cease to be thankful for what I had. For me, every day was Thanksgiving.

Just when I settled in, intending to remain in Fort Wayne until it was time to return to Kurt, things began to change. I was sitting in Clarence's living room listening to a football game on the radio with Clarence, his dad, and his uncle when Mrs. Mason interrupted us.

"Mother is ready to go home," she announced.

Mr. Mason stood, fingering his keys in his pocket.

"Please go with your father, Clarence. I'm sending Mother some leftovers, and you can carry them in for her."

"Mom, couldn't Dad—"

"Clarence," said Mrs. Mason in a warning tone.

"I'll be back in a while," Clarence said. "Don't leave while I'm gone."

"I won't," I said.

"I should be going, too," Clarence's uncle said.

Clarence's other grandmother had departed earlier, so that left only Mrs. Mason and me in the house. I turned off the radio, since I had no real interest in the game.

"Angel, could we have a talk?" Mrs. Mason asked.

"Of course," I said.

"Join me in the kitchen. Would you like another piece of pie?"

"Yes. I would. Thank you. I would have eaten another piece at dinner, but I was just too full."

Mrs. Mason and I were soon sitting at the kitchen table. A big piece of coconut-cream pie sat in front of me. Both of us had iced tea.

"How long have you been away from home, Angel?"

I froze. *She knew.*

"I...um... How did you know?"

"I can read the homesickness in your eyes, Angel. I particularly notice it during dinner. Being with our family reminds you of yours."

I nodded.

"Don't be angry with Clarence for lying to you," I said. "He did it to protect me. I was afraid if you knew I was a runaway that you might turn me in. Are you going to turn me in?"

"No, but I am worried about you, Angel. You seem like a fine boy, and I don't like thinking of you on your own."

"I have a good job, a place to stay, and plenty to eat."

"What about your family, Angel? I know I'd be worried sick if Clarence was who-knows-where and all on his own. I'm sure you're mother is very worried about you, too."

"I'm not sure about that."

"Why not, Angel?"

"I'm just not sure how she feels about me now. I left behind a letter that told my parents something about me they didn't know. Now that they know, I'm not sure they...love me anymore."

"Maybe you should have given them a chance, Angel. Maybe you should have told them before you left. If you'd done that, you would know how they feel."

"You're probably right, but I couldn't stay to find out. There wasn't time."

Clarence's mom took a deep breath.

"At the risk of being nosey, why did you have to leave so quickly, Angel?"

"I didn't do anything wrong, if that's what you're thinking. Don't worry. I won't do anything to lead Clarence astray. I had to leave because my life was in danger. It's a long story, but I turned in some guys who did something horrible. If they had found me before I left…well, it wouldn't have been good."

Mrs. Mason looked truly worried. I was glad I'd sugar-coated the situation. She would probably have lost it if she knew Adam and his gang would have killed me if they'd caught me.

"Oh, Angel. Someone so young shouldn't have to deal with such things."

"I can take care of myself," I said.

"Why don't you go home, Angel?"

"When I left I…helped out a friend. In doing so, I revealed something about me. If I go back everyone will hate me."

"Hmm," Clarence's mom said, thinking. "Do you mind telling me what it is that you think will make everyone hate you?"

I gazed at Clarence's mom for a few moments. Was I telling her too much? Something made me trust her.

"I'm a homosexual," I said.

Mrs. Mason's eyes widened in surprise, and her mouth dropped open. I tensed. I knew that she might very well order me out of her house. I hoped Clarence would understand if he returned and I was gone. Clarence's mom took another deep breath. She started to open her mouth to speak, but then closed it again. Another few moments passed before she spoke.

"Is that why you're unsure about how your parents feel about you?"

"Yes. They didn't know I was a homo."

"Why did you feel it necessary to tell them?"

I opened up to Clarence's mom. She hadn't ordered me out of her house. Instead, she gazed at me with compassion. I told her about Kurt, about the rumors that started about him, and about the letter I left, turning the hatred of my classmates upon myself to save him. By the time I'd finished, Mrs. Mason had tears in her eyes.

"You're a very brave boy, Angel."

"I love Kurt. I would do anything for him. I just did what I had to do."

"I bet he misses you."

"I know he does. I miss him so bad I can't stand it sometimes."

"I'm sure your parents miss you, too."

"I'm not sure," I said.

"I don't know your parents, Angel, but if they are anything like their son, I can't imagine them turning their backs on you. I know also that if I found out that my son was…homosexual…that I'd still love him. I wouldn't be happy about it, but I would love Clarence no matter what. I also know that if he ran away, I'd be hoping and praying for him to come back. I would beg God to return him to me. Angel, you aren't a parent, so you can't truly understand, but there is nothing worse than seeing your child in pain. Not knowing where he is or if he's safe is nothing less than torment. I'm sure your mother is worried sick about you, Angel. On her behalf, I'm pleading with you to go home."

I actually began to cry. I couldn't bear to think of my mom suffering like that. The kind, sympathetic tone of Clarence's mom reminded me so much of my own mother. Clarence's mom stood and walked around the table. I stood up, hugged her, and cried on her shoulder.

When Clarence and his dad returned later, Mrs. Mason and I were sitting at the kitchen table, still eating pie (our second piece by then). There was no sign that anything out of the ordinary had happened between us, but Clarence's mom had given me a lot to think about.

Clarence and I went to his room to hang out. If his mom had any reservations about allowing her son to be alone with a homosexual, she didn't show it. Did she suspect her own son was homosexual? I had no idea. Her acceptance of me gave me hope that she would be accepting of Clarence if he one day told her the truth about himself. Her own words reassured me further.

I told Clarence about the talk I'd had with his mom. He was at first alarmed, then relieved. I told him I'd explained everything to her, leaving out Clarence's advances and interest in me as more than a friend, of course. Clarence drew strength from what his mother had said about still loving him even if he was a homosexual.

"Do you think she suspects I am?" Clarence asked.

"I don't know. She seemed plenty shocked when I told her I was, so I think not."

"I hope she doesn't. I feel better knowing that she'll still love me if she finds out about me, but I just don't want her to know—not yet, anyway."

I nodded. I understood.

Clarence drove me back to the Hotel Indiana later. I almost walked, because I had a lot to think about, but Clarence wanted to drive me.

I was stuffed from dinner, but I picked out a corner seat in the café and ordered a cup of hot tea. Clarence's mom had been truly shocked to discover I was a homo. That wasn't the first time I'd witnessed such surprise. I had told precious few people about me, but without exception, they all had the same stunned looks on their faces. They just couldn't believe it, at first. A homosexual was supposed to be a monstrous deviant, incapable of disguising himself and appearing normal. Most people just couldn't believe a normal boy could possibly be "one of those." What they didn't understand was that homosexuality was normal. True, most people were heterosexual, but there had always been and would always be homosexuals. I'm not sure how I knew that; I just knew.

I was accustomed to the stunned expressions of those I told about me, but I was not accustomed to the acceptance I'd found first on the Selby farm and now with Clarence's mom. I knew I couldn't expect that acceptance from most. I hadn't expected it from anyone. I was glad there were people like the Selbys and Clarence's mom. They gave me hope for the future. It was nice to know that at least a few people out there didn't think I was a monster.

I marveled at the ability of Clarence's mom to toss aside so quickly what she had heard about homosexuals and replace it with what she knew about me. That was truly amazing. Most people wouldn't even say the word "homosexual," and yet she had seen through all the lies and ignorance. She didn't assume I was a monstrous deviant. Instead, she took me as I was and decided I was okay—just like that.

I smiled. I'd liked Mrs. Mason from day one. Now, I liked her even more. She reminded me of my own mom. I sighed. I liked to think of myself as independent, but the truth was I missed my parents terribly. I was on my own and making my own way, but I didn't feel quite grown up yet. I felt as though I'd left home too soon. I'd had no choice in the matter, however. I'd done what I had to do.

I finished my tea and returned to my room. I didn't have to work until the next morning. It was nice to spend time in my own little room. It was quiet, comfy, and cozy. I'd settled in quite nicely.

I didn't have many possessions, but then I didn't need much. When I went to buy work clothes at a resale shop, I'd found a few old baseball magazines and a copy of *Catcher in the Rye*. I liked to read during my off hours and lose myself in another world. It's not that this world was such a bad one, but I loved to explore other places and lives.

I lay back on my bed and began to read. The walls around me disappeared, and soon I fell fast asleep.

***

My life continued as it had since I'm come to Fort Wayne. The only change was a growing sense of urgency about returning home. Clarence's mom had given me a lot to think over. The thoughts and feelings she had stirred up were disquieting and uncomfortable. Guilt gnawed at me. I felt selfish for making my parents worry.

Still, I mostly just went about my business. Nothing very exciting happened, but that was a good thing. Excitement is often linked to danger. The expected trouble with Hal and his buddies never materialized. I was glad, mostly for Clarence's sake, that there was no excitement on that front. I hadn't forgotten what things were like for Kurt when he'd been pegged as a homo.

An internal debate raged in my mind while I showed guests to their rooms, ran errands, vacuumed carpets, and performed the dozens of little odd jobs that made up my work day. The debate continued as I took my meals in the hotel café, at Sarah's, or at Clarence's home. No matter where I was or what I was doing, the same thoughts were playing out on the edges of my mind. Finally, after many days of considering the situation, I reached a decision.

"I'm going home, Clarence."

Clarence looked up from where he sat at his desk. It was a Saturday morning. We were assembling a model of a boat-tail Duesenberg while waiting on his mom to cook us breakfast. I was assisting by reading the directions.

"What?" Clarence stood, his model forgotten. "Angel, you can't!"

"I have to, Clarence. I've been thinking about it a lot. Running away just doesn't feel right. I have to go back."

"Are you sure that's wise, Angel? What if…what if your classmates do something nasty to you? They all know about you. You know how people feel about guys like us. I can't bear to think what they might do to you."

"I know how they feel. I know things will be rough. My life is in Blackford, though, and I've got to return to it. I can't hide out forever."

"I love you," Clarence said.

I took his hand. "I love you, too, Clarence. If things were different there could be something between us. I think you would make a wonderful boyfriend."

"Please stay, Angel. Forget about Kurt. Stay here with me. You'll be safe here." There was a pleading tone in Clarence's voice that nearly broke my heart.

"I can't do that, Clarence. I do care about you, but I love Kurt. And, if I stayed, people would find out about you. It would be rough, Clarence, rougher than you can probably imagine."

"I'm willing to face it, Angel. I'll face it to be with you. Stay with me. Or, I'll go away with you. I'll travel with you so you won't have to be alone anymore. We can…"

"No, Clarence. I care about you. I love you. But Kurt has my heart. I could never forget about him. I could never abandon him. I couldn't live without him. I'm sorry if that hurts you, but you deserve the truth."

"Your loyalty to him only makes me want you more," Clarence said. "I understand, though. I shouldn't have asked you to forget about Kurt, but I had to. I had to at least try. You understand, don't you?"

I nodded.

"You will find someone, Clarence. Like I said, if things were different, then I'd be very interested in you. I have no doubt that others will be just as interested. Be patient. There is someone out there for you."

"I hope so, Angel."

"I know so. In fact…um…I hope you don't mind, but I gave your number to someone."

"You *what*?"

"Relax. He's just going to call, talk to you, and see if you want to go out. I told him a lot about you, and well…he's interested."

"In me?"

"No, in your mom. Of course, in you!"

"Who is he?"

"Fife. I worked with him at the hotel. He's a little older, twenty, and he's very handsome. He's also very nice. I think you two might hit it off."

"So, he's…like us, right?"

"Yeah."

"Wow. So…what's he look like?"

"He's on the small side: I'd say about 5'4" and 110 pounds. It suits him, though. He's very good-looking and has a nice body. He's also got a Scottish accent that is sexy as hell."

"I won't know what to say when he calls!"

"Just talk."

"That's easy for you to say."

I laughed.

"Thanks, Angel."

"You're welcome."

Clarence took a deep breath.

"What made you decide to go back?"

"Your mom."

"My mom?"

"Yeah. Remember that day I was alone with your mom for a while? The day I admitted I'm a runaway? She talked to me about how my mom must miss me. She told me how she'd feel if you ran away. I haven't been able to get the things she said out of my mind."

"Do you really have to go?"

"Yes. Today."

"Today?"

Clarence began to cry. I took him in my arms and hugged him. His body shuddered. I felt guilty for bringing him such grief, but I couldn't stay in Fort Wayne forever. That life couldn't be mine. Even if I lingered until Kurt's graduation, I'd have to go back home some day. It's where I belonged, and, more than that, it's where I wanted to be—with Kurt.

Clarence quieted after a while. I released him, and he took a step back.

"It's going to be really hard to say goodbye, but I'm glad I met you, Angel."

"I'm glad I met you, too—and your mom. Now, come on. I'm hungry, and I bet your mom is nearly finished with breakfast. Go wash your face, and we'll go down to the kitchen."

Clarence wiped the tears from his eyes. I waited outside the bathroom while he erased most of the evidence of his tears. We walked together to the kitchen. A breakfast of blueberry pancakes, omelets, and bacon was nearly ready. Soon the three of us sat down at the table.

I was both happy and sad as I sat there. I was going to miss Clarence and his mom, too. I hadn't expected to find such a good friend in my travels. I hadn't expected to find a mother so much like my own, either.

I looked across the table at Clarence's mom as we ate.

"I'm going home," I said.

Mrs. Mason's eyes filled with tears. She stood up and walked around the table. I stood, and we hugged each other. I gave her a kiss on the cheek as we pulled away from each other.

"You've made the right choice, Angel."

"Thank you for helping me make that choice."

"That's what mothers are for."

I grinned.

We sat down and finished breakfast. Clarence tried not to let his sadness show, but he just couldn't help it. His mom reached out and grasped his hand. Somehow, I knew he'd be okay.

Clarence and I walked back to his room after breakfast. I pulled on my leather jacket and my toboggan.

"Do you have to go right now?"

"Yes. I've already given Mr. Howard notice and received my final paycheck. I'm leaving this morning. I would have told you before, but I thought it was best this way. I didn't want to ruin our last days together."

Clarence's eyes once again filled with tears. He wrote out his address and gave it to me, even though I already knew it by heart.

"You'd better write me," he said, wiping his tears away with his forearm.

"I will as soon as I get home. Before, if I can manage it. Don't worry about me, though. It might be a long trip back. You'd better write me back, too. I want to know how things work out with Fife."

"Will you remember me?"

"I couldn't forget you if I wanted to, Clarence."

Clarence gazed into my eyes. I pulled him to me, hugged him close, and then kissed him on the lips. I knew Kurt wouldn't mind.

"I'll never forget you," I told him.

"I'll drive you to the hotel."

"No. I'd rather say goodbye here. This is how I want to remember you: here, where we've had so much fun together. Don't worry; we'll see each other again—some day."

"You promise?"

"I promise. We're friends, Clarence. This is only goodbye for now. Some day, I want you and Kurt to meet each other—but no hitting on my boyfriend!"

Clarence smiled. I zipped up my jacket. We walked to the living room. Clarence's mother awaited us there with a big grocery bag.

"I made you some sandwiches and a few other things for your journey."

"Thank you," I said, taking the bag from her. "From the weight of this I think you made me enough for the whole trip." I grinned.

"I don't want you going hungry."

"Don't worry about me. I've got a pocket full of money from my job at the hotel. I'm in much better shape than I was when I arrived. I'll be fine. I know how to take care of myself," I said.

"I'm sure you can take care of yourself, Angel, but you get home and let your mother take care of you. She won't have many more years to do that."

I gave Clarence's mom a hug and another kiss on the cheek.

"Thank you, for everything," I said.

I turned to Clarence, and we hugged.

"Goodbye."

"Goodbye."

"Don't forget to write me," Clarence said.

"I won't forget."

I stepped out the door and walked down the sidewalk, looking back only once when I reached the street. Clarence and his mom were standing in the window, waving. I waved back and then began my long journey home.

Kurt

The whole school was buzzing about Martin Wolfe. The boy who had been invisible to nearly everyone had become famous—legendary, even. No doubt he'd be remembered forever as the boy who took his own life by wrapping a rope around his neck.

I was quite sure Martin Wolfe didn't kill himself to achieve fame. There were any number of reasons he might have committed suicide, but I guessed no one would ever know for sure.

I wondered if Martin had hung himself right in the school to send some kind of message. Was it his way of telling his classmates, "You did this to me"? Maybe he just wanted everyone to finally see him. I didn't know. I had no answers when it came to Martin Wolfe.

I felt as if I'd failed him, but what else could I have done? I reached out to him, but he had repulsed all my efforts. It was almost as if he wanted to suffer, but why would anyone want that?

Tyler was strangely quiet. He didn't smile. He had a faraway look in his eyes whenever I saw him. At lunch he responded when spoken to, but he said little and volunteered nothing. The students in the cafeteria were rather subdued, but Tyler was eerily so. A scary image formed in my mind—an image of Tyler withdrawing from his friends and becoming just like Martin Wolfe.

I banished the thought from my mind, but decided I would confront Tyler as soon as possible.

My chance came just after school. I spotted Tyler at his locker. I quickly stuffed what books I didn't need into my own locker and joined Tyler.

"Hey, can we talk?" I asked.

"Yeah, okay," Tyler said without much enthusiasm.

"Why don't you walk home with me? You can have supper at my house. Mom or Dad can drive you home."

"Um, I'd have to call home and ask."

"Please?"

"Okay. Meet you at your locker in a few minutes?"

"Sure."

I returned to my locker. Tommy showed up soon after.

"Hey," I said. "Would you mind if we didn't walk home together? I've asked Tyler to come home with me. I'm going to try to find out what's up with him."

"He has been behaving a bit oddly."

"Yeah, since Martin hanged himself."

"You think that's what's wrong with Tyler?"

"Yeah, but I'm not sure. I want to find out."

"Well, good luck. I'll see you tomorrow morning, okay?"

"You know it. Bye, Tommy."

I didn't have to wait long for Tyler. He was quiet as we walked out of the school. It was plenty cold out, but we were accustomed to that and paid it little mind.

"Tyler, you've been really quiet since Martin died. I know you're upset. Do you want to talk about it?"

"I don't know. I guess."

"There was something between the two of you, wasn't there?"

"Yeah, there *was*, but that was a long time ago."

"Were you…boyfriends?"

"No. It wasn't quite like that. We were too young to be boyfriends, you know?"

"So you were close?"

"Yeah. We used to hang out some. There was this creek with an old bridge across it..."

"Morton's Bridge? Across Morton's Creek?"

"Yeah."

"I went out there to fish one day in the summer when I was eleven. I thought it would be a nice quiet place to think. Well, Martin was there, fishing with his cane pole. I'd seen him at school, but hadn't really talked to him. He was just as quiet back then as he is...as he was until..."

"Yeah."

"I asked if he minded if I fished, too. He said "no" but that was all he said. We just sat there near each other fishing in silence. We were probably there for two hours, just fishing and thinking. It was getting near suppertime so I called it quits. I told Martin goodbye. He said "bye." That was it. "No" and "Bye." He only spoke those two words that whole time.

"I came back a couple of days later, and Martin was there again. I got him to talk just a bit more. I asked if he came there often, and he told me he was there almost every afternoon.

"I started going to the bridge to fish and sit there with Martin about every day. Slowly, very slowly, he began to talk more. He never said very much, just a few sentences at most, but that was talkative for Martin."

"What happened?" I asked.

"Well, we got kind of close. I told him about things...my life, you know? He never said much, but he was a good listener. He seemed interested, too. I kinda started liking him...you know...*liking* him. Martin wasn't all that good-looking, but there was something special about him, something kind of sexy."

Tyler sniffled. A tear ran down his cheek.

"I knew I liked guys even back then. One afternoon, I leaned over and kissed Martin on the cheek. It startled him. I tried to kiss him on the lips, but he jerked away from me as if I'd tried to hit him. I told him I was sorry, but he grabbed up all his stuff and ran. I kind of thought that maybe he was like me, but I guess I was wrong. I didn't really want much more from him than a kiss. We were just eleven, after all. The kiss freaked Martin out.

"He didn't show up at our spot the next day, nor the day after, nor the day after that. For more than a week I went to the bridge every day and stayed there until it was almost dark, but no Martin. I spent a lot of my time crying, wondering why he didn't like me. I went less frequently after that, and I never saw Martin there again.

"When school started up, he wouldn't speak to me for the longest time. When he finally did it was a mumbled "Hi" or something like that. It really hurt me. You might think this is stupid, but I had the biggest crush on him back then. It broke my heart when he ran away from me and refused to talk to me. I tried to get him to talk, of course, but he never would. He never said so, but he seemed angry. I guess he was mad because I'd tried to kiss him.

"I think the worst part of it is that I didn't stop caring about him. Even though he obviously didn't like me, I still had a crush on him. Every time I looked at him, I thought about what it could have been like between us.

"That was a few years ago, but I still cared about Martin. I don't have that same schoolboy crush on him I had as a kid, but I never stopped caring. I wanted to help him, draw him out, and at least be friends with him, but the more I tried, the angrier he became. That's why I told you that you were wasting your time and warned you that he might be dangerous."

"What made you think he was dangerous?"

"Well, at first I thought Martin wasn't like me, that he didn't like guys. Later, I came to think that he was like me, only he couldn't deal with it. I think it ate him up inside. It made him hate himself—and me. I think that's why he got so angry when someone tried to reach out to him. He felt he didn't deserve to be liked. Maybe he thought that whoever approached him was trying to take advantage of him, too. I don't know. I guess most of this is just my own theory on why Martin was like he was. I've always had this empty place in my heart—a space that was meant for Martin—but he wouldn't or couldn't love me back. I guess I've dwelled way too much on what could have been. Now, he's gone. I just feel…I don't know…like some kind of opportunity for happiness is gone—for both Martin and me."

"I don't know if I can say anything to make you feel better, Tyler, but I don't think Martin and you would've ever become any closer. You haven't lost an opportunity for happiness. That opportunity wasn't there to begin with. I don't know what made Martin like he was, but I don't think he could care about anyone."

"You're probably right, but the feeling is still there. Illogical, isn't it?"

"Yes, but you can't help feeling what you feel. When you care about someone, feelings don't have to make sense."

"Martin's life was so sad. Now it's over. I feel really guilty for not trying harder to get to him. I keep thinking that if I'd put a little more effort into trying to draw him out, he would still be alive."

"It wouldn't have made any difference, Tyler. I know. I tried to be his friend. When he rebuffed me, I tried again. You saw what happened that day in the cafeteria. Tyler, I don't think anyone could get to Martin."

"Then why do I still feel so rotten?"

"Because you cared about him. You've lost someone special. Of course, you're going to grieve."

"I guess he's safe from the bullies now. No one can ever cause him trouble again."

"Yeah, there is that. Freedom from pain is worth a lot, but still… it's sad. What a waste. Think of all the good things Martin will miss out on."

"Yeah. Thanks for helping me through this. I actually feel better. It's going to be a long time before I get over what's happened, but it helps just to talk about it."

"You're welcome."

We had talked during our entire walk. We turned into the drive just as we finished our chat. I led Tyler inside and into the kitchen. As I'd hoped, Mom had some freshly baked cookies waiting on us. Mom prepared all our baked goods, even bread. She baked cookies nearly every day in an effort to keep up with the voracious appetites of our family.

"Hi, Mrs. James," Tyler said, smiling.

"Hello, Tyler? How are you today?"

"Yeah. I'm Tyler. Better, thanks to Kurt. I've been kind of upset because of Martin."

"Yes, that poor boy," Mom said. She looked at me for a moment, probably wondering how I was dealing with the discovery of Martin's corpse. I'd had a couple of bad dreams about it, but not quite bad enough to be considered nightmares.

"How about some cookies and milk?"

"That sounds great!" Tyler said, perking up considerably. Mom's cookies had that effect on people.

Mom poured us glasses of milk and set a big plate of chocolate-chip cookies with pecans in front of us. Mmm. I loved all Mom's cookies, but her chocolate-chip cookies were the best!

Tyler and I left our talk of Martin behind. We'd said enough. What we both needed now was not to think about him. Instead, we talked about school and the approaching baseball season. It was still distant, but growing ever closer. Time was slipping away, and I was grateful. Every day that passed brought me one day closer to my reunion with Angel.

Angel

I wanted to get back to Blackford as soon as possible, but I didn't take the most direct route. I had two stops I wanted to make on my return trip: Grandmother's cabin and the Selby farm. Of course, it wasn't the places I wanted to visit, but rather those who lived there. I would always remember what Grandmother, Laura, Emma, and particularly Jack had done for me.

As January turned to February, the coldest winter weather had begun to loosen its grip. February was usually just as cold, or colder, than January, but luckily this year was different. As February got on, it began to get warm—by northern Indiana standards, at least. It would have perhaps been wiser to wait for spring to make my journey, but once I'd made the decision to return to Blackford, I couldn't tolerate much of a delay.

At first, my journey would take me west, but after Verona I would finally turn south—towards home. I reminded myself that every step, no matter in which direction, brought me closer to Kurt.

I was a good deal better off on my return journey than I had been on my flight from Blackford. I'd saved most of the money I'd earned at the Hotel Indiana, so I had little doubt I could make it last until I was back home again. Still, I intended to be frugal, for I had no real idea of what awaited me back in my old hometown. I might very well be forced to set out again shortly after my arrival. I was reassured somewhat that Mr. Howard said I could have my job back any time I wanted it. He had taken me in as a favor to Jack Selby, but he'd been impressed with my work. I had more than ample motivation to do the best job possible. Life on the road had taught me the value of security.

I quickly settled back into walking for long stretches. I was afraid I might've gotten a bit soft during my stay in Fort Wayne, but I guess running all those errands and traipsing all over the hotel had kept me in shape. I hitched a few rides—one in an old farm truck that smelled like hogs, another with an old lady who admonished me for playing hooky from school, and another from a middle-aged man who might have had a thing for me. Hitching a ride was always a bit of a risk, but I never found myself in a situation I couldn't handle. Still, I was cautious.

Grandmother's cabin was naturally my first destination. My journey there was rather pleasant. I was warm enough in my leather jacket, toboggan, and scarf, except sometimes at night. Even when I was chilled, I loved to lie out under the stars, just staring off into the sky. I listened to owls hooting and the noises of the forest. Whenever the road took me through an outpost of civilization I replenished my stock of food. Sometimes, if there was a restaurant, I even splurged on a burger and fries.

Several days' journey brought me to a familiar neck of the woods. I followed the old country road and then turned off on the well-worn trail. Before long, I could see Grandmother's cabin in the distance. Smoke curled from both its chimneys, and I felt as if I was home already. How different the cabin looked surrounded by greening grass instead of snow—both familiar and unfamiliar at the same time.

I walked up to the cabin door and knocked. Moments later, Laura opened the door. She squealed when she saw me and jumped into my arms. I walked inside, toting my admirer. I noted she was wearing the gold chain I'd given her at Christmas.

"Well, I'll be," Grandmother said.

I released Laura and gave Grandmother a hug.

"I'm on my way home," I said. "I couldn't pass by without a visit."

"Can Angel stay the night, Grandmother?" Laura asked.

"What a silly question. Of course, he can. Angel can stay as long as he likes."

"I might stay a couple of days. I can't stay too long. I'm eager to get back."

Grandmother didn't pry into the reason for my return home, but I could tell she was pleased I was heading back towards my parents.

It was mid-afternoon when I arrived. There was a fire going in the hearth, but the windows were open. Grandmother noted my puzzlement as we all sat down near the hearth.

"This is one of the between times," she said. "It's too warm for a fire, but too cold without one. In a few weeks it will be warm enough I'll just keep a fire in the cook stove."

"It's rather pleasant by the fire, despite the warm day," I said.

"This is rather a warm spell for February. No doubt we'll have more cold before the temperature begins to warm up for spring."

It felt good to sit and rest my feet in familiar surroundings. I told Grandmother and Laura about my travels since I'd left them and about my life in Fort Wayne. After a while, Laura dragged me outside for a hike. Walking was definitely not a novel experience for me, but walking through those familiar woods with Laura was something I didn't want to miss. My little friend talked a mile a minute while she told me of all that had transpired since I'd departed: of the cat who had taken to living in their wood pile and the pair of hawks she'd seen flying overhead just the previous day. I grinned as I listened to her, realizing I'd missed out by not having a baby sister.

Laura quizzed me while we were walking, something Grandmother wouldn't have allowed. I didn't really mind, however, and soon I found myself telling Laura about Kurt and how much I loved him. She had a little trouble understanding at first. She couldn't quite understand how I could be in love with another boy. She accepted it soon enough, though. Children are far less judgmental than adults, or perhaps they are just wiser.

Evening was coming on by the time we returned to the cabin. We were greeted by the scent of freshly baked bread as we walked in. It was a scent I remembered well.

"Supper is nearly ready. If you two will set the table, we can eat."

Laura and I got to work, and soon the three of us were seated at the old, worn kitchen table. Grandmother had prepared a pot of chili. There were crackers and peanut butter and jam to go with it. There was also home-baked bread and butter. I hadn't tasted anything so delicious since I'd left Grandmother's cabin on New Year's Day.

We ate and talked, but mostly ate. All that walking had made me ravenously hungry. For dessert there was apple cobbler. It was indescribably delicious.

After supper we sat around the fire, sipping hot tea. There was just something so cozy and comfortable about sitting in front of a fire, listening to the wood pop and smelling the scent of wood smoke. I very nearly fell asleep as I was talking.

"I think you need to get to bed, young man," Grandmother said. "Your pallet is just as you left it, although you might want to move it downstairs if it becomes too warm in the loft.

"Thanks, Grandmother."

I bid them both goodnight and climbed up into the loft of the cabin, feeling a bit like a pioneer boy as I did so. I was reminded that Abraham Lincoln once lived less than an hour from Blackford. Of course, back in his day it would've been quite a journey from his home near Little Pigeon Creek to my hometown.

It was indeed warm in the loft, almost too warm. I stripped completely naked and lay down on top of the covers. I was comfortable enough with my clothes off and rather enjoyed the sensation of being a little too warm. It was much preferable to feeling too cold.

I awakened the next morning to the scent of frying bacon. I lay there for a few moments smiling. How many times had I awakened to that same scent when I'd stayed in the cabin before?

I got up, dressed, and climbed down the ladder. Laura was already up and about. Both she and grandmother were busily preparing breakfast. Laura was obviously in charge of scrambling eggs. There was a large egg basket sitting on the table. I had little doubt the eggs had been gathered that very morning. Laura reached into the basket, pulled out a brown egg and cracked it on the edge of an old spongeware mixing bowl. She repeated the process until she had enough and then began to whip the eggs with a whisk.

"Is there anything I can do?" I asked.

"You can eat these pancakes when they're finished," Grandmother said.

"Oh, I'm always glad to help with that."

Laura giggled.

The table was already set, so there really was nothing for me to do. My idleness left me feeling a bit guilty, but I eased my conscience with my plans for spending the day replenishing Grandmother's wood pile. I'd left Grandmother and Laura a good supply of firewood when I'd departed, but that was weeks ago. I thought I'd spend a few hours at my old task both for old times sake and to give back a little something to those who had given me so much. I had not forgotten that I owed Laura my life.

Soon, my ironstone plate was filled with a stack of pancakes swimming in butter and real maple syrup. A mound of Laura's scrambled eggs rested beside them as did plenty of strips of perfectly fried bacon. There were both hot and iced tea to drink. I hadn't eaten such a breakfast in a long time. The café in the Hotel Indiana and even Sarah's could've learned a thing or two from Grandmother.

After breakfast, I headed out to the woodshed. Despite Grandmother's protest that I had no need to work for my breakfast, I knew she would appreciate an increased wood supply. Chopping and splitting firewood couldn't be easy on either Grandmother or Laura.

Laura tagged along with me, and I was glad of the company. I gathered the old, familiar tools from the shed, and Laura pulled out the wagon they used for hauling wood. The wagon wasn't large, but had high sides. I think it was what was called a goat cart, but I wasn't sure.

We set out into the woods. Laura pulled the wagon along (with some help from me). I walked beside her with an axe slung over my shoulder. The last time I'd cut firewood for Grandmother, I had pulled it through the trees on a sled. There was no snow now, so the sled was useless.

Soon, we came upon some dead wood, and I set about cutting it into lengths suitable for the fireplace and the cook stove. I'd left my leather jacket, toboggan, and scarf behind in the cabin because the weather was mild and I knew I'd be plenty warm working. I soon found I'd underestimated just how warm I would be. In less than two minutes, I'd pulled off my sweater.

It felt good to use my muscles doing manual labor once more. The idea of cutting wood for my livelihood did not appeal to me, but I actually enjoyed it on that pleasant February day. Part of my contentment came from knowing that I was helping someone I cared about. A part of me would have liked to stay there with Grandmother and Laura forever, but my life was elsewhere.

It was odd, but I felt as though I could have settled down on the Selby farm, in Fort Wayne, or at Grandmother's cabin. I could have started a new life in any of those places. If it hadn't been for Kurt I just might have done so. There was little else for me in Blackford, except possible torment. No one in his right mind would have gone back, but I was in love. I definitely wasn't in my right mind. I smiled.

"You're thinking about your boyfriend, aren't you?" Laura asked.

"Yeah."

"What's it like?" she asked.

At first, I thought Laura was curious about two guys dating. Such things weren't even talked about in most places after all. Laura was so accepting of such an unconventional relationship that she gave it no thought. Laura was asking me about love.

"Being in love is wonderful and terrible, joyous and painful."

"It's terrible and painful? Why? How could it be terrible and painful if it's wonderful?"

"When you love someone, you care about them so much that their pain is yours. If they get sick, or hurt, or depressed it hurts you, too. You worry about them. You fear for them.

"You fear losing them. When you're apart, you can miss them so bad it hurts. Missing someone you love can make you sad and lonely."

"Oh! I never thought of that!" Laura said.

"The good more than makes up for the bad. The pain comes from the love. If I didn't love Kurt so much, I wouldn't miss him. I wouldn't be worried about him. I wouldn't be hurt by his pain."

"Is Kurt beautiful like you?"

I smiled.

"Kurt's beautiful, but he's a different kind of beautiful. He's shorter than I am. He has shiny brown hair and brown eyes. When he smiles, I go weak in the knees. He's even more beautiful on the inside. He's good and kind and loving. He's not only my boyfriend, but my friend."

"I'm glad you have a boyfriend."

"Me, too."

Laura shifted topics, talking of the coming spring. Before many weeks had passed, there would be sweet strawberries to pick and, later, blueberries. She and Grandmother would plant their garden—squashes, pumpkins, tomatoes, peppers, green beans, corn, and more. Hearing Laura speak with such enthusiasm made me want to stay.

My old friend Bessie the cow wandered up to us. I took a break from sawing logs to pet her. Good old Bessie; she'd kept me company during the long snowy days when I'd sawn and split wood for hours on end. Laura hugged Bessie, and we made over her as if she was a beloved dog. When I returned to work, Bessie turned her attention to the new grass that was just beginning to sprout up in places.

Sweat ran down my back and chest, which of course gave me a bit of a chill. It wasn't warm out, after all. It was merely warmer than it had been in recent weeks. I thought of pulling my sweater back on, but then I'd be too warm. Sweat plastered my hair to my forehead and ran into my eyes, making them sting. Laura left me alone for a bit, but soon returned with a stoneware jug filled with cold water from the springhouse. I drank it thirstily.

When the wagon was full, I pulled it back to the woodshed. There, Laura stacked the smaller pieces cut from limbs while I spilt the larger pieces with a sledgehammer and steel wedges. When the last piece of wood was split to a useable size and stacked, I headed back into the woods.

I had only Bessie for company on my second trip, for Laura was helping Grandmother prepare lunch. I was already eagerly anticipating the midday meal. Sawing, chopping, and splitting firewood was far more strenuous than working in a hotel or walking mile after mile. I was quickly burning through the large breakfast Grandmother had prepared.

As I worked, I considered sending Kurt a letter, telling him I was on my way home. He was no doubt worried about me. I was still unsure of just how long it would take me to get back, however, and a part of me wanted to keep it a surprise. Kurt wasn't expecting me back for months and months. I wanted to see his face when I suddenly and unexpectedly appeared. For now, at least, I was going to keep my return a secret, but perhaps I could write and let him know I was okay. I had feared writing him before because it might allow someone to find me. Since I was headed back to Blackford anyway, that danger no longer mattered.

When I'd once again filled the wagon, I pulled it back to the woodshed. I split and stacked wood, replenishing Grandmother's wood supply. The sun had risen high in the sky, so I knew lunchtime was near. It couldn't come soon enough for me.

I walked down to the springhouse and washed off in the clear, cold overflow that came rushing out of a narrow trough. I pulled off my shirt. I was already becoming chilly now that I wasn't working. When the cool air hit my naked skin, I wondered if I could endure the chilly water. I definitely didn't want to go into Grandmother's cabin all hot, sweaty, and smelly. I had to be brave. I sputtered when the cold water hit my hot body, but I felt refreshed.

I stood in the sun a bit, drying off. It didn't seem nearly as warm out now, but I knew that was because my torso was wet and I was no longer working. I shivered a bit. I pulled my shirt back on before I was truly dry. I pulled on my sweater and reveled in the warmth. Now that I was all cleaned up, it was time to go inside for lunch.

Greeted by the heavenly scent of fried ham, I entered the cabin. It mingled with the unmistakable scent of freshly baked bread. I was hungry when I came in, but suddenly I was ravenous.

"I was just about to send Laura for you. Lunch is almost ready," Grandmother said.

I could hardly wait. Laura had already set the table, and soon we were all once again seated. There were fried potatoes to go with the ham as well as green beans and delicious hot-out-of-the-oven bread. I lathered a slice of bread with butter and strawberry jam and took a bite. I nearly moaned with sensual delight.

The ham was delicious and the fried potatoes excellent with salt and pepper. Even the green beans seemed more than ordinarily delicious. We washed down our meal with ice-cold spring water. No Coke had ever tasted as good.

After lunch, it was back to work. Laura accompanied me again. We talked as I sawed, chopped, and split wood. It was almost a shame that such a sweet little girl was hidden away in the woods, and yet her isolation was, perhaps, best for her. Laura had a chance to live a unique, peaceful life. I had no doubt life was sometimes hard in the cabin on the hill, but everything seemed more real here. The air was cleaner, the food more delicious, and even the very colors seemed more vibrant. It was as if the world elsewhere was but a poor copy of this original. Time seemed to flow more slowly in and around that cabin. There was no rush. There were no noisy cars belching exhaust fumes. There was no telephone to ring and interrupt things. There were no nosy neighbors or interfering busybodies. Kurt and I could have lived happily in such a place.

I worked steadily until the light failed. I was quite pleased with my progress. In a single day, I could not replace the wood Grandmother had used in my absence, but I had saved her much labor. I was pleased to help her in any way I could.

Supper was as delicious as lunch. I dived right into the fried chicken, mashed potatoes, and corn. We sat around the fire after supper, eating apple cobbler left over from the evening before.

I retired early. I was so exhausted I could barely undress. I swear I fell asleep before my body hit the pallet.

I stayed just two more days at the cabin, working most of the time on increasing Grandmother's wood supply. My heart yearned to remain longer, but it yearned more strongly to return to Kurt.

It was a sad goodbye when I left, for I wasn't sure if I'd ever return. I planned to do so, but who knew where life would take me? My life had already taken so many unexpected twists and turns that I'd learned to take nothing for granted. I could write Grandmother and Laura, at least, and that I promised to do. I would not allow myself to lose touch with those I had come to love.

I walked down the hill with a backpack filled with baked goods that would keep for a few days—a parting gift from Grandmother and Laura. Grandmother had also sent along a ham sandwich for my lunch. I could barely keep from eating it, even though it was only half past ten.

I walked along, saddened to be leaving Grandmother and Laura behind, but happy to be heading for the Selby farm and ultimately to Kurt. The weather had gone a bit chilly—more like the temperature one expects in February. Still, it was a rather pleasant day. The warmer temperatures would soon return; March was coming. Before long, spring itself would burst upon us.

I stopped for lunch on a sunny, grassy hillock not far from the road. The ham sandwich was heavenly. I devoured every bite. I ate a yeast roll as well. Even without butter and strawberry jam, it was sweet and delicious. When I'd finished, I was ready to set out again. My next destination was the Selby farm on the outskirts of Verona.

My journey along the country roads and highways of northern Indiana was rather pleasant—even more so than my trek in the opposite direction. There was no blizzard for one thing! My journey was far more pleasant, too, than those early days when I first left Kurt behind. Traveling toward him was much preferable to growing more distant with every step. My heart was filled now with eager anticipation instead of sadness.

I was eager to see Jack and Emma once again. I knew I wouldn't linger long on their farm. I hadn't even arrived and I was already antsy to turn my feet toward home. I could just imagine Kurt's surprise when I showed up in Blackford months and months before he expected me to return! That day was still a long way down the road, so I focused instead on the journey at hand.

I almost felt as if I'd been hiking along country roads for my entire life. My school days back in Blackford often seemed like nothing more than a distant memory. It was as if I was remembering another life I'd once led, or even the life of someone else. Kurt stood out in stark contrast to everything else, however. He was far away, but he was as much a part of my life now as he'd ever been. The mere thought of him was enough to make me smile.

The grass was beginning to turn green on the slopes of the old gravel road I followed. The honeysuckle was beginning to green up, too. Already its leaves were changing from the dark green of winter, to the light green of spring. It wouldn't be long before the honeysuckle would put on new growth. Then, the fragrant blossoms would set on. Oh, how I loved their scent!

I knew the scent of honeysuckle would remind me of home, as would the call of the whippoorwill. One of my strongest memories of my boyhood was lying in my bed at night with the window open—the call of the whippoorwill and the scent of honeysuckle wafting through the open window. In deep summer, the cicadas and hundreds of other insects made their presence known. Maybe I remembered more of my life in Blackford than I thought. Perhaps more than Kurt was drawing me back there.

In only a few days time I was once again walking through the streets of the little town that reminded me so much of Blackford. Soon, my feet were on an old country road and then on the long gravel drive that led to the Selby farm. Emma rose from her perch on the porch swing and rushed toward me when she spotted me. She had her arms wrapped around me even before the screen door of the porch slammed shut behind her.

It was mid-afternoon, and Jack was busy at work in the fields, but Emma drew me onto the porch and pushed me onto the old swing. I sat there swinging back and forth, looking out over the fields while Emma made us mugs of hot tea in the kitchen. I had insisted I was fine when she asked me if I wanted something to drink. I offered to accompany her to the kitchen when she wouldn't take no for an answer. Emma wouldn't hear of it. I was told to sit right where I was and rest my feet.

My feet sure did need a rest. I was accustomed to walking for miles without stopping, but my feet were still tired and my legs faintly ached. Nothing feels quite as good as sitting down after having been on one's feet for a long stretch.

The gentle breeze brought with it the scent of newly plowed earth. Jack was getting an early start. Dad didn't usually begin the plowing quite so early in the season. The scent of plowed earth stirred up memories of home, and I grew a little homesick. I had long ago resigned myself to being away from home for months upon months, but now that I was about to return, I was more homesick for the old family farm than ever.

Emma returned soon, and I gratefully accepted the steaming mug. It was a rather pleasant day but with a bit of chill, and the warmth of the mug and the tea were most welcome.

"I've been watching for you for days," Emma said. "I'm so glad you've made it at last."

"I stopped and visited Grandmother and Laura for a couple days, and it's a long walk from Fort Wayne. I could have taken a bus, but… well…I don't know. I guess I still need some time to think."

Emma nodded.

"You mentioned Grandmother and Laura in your letter. Tell me about them. Their life sounds fascinating—like something out of the past."

I told Emma about becoming lost in the snowstorm and nearly meeting my end. I also told her how it was the red scarf she had given me that Laura spotted from the cabin. Who knows? If Emma hadn't given me the scarf, I might've died in the blizzard.

Emma was rather distressed by my brush with death, so I quickly moved onto my rescue and the pleasant days that followed. I told her of Christmas in the cabin and of my eventual departure. Next came my tale of the journey to Fort Wayne, meeting Clarence, and my days at the Hotel Indiana. Soon, I'd worked my way right up to the present.

It was time for Emma to begin preparations for supper, so we moved into the kitchen. I sat at the old kitchen table and peeled potatoes while Emma did all the real work. Mostly, I kept her company. I knew Emma was alone for long stretches of time while Jack was out working the farm. I know she was accustomed to it, but I knew she appreciated my companionship. It was too bad she didn't have a close neighbor who could come and visit, but I guess all the other farm wives were just as busy as Emma. I knew from my limited experience that there was as much work to be done in and around the house as there was in the fields and barn. The manual labor of farm work was more strenuous, but I think that housework was actually more difficult. Preparing meals, cleaning, and doing laundry might sound easy, but I'd done enough of it on my previous visit to know that ease had *nothing* to do with it.

I looked around the old kitchen as I sat there. Everything was spotlessly clean from the floor to the counter tops to the windows. There were old prints on the walls, pale, checked curtains on the windows, and old china lovingly displayed; I could see Emma's touch everywhere.

The minutes slipped by. Emma showed me how to roll out pie dough and form it into a crust. It wasn't as easy as it looked. About the only part of pie making I was good at was dumping in the cherry filling. Cutting the narrow dough strips and forming them into the crisscross top of the pie was particularly difficult. I quickly realized that my pie talents rested in devouring rather than making them. At least I was good at something, right?

The scents coming from the range were heavenly. Even the green beans smelled delicious. The most appealing scents came from the roasting chicken, the cherry pie, and, near the end, from the yeast rolls. I had been eating fairly well on my journey from Fort Wayne, but I was ravenously hungry by the time supper rolled around.

Everything was ready, but there was no Jack. Emma sent me out to ring the old dinner bell located not far from the back door. I'd seen the bell on my previous visit, but had never heard it. I gave the rope three strong tugs and was nearly deafened by the bell. I gave it three more just in case Jack didn't hear the first time. Emma said Jack could hear the bell even when he was quite distant. It was usually reserved for emergencies, but at this time of day, it meant supper was ready.

Jack shook my hand when he walked into the kitchen just a few minutes later. Emma set out supper, and the wonderful scent in the kitchen grew more powerful than ever. We all sat down and began to pass around the platter of roasted chicken and bowls of steaming corn, green beans, and mashed potatoes. Emma had roasted the chicken with rosemary and a touch of sage, so it was particularly delicious. Everything was always delicious on the Selby farm.

I told Jack about my experiences in the Hotel Indiana, the kindness of Mr. Howard, and the wonderful little room I'd been given there. I wanted Jack to know I truly appreciated the job. I had thanked him, of course, but I didn't think just saying "Thanks" was enough.

Jack and Emma seemed to enjoy my company. They treated me like family, even though I was just a stray Jack had found on the side of the road. I found myself wishing they could have another son to replace the one they'd lost. They would make great parents, and I couldn't think of a better place to grow up than on the Selby farm—except maybe Grandmother's cabin. My own time there had increased my appreciation of farm life more than my previous fifteen years of living on my own family farm. For the first time, I thought I might want to follow in my father's footsteps.

I frowned. My father might not want to have anything to do with me. I had no idea about how he felt about me now. I might return only to discover I'd been disowned. More likely than not, that's exactly what I would find in Blackford, but I had to go back. I had to face whatever awaited me.

I only allowed myself a two-night stay with the Selbys. Part of me wanted to linger there forever, but the sooner I headed south the sooner I'd be with Kurt again. During my time with the Selbys, I visited with Jack and Emma and helped out as I could. There isn't really much to tell about my visit. Those days were some of the most pleasant I'd experienced, but they were definitely not what I'd call exciting. Feeding chickens, driving a tractor, eating delicious meals, and sitting on a porch for long spells are pleasant enough things to experience, but they don't make a good story.

On the morning of my departure, Emma prepared a huge breakfast for my sendoff. I walked downstairs to find stacks of pecan pancakes and mounds of bacon and scrambled eggs. I was a bit surprised to see Jack sitting at the table, but then again, I figured he was there to bid me goodbye before he began his day's work. I spread butter on my pancakes and drowned them in maple syrup. Emma's pancakes were the best! I loved the scrambled eggs, and the bacon was just right—chewy, but not underdone. Everything was delicious, but then I had yet to taste anything made by Emma that wasn't.

By the end of breakfast, I was quite stuffed. I knew I wouldn't be hungry for a good long time, even with hours and hours of walking ahead. Unbeknownst to me, a pleasant surprise awaited me. Jack was driving me all the way to Kokomo!

"You don't have to do that," I said when he told me. That's got to be three hours of driving, round trip."

"I have a part to pick up in Kokomo," Jack said. "For once even Wahlberg's Farm Store in Verona didn't have the tractor part I needed. They can have it shipped in, but I need it now. If I drive to Kokomo I can pick it up today."

I suspected Jack could wait for delivery of the part, but I didn't say so. He had obviously made up his mind, and there was no use arguing. Besides, that hour-and-a-half drive to Kokomo would save me days of walking. I felt closer to Blackford already.

Emma loaded me down with food for the trip, enough to last me for a few days. I had plenty of cash with me and had no worries about going without, but anything prepared by Emma was better than what I could pick up during my journey. I knew I'd have fond memories of the Selby farm whenever I dipped into the supplies sent by Emma. I was getting nostalgic about the farm even as Emma gave me a goodbye hug.

Jack and I were on the road before ten, headed for Kokomo in his shiny green Ford pickup. At first, we just looked at the passing scenery, but then we began to talk.

"How do you feel about going home, Angel?" Jack asked. I had the feeling he asked me that question more to draw me out and give me advice than to satisfy his own curiosity.

"Excited, nervous, and frightened."

"What frightens you?"

"The reception I may receive. My life may be a living hell when I return. What scares me the most are my parents. I don't know how they'll feel about me. Clarence's mom said that if Clarence ran away, she'd be glad to have him back no matter what. I have a feeling my mom will still love me, but my dad…well…I just don't know."

"It's hard to know how anyone will react to such a thing. I won't even pretend to know how your parents feel. Having lost a son myself, I think your parents may be so relieved to have you back home safe they'll be a good deal more understanding than they would've been otherwise. Your absence and not knowing if you would ever come back, has given your parents a lot of time to think through things. Of course, that in no way guarantees they'll welcome you back, but there is hope."

Jack took his eyes off the road for a moment to look at me.

"If things don't work out so well for you, Angel, you are welcome to come back and stay with Emma and me as long as you'd like. You'll always have a home with us."

I wasn't one to cry easily, but that did it. Tears welled up in my eyes and flowed down my cheeks as a sob escaped from my throat. Jack reached over and patted my knee.

"I will say I think you're doing the right thing by going back. However things work out, I think it's important for you to resolve things with your parents. You'll know where you stand. That's important."

"I'm going in expecting trouble—not from my parents so much, but from others. I pretty much told the entire school off when I left. I made plenty of enemies."

"It's best to be prepared," Jack said. "I'd like to tell you that everything will be all right, but I just don't know. People can get very unreasonable about some things. They can be very ugly. I'm afraid you've got a hard road ahead, Angel. I'm not just talking about the reception that awaits you, but your whole life."

"Yeah. I know. I also know I am what I am. I don't know if I would've chosen to be what I am—probably not, because it's a hard road as you said—but I'm not ashamed. I figure I was meant to be this way. For what purpose, I don't know, but there has to be some reason."

"You may well be right about that. I know you're right about one thing. You have no reason to be ashamed. You should be very proud of yourself, Angel. You're a fine young man. I like to think that if my Angel had survived, that he'd be as strong-willed and confident as you."

"Thank you," I said, meaning those two words far more than I usually did. Jack had just paid me a huge compliment, and I knew it. I hadn't known him long, but I had the feeling he didn't give out praise lightly.

I hoped that someday Jack would have his own son. Even if he and Emma were afraid to try again, perhaps Jack would pick up another stray boy like me and take him in. Of course, if things didn't work out with my parents I might very well be back. If my family didn't want me, I couldn't think of a better place to be than the Selby farm. Even living in Fort Wayne wouldn't be as good as living with Emma and Jack. Just knowing I could go there if I needed to made me feel much more secure.

Jack and I talked about farming most of the rest of the way to Kokomo. Jack had a real love for farm life. I had no doubt he was exactly where he was supposed to be. He was rather lucky, despite his misfortunes, because he spent his days doing what he loved.

Jack and I didn't immediately part company when we reached Kokomo. Over my protest, he took me to a café and bought me lunch. I didn't put up much of a fight. It was hard to say no to Jack.

Sadness enveloped me when it was time to say goodbye. There were few truly good people in the world, but Jack was one of them. I hugged him tightly after we said goodbye, and he hugged me right back. I watched as he climbed into his Ford, waved, and drove away. I wondered if I'd ever see him again.

It wasn't quite one p.m., so I turned to the south and began the last, long leg of my journey home. Miles and miles lay ahead, but at the end of those miles was Kurt. I would've walked to the ends of the earth to hold him in my arms once more.

Kurt

Tommy, Tanner, and I took it upon ourselves to keep Tyler occupied after the death of Martin Wolfe. With Tyler's permission, I'd told Tommy about his relationship with Martin, such as it was. Tanner already knew.

In a way, I felt as if Tyler shouldn't have been so shaken by Martin's death. There was never that much of a relationship between them in the first place. It's not as if they'd dated. They hadn't even been close friends. There had been nothing between them at all for some four years now—not since Tyler was eleven. I guess death can affect people in strange ways, though. In Tyler's case, it made him miss something he never really had in the first place. I've heard that the words "might have been" are the saddest of all. Perhaps it's true. In any case, the sadness Tyler felt was quite real, and so those of us who cared about him tried to help him through the rough times. After all, isn't that what friends are for?

Tommy, of course, was heavily involved with his woman. He didn't have as much time to spare for Tyler as Tanner and I did. He didn't have as much time for me as he did in the old days. I guess it was inevitable that a girl come between us. I don't mean our friendship suffered, just that we didn't spend nearly as much time hanging out as we once did. We walked home together after school less and less, but we still walked to school together each morning.

Tommy's absence from my life could have been a problem, but in helping Tyler, I helped myself. I didn't have time to sit and miss Tommy, because I was too busy making sure Tyler wasn't getting down in the dumps. Tyler became a replacement for Tommy in a way. He filled many of the hours formerly occupied by my best friend.

Sometimes, Tyler came home with me after school, and we did our homework in my bedroom. Sometimes, we went to his house and played Monopoly or card games with his brother. Often, we went out for supper to the Black Heifer or caught a movie at the Delphi. Tyler loved movies. He was capable of becoming completely lost in the images on the screen. That was exactly what Tyler needed: to lose himself and forget about Martin Wolfe.

I had a ton of fun with Tyler. I definitely wasn't making a big sacrifice by hanging out with him. Tyler and I became close. Tyler's friendship brightened up my life and made it much easier to keep myself from pining for Angel. Whenever I started to get sad about the absence of my boyfriend, I remembered Ryan's words and lost myself in life—just as I was trying to help Tyler to do.

Tyler and I caught *The Greatest Show on Earth* at the Delphi on a Friday evening. Tanner was supposed to join us, but something came up at the last minute. Tyler told me he suspected *someone* had come up. Tanner had been spending a lot of time away from home. Tyler suspected he was hanging out with someone—that perhaps his brother even had a boyfriend.

The movie was great. I loved anything with Jimmy Stewart in it. Stewart wasn't one of the main characters, but I didn't care. I even spotted Bob Hope and Bing Crosby as spectators in the audience—of the circus, not the movie. I was quite sure neither Hope nor Crosby would ever come to Blackford, Indiana.

Tyler and I shared a big tub of popcorn during the show. We also pigged out on candy bars and taffy. We'd planned to eat after the movie, but neither of us was hungry when we walked out under the flashing marquee. Instead of heading for the Black Heifer, we walked toward my house instead.

"I wonder what Tommy's up to tonight," I said. "It's a Friday, so I bet he's probably with Alicia."

"Didn't you see them? They were at the movie," Tyler said.

"They were?"

"Yeah, about eight rows back. I doubt they noticed us. Every time I looked at them they were making out."

I laughed.

"And poor Tommy thought he'd never find a girl."

"Do you really think there's someone for everyone, Kurt?"

"Sure. I don't see why not. If I can find someone, surely anyone can."

Tyler rolled his eyes, but it was a bit hard to see in the darkness.

Sam wasn't home yet when Tyler and I walked into my room, but that was no big surprise. He was most likely out on a date as well. He and Betty had been going out for quite a while. I wondered if they'd get married some day. For some reason, I just couldn't picture Sam married.

"Maybe we should run away and join the circus," Tyler said as we both flopped down on my bed.

"Yeah. I could have a great career selling popcorn and peanuts. If I want to do that, I'll just apply for a job at the Delphi."

"I was thinking of something a bit more exciting—like lion tamer or trapeze artist."

"I don't think I'd much like climbing in a cage with a lion or walking on a high wire. I'll just stay on the ground and away from the wild animals, if you don't mind."

Tyler and I were lying on our backs. He turned his head and gave me a smirk.

"Maybe we could get you a job as a bunny tamer. Think you could handle that? Or are bunnies too scary for you?"

I poked Tyler hard in the ribs. He pounced on me. We struggled on the bed.

"I'll show you a bunny tamer. You think you're funny, don't you?"

I wrestled Tyler onto his back and tickled him. He laughed and squirmed beneath me, but kept repeating "bunny tamer" in between laughs. Suddenly, he pushed me off. A few moments later, I found myself on my back with Tyler holding my wrists over my head. I feared he'd tickle me. Oh, how I hated that! Sam used to tickle me until I couldn't breathe.

Tyler looked down at me and smiled. His face became more serious. He leaned in toward me, pressed his lips to mine, and kissed me. I kissed him back. I felt his tongue slip into my mouth.

"No," I said, although the word was muffled. "No!"

I squirmed out from beneath Tyler and stood. My breath came hard and fast.

"Please," Tyler said. There was a pleading tone in his voice that tore at my heart.

"No. We can't. I love Angel."

"What if Angel doesn't come back? We could…"

"Don't say that!" I yelled. "Don't you ever say that! He is coming back! I know he is!"

"I just meant…I'm sorry…I just…"

Tyler lost it. Tears sprang from his eyes, and he began to cry.

I crossed the distance between us and took him in my arms. Tyler hugged me and cried on my shoulder.

"I'm sorry," he said between sobs.

I held Tyler. His tears didn't last long, but his racking sobs bore witness to the pain inside him. When he quieted, he stepped back and wiped his eyes.

"I shouldn't have done that," Tyler said.

"No. You shouldn't have."

Tyler's pain weakened my anger toward him, but it did nothing to take the edge off the anger I felt toward myself.

"I shouldn't have kissed you back," I said.

"You didn't…Well, not for more than a second."

I turned away from Tyler, a scowl upon my face.

"Kurt, you didn't do anything wrong."

"I kissed you."

"No. I kissed you. You kissed me back for a moment only."

"I still did it."

"It was just a reaction. As soon as you realized what you were doing, you pulled away. I saw it in your eyes."

"I still feel like a jerk."

"I'm the jerk, Kurt. Damn. I'm sorry. I'm really sorry."

I smiled slightly.

"Yeah. I guess you are a jerk."

Tyler gave me a goofy grin.

"It's just that…I *really* like you, Kurt. I *really* need someone."

"I can't be that someone, Tyler. I love Angel. I'm in love with him."

"I know."

Tyler turned away for a moment, and then turned back to me.

"Kissing you like that was stupid. I knew it was wrong when I did it. I just couldn't stop myself. I feel really awful now that you feel so bad about it."

"I guess it wasn't that bad," I said. "I'm sure Angel would tell me to just shut up and forget about it."

"You're not going to tell him, are you?" Tyler's voice shook.

"No."

"Good. He'd probably kick my ass."

"I don't think he'd do that. I think he would understand."

"You don't know how lucky you are, Kurt," Tyler said. Tears welled up in his eyes again. "Angel isn't here now, but you still have him."

"Sometimes I don't feel so lucky. I miss him."

"I'm sure you do. The point is: you have someone to miss."

We stood there in silence for a few moments.

"Tyler, I…for what it's worth…if I didn't have Angel…well, I'd be interested in you."

"Yeah?"

"Yeah."

Another silence followed. I was reluctant to bring up the topic that had entered my mind, but I sensed Tyler needed to talk about it. I forced myself to speak.

"Tyler, um...what about Tanner? I mean, you guys...mess around, right?"

"Yeah."

"Isn't he kind of...like a boyfriend?" I asked.

I just knew my face was turning red.

"No. It's not like that. We love each other, sure. We're brothers. More than that, we're twins. We're closer than most people imagine, and I'm not just talking about sex. I love my brother, but he's not the same as a boyfriend. You know? I don't think I can explain it."

"I...don't know what to say."

"Talking about it kind of freaks you out, doesn't it?"

"Yeah."

"We don't have to."

"No. It's okay. You're my friend, Tyler. I care about you. You can tell me anything."

"Thank you."

I smiled at Tyler.

"I love Tanner, but...sometimes I think it's wrong. Brothers aren't really supposed to do that. Are they?"

I shrugged my shoulders.

"I don't think they are, even twins. I like it. It makes me feel good. It makes me feel loved and yet...it makes me feel kind of unnatural."

I didn't say anything. What could I say? I knew nothing of such things.

"I'm glad Tanner and I are so close. I feel like we've shared something special. I don't want to stop, but then again I do. The older we get, the more wrong it feels. I don't want to hurt him by saying no, but sometimes I think it would be better if we didn't have sex."

"Maybe you should tell Tanner how you feel."

"Maybe. I don't know. I do know that I need someone else in my life. I mean, what am I going to do? Date my brother? I wish Tanner and I could both find boyfriends."

"You probably will."

"I don't know about that. You know what it's like for guys like us—homosexuals, I mean."

I nodded.

"I still think you'll find someone."

"I hope so, but what about Tanner?"

"He loves you, Tyler. I'm sure he wants you to be happy. I'm sure he'll be happy when you find a boyfriend, even though it will mean the end of a physical relationship between you. You'll still be close. You'll still love each other."

"Yeah. I'll always love Tanner. I don't think I could have made it this far without him."

"So talk to him. Tell him how you feel. Maybe you can just ease off a bit."

Tyler grinned. "Thanks, Kurt. You're a really good friend for talking to me about this. I know it's uncomfortable for you."

"Well. It's… yeah."

Tyler giggled.

"I don't think most people could understand. They would just think we were nasty, but it's not like that."

"I've never thought that. If you want the truth, the thought of you and Tanner together both attracts and repels me at the same time. I can't really put it any plainer than that. I don't understand it myself."

"I appreciate your honesty, Kurt. I'm really sorry about kissing you. Well, mostly sorry. Part of me is glad I did it. At least I got to kiss you once."

"Just don't do it again or Angel will kick your ass when he comes back."

"Don't worry. I'm not about to cross your boyfriend or to risk messing up what you've got with him. I'll say it again. You're very lucky, Kurt."

"Yes. I am."

Tyler hugged me. I held him in my arms for several long moments. I waited until he released me. Tyler needed to know that someone cared about him. Sometimes words aren't enough.

Angel

I walked along the lonely road, and yet I was not alone. I could feel Kurt as if he was beside me, or perhaps inside me. He was a part of me. Maybe I'd made a mistake when I'd left. I should at least have given Kurt the opportunity to come with me. I'd sought to spare him from the pain I experienced at parting from my friends and family, but perhaps I'd introduced a far worse pain. My intentions were good, but, as they say, the road to hell is paved with good intentions.

I hoped Kurt understood why I'd done what I'd done. I wondered if he'd be angry that I left like I did. I left to save him, but how would I feel if our roles were reversed?

There was no use dwelling on the past. I couldn't change it. However, I could alter the present. That, I was doing by going home.

I walked along under sunlight and starlight—thinking—always thinking. I could have made the journey much quicker by bus. I had plenty of money. Sometimes, I was tempted, but something kept me from buying a ticket. I guess I just needed to think things out. Despite all the solitary hours of the last few months I still had a lot of thinking to do—about Kurt, me, Kurt and me, my home, my family, and my life. I yearned to rush to Kurt, but I knew in my heart that it wasn't time to be with him—not quite yet.

The miles slipped underfoot. There was no need to stop and earn my keep now. I had plenty of funds to see me to Blackford and away again if necessary. If I did have to flee a second time, I knew I was welcome on the Selby farm and at the Hotel Indiana. Grandmother would welcome me, too. Knowing I had somewhere to go made the unknown that lay ahead far less frightening.

Even so, I wondered what awaited me in my old hometown. Most important was Kurt, of course, but I had little doubt he'd welcome me back. Even if he was angry with me, he'd still love me. I knew it in my heart.

I was less sure about my parents. I could probably count on my mom to love me, even if she didn't approve. I wasn't so sure about my dad. He knew I was something that most people considered disgusting and vile. Was he ashamed of me now? Did he wish he had no son?

If they rejected me, then my parents' love didn't matter anymore. Yet, it did. If my father told me to leave and not come back, a part of me would always hurt. I could tell myself he didn't matter. I could let anger burn away love. Still, some little part of me would carry the pain of rejection with me—forever.

As far as my friends were concerned, well, I didn't have any. Adam and the gang had never really been my friends. They were teammates and barely that—nothing more. The team had been my life—first by choice and then by necessity. Most of them were gone now. Good riddance. The few that remained surely hated me. Everyone hates homos. That's just the way it is. It's not fair, but then life isn't fair. If I were to list the unfair things in life, I could do so all the way back to Blackford. When I arrived, I still wouldn't be finished.

I didn't want to dwell on the unfairness of life. I planned to spend my time more pleasantly. Every step took me closer to Kurt. The very thought of Kurt made me smile. The weather was a bit chilly, especially at night. As expected, the warm spell that had hit when I visited Grandmother's didn't last. As Robert Frost said: nothing gold can stay. Still, the chill was welcome in its way. It was an incentive to start out early each morning. Walking in the sun warmed me. Every time I reached a little town with a café, I stopped for a bite and some hot tea. Such rest stops were a welcome respite from my long hike.

I stopped for other rests, too, but I walked as long and far as I could each day. I walked on into the night. When I stopped at last, finding some comfy spot in the grass or upon the moss, my legs sighed with relief. I loved to lie back and look up at the stars. No matter how far I walked, they were the same each night. I sometimes wondered if

Kurt was looking up at the stars, too. If so, we were looking upon the exact same sky. That thought brought me comfort.

Slowly, the miles passed. When I reached Cloverdale, hills began to rise up out of the flat plain. By Spencer, I was truly in hilly country again. Each small town was a mile marker, indicating I was closer to home—Freedom, Worthington, Newberry, Elnora, Plainville, and other even smaller places. Finally, I walked through Washington and several miles later, Petersburg. I was back in familiar territory. Blackford was but a few miles distant. My heart beat faster with each step I took. I was returning home, but I felt as if I was beginning a grand adventure.

Kurt

Spring came early. Well, it wasn't truly spring yet, but it felt like it. In mid-March, the daffodils and tulips popped up. The increasingly warmer weather fooled us all into believing the winter was truly behind us. I should've known better. Winter made a surprise comeback near the end of March—not long before baseball season was scheduled to begin, no less! The surprise attack was a particularly nasty one, coming on the heels of such excellent weather. One day the temperatures were in the mid-60s, and the next they plummeted to freezing. I woke up that morning and looked out my window amazed. Snow! It was snowing!

I nearly froze my face off walking to school, even though I was wearing a toboggan and scarf. The cold felt especially brutal after such wonderful warmth. What a cruel joke Mother Nature played on us all. I was definitely going to hit Sam up for a ride the next morning if the temperatures didn't climb significantly. I couldn't take this winter weather in spring! I thawed off somewhat while waiting for Tommy to finish breakfast, but the short walk from his house to school threatened to freeze us both solid.

The warmth of the school was cozy and inviting. So many of us took simple things like warmth for granted. As they so often did, my thoughts flowed to Angel. Was he safe and warm somewhere, or had the sudden reappearance of winter weather taken him unawares? Perhaps he was somewhere far to the south where it was warm, but he could just as easily be somewhere far more cold. I knew I'd never truly rest easy until we were back together, but it seemed as if that time would never come.

I had a pleasant enough day in school. I was caught up on all my schoolwork and even had some reports written up ahead of time. That was somewhat surprising, as I had spent so much time outside. I was often with the Nudo twins, especially Tyler. Tyler and I were closer than ever after our talk. We were more relaxed around each other, too. Getting everything out in the open had cleared the air. Spending time with him and my other friends was so much fun I was constantly tempted to let my schoolwork slip, but I resisted the temptation. I liked most of my classes and loved some. I was glad I wasn't one of those kids who hated school. Walking through the front doors of the school every day must have been dreadful for them. Me? I had fun!

Tommy was, of course, still disgustingly happy about dating Alicia. There were times when I, and sometimes others, had to tell him to shut up, because he talked about her *all* the time. On those occasions, when we did tell Tommy to shut up, he giggled and a dreamy look crossed his face. The boy was obviously in love. I was happy for him. The annoyance of listening to Tommy talk about Alicia-this and Alicia-that was more than offset by his happiness.

The sudden appearance of winter in spring was nothing to the surprise that awaited us when Tommy and I walked out the front doors at the end of the day. There was a blizzard outside! I'd been admiring yellow daffodils and new green leaves only the day before. Now snow was falling so thick and fast that white was the only color I could see! To make matters worse, the wind was swirling the snow around like crazy.

"This is insane," I told Tommy.

"I can't even see the street!" Tommy said. "Maybe you'd better go back in and see if you can find your brother. You can't walk home in this. Kurt? Kurt?"

I just stood there staring at the ghost emerging from the whirlwind of white. I could hear Tommy, but I wasn't paying the slightest attention. The blizzard was completely forgotten as well; I could not believe me eyes.

"Kurt?" Tommy asked. "Kurt!"

No. It couldn't be. My eyes were playing tricks on me again. How many times had I thought I'd caught a glimpse of him?

I stood completely still, staring hard into the snow. My heart began beating faster.

"Kurt, what is it?" Tommy said at my side, his voice trembling.

I ignored Tommy and kept staring into the swirling snow. The mirage that had disappeared so many times before wasn't going away. It was getting bigger and clearer. Angel was walking toward me, his long hair flying in the wind. Beside me, Tommy drew in a sharp breath.

"Angel," he whispered.

I wasn't going crazy. Tommy saw him, too. I began to run toward him. Have you ever seen a movie where a pair of lovers runs toward each other in slow motion? Well, this wasn't like that at all. Nearly blinded by my own tears, I darted toward Angel with all the speed I could muster. I slipped, slid, and nearly went down, but I kept right on running. Angel ran toward me, and we collided with each other, wrapped our arms around each other, and hugged as if we would never let go.

"Angel. You're here. You're really here!"

I lost it. I couldn't help it. Tears flowed down my cheeks. I hadn't expected to see Angel again for two more years, and there he was! I was so happy I couldn't stand it.

Tommy trotted up beside us and smiled.

"Am I dreaming?" I asked. "This has to be a dream."

"No, Kurt. This is no dream. I've come home," Angel said.

I couldn't believe Angel was really, truly there. I just knew I'd wake up and find myself alone in bed. I held onto Angel for dear life.

"I've missed you so much. I love you! Don't ever go away again!"

"Um, guys," Tommy said. "This isn't the place."

Tommy's warning was a little bit of reality that gave me my first real hope that this was not a dream. I looked around. The snowstorm all but hid us from view. I pulled away from Angel, and we stood there smiling at each other.

The Nudo Twins bounded up behind us, smiling identical smiles as they spotted Angel and me together.

"Whoa! You're back!" Tyler or Tanner said. I couldn't tell which.

I just kept staring at Angel. I couldn't believe it was really him!

"Let's go somewhere and talk," Angel said, still grinning at me.

"Yeah, but where? My parents are sure to be home."

"You could come home with me, but my mom will be home," Tommy said.

"Our parents are gone for the evening," said one of the twins.

"Could we come to your house?" Angel asked. "We could go to a restaurant or something, but someone would be sure to see us."

"Of course you can come," said one of the twins. "We homos have to stick together."

Angel gazed at the twins, probably wondering just how much they knew.

"You're welcome, too, of course, Tommy, even though you like girls," said the twin.

Tommy laughed. "Thanks, but I've got homework, and I'm afraid my parents have my evening planned for me. Why do you think I'm not with Alicia?" Tommy turned toward me and grinned. "I'm very happy for you, Kurt."

"Thanks," I said, wiping tears out of my eyes. Tommy knew what this meant to me.

Tommy looked at Angel and nodded.

"I'm glad you're back, Angel," Tommy said. "Now Kurt can quit mooning over you."

Angel smiled. "Thanks, Tommy."

"Go hang out with your woman, Tommy," I said. "You haven't seen her for ten minutes. You're probably suffering withdrawal."

"If only I *could* see her now," Tommy said wistfully.

Tommy drew his coat around himself and trudged toward his house. Angel and I followed the twins as they walked toward home. I kept looking over at Angel, still not completely sure this wasn't a dream. What a cruel thing dreams could be: pretending to give us exactly what we wanted only to snatch it away again. On the other hand, I sometimes felt as if I was really with Angel in my dreams. Those dream visits had kept me going for all the long months of waiting for Angel's return. I hoped and prayed this was no dream, but if it was, I intended to enjoy it as long as it lasted and use it as a reminder of the day when Angel would return to me.

As dreamlike as the idea of Angel returning might be, the biting cold, the snow stinging my eyes, and the regular passing of time weren't dreamlike at all. The twins remained the twins as they trudged along in front of us. Angel remained Angel. Culver Street remained Culver Street as we walked away from the school. The scene didn't suddenly shift to another place or time. The snow didn't change into rain. Everything remained reassuringly constant. Two things bothered me, though. The winter storm in spring was far too unreal, and Angel's return was too good to be true.

My cheeks were numb by the time we reached the Nudo home. The warmth surrounded us as we entered, and it felt good to shut the snow and wind outside. We pulled off coats, gloves, scarves, and toboggans as we stood in the entranceway. All the while Angel and I gazed at each other. When we were at last free of our excess clothing, Angel and I grabbed each other and held each other tight.

"You're really here," I said. "This isn't a dream. You've really come back."

"I've really come back."

Angel and I pressed our noses together and stared into one another's eyes. We grinned and tears ran down our cheeks.

"Why don't you take Angel to our room, Kurt?" one of the twins suggested. "I know if I had a boyfriend and hadn't seen him in months, I'd want some time alone with him. Tanner and I will stay down here. You can join us when you're finished."

"Just remember we've got school tomorrow," Tanner said, grinning. "And, Mom and Dad will be back by ten."

I'm sure I turned red, but I smiled at the twins.

"Thanks."

"Could I take a shower first?" Angel asked.

"Sure. Use our bathroom. Washcloths and towels are in the cabinet."

"Thanks, guys," Angel said.

I took Angel by the hand and led him upstairs.

"The twins seem to know all about us," Angel said as we walked to Tyler and Tanner's bedroom.

"They do. I told them everything not too long ago. I needed someone to talk to, and I saw no harm."

"I'm glad you've had someone to talk to while I was gone."

We'd reached the bedroom by then. We walked inside and closed the door. Angel pulled me to him and kissed me.

"I want you right now, Kurt, but I'd better shower first. There aren't many opportunities to bathe on the road, and you don't need a smelly boyfriend."

"I guess I can wait a few more minutes," I said. "But, hurry!"

Angel laughed. It was a laugh of joy. I knew without a doubt he was as glad to be back as I was to have him back. Now, that's saying something!

I paced the room while Angel showered. I was tempted to jump in with him. It was funny how impatient I was. After all, Angel had returned months and months before I expected him. Part of me wondered why and what this would mean for us, but all that truly mattered was that Angel was back!

At last, Angel walked out of the bathroom wearing only a towel.

"Oh, my gosh! You're beautiful," I said.

I ran to him, took him in my arms, and kissed him.

We were all over each other from that moment on. Angel ripped my shirt over my head. I jerked away his towel. We kissed while Angel pulled off my remaining clothing. Soon, we were naked together on the bed. Our hands, lips, and tongues were everywhere.

We couldn't get enough of each other. It had been so long since we'd been together. I'd been so worried about Angel. Now here he was, in my arms. We must've have made wild, passionate love for at least an hour. When we finished, we were both panting.

Angel pulled me to him and kissed me. I began to cry.

"I missed you soooo much."

We hugged and kissed a bit more, but the twins were waiting on us. We climbed out of bed, dressed, and walked downstairs. We found the twins in the kitchen cooking spaghetti.

"Did anyone get hurt?" one of the twins asked.

"No," Angel said, grinning. He wrapped his arm around my shoulder as we stood there.

"I'll put in the garlic toast, now that you two have come up for air. Have a seat guys. Supper will be ready in just a few minutes."

"Thank you for being so kind to me," Angel said. "And thank you for looking after Kurt while I was gone."

"Hey, as I said, we homos have to stick together. Besides, who wouldn't want to help a guy as cute as Kurt. If he wasn't your boyfriend, I would've been all over him."

I knew then it was Tyler speaking. Angel smiled.

Now that Angel and I had satisfied our mutual physical need, I asked the question that had been preying on my mind.

"Why did you come back, Angel? I'm so very glad you're back. I've hoped and prayed for your return. But, I wasn't expecting you for two years!"

"It's a long story," my boyfriend said. "I'll tell you everything when we have the time, but I realized I couldn't keep running forever. I realized, too, that running wasn't solving my problems. Sure, it kept me safe from whatever awaited me here, but sooner or later I'd have to come back and face the music. I decided on sooner. Life on the road is hard, and every moment away from you was torment. I know things are going to be rough for me here, but I've got to face my problems. I've got to take the adventure life has planned for me."

"I'm just so glad to have you back," I said, taking Angel's hand.

"I'm glad to be back."

"Adam and his gang are in jail," I said.

"Yeah. I managed to get hold of some newspapers and find that out quite a while back."

"So, at least they won't try to kill you."

"True, but others might. If you remember, I told the entire town to fuck off when I left."

"I remember."

"That was the best!" Tanner said. "Some of the guys were so pissed! I laughed my ass off."

"Yeah, and they'll be more than happy to beat my ass now that I'm back," Angel said.

"Angel…" I said.

"It will be okay, Kurt. I'm not going down without a fight, and I know how to take care of myself. I'll just have to deal with most of the school, and the town, hating me."

"Oh, I don't know," Tanner said. "Word has gotten around about how you saved Kurt from Adam and those jerks. Some people think you're a hero. Noah Taber has been taking up for you in your absence, too. Big time. He's told everyone how you tried to save his little brother. That came out in the trial, too."

Angel smiled.

"You're going to find that most people don't believe you're a homosexual," Tyler said.

"After reading my letter, how could they not believe it?" Angel asked.

"Think about it. Most people won't even say the word 'homosexual' out loud. Homosexuals are only shadowy mythical creatures in a far-off land. Most people around here simply don't believe they exist. They're naïve, true, but that's the way it is. As far as most of Blackford is concerned, you might as well have announced you were an elf or a leprechaun."

Angel actually laughed out loud at that.

"That's good news. Great news. I figured the whole town would be ready to lynch me."

"Not even close," Tanner said. "A lot of people consider you a hero. At the very least, most admire your courage in going up against

Adam's gang. Few believe that a guy with that kind of courage can be a homosexual."

"Here's to stereotypes!" Angel said raising his glass.

We all clinked our glasses against his.

"Yeah, this is great news," Angel said. "I'm sure there will still be plenty of guys more than willing to use me as a punching bag, but at least everyone isn't against me."

"Maybe your badass reputation will help," Tyler said. "I know I was always scared of you."

"I'm going to need all the help I can get."

I was about to cry again, and this time not for joy.

"Don't worry, Kurt," Angel said, squeezing my hand. "No matter what happens I'll be happy because I'm with you."

I managed a weak smile.

"I don't want anyone to hurt you," I said.

"You're going to have to be strong, Kurt. This isn't going to be easy. My first task will be to face my parents."

"What will you do if they won't let you come back home?" Tanner asked.

"I'll live in a barn. I'll do whatever I have to do."

I was frightened for Angel, but he didn't seem frightened at all. How could he be so strong?

"The toast is ready!" Tanner said, pulling it out of the oven. "Let's eat!"

We all filled our plates and got right down to the business of eating. The scent of oregano had made me ravenously hungry.

"This is so good," Angel said. "I've been mostly living on stale rolls for the last three days."

I looked at Angel. All the fears I'd had when he was gone came back.

"It's okay, Kurt. I didn't exist on stale baked goods all the time. I have some stories to tell you about that! Sometimes I ate like a king!"

I relaxed. Whatever Angel had been through had not changed him. Whatever hardships he'd faced were over. If Angel had to run for it again, I was going with him. No matter what, I refused to be parted from him again.

I could barely finish my big plate of spaghetti, but Angel had two. I wondered how long it had been since he'd had a good meal. I was going to make sure he never went hungry again. If his parents wouldn't take him back in, then I'd find a way to bring him food, wherever he was.

"So, what's the plan?" Tyler asked once we'd finished supper.

"I walk Kurt home and then go to see my parents."

"And if they slam the door in your face?" Tanner asked.

"Then I'll sleep in the barn tonight. Either way, I'm returning to school tomorrow. I've missed nearly an entire school year, so I'll see what I can do to make that up, if I can make it up. I wouldn't be surprised if they don't stick me back in my freshman classes."

"It's too cold to sleep in a barn," I said.

"Don't worry, Kurt. I've slept in a lot of barns. Believe me, I won't freeze to death. The last few months have toughened me up considerably. Besides, this is spring! This freak winter weather can't possibly last more than a few days. I couldn't believe it when it started snowing."

"You were tougher than anyone else I knew before you left," Tanner said. "If you're tougher now, you must be invincible."

Angel grinned.

The twins gathered up some food for Angel to take with him. "Just in case," they said.

"Thanks, guys."

I had always liked the twins, but my opinion of them went way up because of what they were doing for Angel. I'd never forget it.

"Well, I might as well get this over with—one way or another," Angel said.

We thanked the twins for supper and for the use of their bedroom. Angel and I walked out into the blizzard. The snow was still coming down fast and hard and swirling around like crazy. It was a good thing I'd called home and told my parents I'd be at the Nudos for a while. Otherwise, they would have had the cops searching snow banks for me.

"Angel, no matter what happens, don't ever run away and leave me behind again. Okay? No matter how bad things get, don't leave me. What you did for me by leaving that letter was beyond incredible. You managed to turn back time and make everything okay for me, but the price was too high, Angel. Being without you was worse than anything that's ever happened to me. It was worse than anything that could happen. I tried to make the best of it, because I knew that's what you would want. I did a fair job, I guess, but I never stopped missing you. I felt as though part of me was gone. So, whatever happens, don't ever leave me behind again. Even if it's for my own good. Even if it's to save my life. If you have to run again, take me with you. Promise me."

Angel looked at me through the flying snow. I could sense his reluctance.

"Promise me."

Angel nodded. "I promise."

I smiled. I knew that once Angel made a promise, he would keep it. Angel smiled back at me. I think that promise made him feel secure. He knew that no matter what, we'd be together. Only death would part us. Maybe death itself wouldn't even pull us apart.

"Are you scared?" I asked. "About talking to your parents?"

"A little. No matter what happens, my life is about to change. Whether they accept me or not, nothing will ever be the same again. Life on the road was an adventure, but I think life back in Blackford is going to be an even bigger adventure."

"Whatever happens, we're in it together."

"I think it might be best if you kept a little distance from me, Kurt. Being associated with me is going to be dangerous. Things could get ugly."

"I've kept my distance from you for long enough. As Tanner said, we've got to stick together."

"Kurt, people will get suspicious if you're too friendly with me. I'm walking back into that school tomorrow as an outcast. Whatever friends I had are my friends no longer. I'll be an outsider. Anyone who is the least bit friendly to me is going to be noticed. If people see you being chummy with me, they may begin to wonder about you, too. You could be right back where you were before I left town."

"Then, that's what will happen. We'll be outcasts together."

"Kurt, I don't want to see you get hurt!"

"I know the danger I'm facing, Angel. I'm not going into this blind. I've faced the danger before. I know it's going to be unpleasant. I know it may very well get ugly. There's only one thing worse I can imagine, and that's being separated from you again. I appreciate what you did for me, but all the time you were gone and I was safe, I kept wishing I had you back. There wasn't a moment I wasn't willing to trade in that safety to have you back in my life again. My wish has been granted. You're back with me. This is how I want things to be, Angel. Even if they kill us, I'm going to spend my last moments with you. Whatever time we've got is worth more than a life without you, Angel."

"What did I do to deserve such an incredible boyfriend?" Angel asked.

"Hmm. You saved my life. You sacrificed yourself for me. I can go on if you like."

Angel stopped, pulled me to him, and kissed me. The swirling snow hid us from view. It was as if angels were hiding us from prying eyes. I hoped the angels were watching over us because we were going to need all the help we could get.

Angel

I kissed Kurt near the driveway to his farm and then continued along the old country road toward my own home. I had one incredible boyfriend. I had wondered if returning to Blackford was a wise idea, but after talking to Kurt, I knew I'd made the right decision. I'd left to spare him pain, but my absence had brought him another kind of pain—a pain that was, perhaps, more difficult to endure than verbal and physical abuse. Kurt would never know how relieved I was when he made me promise never to leave him again. I wanted to protect him, but the truth was I needed him. I didn't see how I could survive without him.

Soon, I was standing by the familiar old fence, peering through the swirling snow at my old home. I could barely see it through the blizzard. I didn't know what awaited me when I walked through the door, but I'd faced a lot of dangers in my life, and there would likely be many more to come. Somehow, walking through the doorway of my old home seemed more frightening than anything I'd faced before.

I took a deep breath and stepped up the driveway. Golden light shone through the windows, illuminating the falling snow. I suddenly felt very young again—a mere boy—and trembled with the thought that my parents might not love me anymore.

As I waded through the snow, the back door flew open and my mother came running toward me in her housecoat and slippers. She was both smiling and crying. Before I knew what hit me, she had wrapped her arms around me and hugged me close.

"Angel! Angel! I thought I'd never see you again."

Mom truly began to cry then.

"Get yourselves in here. It's freezing out!" my father called from the doorway.

Mom led me toward the house, her arm wrapped around my waist. She wouldn't let go of me for anything.

"I'm glad to have you back, Son," my dad said as we walked through the door. I smiled.

Once inside the kitchen Mom hugged me, kissed me and repeated my name over and over. She was still shedding tears, making me feel horrible for causing her to worry. At the same time, her tears made me feel wonderful. My mom still loved me.

"Betsey, get off the boy for a minute. At least let him take his coat off," my dad said.

Dad wasn't big on showing emotion, but after I'd taken my coat off and hung it on a hook, he grabbed me and gave me a hug.

"I should tan your butt for making your mother worry," he said. "Gone for months and not a word!"

I couldn't help but smile.

"I'm sorry, but I had to leave."

"I know, Son. We heard all about what you did to save your friend, Kurt. We're very proud of you."

"Kurt is more than a friend," I said. I thought I might as well get it all out there while I was doing it. There was no reason to hold anything back. "I don't know how you feel about that, and about me, but I'm not going to lie to you. I'm not going to pretend to be something I'm not. I hope you can accept who and what I am. If you can't, I'll understand."

"I would think the welcome we just gave you should tell you something about our…feelings," Dad said.

"We love you, Angel," Mom said. "I was so worried when you were gone. Your father and I did a lot of soul-searching. We couldn't understand what you told us in the letter you left. I couldn't even bring myself to say the word out loud at first. I had never thought much about…homosexuals before. What little I had heard was…well, not very nice."

"Your mother and I discussed it," Dad said. "It wasn't easy to talk about, but then the most important things in life often aren't. We came to the conclusion that we don't really know anything about homosexuals. What little we have heard doesn't match what we know about you. I guess the bottom line is that you've always been a good son. You're not perfect, God knows, but, then, no one is perfect. What you are is good and kind and decent. You're courageous. I was so proud when I heard how you faced those murderers to save Kurt. Most men twice your age don't have the courage to put themselves on the line like that. Some people around here call you a hero. Others have some very unpleasant things to say. We know what kind of a boy you are, Angel, and what kind of man you will become. There are things we don't understand, but we're very proud of you."

"You're our son, Angel, and we love you," my mom said. "That is the real bottom line. Whatever you are, we love you."

I grabbed my mom and hugged her. "Thanks, Mom." I looked at Dad, and he nodded.

Mom had to be assured that I was really okay over and over again. She couldn't keep her hands off me. It was as if she had to check for herself that I hadn't been maimed during my travels. Dad had to convince her to give me a little breathing room. I didn't mind being smothered for a bit, though. My return home had exceeded my most hopeful expectations. I bet not one guy in a hundred had parents who were so accepting and understanding.

I called Kurt as soon as I finished talking with my parents. I gave him the good news, told him I loved him, and then headed upstairs.

Walking into my room was a truly odd sensation. Everything was exactly as I'd left it on that night that now seemed so long ago. I don't think it hit me until then that I wouldn't have to sleep in a barn or huddled up under a pine tree tonight. Tomorrow morning, I'd walk downstairs, and breakfast would be waiting. I wouldn't have to survive on stale rolls anymore. I wouldn't have to wonder what I was going to do when I ran out of money and food.

My future was anything but certain, but I felt more secure than I had in months. My parents knew the truth about me, and they still loved me. I had a home. Kurt was back at my side. I even had a couple of friends in the Nudo twins. Things were going to be rough, but I wasn't alone anymore. I truly felt as though I could face anything.

My parents still loved me. My thoughts kept coming back to that. Nothing was so important—except Kurt, of course. I planned to write Clarence's mom soon and give her the news. I'd write Grandmother and the Selbys and share the news with them, too. Of course, I'd write Clarence and Laura—just to let them know I was home safe and that I missed them. I wondered how Clarence and Fife were working out. I hoped they had hit it off. I knew Clarence would find someone eventually, but sooner would be better than later.

I was so tired my muscles ached. All those letters had to wait—at least until tomorrow. I undressed and climbed into bed. I can't even begin to describe the luxury of sleeping in a real bed—my bed—with real sheets, a soft pillow, and comforters. I was home at last. I was in heaven.

Tomorrow, I'd return to school. Oddly enough, I wasn't frightened by the prospect. I knew I could expect some rough times ahead, but I was as much excited as anxious. I just wondered how it would all end. Would I live happily ever after or die a gruesome death?

I went to sleep while the snow fell outside. The cold wind clawed at the window panes, but I was safe from its clutches. I awakened a few times during the night, unsure of where I was. Once, I thought I was back in Clarence's bedroom, but when I looked to my side, no one was there. Later, I thought I was in the cabin with Grandmother and Laura. Each time, I drew in a breath, and the familiar scent reminded me I was home.

I awakened in the morning about seven. I climbed out of bed and sorted through my closet and chest of drawers. I'd forgotten how many clothes I had! I'd worn the same things day after day for so long it felt odd to face new colors and materials. I chose one of my favorite pairs of jeans and a white button-down shirt and then walked down the hall to the bathroom.

I'd taken a shower the evening before, but the hot water still felt luxurious pounding down upon my body. No one who hadn't been on the road as I had could appreciate the sensual pleasure of a good, hot shower.

I thought about making love with Kurt as I stood in the steaming shower. Our time together had completely relaxed me. I'd almost forgotten that content, mellow feeling that comes after making love. I hadn't had sex since May of last year—the last time I was with Kurt before I left Blackford. I'd had a few opportunities for sex in my travels. A couple of times I was offered money for sex, but I didn't want to be like that. I didn't want to have sex with anyone I didn't love. I loved Kurt with all my heart, so I'd denied myself sex during all those long months when I was separated from him. The closest I came was when I slept with Clarence, but that was just sleeping. I had kissed Clarence when we said goodbye, too, but that wasn't sex, either. Soon, I'd tell Kurt about Clarence. I'd tell him everything. I knew he would be okay with it.

Mom made pancakes, bacon, scrambled eggs, and toast for breakfast. I'd almost forgotten what the usual Egler family breakfast was like. It was nearing eight by the time I made it downstairs. That was late in the morning by farm reckoning. I was surprised to see Dad sitting at the kitchen table drinking coffee and reading the paper. He was usually out and about before I came down for breakfast, and I was behind schedule. Andy and Bob, the field hands who were a lot like family, had already come and gone. They lived in a separate little house on the farm, but came in and ate most meals with us.

"Good morning, Angel," Mom said. She was all smiles, and I couldn't help but grin back. The smile on her face meant everything to me just then. Above all, it meant I was accepted and loved. Mom hugged me.

Mom fixed me a big plate, and I sat down and began to eat.

"As soon as you're finished, I'll drive you to school," Dad said. "We need to see about re-enrolling you. You've missed half the school year."

"Thanks, Dad."

I was relieved Dad was going in with me. I thought I might be facing Principal Kinsley alone. I didn't find Principal Kinsley especially forbidding, but I wasn't sure how to get myself back in school, either. Things would go more smoothly with Dad there.

My life sure wasn't going to be boring from here on out. Most guys would've been shaking in their boots, but most guys never had to deal with Adam and his gang. Those guys were hard core. I'd feared for my life when they were around. Now that they were out of the picture, even the prospect of half the school hating me wasn't nearly as frightening as it should have been.

Perhaps far fewer than half of my classmates would hate me if the twins were to be believed. I guess it stood to reason that a good many people simply didn't believe in homosexuals. I could also see how my actions in saving Kurt made it impossible for others to believe I was some kind of pervert. That's how people thought of homosexuals: as mentally ill perverts. The ignorance of my peers might well work to my advantage. I'd never considered that when I was on the road.

I finished breakfast. Mom hugged me and kissed me as if I was going off to war. Dad restrained himself from telling her again not to smother me, but I could tell it took some effort.

Dad and I walked out to the old truck, a dark-green, 1938 International Harvester pickup. It was in surprisingly good shape for its age and only had about 40,000 miles or so on it. We climbed in and Dad started her up.

"I want to talk to you about something, Angel," Dad said as we started down the drive. "I didn't want to say this in front of your mother, because it would worry her, but a lot of people around here don't understand and don't approve of...the way you are. I don't completely understand it myself, but when I was your age, I did have an uncle—your great-uncle Eustace—who was homosexual. The family didn't talk about it and never came right out and said it, but everyone knew. Out of all my relatives, Uncle Eustace was by far the kindest. He spent quite a bit of time with me. I think that made my mother nervous, but my father trusted him. Uncle Eustace never betrayed that trust. My father never had time for me. He was much too busy with farm work. Uncle Eustace took his place in some ways. He taught me how to play baseball and even how to fight. I think he had to do quite a bit of fighting growing up, because he was different. I'm getting off track here, though. Our family was mostly okay with Eustace being the way he was, but others weren't. Eustace faced a lot of hard times. Things are going to be hard for you, too, Son. I hope you understand that."

"I understand. I expect things to be rough, especially at first. I can handle them."

Dad looked over at me for a moment.

"I expect you can, Angel. Fighting should always be a last resort, but it will come down to that, I'm afraid. If you're cornered, and especially if they gang up on you, don't be afraid to use everything you've got."

"I won't, Dad."

"I don't want to see you get hurt, Son. I can't fight your battles for you, except for this one with Principal Kinsley, but if there's anything I can do to help, you let me know."

"Thanks, Dad. Don't worry about me. I know things may get ugly, but I can take care of myself."

"I'm very proud of you, Angel."

Dad meant it. I could tell. There was a time when I thought he might kill me if he found out I liked boys instead of girls. I'd been wrong about that, however, about as wrong as I could be. I was truly lucky when it came to parents. Most parents would have turned their kid out if he told them he was a homosexual. It was an ugly truth.

"A couple of guys I know from school say that most people just don't believe I'm a homosexual." I paused. It was surprisingly hard to say the word in front of my dad. "They say that I might just as well have claimed to be an elf or a leprechaun."

"They have a point."

"They also said that a lot of people don't believe I can be a homosexual, because I saved Kurt."

"I suppose it would be hard for some to reconcile those two things. There are probably some who believe you're just going through a phase."

"At least everyone isn't against me."

"You can always count on your mother and me, Angel."

"Thanks, Dad."

Dad parked the truck in the school parking lot. School was already in session for the day. Kurt was sitting in a classroom somewhere, probably wondering how things were going with me. I couldn't wait to see him again.

Dad asked to see Principal Kinsley. Soon I was sitting in the outer office, and Dad was inside with the principal. I wondered what they were saying. I had expected to go in with Dad, but he'd asked me to stay outside. I wondered if he was talking to the principal about more than re-enrolling me in school.

I was called in to join Dad and Principal Kinsley after about half an hour. I sat in a chair beside Dad. My school records were spread out on the desk.

"Let's talk about your freshman year," Principal Kinsley said. "You were very close to completing the year when you…left. I'm aware that the circumstances were unavoidable, and your grades are generally good, so I'm going to pass you for your freshman year. You won't have to repeat it."

"Thank you, sir," I said.

"Your sophomore year is another matter. You've missed several weeks of classes, half the school year. Your father and I have discussed it, and there are two options. The first option is that you begin your sophomore year this fall. If you choose that option, you can either sit out the remainder of the school year, or come to classes as usual. If you do choose to attend the rest of this school year, I'm sure some of your school work can be counted toward next year—as far as reports, projects, and such are concerned. The other option is that you attend the rest of this year as your sophomore year. That will mean summer school, however, extra homework, and an extra class instead of a study hall. You'll be expected to maintain a B average or you'll have to repeat your sophomore year. If you need some time to think about it…"

"I don't. I'd like to pick up where I left off and make up what I've missed."

"Very well."

There was a bit more discussion, mostly of the boring sort, but soon we departed from Principal Kinsley's office. Dad went home. I was taken to the school guidance counselor to have my schedule set up, my locker assigned, and so on. By the time the guidance counselor was finished with me and I had picked up my books, it was nearly lunch time. I dumped all my books in my locker and spent the few minutes remaining before lunch scouting out the locations of my afternoon classes.

Doug Finney and John Hearst slammed to a halt when they spotted me in the hallway. They eyed me as if they'd like to kick my ass, but they didn't say a word. They continued on, looking back now and then, as if they couldn't believe I had the balls to return. I knew my presence in the school wouldn't be a secret much longer. They would tell everyone I was back. Of course, when I went to the cafeteria, that secret would end anyway.

The bell rang, and the hallways filled. More than a few of my classmates noticed me. The whispering began. I smiled to myself when I remembered the letter I'd left behind. I had basically told everyone who had treated Kurt so badly that they could go fuck themselves. I'd made plenty of enemies to be sure.

"Angel!" Angela Yates said when she spotted me.

"Hi, Angela."

"I didn't think you would come back."

"I live for danger," I said.

From the look in her eyes it was obvious Angela still wanted me. She either didn't believe I was a homo or just didn't understand the concept.

"Are you going to play baseball? Tryouts are later this week. You look so good in that uniform."

"I haven't thought about it."

"I guess you have had a lot on your mind."

"Uh, yeah."

"Now that you're back, maybe we could…go out sometime."

"Angela, did you read that letter I left?"

"Well, yes, but I don't really believe it. I mean the idea that you could be…one of those. The more I thought about it, the more ridiculous it seemed."

"You never know, do you?" I said in a mysterious tone.

Angela giggled. "You're so funny, Angel."

I considered telling her that I was indeed a homo, but that would've been crazy. While I didn't want to live a lie, I didn't see any way I could fight everyone. It was going to be hard enough fending off those who believed I was a homo. I hadn't expected so many people to refuse to accept the truth, but I wasn't about to rock the boat. That disbelief just might allow me to survive.

"I have to get going," I said.

Angela reluctantly allowed me to depart. I was on the receiving end of a few hostile glares as I made my way through the noisy hallways. Those glares were a warning that too many did indeed believe I was a homo. I knew I'd be lucky if I made it through the day without getting jumped. An attack was inevitable. When it came, I was gonna use everything I had. My only hope was to inflict such pain on my attackers that they would think twice about attacking me again.

Before I'd walked fifty feet, someone shouldered me hard, hard enough I should have been knocked down.

"Egler," Sidney said. I remembered him well. He always was a jerk.

"Hey, Wanker."

"That's Winker."

"Oh, I forgot. Easy mistake to make."

Sidney scowled and said something under his breath.

"What was that? You have something to say to me? Do you?"

I poured on the menace. I was going to start as I intended to go on. I might get my ass kicked daily from now on, but I wasn't taking any crap. No matter what anyone did to me, I'd come right back at them. Sidney was nothing more than practice.

"I'll say it later," Sidney said.

"Yeah, when you have some buddies to back you up. Coward."

Sidney was grinding his teeth. "I'll deal with you later, Egler."

"Be sure to bring your friends, Wanker, or I'll kick your ass!"

Sidney stalked off. If circumstances hadn't been so dire, the little scene with him would've been funny. I take that back. It was funny, anyway.

I walked on toward the cafeteria. It was so weird to be back in school. I felt as though I'd been gone for years, and yet I also felt as if I had never left. There were familiar sights, sounds, and faces. There was even the familiar scent of pencil shavings and chalk dust. I was in danger walking down those old hallways, but I was a lot safer than I had been out in the big, bad world.

Kurt spotted me as he walked down the hallway with Tommy. He made a beeline for me. I could tell he just barely stopped himself from hugging me. I'm glad he restrained himself. There was no reason those who believed I was a homo should think Kurt was one, too. He would be in deep enough shit just for being friendly to me.

"Angel! So how did it go?"

"Extra work, a class instead of a study hall, and summer school, but I'm officially a sophomore."

Kurt smiled. "Great! Come on. Let's get something to eat."

I swear everyone in the cafeteria was staring at me as Kurt, Tommy, and I went through the line. I don't mean the way you think everyone is looking when you have a hole in your sock or have just discovered your fly is unzipped. They were actually staring, at least until I began staring back.

The old varsity-baseball table was no more. A few guys from my old team were still sitting in their old spots, but much of the team was in jail, and their places had been taken by others. Kurt led me to my new home—his table. I sat down right across from him. Tommy sat next to Kurt. Soon, the Nudo twins arrived and sat on either side of me. That drew a lot of attention. There were whispers all over the cafeteria, and I'm reasonably sure they were talking about me.

I'd never had a lot of friends, so being an outsider wasn't as uncomfortable for me as it would've been for others. Besides, I had Kurt & Company with me, and that was better than the old Adam & Company any day. For one thing, no one sitting with me was a murderer. For another, none of them would cut my throat if I revealed their dark secret. The friends I had now were true friends, not barely disguised enemies.

A few others dared sit near me. I think they were regulars at the table, however, as I recognized several members of last year's junior-varsity baseball team. I was sure many of them would be moving up, since Adam, Danny, Chuck, Joshua, Jesse, and Travis wouldn't be playing from jail. I bet they hated that. They were all baseball freaks. I'm almost certain they would've killed me the night they murdered Matt Taber if I wasn't such a kickass first baseman.

"How is your day going?" one of the twins asked.

"Sidney Wanker tried to give me some shit, but I put him in his place."

Kurt, Tommy, the twins, and a few others laughed. They didn't fail to notice I'd said "Wanker" instead of "Winker." I had the feeling the name would stick.

I was amazed so many guys were willing to be associated with me. That fact, more than anything else, proved to me that most people really didn't believe I was a homo. Perhaps the stares I received weren't as belligerent as they seemed. Perhaps I was an object of interest merely because of my long absence.

"Guess what I heard about you this morning, Angel," Tommy said.

"What?"

"Some girls were saying they heard you joined the circus as a tiger tamer."

I couldn't help but laugh.

"I heard you ran away to look for Rebecca Foerster and your baby," Tyler said.

"Where do people come up with this stuff?" I asked.

Months before there was a rumor Rebecca left town because I'd gotten her pregnant. That rumor was, of course, false. Now rumors were building on rumors.

"When there's a lack of information, people just fill in the blanks with whatever they can come up with," Tommy said.

"I heard Adam hired a hit man to kill you," Fred said. I didn't know Fred very well, but I recognized him as one of Kurt's teammates. "And get this, I heard you set up a trap for the hit man and killed him."

"Damn, I am dangerous, aren't I?" I said.

"Why were you really gone, Angel?" Fred asked.

Kurt and I exchanged a look for a moment.

"Mainly because I knew Adam and the gang would kill me if they got the chance. I only found out recently they'd been put away."

"I would've hauled my butt out of town if those guys were after me," Tommy said, playing along with my half-truth. Tommy knew the real reason I'd left—to crush the rumors about Kurt by taking them onto myself.

"I still can't believe they killed Matt Taber," Tanner said.

"Believe it," I said. "I was there."

A hush fell over the table.

After hearing some of the rumors going around about me, the stares of my class-mates seemed less malicious. I wondered how many actually believed the ridiculous rumors now circulating. No matter. Those rumors would further hide the truth. Some of them enhanced my reputation as a badass, too. That reputation would likely prove valuable.

Not all was well, of course. When I returned to my locker with Kurt after lunch, I discovered someone had written "cocksucker" on it.

"I bet it was Wanker," I said.

"Are you okay?" Kurt asked.

"Sure I am. This is nothing," I said, pointing to the slur.

"Keep your eyes open, Angel. Some of these guys are out to get you."

"You mean not everyone believes I'm a tiger tamer who killed a hit man while searching for my girlfriend and baby?"

"I'm serious, Angel."

"I know. You keep your eyes open, too. I'm sure word is out that you sat with me at lunch."

I wanted to kiss Kurt on the lips, but doing so would definitely expose him to pain and torment. I settled for a smile and the knowledge that I could kiss him soon enough. After months without him, waiting a few hours was nothing.

I found my way to my 5th period American Lit class without trouble. Mrs. Ryan was the teacher. I'd had her for European Lit my freshman year. I handed her the form adding me to her class, and she assigned me a seat next to John Hearst. There were whispers as I took my seat, just as there had been when I entered. As more kids came into class each of them stared at me for a moment.

John Hearst leaned over and whispered into my ear. "You're dead, homo."

"What?" I said, loud enough for those near to hear. "No. I won't meet you after school. You're not my type, John."

John's eyes bulged out of his head, and he sputtered. He began to rise out of his seat, but remembered where he was. Some of the kids around us laughed, which infuriated John even more. He glared at me.

"You are so dead," he said, loud enough this time to be heard by others.

"Bring your friends. You're gonna need some help."

I stared right into his eyes. If he thought he was going to frighten me, he was dead wrong.

I observed my fellow students as class began. A few of the guys glared at me with contempt and hatred, others with respect or fear, or both. The girls seemed more curious than anything, although some of them looked a bit frightened of me, too. My former badass reputation was obviously still in effect. I no longer had to play that role to protect myself from Adam & Company, but now it was a means of defense against all those who hated homos. If they feared me, they would hesitate to attack. The more guys I could keep at bay with my reputation, the better.

I was glad to be back in school. Wandering around for months had a downside. I was often cold, often hungry, and I'd been in some dangerous situations, besides nearly dying. The worst part was being away from Kurt and my family. I was glad to be back.

My 6th and 7th period classes were roughly similar to American Lit: stares, glares, whispers, and looks of curiosity. I received no more death threats, but more than one of the guys looked as if he'd love to kick my ass. Horace Stipleton in particular made his desires obvious. He kept glaring at me, hitting his palm with his fist. Horace would no doubt have been part of Adam's gang had he possessed any athletic ability. He was all muscle and had the proper badass attitude, but he couldn't hit a ball to save his life. He'd tried out for the team, and he was pathetic. I think he hated me as much for being on the varsity team as he did for being a homo.

By the time I returned to my locker at the end of the day the slur had been cleaned away. Removing it was probably a waste of time, because I was almost sure someone would just write something else there.

I had to take my books for my 5th, 6th, and 7th period classes home with me. I had tons of catching up to do. The only thing that saved me from having to haul the books for my morning classes home was the fact I hadn't attended those classes yet. Tomorrow afternoon I'd have my arms full.

Kurt met me at my locker. Tommy joined us. We walked out the front doors together. The freak winter weather had disappeared while we were inside. It was way above freezing and there was barely a trace of the snow that had blanketed the ground. The three of us almost made it safely off the school grounds, but just as we neared the sidewalk Horace Stipleton stepped in front of me, blocking my path.

"You're late," I said. "What took you so long?"

"Huh?"

I rolled my eyes. "You're just not too bright, are you, Simpleton?"

Enraged by the oft-used variation of his last name, Horace swung at me. I was ready for him. I dropped my books, but didn't quite manage to step back far enough to keep his fist from connecting with my stomach. I grunted in pain.

Out of the corner of my eyes I saw Kurt and Tommy grabbed and held back. Obviously this attack had been planned. At least no one was pounding on my boyfriend and his best friend. They were merely being restrained.

Horace rushed me, infuriated beyond belief. It made him reckless, which is what I was aiming for when I made fun of his name. Angering your opponent ensures he'll come at you with everything he's got, but it also makes his attack wild and poorly thought out. I sidestepped Horace and punched him hard in the side as he flew by.

I slugged Horace in the face as he regained his footing. I followed through with a quick jab to the stomach. Horace smashed his fist into my eye, but I nailed him upside the head.

Horace only had an inch on me in height, but he was far stronger than I was. He had broad shoulders, a wide and thick chest, and arms that bulged with muscle. He should've been able to kick my butt with ease, but where he had strength, I had intelligence. I used his size against him, dodging and spinning out of the way. When his fist made direct contact it did serious damage, but most of his blows were glancing. By the time his fist reached its target, I was nearly always gone.

I delivered a couple of quick jabs to Horace's face and his nose began to bleed. I could have taken him out, but Doug Finney jumped on me from behind. I was in serious trouble after that.

Kurt and Tommy wanted to help, but they were being held with their arms pinned behind their backs. They struggled, but couldn't break free. Doug held me for a moment and Horace landed a solid punch to my stomach that doubled me over. Then, Horace nailed me with a sharp uppercut that nearly took off my head.

"Angel!" Kurt screamed at the top of his lungs.

I stomped on Doug's foot and he released me. He hopped up and down. I darted to the side, barely escaping another punch from Horace and falling in the process. Unfortunately, that put me on the ground with Horace standing over me. The bastard actually tried to smash the heel of his shoe into my stomach. I rolled away just in time to avoid it. I stumbled to my feet, but Horace came in and smashed me in the jaw. I nearly went down.

Suddenly, Horace was knocked to the side. It took me a moment to realize that someone else had joined the fight. I recognized Noah Taber as he quickly punched Horace in the face twice. Doug rushed to Horace's rescue, but I tackled Doug. I got him on his back and delivered one quick blow after another. The fight went out of Doug fast.

Horace had managed to punch Noah in the face, but I jumped up and tackled Horace as I had Doug. We went down, a mass of flying fists. Whoever was holding Kurt and Tommy (I found out after the fight it was Sidney Winker and John Hearst) let them go to join in. It would've been four against two, but Kurt and Tommy naturally came in on our side.

Doug was no longer in fighting form, so we actually had our opponents outnumbered. Kurt was a better fighter than I'd imagined. Tommy was on the small side, but fearless. He yelled like a wild boy as he attacked, throwing Sidney off balance.

Horace moved slowly, losing effectiveness. He wasn't landing any blows, but he was taking them. Soon, our enemies began to retreat, and we let them. I was winded and all of us were more than ready to stop. I stood there with my hands on my knees, gasping for breath, smiling at Kurt, Tommy, and Noah.

"Thanks, guys," I said.

Noah shook my hand. "I'll always be here to help you, Angel. I'll never forget you tried to save my little brother."

The excitement was over. Noah departed, and the rest of us continued down Culver Street. I rubbed my cheek.

"Oww."

"Are you okay, Angel?" Kurt asked.

"I'm good enough. I've been hurt worse. How about you?"

"I've taken worse beatings wrestling with Sam."

"Tommy?"

"I'm okay. That was actually kind of fun."

I laughed.

"I'm sure there will be plenty more fun where that came from."

"I'll be there!" Tommy said. He was sure a scrappy little guy.

We reached Tommy's house soon after that, and he veered off.

"See you tomorrow, guys!"

"Bye, Tommy! And thanks!"

Kurt and I continued on.

"You think those guys will jump you again?" Kurt asked.

"Almost certainly. That was just the opening act."

"Angel, I'm worried."

"Whatever is going to happen is going to happen. Don't worry about it. Tomorrow, I'll go into school with my bruised face and stare those jerks right in the eyes. I'll let them know they don't scare me."

"Yeah, but that won't keep them from attacking you again."

"Probably not, but they'll fear me, and that will work to my advantage."

"Aren't you scared at all, Angel?"

"Sure I am. Only a fool is never afraid. Fear is a part of life. I'm just not going to let it run my life. I'm not going to let my enemies see my fear."

"You're really brave."

"I'm just realistic. If I'm going to stay here, I've got to stand my ground. Those jerks will do their best to beat me down, but no matter what they do, I'll keep going back. I only lose if I run away. I'm not going anywhere."

"I don't care if you agree or not, you're the bravest guy I know."

I looked around. No one was in sight. I leaned over and kissed Kurt on the lips.

"You're a good fighter, Kurt."

"Well, I got some practice when that rumor was going around about me. Angel, watch out for Doug and John. They're dangerous."

Kurt shuddered.

"What do you mean?"

"I never told you this because I didn't get the chance before you left. I don't like talking about it either, but Doug and John tried to do something to me when they thought I was a homo. Well, they tried to make me do something."

"What?"

Kurt looked as if he was trying to force himself to speak.

"They cornered me in the restroom and tried to make me blow them."

"*What?*"

"Doug forced me down on my knees. He was going to make me blow him, but Coach Douglas walked in."

"Did he see anything?"

"No, but his timely arrival saved me, otherwise...well, you know. I wanted you to know because they might try the same thing with you."

"They are sick bastards, aren't they?"

"I steered clear of them after that. Doug beat on me some, but he never got the chance to try to force himself on me again. After you left that letter, he backed off."

"You need to be careful even now, Kurt. He may decide that being friends with me is enough of an excuse to try to force you again."

"I know. I don't go into the restroom alone."

"Just be careful, Kurt."

"You, too."

We reached Kurt's driveway. We bid each other goodbye, and I walked on alone. My stomach ached a bit and my face was tender, but the day had gone far better than I'd expected. Of course, tomorrow might be a good deal worse. No matter what, I was going back to school. I wouldn't let the bastards get me down.

Kurt

The day after Angel's return to school was rough. I'd been spotted not only sitting with him at lunch, but walking with him after school. Doug, Horace, and that whole crowd considered me an enemy by association. They shoved me around in the hallways between classes and were generally big jerks. Still, it wasn't nearly as bad as when they pegged me as a homo.

Doug and John frightened me—particularly Doug. Finney eyed me as if he would very much like to force me into doing what he'd tried to force me to do before. There was no way I was going to let him get me alone. He was a lot bigger than I was, and if he got his hands on me, I was doomed.

Horace got me right before 5th period. It was a lightning attack. I had no idea Horace could move that fast. I was hurrying down a deserted stretch of hallway when he darted in and punched me in the face. I was so stunned the pain didn't even register for a moment. I didn't enjoy it when it did. Oww!

"Stay away from Angel or there'll be more where that came from."

Horace stalked off, leaving me clutching my face. I could feel the area around my eye swelling. I glared at his back as he walked away. If Horace thought he was going to scare me off, he was sorely mistaken. I was in this with Angel to the end—bitter or otherwise.

At the end of 6th period, Tommy and I met in the hallway. He was sporting a black eye, too.

"Sidney?" Tommy asked, nodding at my blacked eye.

"No. Horace."

"Sidney told me to stay away from Angel…"

"…or there'll be more where that came from," I finished for him.

"I'd say someone, or rather a group of someones, doesn't like the fact we're hanging out with Angel," Tommy said.

"Well, if they think a black eye will change my mind, they've got a lot to learn."

"Talk to you later, Kurt. I've gotta run or I'll be late."

"Bye, Tommy, and I'm sorry."

"Not your fault!" Tommy yelled as he rushed down the hallway.

My path crossed those of the Nudo twins between 6th and 7th periods. They now possessed matching black eyes. It didn't take a genius to see a pattern emerging.

By the end of the day I discovered that Noah Taber and a few members of the J.V. baseball team were all sporting black eyes—everyone who sat near Angel at lunch or was the least bit friendly with him in fact.

When I met Angel at his locker, I noticed his other eye was blackened, too.

"Noah Taber told me what happened to you, and him, and the others," Angel said. "Are you okay?"

"I've been better, but I've been a good deal worse, too. How did you get your second black eye?"

"Doug Finney and John Hearst shoved me up against the lockers and Doug got me. I kicked him in the nuts, though. You should have heard him scream. Then, John tried to hit me in the face. I ducked, and he smashed his fist into the locker. I think he broke his hand!"

Angel actually laughed.

Noah and Tommy walked up. They wondered why Angel was laughing, so he had to tell his story all over again. As we stood there talking, more and more of the guys who'd received a warning punch in the face showed up until there was a fair-sized crowd around Angel's locker. They were all plenty pissed, but not at Angel.

"We've got to pay these assholes back!" said Noah. "If they think they can intimidate me and tell me who I can and can't be friends with, they're gonna find out real fast that that crap doesn't fly with me."

There were sounds of agreement all around. The bullies' plan had backfired. Instead of scaring Angel's allies off, it had united us.

"I think we should all get together and come up with a plan to strike back," I said. "We've got to stick together. If we don't, we'll all be in for a daily beating."

There were nods of assent all around, as well as a few cheers. I felt suddenly bold and courageous. Angel told the story of how he got his black eye to the later-comers, and everyone had a good laugh at Doug's and John's expense.

"Where can we meet?" Tommy asked when everyone stopped laughing. "We don't want Doug and the other jerks to get wind of this, and I don't think any of us want our parents to know, either."

"I think I might know a place," I said. "Let me check it out, and I'll get back to everyone. Until then, I think it's time to use the buddy system. Let's stick together in pairs, at least."

We broke up and went our separate ways. Angel, Tommy, and I walked out of the school together. I truly appreciated Tommy sticking up for Angel and me. He was giving up prime time with his girlfriend to help us out.

The three of us were alert for any sign of the enemy. It was only the day before that we'd been jumped leaving school.

"What place do you have in mind?" Angel asked.

"Ryan's," I said.

"The guy you do yard work for. Right?" Tommy asked.

"Yeah. He might let us meet at his place."

Angel and I walked Tommy home, then turned around and headed for Ryan's house.

I knocked on Ryan's door. His face lit up when he saw me, and then his expression turned to one of shock.

"Angel! Come in, guys. Come in."

We walked inside and pulled off our shoes.

"I just put a kettle on. Would you guys like some hot cocoa, tea, or some coffee? It's still a bit nippy out, but nothing like yesterday!"

"Hot cocoa would be great," I said.

"Yeah," Angel said.

"I'm glad the weather is getting back to normal. That blast of winter we just had was not welcome. I don't even like to go outside in weather like that," Ryan said. "Winter is best observed through a window. So, when did you get back, Angel? Kurt said he wasn't expecting you for months or years."

"Just a couple of days ago. I had planned not to return until Kurt graduated. I thought that way, if he was still interested in me—"

"If!" I interrupted.

Angel smiled.

"Okay, I thought that by coming back on Kurt's graduation, we could make a run for it, if necessary. Some things happened during my travels that changed my mind, though. I decided I couldn't spend my life running. It was time to come back and make a stand. I just hope it's not my last stand. The name Custer keeps coming to mind."

"That's kind of why we're here," I said.

"Does this have anything to do with those black eyes?" Ryan asked.

"It's connected. Some of the jerks at school have started in on Angel. Quite a few are standing up for him, too. Those of us who are with Angel received a little warning today," I said, pointing to my black eye. "So we're planning to organize ourselves to strike back. The problem is we don't have a place we can meet…"

"I have the feeling this is where I come in," Ryan said.

"Well, we were wondering…"

"Of course you can meet here, Kurt, and I may be able to help you."

Soon, we were sitting and sipping cocoa by the fire. We told Ryan more about our troubles and about some of the guys harassing us. He asked a lot of questions and looked rather thoughtful.

Ryan insisted on driving Angel and me home when we departed a half hour later. I think he was a bit concerned we might get jumped again. I'd told him what had happened the previous afternoon.

Angel and I kissed goodbye when we reached my driveway. I watched as Ryan and Angel drove away, content with the knowledge that Angel would soon be home safe.

***

The bullies wandered the hallways the next day. They were no doubt checking to see if they had intimidated Angel's supporters. They underestimated us. We weren't the kind to abandon a friend to save our own necks.

I received a particularly nasty glare from Sidney Winker when he spotted me walking with Angel between classes. I knew I'd have to watch my back, but then again, I already knew that.

Even if the jerks weren't specifically targeting Angel's allies, I would've been in danger. Some of the guys believed Angel was a homo, and by associating with him I was as good as saying I was one, too. It was obvious to anyone with any sense at all that Angel and I were close. It wasn't too big of a leap from there to figure out we were more than friends—boyfriends, in fact. Once that realization hit, I'd be once again marked as a homo. It was only a matter of time. I was quite sure some had already reached that conclusion.

If our enemies had any doubt their warning was being ignored, that doubt was erased at lunch. I'm sure they had hoped to see Angel abandoned and sitting all alone—an outcast. Instead, we all sat together just as we had the day before.

I think all of us were a bit nervous. Our open defiance would lead to trouble. There was no doubt about it. The bullies knew we weren't backing down. Like any good bullies, they would surely up the ante. If we weren't very careful, someone was going to get hurt.

After school, Angel, Tommy, and I walked towards Ryan's house. All the guys were supposed to meet there by four. Ryan was a good sport. It's not every adult who would be okay with a bunch of teenaged boys invading his home. Some might think Ryan had an ulterior motive—

that he hoped to lure one of the boys into something perverted. I knew and trusted Ryan, though. He might find some of the guys attractive, but he would never make a move on them. He'd had every opportunity to make a move on me and had never done so.

We were welcomed at the door by Ryan and the scent of warm cookies.

"You're the official greeter, Kurt," Ryan said. "I have cookies in the oven."

"They smell delicious. Oh, this is my best friend, Tommy."

"It's nice to meet you, Tommy. Everyone make yourselves at home."

Ryan returned to the kitchen, which was separated from the living room only by a counter. There was a fire going in the big, stone fireplace, despite the fact that it was even warmer than the day before. I loved Ryan's home. It was so comfy and cozy. I just wished he had a boyfriend to share it with.

"Angel," Ryan said. "Can you fill some glasses with ice?"

"Sure."

"The glasses are right up there," Ryan said, pointing to a cabinet. "Help yourselves to cookies, guys."

"You didn't have to go to all this trouble," I said.

"It's no trouble. I rarely have an excuse to bake cookies. There's chocolate chip, oatmeal raisin, and sugar cookies."

There were tons of cookies. Ryan had gone all out.

"The samovar on the counter is filled with hot cocoa."

"The what?" I asked. "You mean this big silver thing?"

"Yes," Ryan said, trying not to laugh. "That's a samovar."

"I've never seen one before."

"Few people around here have. A samovar is used to boil water for coffee or tea, but I prefer my kettle. It's great for keeping things hot, though. Oh, Kurt, could you set out some cups?"

"Sure."

Ryan busily moved about the kitchen, taking trays of cookies out of the oven and putting others in. He was just filling a bowl with marshmallows to go with the cocoa when the doorbell rang.

"That will be some of the guys," I said.

Each new arrival was greeted with hot cocoa and cookies. It seemed more like a party than anything else. Our meeting was about serious business, however.

Everyone arrived by four, and shortly after that we all gathered in the living room. I introduced Ryan, who waved from the kitchen where he was still baking cookies.

"Okay," I said. "We're here to make some plans, but first, did anyone have any trouble today?"

"Horace called me a 'homo lover,' but that's it," Edgar, one of my team-mates, said. "Fred was with me."

"John Hearst was stalking me after second period," Iggy said. His real name was Ignatius, but everyone called him Iggy. "I stuck near teachers until I could meet up with Bart. We've been sticking together since."

No one had anything more than nasty looks and insults to report.

"Okay, sticking together is working, but we're going to have to be extra careful from here on out. We took them by surprise today. They weren't expecting us to defy them, or to pair up. They'll be ready for it tomorrow, so it's best to stick with as large a group as possible."

"How are we gonna get back at these guys?" asked Tanner Nudo.

"That's the big question. Unfortunately, some of the toughest guys in school are against us. I don't know how we can take them on."

"We'll probably get our butts kicked," Iggy said.

"Maybe we could catch each of them alone and beat him senseless," Fred suggested.

"Can I make a suggestion?" Ryan asked from the kitchen.

"Sure," I said.

Ryan walked into the living room, where the guys were sitting and lying all over his furniture.

"You need to think your actions out far ahead. If you use the same tactics as these bullies, you're only starting a war. No one ever wins a war. It's just a lot of suffering and pain. If you use their methods, you'll open yourselves up to attacks from your teachers, parents, and the community."

"What do you mean attacks?" Tommy asked. "I can't really see Mrs. Kendall trying to kick my butt."

Everyone laughed at that.

"I don't mean physical attacks. You have to be very careful. Some people believe Angel is a homosexual, and people don't approve of homosexuals. Many think of them the same way they do murderers. When they find out you're standing up for Angel, a lot of people will be against you. Some of your teachers at school will be among them. If you get into fights, you may find that you get in trouble, while the bullies don't."

"That's not fair!" Tyler said.

"This has nothing to do with fair. Those who are against you will use completely unfair tactics if they can."

"So if we can't fight them, what can we do?" I asked. I'd noticed Ryan said some people *believed* Angel was a homosexual. He wasn't confirming anything. I wondered how many of those sitting there thought Angel was a homo. I wondered if they would still be with us if they knew the truth.

"Strike at them in other ways—ways that can't be traced to you with any certainty. This battle will require stealth."

"Like, how?" Angel asked.

"Use whatever you've got going for you. Are any of you teacher's assistants?"

"I am," Tanner said. "I grade papers and stuff for Mr. Brooks so I don't have to sit in study hall."

"Okay, what would happen if say…Doug's test answers were changed so that he got most of them wrong? Or what if his test couldn't be found at all and he had to take it over?"

Tanner grinned.

"There are ways to make things unpleasant for someone without physically harming them. When I was in school, one of the bullies found the doors and windows of his car taped shut. Another opened his locker to find it plastered with photos of his best friend's girl. Not being caught is extremely important, however, and so is not taking things too far. Property damage isn't acceptable.

"I don't see any girls here, but if you can get some on your side they can make powerful allies."

"What's so powerful about girls?" Bart asked.

"Some of the bullies have girlfriends, right?"

"Sure," Bart said.

"Well, if some of those girls were to start denying the bullies what they want from them, they might be convinced to back off."

"You mean sex, right?" Tyler asked.

"Exactly."

"You're kind of evil. I like you!" said Noah. "If my girl wouldn't... well, I get what you mean."

Some of the guys laughed at that.

"As you get older, you'll find women are very powerful and not just because of sex. We don't have time to get into the other reasons, just take my word for it. Never underestimate women. Those who do are making a serious and foolish mistake. Girls will be your best allies in this. Just be careful whom you recruit.

"I'm sure you guys can come up with lots of ways to make life miserable for those who are harassing you. Just don't forget about defense. Even if they can't pin what's being done to them on anyone in particular, they are going to strike back at you. You've got to stick together on this and watch out for each other."

Ryan truly changed the direction of our discussion. I think all of us had been thinking about a rumble, but Ryan was right: many people would be against us. I could just see Angel or me getting detention while Doug and John got off with no punishment at all.

Once Ryan had shared his wisdom, he stepped back and let us handle it from there. We spent the next hour or so bouncing ideas back and forth. I had no idea there were so many ways to seek revenge. Of course, what we were doing wasn't as much about revenge as it was about deterring our enemies. If we made the price for picking on us high enough, perhaps they would back off.

Ryan sent everyone home with extra cookies. Angel, Tommy, and I were the last to leave. We stayed behind to help Ryan clean up.

"Thank you so much, Ryan," I said. "Letting us meet here was great, but the ideas you gave us were incredible."

"I'm just trying to keep you guys out of trouble. The world can be a very unfair place."

"Why are people like that?" I asked. "Why are they willing to be so unfair and so nasty just because someone is different?"

"We think of ourselves as civilized," Ryan said, "but I'm not so sure we are. The least excuse is all many of us needs to act in a barbaric manner. Look at how the Negroes are treated just because their skin is a different color. Most people talk a good game, but all their high ideas go right out the window when they're presented with someone who isn't just like them. Christians in particular act in the most un-Christian ways when it comes to minorities. In fact, they often lead the fight against them, abandoning all their principles while claiming to uphold them."

"That's scary," I said.

"The world is a scary place, but don't worry, I'm just citing the bad examples. Plenty of Christians are quite true to their beliefs. There are plenty of other good people out there, too. Just look at these boys who came here tonight."

"Most of them weren't even my friends before," Angel said. "They're just taking up for me because Kurt is."

"That makes them all the more noble. Never lose your faith in the goodness of people. Those who you most expect to act with kindness and decency often do not, but others will surprise you."

"Thanks, Ryan."

Ryan drove us all home, despite our protests that we would be perfectly safe. Ryan was incredible. The world needed more people like him.

***

Our plan was put into action the very next day. Tanner fired the first shot. There was a World History exam and Horace's test mysteriously disappeared. Horace was livid when he found out he would have to retake the test. No doubt the fact that it was an essay test was especially galling.

I'm not sure who did it, but one of our number glued Sidney Winker's locker shut. I don't know what they used, but it sure wasn't Elmer's. The custodian still hadn't been able to get Wanker's locker open at the end of the day. I felt a little bad that we put the janitor out, but then again I guess he would've just been sweeping or whatever if he wasn't working with Wanker's locker.

I took part in the best act of revenge of the day. About 9 p.m. I received a call from Tommy summoning me to his house ASAP. When I arrived, we rushed downtown to a side street near the Delphi Theatre where the Nudo Twins were hard at work filling Doug Finney's old Ford Club with water balloons.

"If he catches us, he will kill us," I said.

"All the more reason to hurry," Tyler said, who was giggling.

"What do you think of our idea?" Tanner asked as he carefully filled balloons with a water hose running from the back of the donut shop.

"It's brilliant," I said. "Doug will have a fit."

We worked quickly. With four of us carefully tying off and filling the car with water balloons the interior filled up quickly. Despite the fear of getting caught, we filled the car right up to the roof. I was sure one of the balloons would burst under the weight, but Tanner was an expert at putting in just the right amount of water. By the time we finished there wasn't a square inch of Doug's car that wasn't filled with water balloons.

We quickly dispersed once the deed was done. Doug was probably in the Delphi watching a movie with his girl. I would've given about anything to see his face when he came out, but the danger was too great to risk sticking around. Tommy and I laughed and giggled all the way to his house.

Doug was steamed the next day at school, but of course, he had no idea who had filled his car. He might have suspected it was some of Angel's crowd, but we hadn't harassed the jerks enough for them to catch on to our tactics. Doug made the mistake of telling some of the guys at school what had been done to him, and they howled with laughter. That only ticked him off more. I was delighted.

We were taking our time and staging our attacks with care. Most of our nasty tricks could only be done once or twice. If too many tests from Mr. Brooks's classes came up missing, suspicion would fall on Tanner. If we filled too many cars with water balloons, our enemies would quickly catch on. Doug and his crowd had most of the brawn, but we had the brains. Our strategy was to strike quickly, quietly, and without notice.

I was laughing with a group of guys over yet another retelling of the water-balloon-filled-car incident when I heard a voice behind me.

"Why are you hanging out with that...pervert?"

I turned. It was Derek Spradley.

"Pervert?" I asked.

"Angel."

"He's not a pervert, and you'd better not let him catch you saying that."

"He is, too. He said so in that letter."

"You don't know anything for sure, and so what if it's true?" I asked.

"How can you say that? Dad says homosexuals go straight to Hell. He says all of them should be killed."

"Your dad sounds like a load of laughs," I said sarcastically.

"I'm serious. You shouldn't hang out with him."

"Why are you so concerned whom I hang out with?"

"Because sometimes I hang out with you, and I don't want anyone to think I'm a pervert. People are already beginning to think you're queer for hanging out with Angel. Soon it will rub off on me."

"You hang out with the Nudo Twins, and there have been rumors about them going around for years."

"No one believes any of that. Angel is different. He admitted he was queer himself."

"You know, I like you Derek, but you're not telling me whom I can and cannot have as friends. I like Angel. Hell, he saved my life!"

"I'm just trying to help you. It wasn't that long ago that people thought you were a homo. If you keep hanging out with Angel, people are going to start wondering if maybe you really are one after all."

"So let them wonder. You shouldn't be so afraid of what others think, Derek."

Derek shook his head.

"If you're gonna hang out with him, I can't hang out with you."

"I'm sorry you feel that way," I said. I turned my back on Derek and walked away. Why did he have to be such a creep?

***

The freak winter weather of a couple of days before was but a memory as Angel and I showed up for baseball tryouts. The sun was shining. The green of the grass was deepening. The daffodils, crocus, and tulips were growing so fast I felt as if I could almost see them getting bigger.

"Now, this is what I call spring," Iggy said as he walked along beside us.

"It must be 70. It's hard to believe it was snowing just days ago," Angel said.

"Grandpa says the one thing certain about weather is that it will change," Iggy said.

Tommy, Tanner, Tyler, Bart, Fred, and Edgar soon joined the three of us. Derek Spradley had shown up for tryouts, too, but was keeping his distance. I hoped Derek would get over himself soon. I really did like him. He couldn't fail to notice how many guys were hanging around Angel. Why was he so afraid?

"Here come the bad guys," said Fred.

I turned to see Doug Finney, John Hearst, Sidney Winker, and Horace Stipleton walking toward the baseball diamond in a tight knot. Doug shot us a disapproving glare, but then ignored us. This was going to be an interesting baseball season.

Plenty of other boys showed up, too. There were the remnants of the old varsity team, almost the entire JV team from the year before, and many newcomers, too. Now that Angel was back, I wanted to make the varsity team more than ever. I felt a sense of nervous anticipation as I stood there waiting for Coach Douglas and Coach Marley to get things started. I had improved tons during the last season, but I'd been kind of pathetic at the beginning. Would they remember how I'd played near the end of the season, or would they instead remember the fumbling kid from the start? I had to be on my game today. I just had to be on the varsity team with Angel!

Tryouts took a *long* time. First, we paired off so the coaches could judge our catching ability. Angel and I stuck together of course. We took our places in the long line, facing each other, about twenty-five feet away. Angel tossed me the ball, and I made a great overhead catch. I took care to close my glove and to cover the ball with my free hand, just as Angel had taught me all those months ago. Unfortunately, neither Coach Douglas nor Coach Marley was there to see it. They were checking out other potential players. I just hoped that I didn't mess up when they were watching me.

Angel was amazing, but that was no surprise to me. Even when my throws were off the mark, he still managed somehow to catch the ball. Angel moved so fast at times that he seemed superhuman. There was no way he could fail to make varsity.

Next came batting. Angel was chosen to pitch. Big surprise, huh? He wasn't as expert a pitcher as he was a first baseman, but he had a killer fastball. The coaches had him give each of us a couple of easy pitches and then a couple of deadly ones. I hit the easier pitches with no trouble. The first difficult pitch, a curveball, got past me. I nailed the second pitch, even though the ball came at me so fast I could barely see it.

Coach put me in the infield while others took their turn at bat. Five different hits came my way, and I fielded each of them. Coach Douglas noticed a particularly difficult catch I made. He wrote something on his clipboard right after that. I tried not to let myself get excited, but I was feeling hopeful.

There was a lot of downtime during tryouts, but I was in the field most of the time, so I didn't get bored. I had to stay sharp in case a ball came in my direction, just as if I was in a real game.

When about a third of the guys had taken their turn at bat, Coach Douglas moved Angel to first base and replaced him with John Hearst. John shot Angel a look as if he'd beaten him out for the position. That was ridiculous, because this was only a tryout, and Angel wasn't even interested in being the pitcher. He wanted his spot at first base back.

I have to admit that John was a damned good pitcher. I didn't think he was quite as good as Angel, but then I was biased. I always thought my boyfriend was the best!

After everyone had their turn at bat, the coaches divided us into squads. I wasn't happy when Angel and I were placed on opposing sides: first, because I wanted to be with Angel, and second, because the few remaining varsity players from last season were on Angel's squad, while I was put with the JV players and the completely new guys. To make matters worse, some players from the JV team were on Angel's squad. I wondered if that meant they were being considered for varsity and I wasn't. The hopeful feeling I'd experienced earlier evaporated. I didn't let my disappointment show, and I didn't complain, either.

John Hearst did his best to strike me out. His first pitch was an inside fastball that I could barely see. I didn't so much mind missing it, but I didn't like the smirk on John's face. I was determined to hit the next pitch, no matter what. I was totally focused on the ball as I waited for John to pitch. He whipped another one in, low and away, on the outside corner, right where I thought he'd pitch me, since he'd come inside with the first one. I went with the pitch and slapped it down the right field line. I dropped my bat and ran. Angel was waiting near first base, but the right fielder, Tim Carnes, was still chasing after the ball in the corner. I raced to second and then third and saw that Carnes was having trouble coming up with the ball and took a gamble by heading home. Carnes finally hit the cutoff man but I slid in under the relay throw with an inside-the-park home run.

I showed the coaches that I could not only hit but run as well, and John was not happy. He kicked the dirt on the pitcher's mound in disgust and scowled at me. Angel was delighted. The intersquad game continued, but that was the highlight for me. My hopeful feeling was restored. I grinned as I walked away with Angel at the end of tryouts. I just hoped the coaches were impressed enough to bump me up to the varsity team. There were lots of vacancies, but there was plenty of competition, too. I hoped I made it. I *really* wanted to be on the varsity team with Angel.

Angel

"I want to help."

"Huh?" I said, pulling my head out of my locker. I'd been searching for books. It was the end of the school day, and I was preparing to load up for the walk home.

"Oh, hey, Angela. What do you mean you want to help?"

"I'm not stupid. Doug's car filled with water balloons? John's locker filled with molasses? Sidney's locker glued shut? And, were those Doug's boxers flying from the flagpole this morning? Those guys may be too stupid to figure out what's going on, but I'm not. Bad things are happening to those who are on your butt. So, I want to help."

I grinned.

"I am right, aren't I?"

"How do I know you aren't a spy for the enemy?"

"Listen. I did something really bad a few months ago, and I want to make up for it."

"Huh?"

"Didn't Kurt tell you?"

"Tell me what?"

"I'm the one who started the rumors about him."

"*What?*" I practically yelled.

Angela's face paled, and she stepped back. She took a deep breath and gazed at me.

"I'm sure it comes as no surprise that I'm interested in you. No one else seemed to notice, but you and Kurt were always together. I wanted him out of the picture so I could move in. So, I spread the rumor that he was caught doing it with another guy. I thought you'd dump him as a friend if you thought he was queer."

I wrinkled my nose.

"That was a vile, treacherous thing to do."

Angela's lower lip trembled, and tears rimmed her eyes. I wondered if Angela had suspected Kurt and I had been more than friends back then. But, if so, why was she interested in me?

"I know. It was a rotten thing to do."

"Kurt got beat up because of that rumor. People treated him like shit!"

"I'm sorry. I can't tell you how sorry I am. I had no idea things would get so out of hand. I admitted to Kurt that I'd started the rumor. I apologized. I know that doesn't make up for it. That's one reason I want to help now. That and…well, I do like you."

Kurt showed up just then with Tommy. We met at my locker daily to walk home together. I just stared at Angela for a few moments. I had half a mind to yell at her and tell her to get lost.

"Come with us," I said, finally, still indecisive.

We walked down the hallway and out of the school. I waited until we'd left the school grounds and on the sidewalk before I spoke to Angela.

"Why should we trust you?"

Kurt and Tommy had no clue as to what I was talking about, but I knew they would figure things out soon enough.

"Because I want to make up for what I did to Kurt. I know you guys are…friends."

"Do you think I'm a homo?" I asked. "Do you think I get it on with Kurt?"

Angela was shocked by my directness.

"I don't know, I…"

"I am, and I do. Kurt is my boyfriend, and I love him. What you did to him..." I shook my head slowly, so angry I could almost have belted Angela in the mouth, girl though she was.

I wasn't the only one angry with Angela.

"You know Angel had to leave town because of your rumor," Kurt said.

"I thought he left because Adam and..."

"That was only part of it. Angel could have come back as soon as those guys were behind bars, but because of you, he had to stay away for months!"

"I'm sorry. I'm so sorry. If I'd known...I know neither of you may ever be able to forgive me, but I want to help you now. I know Doug and his friends are out to get you, Angel. I don't want to see you get hurt. I know you may find that hard to believe, but I swear I never meant to cause you or Kurt any pain. I didn't think about the consequences when I started that stupid rumor. Please give me a chance to make up for at least part of the harm I've done."

"So," I said, "let's say I'm interested. How can you help?"

Angela grinned. "I can give you inside information. I know the girls who date your enemies."

"And why would they want to help me?"

"I can get information without them knowing it—girl talk. Some of them aren't too happy about the way their boyfriends are treating you, either. I'm sure at least a few will be willing to help."

"Helping me could be dangerous. If Doug finds out..." I began.

"Oh please. What is he going to do? I'm a girl. He can't hit me."

"I'm sure he could devise ways to make life unpleasant for you."

"My friends wouldn't allow that," Angela said.

"He could spread rumors about you," Kurt said. "Nasty rumors."

"If he does, it wouldn't be completely undeserved, now would it? I'm willing to take that chance. Doug won't find out. If he does, I'll deal with the consequences.

"Please. Let me help. You don't have to tell me anything about what you've got planned. I'll just supply you with information. I can let you know where Doug and the others will be, and when. I can also find out what they have planned for you."

"Are you sure about that?"

"Please. Even though you are…homosexual, you should be smart enough to know that a girl can twist a boy around her little finger if she likes. Anne is dating Doug. She can get him to tell her anything."

"Hmm," I said. "Such information would be useful."

"Are you sure you can trust her?" Tommy asked, eyeing Angela angrily.

"No, but I have a feeling I can." I turned to Angela. "Okay. You're on. I can use all the help I can get."

"You won't be sorry," Angela said.

"I hope not."

"I'm going to get out of here," Angela said. "It's probably best if I'm not seen with you too often. I'll contact you when I have some information for you."

We watched her walk away and then continued on our way home.

"You think she's for real, or do you think this is some kind of trap?" Kurt asked.

"I think we can trust her. I'll be careful. I won't allow any of us to be maneuvered into a dangerous situation. If we are being set up, our opponents are going to find it damn hard to spring the trap."

"You know, if she's for real, things just got a lot easier for us," Kurt said.

"I know."

I smiled. The possibilities were limitless.

We dropped Tommy off at his house. His girl was waiting on the porch. Tommy grinned. Angel and I resisted the urge to tease him.

Doug drove by slowly and glared at Angel and me as we passed the A&W. There were two of us and one of him, so he didn't try anything.

"I wish everyone would just leave us alone," Kurt said.

"Everyone is, for the most part. It's only a few that are causing trouble. I know things are scary right now, Kurt, but the situation is much better than I anticipated. I thought I'd find the entire town against me when I returned. I pictured everyone chasing me with torches as if I was Frankenstein's monster. I really didn't think I'd be able to stay long when I came back."

"Why did you return then?"

"Because I couldn't stand to be away from you for another moment. I knew I couldn't just keep running. As slim as my chances of success were, I had to try. To be honest, I figured I'd be driven back out of town, but at least I'd get to see you again."

"If you're driven out of town, I'm going with you this time."

"I know," I said and grinned. "I don't think it will come to that, though. I never dreamed people just wouldn't believe I was a homo. I never considered for a moment some would actually think of me as a hero."

"You are a hero, Angel. You could very easily have been killed by Adam and the others."

"I'm not a hero. I just did what I had to do."

"Isn't that the definition of a hero—someone with the courage to do what must be done?"

"I don't know, but I sure don't feel like a hero."

"You'll always be my hero."

"You are so sappy, Kurt."

Kurt giggled.

"I'm nervous about the tryouts."

"Tryouts were yesterday, Kurt. Why are you nervous now?"

"Because I'm afraid I won't make varsity."

"You will. You were one of the best players out there, and I'm not just saying that because I love you."

"I hope you're right. I wish the coaches had posted the list today. What's taking them so long?"

"They're posting the list tomorrow. Stop worrying. You'll make varsity."

"I bet I won't be able to sleep tonight."

"Just relax, Kurt."

"That's easy for you to say."

I grinned. We walked along in silence for a bit.

"Come home with me," I said finally.

"Are you sure?"

"Yes. Mom and Dad are more or less okay with what I am. I can't tell you how much that means to me. There's no reason I shouldn't have you there with me."

"Are you going to announce that I'm your boyfriend?"

"Well, they know you're more than a friend. I didn't tell them you're my boyfriend, but I'm sure they've figured it out. It's probably best if we're not too obvious in front of them. Beyond all hope, they love and accept me, but it's still hard for them. I don't want to push what I am at them. They may just not want to think about it. I'm going to respect that."

"I understand. I love you, Angel."

"I love you, too, Kurt."

We walked toward home. I breathed in the moist, spring air. The whole world was coming alive. I couldn't have been happier. Kurt was at my side. Somehow I knew that no matter what happened, we would always be together.

"I still can't believe it," I said, speaking a thought out loud.

"Can't believe what?"

"That so many people refuse to believe I'm a homo. They had no problem believing you were one."

"Yeah, but Angela said she saw me doing it with another guy. You merely left a letter behind."

"I said I was a homo in the letter!"

"True. At first, a lot of the guys believed it, but you had such a reputation as a badass no one could reconcile the two. I think most people think your letter was mostly bullshit—just a way to piss off everyone."

"If they think my letter was bullshit, why didn't they turn on you again?"

"Well, Angela put the word out that she started the rumor about me. She admitted she had made the whole thing up. That's probably why a lot of people think your letter is bullshit. They think that if the rumor about me was made up, then your letter saying you were the queer and not me had to be made up, too."

"What a complicated mess," I said.

"Yes. Unfortunately, not everyone was convinced. Doug and his whole crowd believe you're a homo."

"Angela was a little late in admitting she started the rumor. If only she'd told everyone it was a lie before I wrote that letter! Everything would probably be fine now!"

"True, but it was your letter and departure that made her come clean: cause and effect."

"I guess there's no use analyzing it. I can't believe all this trouble was started by a rumor."

"I bet plenty of trouble is started by rumors. We just don't know about it."

"Yeah."

"At least Angela did the decent thing in the end."

"Yeah, after you'd been beat up and almost killed—after I had to admit I'm queer and then go on the run."

"I know. Admitting the truth cost her, though. Many people were plenty pissed at her. She lost some friends over it. I'm not one bit happy about what she did, either, but she has tried to make up for it."

"I guess I can forgive her if you can."

"Now that you're back, I can forgive anything."

I put my face against Kurt's and nuzzled his nose. We were on a stretch of lonely country road, so I kissed him. We rubbed our noses together again, smiled, and continued on.

"Maybe all this will work out for the best," I said. "It was probably inevitable that we be found out sooner or later. Now, we have been found out, but most people don't believe it. Even if someone was to see us making out and told everyone, most people would just think it was a baseless rumor."

"Or the same old rumor recirculating again," Kurt said. "I hadn't thought of that."

"That's the bright side. The dark side is that Doug & Company is out to get me and anyone who sides with me."

"True, but there's a bright side to even that: Doug & Company aren't half as dangerous as Adam & Company."

"Yeah. I think a severe beating is the worst Doug and his crowd would do. Adam and his bunch would have killed us."

"I still don't find the thought of a severe beating, or any kind of beating, appealing."

"That's why we've got to take care of these guys."

"Do you think our life will ever be boring, Angel?"

"Perhaps it will cease to be dangerous, but it will never be boring."

We had already passed Kurt's house and were nearly home. Soon, the fence came into view, as did the barn, and the outbuildings. We turned onto the drive and walked toward the house.

We entered through the back door, pulling off our shoes. Dad was nowhere about, but Mom was in the kitchen, already beginning the preparations for supper. Every day Mom cooked for Dad, Andy, Bob, and me. Mom stopped peeling potatoes long enough to give me a hug.

"Hello, Kurt," she said.

"Hi, Mrs. Egler."

"You boys help yourself to some cookies. I just took a batch out a few minutes ago. They're probably still warm."

"Thanks, Mom."

"Thanks, Mrs. Egler. Oh. I should call my mom."

I poured Kurt and myself glasses of milk while he called home. We sat at the kitchen table, snacking on chocolate-chip cookies while chatting with my mom. Mom gazed at Kurt with renewed interest. I can't go quite so far as to say that I got the impression Mom approved of my relationship with Kurt, but she didn't seem to disapprove. Perhaps she thought that if I was going to be involved with another boy, it might as well be with a nice boy like Kurt. Perhaps I was seeing more than was there, too. Maybe Mom didn't get what "more than friends" meant. She probably did get it; Mom was far from stupid. Mom invited Kurt to stay for supper. I found that encouraging.

As we sat there, I thought again of how lucky I was in the parent department. I probably had Great Uncle Eustace to thank for my dad's level of understanding. Most people had never met a homosexual, but Dad was exposed to Uncle Eustace at an early age. I was thankful Dad had had such a positive experience with his uncle.

Kurt and I retreated to my room after we'd eaten a few cookies. I was tempted to lock my bedroom door so Kurt and I could make love, but that might have been going a step too far. My parents knew I liked boys, and Kurt obviously was a boy, so…well, you get my point. That didn't stop me from grabbing Kurt, pulling him to me, and slipping my tongue into his mouth. We stood there, holding each other so tightly that we could barely breathe, while we made out like crazy.

We both got all worked up in seconds, but we controlled ourselves. It was a good thing, too, for after about five minutes there was a knock on the door, followed quickly by my mother delivering clean laundry. Kurt and I had no trouble pulling apart in time, but had we been undressed there would've been no hiding what we were doing. If I'd locked the door, Mom would have been suspicious ever after.

I think Mom might have been a bit suspicious anyway, but Kurt and I looked innocent enough as she entered. Mom left the basket of laundry and returned to the kitchen, closing the door behind her.

"Do you think she was checking up on us?" Kurt asked.

"What do you think? Mom quit in the middle of preparing supper to deliver laundry I could have brought up myself. She was definitely checking to see if we were up to something."

"I'd very much like to be up to something," Kurt said.

"Me, too," I said with longing.

"I guess we should look at the bright side. Waiting will make it that much hotter."

"Yeah, but I just might explode if we have to wait too long."

Kurt laughed. "Welcome to my world."

Kurt and I began to kiss again. It was amazing how sexy making out made me feel. It was amazing how my body reacted to it. You'd think my lips were directly linked to my penis. Running my tongue along Kurt's while our lips caressed drove me out of my mind with need.

We sank onto the bed and continued kissing. As much as we wanted to, we went no further. It was frustrating in the extreme, but just being able to hold Kurt and kiss him filled me with bliss. We kept making out for a good half hour.

Not two minutes after we finished, Mom knocked on the door and quickly entered—this time to ask if Kurt preferred his iced tea with sugar or without. Kurt and I were innocently sitting apart on my bed, giving no indication we'd just been making out. Mom departed, hopefully convinced we hadn't been doing what we'd been doing.

"Definitely checking up on us," Kurt said.

I laughed.

"I guess it's to be expected. If I liked girls, I probably wouldn't even be allowed to have one in my room."

"Wow, so there are advantages to being a homo?"

"Many."

An hour later, Mom called Kurt and me down for supper. We had taken pity on her and opened my bedroom door, so her checks were limited to occasionally walking past. Serious lovemaking was going to be a problem. We'd have to do it outside, in some remote spot. There was not enough privacy indoors. We might make use of the tree house, but if we went there often, suspicions would be aroused.

Kurt and I sat down at the table in the kitchen with Mom, Dad, Andy, and Bob. I noticed Andy and Bob checking Kurt out with renewed interest. Andy and Bob were more than hired help; they were like family. They knew I was a homo. There was no keeping it from them. So far, they'd given no indication one way or another as to their feelings about my "deviant sexual desires," as some referred to them.

I hoped Andy and Bob would be okay with my homosexuality. They were kind of like big brothers in a way. We weren't especially close, but you don't live around someone for years without developing at least some closeness.

Supper consisted of fried chicken, mashed potatoes with milk gravy, green beans, corn, freshly baked yeast rolls, and chocolate cake. It was typical fare for the Egler household, where most meals were large. I'd been so accustomed to such meals I hardly noticed them while growing up, but life on my own had given me a new appreciation for them.

Kurt was witty, entertaining, and outgoing at supper. I was surprised he spoke up so easily. He'd been to my house before and had eaten supper with us, but he seemed more at ease than ever before. I could tell everyone liked him.

I walked Kurt home after supper. I wanted to make sure he arrived safely. Besides, it was an opportunity to spend yet more time with him and sneak in a kiss or two.

"I'm glad your mom was okay with you coming home with me," I said. "I feared your parents might not like you hanging out with me."

"Are you kidding?" Kurt asked. "You saved my life. If Adam and his crew had killed me, my parents would've been stuck with Sam as their only son. That's a fate worse than death. I'm sure they're eternally grateful."

"Sam's not so bad."

"Yeah, I know, but he's my older brother, so I have to run him down some. It's tradition."

"I'm an only child, so I wouldn't know."

"Yeah, all the good genes in your family are concentrated in you, not spread out between three kids."

"I don't think it works that way, Kurt. Otherwise, kids in big families would really have a hard time."

"I wish we could do it again."

"Do what again?" I asked, playing dumb.

"You know what: make out."

"Well, it is getting dark. Mom will expect me back soon, so we don't have much time, but I think we can risk a short make-out session."

I pulled Kurt into my arms, and we kissed. We held each other tight as we began to make out. I wanted to rip his clothes off and just go at it, but I controlled myself. I sighed with contentment. I loved the feeling of closeness that being with Kurt gave me. Whether we were making out or making love, I felt as if we were connected. Maybe that was the whole idea of sex. Maybe that's why sex created such intense physical pleasure. Perhaps it was meant to create an intimate bond that continued long after the sex was over. I felt that connection to Kurt—both now and when I'd been far, far away. Kurt was why I'd returned. I was glad I did.

Kurt

Despite the constant danger from Doug and his crowd, I felt relaxed the next morning as I hadn't in ages (other than worrying about making the varsity team, that is). It was as though my body needed contact with Angel, as if he was a necessary part of me. I replayed our time together in his room over and over. Being with Angel was worth all the bad stuff that had ever happened to me.

I could swear the clock stood still as I sat in each of my classes. Seconds refused to pass. Minutes just would not budge. I usually enjoyed my classes, but today they were an obstacle. The team lists would be sadistically posted *after* school. I knew I had a good chance to make varsity, but it was nowhere near a sure thing. I wouldn't rest easy until I read my name on the list. Waiting was agony.

Failing to make varsity wouldn't be the end of the world, although it might seem like it. If I was stuck back on the JV team, I'd probably be one of the better players. I might even be assigned a choice position like shortstop. I wasn't sure I'd be up to the pressure, however. I wanted to play, but I didn't want too much responsibility. I wasn't like my boyfriend. Angel could handle anything.

At the end of the day Angel, Tommy, Alicia and I walked to the bulletin board near the entrance to the locker room. Angel was an essay in cool confidence. Coach Douglas tacked up two sheets of paper on the bulletin board just outside the gym. Guys crowded around. Some walked away smiling. Others weren't so happy.

"Good luck, Kurt," Angel said, patting me on the back. He leaned in close and whispered into my ear. "I'm sure you made it, but remember I'll always love you, no matter what."

I smiled at him. I wanted to hug him.

Angel, Tommy, and Alicia watched as I nervously approached the varsity roster. It was in alphabetical order by last name. I started at the top, almost too scared to read down the list. Brody was one of the first names I'd read. Tommy had made the team! Egler came up soon after. There was no surprise there, but I was happy for my boyfriend. I read on down the roster, almost forgetting to breathe. There it was. James! Kurt James! I'd made it!

"I made varsity!" I yelled, turning around.

I was so happy I grabbed Angel and hugged him before I realized what I was doing. To cover, I grabbed Tommy next and hugged him, too. Last, I hugged Alicia.

"You made it, too, Tommy! You're on varsity!"

"What?" Tommy asked, incredulously. "Are you kidding me?"

"I guess they've lowered the standards," I said. Tommy punched me in the shoulder.

"Congratulations, Tommy," Alicia said. She kissed him on the cheek. Tommy went all dreamy and probably completely forgot about baseball for a few moments.

"The Nudo Twins are in!" one of the twins announced as the pair walked toward us.

"This is great! Beyond great!" I said.

"I made varsity?" Tommy asked, still in a daze. "I didn't think I had a chance!"

"If they'll let Tanner in, they'll let anyone in," Tyler said.

"Shut up, Tyler," Tanner said, grinning.

"Let's celebrate!" Tommy yelled, holding his arms above his head.

Bart, Edgar, Iggy, and Fred all walked up after reading the lists.

"How did you guys do?" Tommy asked.

"We're all on JV except Iggy here," said Fred. "Poor Iggy will be stuck with you guys."

Fred, Bart, and Edgar all seemed quite content to be on the JV team.

"We're going to celebrate making the team," I said. "Why don't you guys join us?"

We all made our way to the Black Heifer. We pulled a table up to a booth so we could all sit together.

"Guess what?" Edgar said when we'd all ordered. "Sidney and Horace didn't make varsity. They are going to be so ticked off."

"Doug and John made varsity, right?" Angel asked.

"Yeah."

"That's going to be fun: playing on the same team with *those* guys."

"I don't envy you," Edgar said, "but we're stuck with Wanker and Simpleton. We're doomed."

Everyone laughed.

Tommy sat there stunned as we celebrated. He joined in on our rowdy celebration, but I could tell he couldn't quite believe his good luck. The guys who didn't make varsity truly didn't seem to mind. I hoped that was true and that they weren't just putting on a brave face. I would have been upset if I hadn't made varsity, but that was mainly because I wanted to play on the same team as Angel.

We celebrated for a good hour. I couldn't wait for our first practice. Baseball was so much fun!

"Well, Fred, Bart, Edgar, and I need to go make some plans. We have a mission tonight," Iggy said.

"Mission?" Tommy asked.

I already knew what was up, but not everyone did. Iggy leaned in conspiratorially, although none of the enemy was about.

"Our spy has passed us some vital information. John Hearst leaves his bike on his back porch, and he and his family will be gone for the entire night."

The twins grinned as one.

"What are you going to do?" Tanner asked.

"We're going to take it apart," Iggy said and then grinned.

"John will be so ticked off!" Tommy said.

"That's the plan," Iggy said.

"Just be careful," Angel said. "It could be a trap. Do you guys want me to go with you?"

"No. We've got it covered. Don't worry, we'll be on the lookout for treachery."

We all paid our checks and went our separate ways after that. I could tell that Angel was concerned. The tip about John's bike was the first bit of information Angela had passed us. What if it was a trap?

We had our answer the next morning. The mission was a success. Iggy reported that all was just as Angela had said. Iggy and Fred watched for twenty minutes to make sure the coast was clear, then slipped in with pliers and wrenches to completely disassemble John's bike. Bart and Edgar were also on the scene, acting as lookouts. Iggy and Fred left John's disassembled bike lying on the porch like a giant jigsaw puzzle. I wondered how long it would take John to put it back together.

Despite our group's success, Angel advised caution. He felt we could trust Angela, but she was in a position to set us up big-time. Just because the first bit of information she gave us was accurate didn't mean we could count on whatever information she gave us next. Angel spread the word to proceed with caution. If Angela was some kind of double agent, she would probably give us several bits of accurate information to gain our trust before setting us up for a fall.

Our first baseball practice was that afternoon. After a short speech by Coach Douglas about teamwork and dedication, we were given our uniforms. Yay! The uniforms were identical to the JV uniforms, except they said "varsity" on them. I felt so proud when Coach Douglas handed me mine and told me he was glad to have me on the team. I had been a screwup at the beginning of the previous season, but with Angel's help I'd improved dramatically. If someone had told me last season I'd be on the varsity team in a year, I would've thought they were crazy. Of course, if someone had told me about most of the things that were going to happen last year, I would've thought they lived in some kind of fantasy land. Me dating Angel Egler, the bad boy of B.H.S.? Impossible! Life was weird.

Our first practice was much like the tryouts. Coach announced that most of the positions would be filled in the next few days, once he'd had a chance to assess our strengths. He did announce that Angel was the first baseman. No surprise there. Angel was the best first baseman ever. What did come as a bit of a surprise was when Coach announced that Doug would lead our pitching rotation. Angel and I looked at each other. Like me, he was no doubt wondering how sworn enemies would work as teammates.

Coach had me playing second base during practice. On the one hand, I was excited that I might get the position. On the other, I wondered if I'd be better off in the outfield where there was less pressure. I kept seesawing back and forth. I wanted to play second, but I didn't want to screw up.

Practice went smoothly. Doug and John shot Angel and me a few glares but did nothing overtly hostile. Still, a wave of fear passed through me when Angel walked right up to them at the end of practice. Tommy, the twins, and Iggy watched nervously from a distance. Like me, they no doubt feared a showdown right there on the baseball diamond.

"We need to talk," Angel said.

Doug looked more like he wanted to spit on Angel than speak to him.

"So talk," Doug said finally.

"You don't like me, and I don't like you," Angel said, "but we're on the same team. If we fight each other we might as well just forfeit to the other team."

"So what are you proposing, homo?"

"A truce—on the field and in the locker room and showers. You don't bother my guys, and we don't bother you. When we're practicing and when we're playing, we act as a team."

Doug looked Angel over.

"And elsewhere?" Doug asked.

"Anything goes."

"Deal," Doug said.

Angel extended his hand. Doug hesitated and then shook it.

"I just hope Coach has a backup first baseman," Doug said, "because you're not gonna be able to play out the season. You're dead, fag."

"We'll see about that," Angel said, not so much as flinching.

Doug and John walked away without so much as another word.

I was worried. I didn't like the sound of "You're dead, fag." I was sure Doug didn't mean it literally, but it was clear he meant to hurt Angel. If Doug and his bullies ever got Angel alone, I shuddered to think what they'd do. I was determined that would never happen.

"It will be okay, Kurt," Angel said, gazing at me.

"Be careful, Angel."

"I'm always careful. Besides, Doug and his crowd are little league. They aren't a tenth as dangerous as Adam and his thugs. I survived playing with the big boys. I'm sure I can handle Doug."

I was still uneasy, but I felt a bit better. Angel was right. Doug was a bully, but Adam had been a murderer. As dangerous as our current situation was, we'd already been through much worse. If Angel could handle Adam, he could surely handle Doug.

***

A truce was declared for baseball practices and games, but otherwise it was business as usual. We continued our campaign to make our enemies' lives miserable. Unfortunately, there were only so many things we could do to strike back at them. Opportunities were severely limited, so we tried to take advantage of every one as it presented itself. We also had to be creative. Our revenge could only go so far and couldn't stray into property damage or bodily harm. Doug and his thugs thought nothing of resorting to physical violence, but we were better than that. Our efforts could best be described as annoyance and harassment.

Our masterpiece made filling Doug's car with water balloons and disassembling John's bike look like child's play. The target was Sidney Winker this time. Wanker was the lucky winner because Angela tipped us off that Sidney and his entire family would be gone for the weekend. That would give us plenty of time to do our dirty work.

The whole gang was involved in Operation Wanker. We rendezvoused at the entrance to the cemetery and waited for dusk to settle into night. When we could count on the cover of darkness to hide us, we set out for Wanker's house. Iggy acted as lookout while the rest of us got busy. We slipped into Wanker's house and made our way to his room. Our first task was to cover his windows with thick, black cloth so that no light would escape and reveal our activities. The last thing any of us needed was to explain to the police what we were doing in Wanker's house. Once the blackout curtains were tacked up we began to move the contents of Wanker's bedroom onto the front lawn. We split the task between us with each little group in charge of one small area of the bedroom. Everything was reassembled on the lawn exactly as it was in Wanker's bedroom. Angel and I took care of Sidney's dresser. We made sure his framed photos and even his comb were placed just as he'd left them. With all of us working together, the task was completed in just under two hours. When we were finished, Sidney's bedroom looked exactly as it did when we found it, only now it was on the front lawn.

Once the job was done, we broke up into smaller groups and went our separate ways, giggling and laughing at Wanker's expense. If only we could've seen his face when he returned from his weekend trip.

When Angel, Tommy, and I walked into school on Monday morning, the story of Sidney's bedroom was already running up and down the corridors. The halls were filled with more than the usual amount of laughter. It was difficult not to take credit for what was being proclaimed as the best practical joke of the year. Sidney and his friends were not amused. I imagined it took them just as long to carry all Wanker's stuff back into his room as it had taken us to carry it out. I'm sure it wasn't nearly as fun either.

Doug & Company weren't especially bright, but our last bit of mischief made our intentions obvious, even to them. When Doug's crowd started to tally up the acts of sabotage, it didn't take them long to figure out who was behind them. They had no proof, of course, but they were mad as hell.

"Here's where it gets ugly," Angel said as we walked toward the cafeteria the day after Doug & Company finally figured out what was going on. "They'll be after us hot and heavy now."

"Yes, but it's also where they begin to realize that harassing us comes with a price."

"The question is: how far are Doug and his thugs willing to go? We may have only succeeded in stirring up a hornet's nest."

"Possibly, but you're forgetting one thing."

"What?" Angel asked.

"It's been a lot of fun."

Angel laughed.

Moments later, Doug Finney himself stalked up to Angel as if he'd been summoned by our conversation. He poked Angel in the chest.

"I know you're behind all this!"

"All what?" Angel asked, innocently.

"My car! Sidney's locker! Sidney's bedroom! All of it!"

"You think I did all that?"

"No. I said you're behind it. Your little pack of homo-lovers is helping you—like this one here!"

Doug pushed me, and I staggered back a couple of paces, nearing falling on my butt. Angel stepped in between us. Doug had just made a *big* mistake.

"You ever touch him again and I'll break your arm!" growled Angel.

It was Doug's turn to take a step back, out of fear. He quickly regained control, angrier than ever that Angel had frightened him.

"Protective of your little boyfriend, are you? You'd better be careful, Angel, or something bad might happen to him."

Angel took a step forward. I feared he was going to belt Doug in the face.

"I promise you, if you ever hurt Kurt, I'll make you sorry you were born."

The menacing tone of Angel's voice frightened even me. He was in badass mode and quite convincing. Doug's face blanched for a moment.

"Yeah, well. We'll see about that," he stammered.

Doug beat a hasty retreat. He was a badass, but he was nothing compared to my boyfriend. Doug needed his thugs to back him up. Angel was quite capable of standing alone.

"Don't even think about going anywhere alone, Kurt," Angel said.

"I'm not stupid, you know."

"I know. I just don't want to see you get hurt."

I'm sure Angel wanted to hug me just then. I definitely wanted to hug him. We were in plain sight of everyone in the hallway, so our embrace would have to wait.

Angel and I walked on to the cafeteria. We were greeted with the scent of meat loaf and green beans. The cafeteria was noisy as usual, with lots of chattering kids, clinking silverware, and trays scooting across Formica tables. Angel and I went through the line together and made our way to our usual table. When we sat down with our trays, we immediately noticed Tyler had a fresh black eye.

"What happened?" I asked.

"Doug, Horace, and Derek got me in the hallway between classes. Fred was with me, but we were outnumbered."

"We have to be especially careful from now on," Angel said. "I was just telling Kurt that this is where things get ugly. Doug and the others have figured out what's going on, and they're going to strike back."

"You think?" Tyler asked with just a trace of humor. I admired him for his bravery.

"If anyone wants out, this is the time to distance yourself from me," Angel said.

I looked around the table. I was relieved that no one showed any sign of abandoning Angel. This was when he needed his friends the most.

"Till death do us part," said Noah in a serious tone. I had no doubt he meant it literally. Noah would never forget that Angel tried to save his little brother.

Angel nodded. He knew he could count on Noah, no matter what.

Just as the battle was heating up, help came from an unexpected direction. The girls at B.H.S. joined our cause. They were not at all pleased that Doug, Horace, and Derek had attacked Tyler. Despite the rumors about them, the girls had a special affection for the twins. They seemed to think of Tyler and Tanner as pets. Now that I thought of it, the twins were cute and cuddly, kind of like puppies. I grinned at the thought.

The first sign that the girls were coming over to our side was subtle. At first, I didn't even notice they were giving Doug & Company the cold shoulder. Once I picked up on it, however, it became apparent. Doug and his thugs found themselves on the receiving end of icy stares from the females. Their greetings were met with silence, or frowns. When Wanker tried to his hug his girl she slipped out of his grasp and walked away. I smiled at the sight of him standing there with a confused look on his face.

Horace Stipleton paid a higher price than the others for his part in hurting Tyler. Angela spread rumors about him—the kind of rumors guys dread. I overheard two girls talking about him as I was getting books out of my locker. I couldn't help but eavesdrop.

"He is really built," Alicia said, "but Angela said he works out all the time to make up for what's lacking in his pants."

"You mean…?" said Betty.

"Yes," Alicia said, waving her pinky in the air. "He's hung like an eight year old."

The girls giggled. I had to stifle a laugh myself. I almost pitied Wanker—almost.

"It gets worse,' Alicia said. "Apparently what little he's got isn't of much use. Angela said she talked to a girl who was with Horace, and he couldn't get it up when the time came."

Betty looked supremely embarrassed. Alicia was a little red-faced, too. I wasn't surprised. I had no idea girls talked about things like that.

Word about Horace, true or untrue, spread like wildfire. Whispers began to follow him, and girls giggled when he was near. I spotted him hurrying down the hallway, red-faced with embarrassment. I wondered what his chances of getting a date were now. Rumors could be brutal. I knew.

The girls' tactics, added to our own harassment, made Doug and his crowd increasingly bitter and resentful. Doug crossed my path between classes, and there was murder in his eyes.

Just after school, Tommy and I found Sidney, Horace, and John waiting on us at my locker. If we would've spotted them in time, we would have made a break for it, but I was too busy telling Tommy about the Horace rumor. Tommy was too busy listening and laughing. By the time we spotted the enemy, it was too late. To his credit, Tommy stood by me, even though it would likely cost him bodily harm.

Horace grabbed me and shoved me up against my locker. He snarled at me. I wondered if he knew we'd just been laughing at his expense. Horace pulled his fist back for a punch, but Tommy flung himself on Horace's arm. It was like a miniature Yorkie attacking a Doberman, but it threw Horace off balance. He swung, hurtling his fist toward my face with Tommy still clinging to his arm. The blow went wide and I had time to duck, squeeze past Horace, and get some maneuvering room.

Sidney and John were on me in a second. I struggled to break free, but they were ten times stronger than I was. Horace tossed Tommy away and came for me as I writhed and squirmed, trying to escape the clutches of Sidney and John. Horace was only three feet away and closing. I said a silent goodbye to my face.

The wide shoulders of my brother, Sam, suddenly blocked my view. He shoved Horace back, then turned and punched Sidney in the gut. I stomped on John's foot as hard as I could manage and broke free.

Tommy and I quickly stepped up on either side of Sam and faced our attackers. Horace, Sidney, and John were no longer so eager to attack now that there were three of us. In moments, Angel arrived on the scene and our enemies were outnumbered. They made a reluctant and resentful retreat.

"Trouble, little brother?"

"Nothing I can't handle," I said.

"Yeah, right."

Sam gave Angel a sideways glance. He knew what was up.

"I guess the battle has begun, huh?" Sam asked me.

"Actually, it's been going on for while now. It's just reaching the serious phase."

"I heard about Winker's bedroom. That was a good one."

"Whatever do you mean?" I asked.

"Don't play innocent with me, little brother. I know you too well."

I smiled.

"Thanks for saving my face, Sam."

"Well, there's not much there to save, but you are my little brother. Just remember I can't be everywhere at once. We talked about this long ago."

"I've got allies," I said, looking at Tommy and Angel.

"Oh, how I long for the days when I was an only child," said Sam as he walked away.

The following days were all pretty much the same, so I'll condense them for you. Doug & Company were hot after Angel and the rest of us. There were always at least three of them, so we tried to stick in groups of three or more as well. That's not nearly as easy as you might imagine. We all had lives, after all. There were times between classes when we couldn't manage it at all. I even found myself rushing down the hallways alone now and then. That would've been suicide, but the girls were watching out for us. Once, Horace spotted me alone in the hallway and made for me, only to be blocked by a group of four girls. They mysteriously got in his way and moved in whatever direction he did. By the time he'd freed himself, I'd slipped away. For a homo I sure liked girls!

There were no major showdowns. Doug and his crowd were trying to catch us when they had us outnumbered. They didn't want a fair fight. They wanted easy pickings. We weren't about to make it easy for them. You wouldn't either if your face was on the line.

We had few opportunities to harass our enemies. With Doug and the others hot after us, we spent our time on defense. Each of our enemies did find the inside of his locker dripping with honey or molasses, but there was no time for any truly creative revenge.

Our female allies made the real progress. Doug & Company found them aloof at best, hostile at worst. Doug, John, and the others had shown their ugly side by giving out pain and black eyes like candy on Halloween. That didn't go down well with most of our classmates. The girls, in particular, were turned off by it. Doug and the rest found their very own girlfriends giving them the cold shoulder and denying them so much as a kiss. That had to be frustrating for those poor heterosexual boys. Unfortunately, it made them meaner, as if their testosterone was building up to toxic levels.

I was pushed around some in the halls, but none of the enemy had the opportunity to do any real damage. If looks could kill, I would've been dead. Hate-filled glares were frightening, but they didn't hurt like a fist in the face.

Everything pretty much continued along the same until Sam dropped Angel and me off at Tommy's house on Wednesday morning. Sam drove us to Tommy's house most mornings now. He would've driven us home, too, but he usually worked at the Marathon station right after school.

I could tell something was wrong when Tommy's mom met us at the door. One look at her worried face told me something bad had happened.

"Tommy isn't going to school today, but I'm sure he would appreciate a visit."

A cold chill went up my spine as I entered the Brody home. I walked to Tommy's room and knocked on the door.

"Come in."

Tommy was sitting on his bed. He had a black eye, bruises on his face, and his left arm was in a sling.

"Tommy, what happened?"

"John Hearst happened. I ran to the store for Mom and…"

"Alone? Why didn't you call me?"

"Mom was making spaghetti for supper and discovered we were out of spaghetti. The sauce was almost ready, so…"

"Are you okay?" I asked, interrupting. I couldn't stand seeing him like that. He'd been beaten up badly.

"I'm kind of sore and my shoulder hurts."

"Oh, Tommy, I'm so sorry."

"You didn't beat me up, Kurt."

"If it's anyone's fault, it's mine," Angel said. "You wouldn't have been hurt if it wasn't for me."

"This isn't your fault, Angel, and you know it. The blame rests solely on John."

"Yeah, but…"

"No buts. I knew the risk going in. This changes nothing. If anything, I'm more determined that ever to stick it out. Those jerks are not gonna win!"

I smiled. "You're very brave."

"I'm not brave. I just stick by my friends," Tommy said.

"And I'm lucky to be your friend," I said.

"Oh, don't go all gushy and homo on me," Tommy said.

Angel laughed. I was relieved that Tommy was teasing me. That meant he didn't feel too horrible.

"Is your shoulder going to be okay?" I asked.

"Yeah, the doctor said it was sprained."

"So what happened?"

"John spotted me on my way to the grocery. I ran for it, but he's fast. He got me in an alley."

"You must have been terrified."

"I wasn't having any fun, that was for sure. He started beating on me, calling me names, the usual."

"How did you get away?"

"I kicked him in the nuts. That stunned him, so I did it again. He sank to his knees, and I staggered out of the alley. Iggy, Fred, and Bart spotted me and took me home."

"Do your parents know why you were beaten up?"

"I told them some guys are picking on you and Angel and that the rest of us are sticking up for you."

"Your parents must hate us."

"Don't be silly. They don't hate you. Dad is rather proud of me, actually, so the beating might just have been worth it."

Tommy was smiling.

"Is there anything I can get you?" Angel asked.

"Nah, I have room service here. I intend to milk this for all it's worth."

Tommy smiled again.

"Anything I can do for you, then?"

"Just relate my heroic exploits to the guys. Be sure to make me sound as brave and manly as possible."

"I won't have to add anything to the story for that," Angel said.

Tommy looked very pleased.

"Well, we'd better get to school," I said. "I'll bring your books and homework by this afternoon."

"Some friend you are."

I laughed.

"See you later, Tommy."

"Go on, get out of here. I have comic books to read! Later, I have a nap scheduled."

We left somewhat reassured by Tommy's cheerful attitude, but still concerned by the attack. What if Tommy hadn't managed to kick John in the balls? How badly would John have beaten him?

The walk from Tommy's house to school was very short, but Angel and I were sitting ducks. Luckily, none of the bad guys spotted us. Tyler and Tanner were lingering near the entrance.

"Where's Tommy?" one of the twins asked.

"John Hearst beat up Tommy last evening," I said. "Tommy's going to be okay, but he's staying home today."

"Is he in bad shape?"

"He's got a black eye, some bruises, and his shoulder is sprained, but he'll be okay. He actually seems to be enjoying himself. Get this: he nailed John in the balls—twice. That's how he got away."

Both twins laughed for a moment, but quickly became serious once more.

"Who was with him?"

"Tommy? No one."

"We're getting sloppy," Angel said. "Someone is going to get hurt. Someone has."

"Yeah, we can't take any chances. Tyler and I stick together always."

"Even in the shower," Tyler said, wiggling his eyebrows.

I had to stifle a giggle. Tyler most likely wasn't kidding.

"So, Tommy nailed John in the balls, huh?" Tanner asked. "That explains why he was walking funny this morning."

"I told Tommy I'd relate his heroic story to everyone," Angel said.

"We will help spread his epic tale," Tyler said dramatically. "When we're finished, all will quake before the fearsome Tommy Brody and his kick of pain."

I shook my head, but grinned.

The four of us walked inside, and then parted. Angel and I made our way to my locker. Angela walked up as I fumbled with the combination lock.

"They're going to set you guys up for an ambush tonight," Angela said.

"How?" Angel asked.

"They plan to grab one of the twins and allow whoever is with them to see it happen. When you go to rescue him, they'll all be waiting—with chains and baseball bats."

I swallowed hard. I didn't like the sound of that at all.

"Thanks, Angela," Angel said.

"I just wanted you to know."

"What are we going to do?" I asked when Angela left.

"We're going to make damned sure there are enough of us with the twins this afternoon to keep them safe. The problem is, the enemy could spring this trap at any time. Say we stop them tonight; there's nothing to keep them from grabbing someone later. The rest will have no choice but to attempt a rescue. Who knows what they'll do to whomever they catch?"

That was a truly unpleasant thought. I felt almost as if I was within the clutches of Adam and his brutes again. Doug and his crowd were becoming nearly as bad.

Doug walked past, and I couldn't help but look at him in fear. He glared at us. I had to fight to keep myself from shaking. This was getting too serious.

***

Angela's information proved accurate. Doug, John, Horace, and Sidney were waiting for the twins on their usual path home. What they weren't expecting is that the twins would be escorted by Angel, Iggy, Noah, and me. Doug was clearly pissed off.

I was relieved we had prevented the enemy from kidnapping one of the twins. I was sure the twins were relieved, too. The problem was that any of us could be next. We couldn't travel around in large packs all the time.

Doug & Company were intent on carrying out their plan. Angela tipped us off two days later that I was to be the target on my way home from school. We were therefore prepared and foiled Doug's plan. There were two additional attempts Angela didn't get wind of; the targets were first Iggy and then Tommy. We tried to stay in larger groups, and we lucked out both those times. How long would our luck hold, however? How long would it be before someone slipped up?

At the end of the school day on Friday, I walked to my locker to meet Angel and Tommy for our usual trip home. They hadn't arrived yet, so I opened my locker to gather my books. I spotted an envelope lying on the bottom. Someone had stuck it through the vents of my locker.

I opened up the envelope, and my breath caught in my throat. The words I read terrified me more than any I'd ever read.

The note said, "You're being watched. Look towards the restrooms if you don't believe me." I looked. Derek Spradley stood there grinning evilly at me. "We have Angela. We know she has been giving you information. If you don't do as you're told, something very, very bad will happen to her."

I paused for a moment, suspicious. Angel had warned me that Angela might give us accurate information to gain our trust and then lead us into a trap. Was this it? Was that what was happening now, or was this for real?

"Saying nothing to anyone," the note continued. "Walk to the rear entrance of the school. There you'll be met by an old buddy of yours. If you try to get help from any of your friends, Angela will suffer for it. Go to the back entrance now."

I looked toward the bathrooms again. Derek glared at me. I made a show of slipping the envelope into my pocket, but discreetly dropped the note itself on the floor. I hoped Angel or Tommy would find it and realize what was up. I walked away.

As I neared the end of the hallway I looked back. Derek was bending down and picking up the note! He shook his finger back and forth as if to scold me. Now what was I going to do?

I was in a tight spot. Maybe Angela was in league with Doug after all, but if she wasn't, she was in real danger. What might Doug and the others do to Angela if I didn't do as I was told? The possibilities made my skin crawl. I walked on towards the back entrance, shaky with nerves and fear.

I walked along, trying to think myself out of the situation. If I didn't do as I was told, something nasty would happen to Angela. If I did what the note said, I'd be at the mercy of Doug. I began to slow. Finally, I stopped.

I'm an idiot, I thought to myself.

I turned and walked back the way I came. Derek soon blocked my path.

"Where do you think *you're* going?"

"I'm sure not going out the back entrance to be grabbed by whoever is waiting."

"You must not care very much about Angela. When Doug found out she was tipping you guys off to our plans, he was plenty steamed. Who knows what he'll do to her if you don't come."

"Yeah? How will handing myself over to you guys help Angela, huh? This isn't a trade: me for Angela. If I walk out that back door, you'll have Angela and me. I'm not gonna do it. I'm not *that* stupid."

"You coward. You're going to let a girl suffer because you're too afraid to face Doug?"

"Don't try that crap on me. You and I both know that I'll accomplish nothing if I give myself up."

"I guess we'll have to do this the hard way," Derek said.

Derek grabbed the front of my shirt. He began to pull me toward the back entrance, but I knocked his hands away. Derek swung at me, but I blocked his punch with my forearm and jabbed my fist into his stomach. I wasn't able to hit him full force, but he doubled over in pain nonetheless. He came right back at me and slugged me in the face. I punched him in the stomach, harder this time.

Unlike most of Doug's crew, Derek was more or less my size. He was still tough, and I wasn't much of a fighter. If any of his buddies came along I was going to be in serious trouble. I might be even if they didn't come.

Derek jabbed me in the side. The sharp pain just about took my breath away, but I hit him in the face. Soon, we were down on the floor, rolling around, punching the crap out of each other. A small crowd gathered to watch. I just hoped no teachers would come along, or worse, one of Derek's buddies.

I got Derek on his back and slugged him in the face three times in quick succession. He stopped trying to fight and concentrated on protecting his face. I got off him and stumbled to my feet. The crowd parted for me as I walked away. I could hardly believe it. I'd actually won!

I hurried back to my locker. Angel and Tommy were waiting.

"Where have you…Kurt you're bleeding!" Angel said.

"I just beat the crap out of Derek Spradley," I said smiling. My smile faded quickly. "There was a note in my locker. They've got Angela."

I quickly explained the note and what had happened.

"You're right. Giving yourself up to them would've been stupid," Tommy said.

"Do you think they've really got her, or do you think this is a trap?" I asked Angel.

"It's a trap either way. Perhaps Angela has betrayed us. Perhaps not. Regardless, we've got to check this out. If Angela is in trouble, we've got to help her. Kurt, you and Tommy round up the guys. I'm going to find Angela."

"What do we do when we get everyone together?" Tommy asked.

"Find me. I'm going to need help."

"I don't like this," I said. "Angel, you can't go running around by yourself. It's dangerous. I'll come with you."

"No. We need help, and it's not safe for Tommy to go for help alone. Some of Doug's crowd might grab him before he got the others. Then there would be no help and no Tommy."

Tommy swallowed hard. I knew I had to go with him. He wasn't fit to fight off even one guy. He only missed one day of school because of his injuries, but his arm was still in a sling.

"How are you going to find Angela?" I asked. "They could have her anywhere!"

"I don't have to find her. I just have to find Derek."

Angel grinned. I would not have wanted to be Derek when Angel tracked him down.

"Be careful, Angel!" I said.

"Hurry. Get the cavalry. I have a feeling I'm going to need all the help I can get."

Angel took off toward the back entrance of the school. I was desperately worried. I knew he could handle Derek, but what about all the others? I fought back tears as I turned to Tommy.

"Come on. Let's go."

Angel

I raced toward the back entrance, bracing myself for the struggle to come. Who knew how many of Doug's guys were waiting there? Perhaps I was being stupid, but the only way to find Angela was to grab Derek and make him talk. I knew very well I might be the one to be grabbed, but I had to take that chance.

I grinned when I spotted Derek in the hallway ahead of me. He turned at the sound of my sneakers squeaking on the wooden floor. He gave a small cry and bolted. My longer legs allowed me to catch him before he could make it to the door.

"Guys! He…"

That's as far as Derek got in his cry for help before I clamped my hand over his mouth. I looked fearfully at the rear entrance. No one came rushing through from the outside. I turned Derek around and pushed him up the hallway. I directed him to an empty classroom and shoved him inside. I closed the door behind me. Derek looked at me with terror in his eyes.

"Where is she?" I asked.

Derek shook his head.

"You're going to tell me, Derek. Your only options are whether to tell me with or without pain." I was in badass mode. Derek trembled, but he shook his head again.

I took a step toward him. I filled my eyes with menace. Derek cracked.

"Down on the river! Doug's parents have a fishing cabin!"

"Where?"

Derek told me.

"Who's there?" I asked.

"I'm not sure. Doug is, but I don't know about the others. Sidney is waiting out back. I don't know about John or Horace."

I gazed at Derek, sizing him up.

"If you're lying to me, I swear…"

"I'm not! I swear I'm not! Please don't hurt me!"

Derek was shaken. I believed he was telling the truth. Either that or he was a talented actor and liar. I looked around the room. I spotted a closet.

"Get in there," I said.

"No, please!"

"I won't have you telling the others I'm coming. And, if you've lied to me, I want to know where to find you. I can either lock you in the closet or knock you out. Which would you prefer?"

Derek meekly walked toward the closet.

"It could be hours before anyone finds me!"

"You'll live."

Derek was crying as I shoved him inside, but I felt no pity for him. He was a bully, just like the others. He'd hurt Kurt. I closed the doors and tied the handles together with a coat hanger. The janitor would probably find him in a few hours. He would be discovered the next morning at the latest. His short-term imprisonment was no more than he deserved.

I walked back into the hallway, closing the door of the classroom so Derek's cries for help couldn't be easily heard. The hallways were empty. I made for the front entrance.

I needed help. Kurt and Tommy were rounding up the guys, but there was no way to contact them and no way to let them know where I was going. There had to be someone who could help me. Ryan!

I raced down the hallway and out the front doors. I sprinted across the lawn as if I was bolting towards home plate. I ran across the street, dodging cars, ignoring horns sounded by angry drivers, and raced on. The world sped by in a blur. I was accustomed to running fast and to running long distances. I was not accustomed to doing both at the same time. My side ached, and my breath came in gasps. My body wanted to collapse upon the sidewalk, but I pushed myself on. I couldn't stop. I couldn't slow down. Maybe the whole thing with Angela was a setup, but she was in real trouble if it was not. She had put herself in danger for me, and I couldn't, wouldn't, let her down.

I arrived at Ryan's house a few agonizing minutes later. I pounded on the door. Ryan opened it in moments.

"Angel? What's wrong?"

"Trouble," I gasped. "Come."

That's all I could manage to get out. My breath came in gasps. I felt as if my lungs might explode.

Ryan grabbed his keys and led me to his Oldsmobile. We hopped inside, and he started it up.

"Where?" Ryan asked.

"On the river. Old Post Road. Next to the old ferry."

My breath was already beginning to calm a little.

"What's happened? Is Kurt okay?"

"Kurt's okay. It's this girl, Angela." I paused for a moment to catch my breath. I still couldn't speak normally. "She's been helping us. Doug found out. He's got her. At least, I think he's got her. It could be a trap."

"You do lead an exciting life, don't you, Angel?"

"Too exciting sometimes."

"Where are Kurt and the others?"

"I sent Kurt and Tommy to gather everyone. The problem is, our reinforcements won't know where to find us."

"So you sent Kurt off on a wild-goose chase to keep him out of harm's way?"

"I don't want him to get hurt." The very thought nearly made me cry, and I'm not a guy who cries easily. "Maybe it would have been smarter to bring Kurt and Tommy with me, but I just couldn't face what might happen to him."

"You love him a lot, don't you?"

"Yes."

"Enough to send him on a useless errand while you face the danger alone."

"Well, I did come to you for help."

"True, but you would've gone in alone if I hadn't been home." It was a statement, not a question.

"Yes."

"I wish I had your courage."

"You're here with me now, aren't you?"

"True," Ryan said, "but I'm not sixteen years old. I definitely wasn't as tough or brave as you when I was your age."

"Stop!" I shouted.

Ryan slammed on the brakes.

"What?"

"There's Iggy and Bart."

I hopped out of the car, shouted to Iggy and Bart, and quickly filled them in. I told them where Ryan and I were headed. I asked them to find Kurt and the others and bring them as fast as they could manage. Iggy and Bart took off. I returned to the car.

"I've sent for the cavalry."

"So Kurt's useless errand might not be so useless after all?"

"Maybe. I doubt they'll arrive in time to be of any help, but I feel a little better knowing they'll be coming. If we fail, they can at least try to rescue us." I turned to Ryan. "I'm glad you're with me. These guys are tough. They could all be there by now, except Derek. I left him locked in a closet."

"You'll have to tell me that story later. How many guys are we talking about?"

"As many as four. Only one if we're lucky, but I have a feeling we aren't going to be lucky."

"Okay, so worst-case scenario is two against four. The odds could be better, but then again, they could be a good deal worse."

Ryan stopped the car close to our destination, but not so close as to announce our arrival. The element of surprise was an ally we desperately needed. We crept forward, wishing it was dark. Anyone looking out the windows of the little fishing cabin would have had no trouble spotting us. There was nothing to do but proceed, however. We couldn't wait for the cover of darkness. Angela might be in serious trouble.

Our plan was to get close and check out the situation. Our first priority was to determine if Angela really had been kidnapped or if this was nothing more than a ploy to capture the lot of us. Our next priority was to figure out how many of the enemy were inside and how best to attack.

The fishing cabin was less than twenty feet from the riverbank. It stood up on stilts to keep it from flooding during high water. Ryan and I stopped and hid ourselves behind a tangle of bushes to check the situation out. No one seemed to be about. Ryan nodded, and we rushed across what passed for a lawn. We darted underneath the cabin. Hopefully, we hadn't been observed.

We stood under the cabin. There was no sign anyone had spotted us. We could plainly hear footsteps above our heads, but no one was rushing out the door.

"I'd say there's more than one person in there," Ryan whispered.

We heard nothing more than pacing for a while. A set of footsteps crossed the cabin to the front window and then back again. I was relieved we'd approached from the side or we would've surely been spotted. Someone up there was on lookout.

"What's taking so long?" a voice I recognized as Doug's asked. "Those two screw-ups are good for nothing."

"It hasn't been that long," another voice, clearly John's, said. "Maybe Kurt didn't go for it. Maybe they had to nab him."

"I don't like this," Doug said.

Wanker came hurrying along the rock road on his bike. Ryan and I hid ourselves in the shadows as he hurried to the cabin and up the front steps. I noted the third step up squeaked loudly. Sidney rapped on the door.

"Well?" Doug asked, his voice louder for a moment through the open door.

"He never came out! I went in to check after I'd waited twenty minutes, and there was no sign of Derek or Kurt anywhere."

"Dammit!" Doug said. His fist hit a hard surface, a table probably.

"Maybe…maybe Derek will bring Kurt here himself," Wanker said.

"That was not the plan!" Doug yelled.

"I know! I know!"

"I guess all we can do is wait," Doug said. "If he doesn't show we'll have to go to Plan B. In the meantime, let's have a little entertainment. I'm tired of waiting."

"Yeah!" John said. "It's about time."

There was a scuffle above and then a female voice.

"Get your hands off me!"

It was Angela. We hadn't heard her voice before. Had she been gagged? I didn't know.

"Mmm, I love it when they struggle," Doug said. "Don't you, guys? Don't crowd. There's plenty here for all. Just so I get mine first."

Ryan and I looked at each other, our faces stricken. There was more scuffling above. Angela screamed. Ryan motioned toward the stairway with his head. It was time.

If anyone was looking out the window, they would have spotted us for sure. It didn't sound like anyone was interested in the view at the moment, however. Angela's screams encouraged Ryan and me to hurry. I pointed to the third step, the one that squeaked, and Ryan and I stepped over it. I doubt the squeak could've been heard over the noise coming from inside, but there was no reason to take chances.

Ryan grabbed the door handle.

"It's locked!" he said.

Angela screamed "Rape!"

Ryan motioned me to stand beside him. He mimicked kicking the door open with the bottom of his foot. I copied his actions as he planted his left foot firmly on the floor and pulled back his right. Ryan held up three fingers and counted down. On zero, we both kicked as hard as we could manage. The door burst open.

Doug, John, and Sidney were momentarily startled and motionless. I took the scene in at a glance. The three boys surrounded Angela. Her blouse was torn, her face tear-streaked. Cold fury surged within me.

Doug growled and launched himself at me. John and Sidney went for Ryan. Sidney didn't make it, however. Angela jumped on his back and in moments had him on the floor. She slugged him repeatedly. In books and movies girls are always helpless damsels in distress. If Angela was any indication, all the novels and films had it completely wrong. Angela kicked Wanker's ass. I wish I could've watched and laughed at Wanker, but Doug was hurtling toward me, intent on rearranging my face in a most unappealing manner.

Doug's fist flashed just past my face, but his body collided with mine, and we both went crashing to the ground. The second we hit I slugged Doug in the gut. He tried to knee me in the balls, but missed, hitting my leg instead. The sharp pain made me hiss, but I grabbed Doug by the front of the shirt and tossed him to the side. Doug and I rolled around on the floor, wailing on each other with everything we had. I couldn't see what was happening with the others, but soon Ryan pulled Doug off me and took him out with a couple of swift punches to the face. When I staggered to my feet, Angela was standing above Wanker, watching him as he writhed on the floor. I had to remember to take Angela along the next time there was going to be a fight. She could kick ass with the best of them.

Angela ran to me and hugged me, then Ryan, then both of us together.

"Thank you!" she said.

"Are you okay?" I asked.

"I am now, but things were getting ugly when you two arrived. Animals!" she said, kicking Doug in the side. He groaned in pain.

I heard a loud squeak. It was the third step announcing the arrival of the cavalry. I smiled. Better late than never, I guess. I turned, and my smile quickly faded.

"Hello, Angel."

It was Jesse. Jesse who was supposed to be behind bars. Jesse who'd resented me for taking his spot as first baseman. Jesse who had wanted to kill me the night I tried to stop the gang from murdering Matt Taber.

"Adam sends his regards. He's sorry he couldn't be here to greet you, but he had some urgent business to attend to."

I looked down at the pistol in Jesse's hand. I swallowed hard.

"What urgent business?"

"Killing Noah Taber for testifying against him."

Shit. The situation had taken a turn for the worse. That was putting it lightly. Kurt was likely to be with Noah when Adam found him. I couldn't let myself think about what might happen or I'd be paralyzed by fear. I couldn't afford that now. We had to somehow take out Jesse and get to Adam before he found Noah and Kurt.

"You think it's wise to lengthen your sentence by adding another murder to the list?" I asked.

"Two murders, Egler. You don't really think I was gonna break out of jail without paying you a little visit, did you? I heard you'd skipped town. How thoughtful of you to come back."

Jesse looked at Doug, John, and Sidney all lying on the floor. John was out cold. The others were writhing in pain.

"Amateurs," Jesse said in disgust. "Complete failures. Then again, maybe not. You're here, after all. That's what this was all about."

Jesse grinned at me evilly. He looked at Ryan for a moment and then focused his attention on Angela.

"What do we have here? Mmm, I always liked you, Angela. Maybe I'll take you along after I kill Angel."

"Dream on, Jesse Offield! I didn't like you before I knew you were a murderer, and I like you far less now!"

Angela sure had spunk.

Jesse stepped toward her, pointing the pistol at her. Ryan and I tensed, but we were just a little too far away to try to jump Jesse. He'd turn and kill one of us for sure. Either that or he'd gun down Angela for spite.

"Yeah," Jesse said, looking Angela up and down. "I'm sure I can find a use for you. Maybe I'll even share you with Adam."

Jesse grabbed Angela around the waist, pulling her into his side where he could keep the pistol trained on her, but also turn it on Ryan or me at a moment's notice.

I had to do something. We didn't save Angela from her would-be rapists only to let the likes of Jesse and Adam get their hands on her. The seconds were ticking by. I knew Adam could be killing Noah even as we stood there. He could be killing Kurt.

Don't think about it. Just do something!

There wasn't a moment to lose. Jesse was going to kill me anyway, so why not make my death count for something? I tensed to spring at him. He would undoubtedly turn and fire. I'd be dead, but Ryan and Angela could jump him and then go and save Kurt and Noah.

"Say goodbye, Angel. This is gonna be a pleasure."

Jesse pointed the pistol directly at me. I was too late! Why had I stood there thinking when I should have been jumping him? I was so stupid. Now I was going to die uselessly.

No. I could still rush him. I took a deep breath. I closed my eyes to focus myself. I tensed my muscles, ready to spring.

A deafening bang that sounded like a cannon shook the cabin. Splinters from a rafter overhead rained down upon me. Stunned, I opened my eyes and peered through the smoke and plaster dust to see Jesse on the floor, writhing in pain. Angela kicked at him savagely. She had taken him out! There was no stopping that girl.

I glanced up at the ceiling to see a huge chunk missing from a rafter. I looked back at Angela and Jesse. She had stopped kicking him. Jesse had curled up in a ball, moaning in pain. Ryan picked up the pistol with a handkerchief, careful not to disturb the finger prints.

"A .357. This kid wasn't messing around. If he hadn't missed, this would have left a hole in your chest the size of your head."

I gulped. This day was far too filled with excitement. It wasn't over, either.

"We've got to find Noah!" I said. "Now!"

Ryan spied some rope hanging on the wall. Angela, Ryan, and I got busy tying up Doug, Sidney, John, and Jesse.

"Can you handle these guys?" Ryan asked Angela. It almost seemed a stupid question after the way she'd taken out first Sidney and then Jesse.

"Piece of cake. There's a phone. I'll call the police. Once I'm done here, I'll come and save you."

I grinned. If I was attracted to girls, Angela would be the one. Wow!

Ryan and I rushed out the front door, down the steps, and straight to the car. We jumped in and headed back toward town.

"Any idea where Noah might be?" Ryan asked.

"None, but we've got to find him. If we don't, Adam will kill him for sure." My voice broke as a sob tried to escape from my chest. "And Ryan, Kurt is probably with Noah."

Ryan looked at me. I was certain he could read the anguish in my eyes.

"We'll find him. We'll find them both," Ryan said.

I nodded.

"Let's try Noah's house first," I said.

We were there in minutes. Unfortunately, but not surprisingly, Noah wasn't there. His father was home, but had no idea where Noah might be. I quickly executed the unenviable task of informing Mr. Taber than his son's life was in danger. He sprang into action. He was calling the cops even before I was out the door.

"No luck," I said, hopping into the car. "Let's try the school. Maybe Adam went there to grab him."

"If that's true, we're too late already."

Ryan was right, but what else could we do? I racked my brains, trying to think of where Noah might be.

When we arrived at the high school, no one was in sight. The parking lot was nearly empty. I rubbed my temples, trying to concentrate.

"Where could he be?" I asked out loud.

I looked through the window. One of the few vehicles in the parking lot was a milk truck from Valparaiso, Indiana. I stared at it for a moment. Valparaiso—that's where Adam and the others were being held.

"I think I know where we can find Kurt and Noah. I just hope we're not too late," I said.

I jumped out of the car and raced across the parking lot. I ripped open the back doors. The truck was filled milk bottles and milk cans, but there was no Noah.

"Go to the cops," I said. "Tell them to come to the woods behind the school—where Matt Taber's body was found. Tell them to hurry!"

I turned to rush towards the woods, but Ryan's hand clamped down on my shoulder.

"Angel, wait. We'll get the cops and let them take care of this. It's too dangerous."

"There's no time! Adam could be pulling the trigger even now! Noah's parents lost one son. They don't need to lose another. I'm not going to fail them again! And…if Kurt's with him…"

Hot tears stung my eyes. Ryan nodded. I bolted for the woods, and Ryan hurried back to his car.

I prayed Adam hadn't killed Noah already. I prayed even more fervently Kurt wasn't with him. I hoped Adam's sense of the dramatic would take control. He could easily shoot Noah on sight, but he'd want him to suffer. I was guessing he'd take Noah to the very place where Noah's little brother was killed. Adam would make Noah relive his brother's death. I just hoped my hunch was right and that I wasn't too late.

I raced across the baseball field where I'd played so many games. I ignored the clipped green grass and the spring flowers. Such beauty meant nothing to me. Nothing mattered but getting to Adam before he killed again. I ran on into the forest, making straight for the spot where Matt was murdered all those long months ago.

What if I was too late to save Noah? What if I just couldn't manage it? What if Adam had Kurt, too? No. I couldn't allow myself to think like that. I couldn't let myself get bogged down in possibilities, either. I'd deal with the situation as I found it when I arrived. If Noah was still alive, I'd save him or die trying. If Kurt was there…

I slowed to a fast walk as I entered the forest. The carpet of leaves on the forest floor was wet, so I was able to move forward without making too much noise. I wished it was summer, so I could creep close without being seen, but I'd just have to do my best. My heart pounded as I drew near to the site of Matt's murder. So many things had happened there—horrible things. I struggled to keep memories of the night Matt was killed out of my mind. I felt so helpless watching him die. If only I could have broken free, I could have saved him. No, I wasn't going to think about that. I forced my thoughts to the night I rescued Kurt in that very same spot. I hoped that happy ending would repeat itself with Noah. That depended on me. Help was coming, but it would come too late. It was all up to me.

I spotted Adam and Noah some fifty feet ahead. Kurt was nowhere in sight! I breathed a sigh of relief and focused on the task at hand. I slowed and began to circle around so I'd come up behind Adam. Any other approach would expose me to view far too soon. I moved from tree to tree. When I was within twenty feet Noah spotted me, but had the presence of mind not to stare and give me away.

I fought to calm my breath. I didn't want Adam to hear my ragged breathing. Images from the night Noah's brother was killed flashed in my mind. Adam was making Noah dig his own grave—just as he had Matt. It was a nightmare revisited. At least Noah was still alive. If Adam didn't derive such sadistic pleasure from tormenting his victims, Noah would be dead already. I still had a chance to save him.

"Put your back into it, Noah. I don't have all day," Adam said. "Make it nice and deep. We don't want some dog digging you up like your brother."

Noah jerked his head toward Adam. His handsome features were twisted in rage. Tears streamed down his cheeks. I thought for a moment he was going to rush Adam.

Steady, Noah. Steady.

Noah controlled himself, even though Adam laughed in his face. Adam had a pistol trained on Noah. His finger was on the trigger.

I crept forward, intently aware that Adam could whip around at any moment and blow me away. I'm not ashamed to admit I was shaking. I don't know of anyone who wouldn't have been in that situation. I was about ten feet from Adam now. Noah was about another five feet away. I could hear the shovel slicing into the wet earth as Noah dug his own grave.

"You're not blubbering as much as your little brother did," said Adam. "He cried like a baby."

Even from ten feet away I could see Noah tremble with rage. I was so infuriated I wanted to snap Adam's neck. How could anyone be so cruel?

I crept closer. I was only six feet away now. I crouched down, ready to spring.

My head jerked to the side. Adam and Noah both looked to the left as well. They had heard the same twig snap. I spotted figures moving toward us. It was the cops. Ryan was with them, and, shit, so were Noah's parents.

I was both relieved and distressed by the arrival of the cops, but more distressed. If they tried to strong-arm Adam, he'd likely blow Noah away right in front of his mom and dad. He'd do it—just for spite. Adam took several steps forward. He was now fifteen feet away, and there wasn't a single tree standing between us. How could I possibly cross that distance without Adam turning and gunning me down?

Adam grabbed Noah around the throat, thrust him in front of himself as a shield, and pointed the pistol to his head

"Stay back or I'll blow his brains out!" Adam shouted.

Noah's mother screamed. Why had they brought Noah's parents? They didn't want to see this.

"Stay back and throw those guns on the ground. Now!"

What possessed the cops to think they could just walk right up to Adam and arrest him? Didn't these guys know *anything*? Then again, I was being overcritical. They didn't know Adam as I did. They didn't understand the twisted workings of his mind.

I spotted more figures approaching. It was Kurt and the guys. There were a few others, too: Kurt's brother, Sam, and more. Had the whole damned town come out to watch?

"I'm going to show you what happens to people who mess with me!" Adam shouted.

Shit. I'd hoped he'd try to get away, using Noah as a hostage, but Adam's sense of the dramatic had flared up again. I knew exactly what he was going to do. He was going to kill Noah right in front of Noah's parents. Then, he'd fire away until one of the cops managed to shoot him. Adam would likely be killed, but Noah would certainly die. Several others would die or be wounded, too. If only I could get close enough to jump him. It wasn't going to happen. He was too wary now. He kept checking in all directions, expecting to be jumped from behind. The moment I moved out from behind my tree he'd spot me.

"Say goodbye to Noah, everyone!" Adam laughed insanely.

"Noah isn't the one you want!" I shouted as I stepped out from behind the tree. Adam instantly turned his attention to me.

It was either the bravest or the stupidest thing I'd ever done. All I knew was that if I didn't do something Noah would be dead in seconds. I didn't want to go through my life knowing that I'd stood by and watched Noah die. I'd watched his brother die, but I'd been helpless. Nothing was holding me back this time, except my own fear.

"I'm the one who turned you in to the cops, Adam. I'm the one who sent them a letter detailing your sick crimes. Noah's testimony was nothing. If it wasn't for me, you'd still be roaming free." I faked a laugh, hoping to enrage Adam. My laugh sounded convincing to me.

My words weren't quite true, but the truth didn't matter just then. Keeping Adam from killing Noah was all that mattered.

"Did you have fun in jail, Adam? Did you?" I asked in my best smartass tone.

"Why aren't you dead, Angel?"

"Jesse had a little trouble. Angela kicked his ass. You never were that bright when it came to choosing your friends, Adam. They're all losers, just like you."

I was prepared to go on and truly piss Adam off. I wanted to shake him, force him to lose his concentration so someone, anyone, could jump him. Ryan was creeping forward, as was Noah's dad. Kurt and the guys were edging closer, too. The cops didn't seem to know what to do. I infuriated Adam far more quickly than I'd anticipated. He gave a yell something between a growl and a scream, released Noah, and spun around, firing his pistol at me as he turned.

It was probably just more stupidity on my part, but instead of dodging out of the way, I rushed Adam. I heard one shot, two, three. I expected at any moment to feel searing pain, or perhaps to feel nothing at all if I died fast enough. How Adam managed to miss at such close range I don't know. Perhaps it was because he didn't expect me to come straight at him. No one was *that* stupid after all. Adam continued to howl in anger. Perhaps he was so infuriated he just couldn't see straight. I was totally amazed as my shoulders crashed into his chest. Another shot rang out from his pistol, deafening at such close range. My momentum carried us both to the ground—Adam on his back, me on top of him. Adam's right arm slammed into the ground and the pistol went flying. I slugged Adam in the face twice before he could return a punch. He nailed me hard in the lats, but I just kept on slugging. That bastard wasn't going to get up off the ground if I could help it.

I guess I kind of lost it. I punched Adam in the face again and again. I think Adam was punching me back, but I swear I couldn't feel it, not until the next day, that is. I pummeled him until someone pulled me off. Even then, I tried to get back at him. When I finally calmed down I noticed Kurt was hugging me. Noah's parents were hugging their son. The cops had Adam handcuffed and were leading him away. There was quite a crowd. My parents and Kurt's had even shown up. I guess nothing this exciting had ever happened in Blackford before.

Everyone's attention was focused on either Noah and his parents or Kurt and me. I suddenly became aware that I was kissing Kurt right on the lips. I think Kurt realized what we were doing at about the same time. We pulled back and looked at each other—shocked. We turned our heads toward the crowd. No one was jeering at us or calling us names. We had done the unthinkable, the unspeakable, and yet no one was throwing stones. I relaxed just a bit, but was still astonished that Kurt and I had hugged and kissed right in front of everyone!

Noah's dad stepped up to me and hugged me. He was actually crying. Noah's mom was on me next—hugging me, bawling, thanking me, and telling me I was a hero. I was completely overwhelmed.

I heard the word "hero" a lot in the next few minutes. I didn't feel like one. I was so frightened as I'd rushed Adam that I was still shaking. I don't think I'd ever experienced such sheer terror before. I even did a quick check to see if I'd wet myself in those terror-filled moments. Thankfully, I hadn't, but all the hero talk was just a bit much.

It went on and on, though. A reporter from the local paper was soon on the scene taking pictures. He wanted to interview me. Thankfully, my dad stepped in and told him it would have to wait. I was relieved. Now that it was all over, I felt like crying.

The greatest thing ever happened when the crowd began to clear. My parents asked Kurt's parents if they would like to come over and get to know one another better.

"I'm sure the boys will want to be together after this," said my mom. "I just baked a pineapple cake. We can…"

I stopped listening. I was stuck back on "the boys will want to be together…" Had my mom just acknowledged that Kurt was my boyfriend? Had she said it right to Kurt's parents without them recoiling in disgusted horror?

Kurt and I stared at each other, amazed. My parents knew about me. They more or less knew Kurt was my boyfriend. Kurt's parents didn't have a clue about him or our relationship—until now. I noticed Kurt's dad and mom eyeing us, but there was no recrimination in their gazes. Both had to be shocked right down to their toes. Such things were not talked about. Never. Ever. Kurt was a homo, and his parent's now knew it. They knew I was his boyfriend. They had seen us hug and kiss. A mountain had dropped on them, and they took it with barely a flinch.

Noah's parents came and made over me again. They turned to my parents and gushed their gratitude and admiration. They spoke words like "hero" and "fine son" and "amazing act of courage" until I was red with embarrassment. My dad looked proud enough to pop.

My head was spinning as I walked beside Kurt, following his parents and mine. I didn't know quite how to handle what was going on. All kinds of people were shaking my hand and patting me on the back. I couldn't wait to get home and get away from everyone.

Kurt wrapped his arm around my shoulder and gave me a quick hug. We smiled at each other. I knew I'd made the right decision when I'd come home.

Kurt

I walked out of the woods with Angel, but after a quick hug I turned toward my parents. Mom, Dad, and I just stood there by the Nash, gazing at each other. What was going through their minds? My own was racing. I hadn't planned for my parents to find out about me so soon. I hadn't even decided if I'd *ever* tell them. Now, they knew. What did they think of me? Did they still love me? Could they deal with having a homo for a son?

Sam joined us silently. He looked at me, nodded, and smiled. I was glad to have my older brother on my side just then. He understood.

As frightened as I was at that moment, I knew I wouldn't change, even if I could. Angel meant everything to me. If I wasn't who I was, I could never have loved him. I would've missed out on the most important part of my life.

The silence extended. None of us knew what to say.

"I love him," I said, finally. "I love Angel."

My lower lip trembled, and a tear slid down my cheek. I didn't want to cry just then, especially in front of my dad. My parents had just discovered I was a homo. I didn't want them to think I was weak.

Mom stepped toward me and hugged me. As soon as she took me in her arms, I began to cry. All the pain inside me just came out. It wasn't long before I got myself under control, but I felt better. I stepped away from Mom and wiped my eyes. Sam mussed my hair.

"Are you okay, Squirt?"

"Yeah. I think so."

I looked toward Dad. He stepped nearer, put his hand on my shoulder, and said, "I love you, Son."

I knew then that everything was going to be okay.

***

Our secret was out, but no one mentioned it in public or talked to us about it. It's likely a lot of people talked about us behind closed doors, but in public our relationship was something known but never discussed or acknowledged. Our relationship was there, but invisible. Everyone turned a blind eye to it. The exception was Ryan, Tommy, the Nudo twins, my family, and Angel's family. Only Ryan, Tommy, the twins, Sam, and my sister Ida actually talked to Angel and me about our relationship. Only they spoke of it openly and then only around our little group. My parents might ask "How are you and Angel getting along?" or "Is Angel coming for supper tonight?", but they never mentioned words like "boyfriend" or "homosexual" or "queer." Angel said his parents were the same. I would've liked it if Mom and Dad referred to Angel as my boyfriend, but I wasn't about to complain. Relationships like ours just weren't mentioned in our little corner of the world. They were illegal in most, if not all, states. Angel and I were practically outlaws. Maybe I had a bit more of my great, great, whatever grandfather Jesse James in me than I thought. I wished I lived in a world where I could tell everyone about my love for Angel, but it was enough that I could share it with my family and friends.

You wouldn't believe how everyone made over Angel. It embarrassed him to no end, but he deserved every bit of the attention he received. I teased Angel that soon there would be a statue of him in front of the library or town hall. He told me to shut up and then kissed me.

The local paper published several stories on Angel's heroic, death defying rescue of Noah Taber. Many considered Angel a hero even before he rescued Noah, but now his reputation was carved in stone. Even newspapers from neighboring towns covered Angel's story.

I'm sure it was Angel's heroic deeds that made everyone willing to accept, or at least ignore, his queerness. I gained a like acceptance because I was Angel's boyfriend. Not that anyone called me his boyfriend. I was his friend or "special friend." I think a lot of people just couldn't fit the two things together—homosexuality and heroism, that is. Many convinced themselves that Angel and I couldn't be homosexuals. We were just *really* good friends. Others understood the truth and, at the very least, left us alone. I think some even learned that homos aren't the monsters they're made out to be.

Some people wouldn't change their views no matter what, of course. Doug and his whole crowd were some of those. Big surprise there, huh? Derek was the exception. I never once heard him say "homo" or any other slur again. He even started to become remorseful over his actions.

Doug, John, and Sidney were in major trouble. Kidnapping and attempted rape is not taken lightly in Indiana. I was horrified when Angel told me what they almost did to Angela. I laughed my head off when he described how she'd taken out first Sidney and then Jesse. I sure didn't want to tangle with her.

This is the part in most stories where it says: "And they lived happily ever after." I can't say that. For one thing, I'm not dead yet, so I really don't know what's going to happen next. For another, no one really lives happily ever after. Have you even experienced a single day in your life where you were completely happy? I doubt it. Life is stuffed full of problems and pain and unpleasantness. That's just the way it is. Thankfully, it's also stuffed full of fun and pleasure. I, for one, like those parts a whole lot better. I focus on the good and not the bad.

Angel and I may not live happily ever after, but I'm sure happier than I have been in a long time. I think the happiest moment of my life so far was when Angel came back. Of course, the very next moment I began to worry about what would happen to us. I guess I'm even happier now or, at least, more consistently happy. Angel is home. We're together. Our families are more or less okay with our relationship. Adam and his crowd are back in jail where I hope they *stay* this time. The fate of Doug & Company is up in the air, but it's not looking good for them. Even if they could come back to school (and believe me, I'm thrilled that they can't come back) I don't think they'd dare to give Angel or any of the rest of us a hard time. Angel's a hero now, and the rest of us...well...we all stick together. I'm not worried about

Doug and his thugs anymore. They were bad, bad boys. I'm sure they'll be behind bars for a good long time.

Angel stayed over last night. He was allowed to stay in my room, which amazed us both. Angel was supposed to sleep in a sleeping bag on the floor, but he soon climbed into bed with me. I have the feeling my parents knew that would happen. They'd been teenagers once, too. Sure, Angel and I were both guys, but it's pretty much the same as with a girl and guy, really. Then again, I can't imagine Mom and Dad being okay with me having sex, so maybe they thought Sam would act as a chaperone. Silly parents, but I love them, and best of all, they love me.

It was the first time Angel and I made love in ages—at least it seemed that way. I had needed it bad *forever*. I'm not just talking about sex. What Angel and I did was far more than that. I could describe the physical acts, but that wouldn't tell you the half of it. It was as if we became one when we made love. We weren't separate individuals anymore. I loved the intimacy and the closeness. When we were done, we kissed each other until we fell asleep. When I awakened during the night, Angel was pressed up against me. His arm was around me. I snuggled up against him and went back to sleep. That's as close to happily ever after as I'll ever need.

Other Books by Mark A. Roeder Listed in Suggested Reading Order

Gay Youth Chronicles:

Outfield Menace

Outfield Menace is the tale of Kurt, a fifteen-year-old baseball player, living in a small, 1950s, Indiana town. During a confrontation with Angel, the resident bad boy of Blackford High School, Kurt attacks Angel, earning the wrath of the most dangerous gang in town. When Angel finally corners Kurt, however, something happens that Kurt wouldn't have imagined in his wildest dreams. As the murder of a local boy is uncovered, suspicion is cast upon Angel, but Kurt has learned there's more to Angel than his bad boy image. Angel has a secret, however, that could get both Kurt and himself killed. *Outfield Menace* is a story of friendship, love, adventure, and perilous danger.

Snow Angel

Angel rescued his boyfriend, Kurt, from a hellish existence, but at the cost of exiling himself from his hometown of Blackford, Indiana. Fifteen-years-old and on the run, Angel must make his way until he can fulfill his promise to return to Kurt. Along the way he faces loneliness, hardships, and a brutal blizzard, but makes new friends and finds acceptance he didn't expect.

Kurt's life is nearly back to normal, but the love of his life is gone. Kurt is determined not to let Angel's sacrifice be in vain, but how can he wait three long years for the return his boyfriend had promised him? What will happen when they are reunited at last? Can they be together, or will Kurt and Angel have to run for their lives?

Snow Angel is a tale of lovers parted, of survival, and a love that cannot be diminished by distance or time.

Ancient Prejudice Break to New Mutiny

Mark is a boy who wants what we all want: to love and be loved. His dreams are realized when he meets Taylor, the boy of his dreams. The boys struggle to keep their love hidden from a world that cannot understand, but ultimately, no secret is safe in a small Mid-western town.

Ancient Prejudice is a story of love, friendship, understanding, and an age-old prejudice that still has the power to kill. It is a story for young and old, gay and straight. It reminds us all that everyone should be treated with dignity and respect and that there is nothing greater than the power of love.

The Soccer Field Is Empty

The Soccer Field Is Empty is a revised and much expanded edition of ***Ancient Prejudice***. It is more than 50% longer and views events from the point of view of Taylor, as well as Mark. There is so much new in the revised edition that it is being published as a separate novel. ***Soccer Field*** delves more deeply into the events of Mark and Taylor's lives and reveals previously hidden aspects of Taylor's personality.

Authors note: I suggest readers new to my books start with ***Soccer Field*** instead of ***Ancient Prejudice*** as it gives a more complete picture of the lives of Mark and Taylor. For those who wish to read the original version, ***Ancient Prejudice*** will remain available for at least the time being.

Someone Is Watching

It's hard hiding a secret. It's even harder keeping that secret when someone else knows.

Someone Is Watching is the story of Ethan, a young high school wrestler who must come to terms with being gay. He struggles first with himself, then with an unknown classmate that hounds his every step. While struggling to discover the identity of his tormentor, Ethan must discover his own identity and learn to live his life as his true self. He must choose whether to give up what he wants the most, or face his greatest fear of all.

A Better Place

High school football, a hospital of horrors, a long journey, and an unlikely love await Brendan and Casper as they search for a better place...

Casper is the poorest boy in school. Brendan is the captain of the football team. Casper has nothing. Brendan has it all: looks, money, popularity, but he lacks the deepest desire of his heart. The boys come from different worlds, but have one thing in common that no one would guess.

Casper goes through life as the "invisible boy"; invisible to the boys that pick on him in school, invisible to his abusive father, and invisible most of all to his older brother, who makes his life a living hell. He can't believe his good luck when Brendan, the most popular boy in school, takes an interest in him and becomes his friend. That friendship soon travels in a direction that Casper would never have guessed.

A Better Place is the story of an unlikely pair, who struggle through friendship and betrayal, hardships and heartbreaks, to find the desire of their hearts, to find a better place.

Someone Is Killing The Gay Boys of Verona

Someone is killing the gay boys of Verona, Indiana, and only one gay youth stands in the way. He finds himself pitted against powerful foes, but finds allies in places he did not expect.

A brutal murder. Gay ghosts. A Haunted Victorian-Mansion. A cult of hate. A hundred year old ax murder. All this, and more, await sixteen-year-old Sean as he delves into the supernatural and races to discover the murderer before he strikes again.

Someone is Killing the Gay Boys of Verona is a supernatural murder mystery that goes where no gay novel has set foot before. It is a tale of love, hate, friendship, and revenge.

Keeper of Secrets

Sixteen-year-old Avery is in trouble, yet again, but this time he's in over his head. On the run, Avery is faced with hardships and fear. He must become what he's always hated, just to survive. He discovers new reasons to hate, until fate brings him to Graymoor Mansion and he discovers a disturbing connection to the past. Through the eyes of a boy, murdered more than a century before, Avery discovers that all is not as he thought. Avery is soon forced to face the greatest challenge of all; looking into his own heart.

Sean is head over heels in love with his new boyfriend, Nick. There is trouble in paradise, however. Could a boy so beautiful really love plain, ordinary Sean? Sean cannot believe it and desperately tries to transform himself into the ideal young hunk, only to learn that it's what's inside that matters.

Keeper of Secrets is the story of two boys, one a gay youth, the other an adolescent gay basher. Fate and the pages of a hundred year old journal bring them together and their lives are forever changed.

Do You Know That I Love You

The lead singer of the most popular boy band in the world has a secret. A tabloid willing to tell all turns his world upside down.

In ***Do You Know That I Love You***, Ralph, a young gay teen living on a farm in Indiana, has an aching crush on a rock star and wants nothing more than to see his idol in concert. Meanwhile, Jordan, the rock star, is lonely and sometimes confused with his success, because all he wants is someone to love him and feels he will never find the love he craves. ***Do You Know*** is the story of two teenage boys, their lives, desires, loves, and a shared destiny that allows them both to find peace.

Masked Destiny

Masked Destiny is the story of Skye, a high school athlete determined to be the Alpha male. Skye's obsessed with his own body, his Abercrombie & Fitch wardrobe, and keeping those around him in their place. Try as he might, he's not quite able to ignore the world around him, or the plight of gay boys that cross his path. Too frightened of what others might think, Skye fails to intervene when he could have saved a boy with a single word. The resulting tragedy, wise words for a mysterious blond boy, and a unique opportunity combine to push Skye toward his destiny.

Oliver is young, a bit pudgy, and interested in little more than his books and possibly his first kiss. As he slowly gains courage, he seeks out the friendship of Clay, his dream boy, in hopes they will become more than friends. Oliver is sought out in turn by Ken, who warns him Clay is not at all what he seems, but Ken, too, has his secrets. Oliver must choose between them and discovers danger, a link to boys murdered in the recent past, and the answers to secrets he'd never dreamed.

Altered Realities

Marshall only wanted to help his friends, to undo the pain of the past, but a few moments of thoughtless action changed everything. ***Altered Realities*** is the tale of a changed world. All bets are off. Nothing is as it was and what is to be is transformed too. Mark, Taylor, Ethan, Nathan, Brendan, Casper and nearly the entire cast of the *Gay Youth Chronicles* come together in a tapestry of tales as they all try to deal with the consequences of Marshall's actions. The road to hell is paved with good intentions.

Dead Het Boys

Marshall's experiences with ghosts and the supernatural are legendary, but when a boy a hundred-years dead turns up in his bedroom with the cryptic message "Blackford Manor," Marshall realizes his adventures with the other side have only began. As more specters appear to Marshall, he begins to assemble the pieces of a puzzle that lead him to Graymoor Mansion and a set of crimes more heinous than those of modern day serial killers.

Just over a year ago, Sean's best friend, Marty, was murdered and Sean narrowly escaped the same fate. Now, the evil four, a group of boys who were involved with the death of Marty, have returned. Sean, Skye, and the other gay boys of Verona can do little more than watch and wait for the terror to begin again. Soon, Skye learns of a psychopathic homophobe who is in league with his enemies. Things take a curious turn, however, when one of the evil four is brutally murdered. Suspicion turns to Skye. Has he finally gone too far to protect his friends? Skye isn't the only one with a motive, however. All the gay boys of Verona are suspect. This time around, the shoe is on the other foot.

This Time Around

What happens when a TV evangelist struggles to crush gay rights? Who better to halt his evil plans than the most famous rock star in the world?

This Time Around follows Jordan and Ralph as they become involved in a struggle with Reverend Wellerson, a TV evangelist, over the fate of gay youth centers. Wellerson is willing to stop at nothing to crush gay rights and who better to halt his evil plans than the most famous rock star in the entire world? While battling Wellerson, Jordan seeks to come to terms with his own past and learn more about the father he never knew. The excitement builds when an assassin is hired and death becomes a real possibility for Jordan and those around him. Jordan is forced to face his own fears and doubts and the battle within becomes more dangerous than the battle without. Will Jordan be able to turn from the path of destruction, or is he doomed to follow in the footsteps of his father? This time around, things will be different.

The Summer of My Discontent

The Summer of My Discontent is a tapestry of tales delving into life as a gay teen in a small Midwestern town.

Dane is a sixteen-year-old runaway determined to start a new life of daring, love, and sex—no matter the cost to himself, or others. His actions bring him to the brink of disaster and only those he sought to prey upon can save him. Among Dane's new found "friends" are a young male prostitute and the local grave robber who becomes his despised employer.

The boys of ***A Better Place*** are back—Ethan, Nathan, Brendan, and Casper are once again dealing with trouble in Verona, Indiana. Drought and circumstance threaten their existence and they struggle together to save themselves from blackmail, financial collapse, and temptation.

Brendan must cope with anonymity after being one of the most popular boys in school. Casper must face his own past—the loss of his father and the fate of his abusive brother, who is locked away in the very hospital of horrors from which Brendan escaped. Letters from his brother force Casper to question his feelings—is Jason truly a monster or can he change?

Dark, foreboding, and sexy—***The Summer of My Discontent*** is the tale of gay teens seeking to find themselves, each other, and a better place.

Disastrous Dates & Dream Boys

Disastrous Dates & Dream Boys is the story of teenaged boys who want what we all want, to love and be loved. The boys from *A Better Place* are back. Shawn yearns for a boyfriend, but fears his father's wrath if he discovers the truth. Dane, too, is seeking a soul mate and trying to leave his checkered past behind. He yearns for Billy, but if he approaches him will the result be happiness or disaster? Brendan has created a new life for himself and his boyfriend, Casper, but what happened in his old hometown haunts him and he realizes he must face his father if he is to ever be at peace. Nathan also has issues to resolve with the parents who gave him and his little brother up far too easily. *Disastrous Dates & Dream Boys* is a tale of fathers & sons, lovers & friends, and above all love and understanding.

Phantom World

Toby Riester is sixteen, gay, and searching for his first boyfriend. He discovers many potential candidates—Orlando, a cute sixteen year old boy of Latin ancestry who works with Toby at the *Phantom World* amusement park—C.T., a blond, seventeen year old who is obviously gay—and Spike, a well-built sixteen year old from the internet. Each boy has his own seductive qualities and each is more than his seems. One of them, however, is far more dangerous than Toby ever guessed.

Orlando finds himself a girlfriend at ***Phantom World***, but that's only the beginning of his story. When he meets his girlfriend's twin brother, Kerry, his world is turned upside down.

Mackenzie Riester is the athletic younger brother of Toby. He has little respect for his queer big brother and joins with his new found friend, Billy, in playing an elaborate practical joke on Toby that becomes more perilous than he ever dreamed.

Phantom World is the story of three very different boys—their triumphs, heartaches, and their search for love and acceptance.

Second Star To The Right

Cedi, a eighteen-year-old British import to the town of Blackford, Indiana, is determined to be a rock star. No one quite knows what to make of the new wild boy in town with his blue hair and overpowering-enthusiasm—not the jocks he torments in revenge, nor his new friends Toby and Orlando. Cedi is certain of his future until his path crosses that of Thad, a tall, dark, older man who tells Cedi he has no talent. Cedi is infuriated, but intrigued. He becomes obsessed with Thad, who wants nothing to do with him. Cedi isn't about to give up, however, and wedges his way into Thad's life. Cedi finds himself caught between his love for Thad and his dream. Just when he has what he thinks he wants, his adventure truly begins…

The Perfect Boy

A specter from the past haunts the halls of Blackford High School, terrorizing anyone who preys on the weak. Rumors say that a Goth/skater boy controls the ghost, but can the rumor be true? A mysterious new boy catches the eye of Toby and his new friend, Daniel Peralta as well. The new boy seems too perfect to be real. Is he or will be become the boy of Toby's or Daniel's dreams?

Cedi is living his fantasy—touring with *Phantom*, the most popular band in the world. Cedi can't quite forget Thad, the older, mysterious novelist he's left behind, but is quickly pulled into a world of concerts, autograph signings, and press conferences. Cedi takes an interest in Ross. Ross has his own demons, however, that may forever prevent him from loving anyone but the man of his dreams.

The Graymoor Mansion B&B

Is turning a haunted mansion into a Bed & Breakfast such a good idea? Sean and his family think so, except for Avery, who believes guests will be scared away by disembodied voices, candles that light themselves, and the ghostly reenactment of the notorious Graymoor Ax Murders.

When the gay boys of Verona went their separate ways, Verona was more at peace than it had been in ages. Skye, the local champion of gay boys, has been gone for five long years, however, and much has changed in his absence. Sean and Nick lived apart during their college years. They've eagerly anticipated their reunion, but what will happen when Ross, the drummer for *Phantom*, comes to stay at Graymoor with the band? Is Nick over his Ross obsession—or is there trouble ahead? Jordan and Ralph have long considered starting a family, but can they surmount the obstacles that stand in their way? The gay boys of Verona, old and new, are together once again.

Other Books

The Vampires Heart

Ever wonder what it would be like to be fifteen-years-old forever? Ever wonder how it would feel to find out your best friend is not what he seems? Graham Granger is intrigued by the new boy in school. Graham's heart aches for a friend, and maybe a boyfriend, but is Josiah the answer to his dreams? Why is Bry Hartnett, the school hunk, taking an interest in Graham as well? When strange happenings begin to occur at Griswold Jr./Sr. High, Graham's once boring life becomes more exciting than he can handle. Mystery, intrigue, and danger await Graham as he sets out on an adventure he never dreamed possible.